T0265539

PROPHET OF BLOOD

Also by Peter Tremayne

The Sister Fidelma mysteries

WHISPERS OF THE DEAD
THE LEPER'S BELL
MASTER OF SOULS
A PRAYER FOR THE DAMNED
DANCING WITH DEMONS
THE COUNCIL OF THE CURSED
THE DOVE OF DEATH
THE CHALICE OF BLOOD
BEHOLD A PALE HORSE
THE SEVENTH TRUMPET
ATONEMENT OF BLOOD
THE DEVIL'S SEAL
THE SECOND DEATH
PENANCE OF THE DAMNED
NIGHT OF THE LIGHTBRINGER *
BLOODMOON *
BLOOD IN EDEN *
THE SHAPESHIFTER'S LAIR *
THE HOUSE OF DEATH *
DEATH OF A HERETIC *
REVENGE OF THE STORMBRINGER*

* available from Severn House

PROPHET OF BLOOD

Peter Tremayne

SEVERN
HOUSE

First US edition published in the USA in 2024
by Severn House, an imprint of Canongate Books Ltd,
14 High Street, Edinburgh EH1 1TE.

severnhouse.com

British Library Cataloguing-in-Publication Data
A CIP catalogue record for this title is available from the British Library.

ISBN-13: 978-1-4483-0981-8 (cased)
ISBN-13: 978-1-4483-1491-1 (e-book)

All Severn House titles are printed on acid-free paper.

MIX
Paper | Supporting
responsible forestry
FSC
www.fsc.org FSC® C013056

Typeset by Jouve (UK), Milton Keynes.
Printed and bound in Great Britain by TJ Books, Padstow, Cornwall.

Praise for the Sister Fidelma mysteries

"[A] multilayered, complex, atmospheric, locked-room mystery"
Booklist on *Revenge of the Stormbringer*

"Fascinating legends and mores of ancient Eire meld seamlessly
with a complex mystery"
Kirkus Reviews on *Revenge of the Stormbringer*

"An impressive achievement"
Publishers Weekly Starred Review of *Death of a Heretic*

"A mystery embedded in a revealing look at the violently differing
theological views of early Christians"
Kirkus Reviews on *Death of a Heretic*

"Tremayne plays fair with the readers while evoking the period in
vivid detail. This long-running series remains as fresh and
inventive as ever"
Publishers Weekly on *The House of Death*

"A complex, lovingly written mystery notable for its historical
detail and strong heroine"
Kirkus Reviews on *The House of Death*

"Tremayne expertly incorporates historical and legal details of the
time into the suspenseful plot. This impressive volume bodes well
for future series entries"
Publishers Weekly Starred Review of *The Shapeshifter's Lair*

"Fans of ancient history, myths, and swashbuckling adventures
are likely to enjoy this tale set in seventh-century Ireland . . . this
is a challenging and unusual but deeply satisfying and enjoyable
historical thriller"
Booklist on *The Shapeshifter's Lair*

About the author

Peter Tremayne is the fiction pseudonym of Peter Berresford Ellis, a well-known authority on the ancient Celts, who has utilised his knowledge of the Brehon law system and seventh-century Irish society to create a unique concept in detective fiction.

www.sisterfidelma.com

Propheta autem qui arrogantia depravatus voluerit loqui in nomine meo quae ego non praecepi illi ut diceret aut ex nomine alienorum deorum interficietur.

But the prophet, who corrupted by arrogance, would speak in my name that which I did not command him to say, or that shall speak in the name of other gods, shall be put to death.

Deuteronomy 18:20
Vulgate Latin translation of Jerome, fourth century

pRINCIpal chaRACTERS

Sister Fidelma of Cashel, a *dálaigh* or advocate of the law courts of seventh-century Ireland
Brother Eadulf of Seaxmund's Ham, in the land of the South Folk, her companion
Dego, a warrior of the Nasc Niadh (The Golden Collar), élite bodyguards to Fidelma's brother, Colgú, King of Muman

On An Abhainn Mór (the Great River)
Duach, a boatman
Docht, his mate

At the Abbey of Dair Inis
Abbot Brocc
Brother Guala, the *rechtaire* or steward
Brother Cróebíne, the *scriptor* (librarian)
Brother Fisecda, the physician
Sister Damnat, his assistant
Brother Scatánach, a novitiate
Sister Cáemóc, *chomairlid,* chief counsellor for the female community of the abbey
Brother Echen, son of Eachdae, a former warrior

By Gleann-Doimhin
Lalóg, princess or *bean-tiarna* of Gleann-Doimhin, ('village at
the mouth of the river of the Deep Glen')
Cathbarr, steward to Lalóg
Tóchell, attendant to Lalóg
Scannail the Contentious, a wandering *seanchaidh* (historian)
and bard of the Uí Liatháin
Tóla, captain of a Déisi merchant ship
Echrí, the horse master and smith
Eachdae, a wagoner

By the River Tuairigh (River of Omens)
Íccaid, a physician
Suaibsech, his wife and assistant
Sárán, a Déisi *seanchaidh* (historian)

Among Cnoic na Taibhsí (Hills of the Phantoms)
Caol, warrior and former commander of the Nasc Niadh (Golden
Collar), élite bodyguards of the Kings of Muman
Cadan, his son
Finnat, a female cottager
Conmhaol, a prince at the *crannóg* by *Cnoc an Fiagh* (the Hill of
the Magic Mist)

At Cúasám Echnach, (Echnach's Caves)
Báine, a princess and farmer

At Dún Guairne
Gobán, a smith
Temnén, a young boy
Tomán, his father

x

At the Abbey of Lios Mór
Fíthel, Chief Brehon (judge) of Muman
Colgú, King of Muman, Fidelma's brother
Finguine, heir apparent to Colgú, King of Muman
Abbot Iarna, Abbot of Lios Mór

Frequently mentioned
Tigerna Cosraigib (Lord of the Slaughter or Carnage) of Dún Guairne, the late Prince of the Uí Liatháin

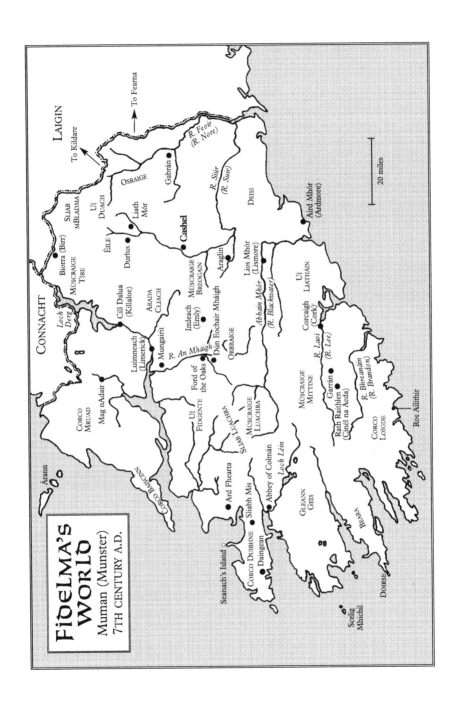

FIDELMA'S WORLD
Muman (Munster)
7TH CENTURY A.D.

LAIGIN

To Kildare

To Fearna

CONNACHT

R. Feoir
(R. Nore)

OSRAIGE

Gabrán

R. Siúr
(R. Suir)

SLIAB
MBLADMA

UÍ
DUACH

Liath
Mór

DEISI

Biorra (Birr)

Durlus

ÉTLE

Cashel

Aird Mhór
(Ardmore)

MUSCRAIGE
TÍRE

Cill Dalua
(Killaloe)

ARADA
CLIACH

MÚSCRAIGE
BREOGAIN

Araglin

Lios Mhór
(Lismore)

Loch
Derg

Luimneach
(Limerick)

Mungairit

Imleach
(Emly)

Dún Eochair Mháigh

Abhain Mhór
(R. Blackwater)

Uí
LIATHÁIN

Corcaigh
(Cork)

CORCO
MRUAD

Mag nAdair

R. An Mháigh

Ford of
the Oaks

Uí
FIDGENTE

ORBRAIGE

R. Laoi
(R. Lee)

Arann

CORCO BAISCINN

SLIAB LUACHRA

MÚSCRAIGE
LUACHRA

MÚSCRAIGE
MITTINE

Garrán

Rath Raithlen
(Cinél na Aeda)

R. Bhreanáin
(R. Brandon)

CORCO
LOÍGDE

Ros Ailithir

Ard Fhearta

Sliabh Mis

Abbey of Colmán

Loch Léin

GLEANN
GEIS

BEARA

Seanach's Island

CORCO DUIBHNE

Daingean

DOIRSE

Sceilg
Mhichil

20 miles

AUThOR'S NOTE

This story is set during the autumnal Irish season called *fochmuine*, the time of sharing the harvest, at the equinox. The year is AD 672.

The main locations are in the territory of the Uí Liatháin, the Descendants of the Grey One (roughly south-east Cork). The story commences at Dair Inis, the Oak Island now called Molana Abbey. It stands at a bend of An Abhainn Mór (the Great River) now anglicised as The Blackwater. No longer an island, Dair Inis is two and a half miles upriver from the township of Eochaill (the 'place of yews') Anglicised as Youghal.

The Abbey of Dair Inis was founded in AD 501 by an Uí Liatháin noble named Máel Anfaid (from which name the Anglicised Molana derived). For a long time it was an isolated Christian outpost surrounded by a population determined to cling on to their Old Faith. Yet within two centuries of its foundation, Dair Inis had grown to be a prominent Christian learning centre with a celebrated library. Its scholars were recorded even in the *Annals of Ulster*: scholars such as Reubin Mac Connadh (d. AD 725) who was one of the great theoreticians of the Celtic Church.

Readers of this series will find references to the coup attempting to overthrow Fidelma's brother, Colgú, King of Muman, in *The House of Death* (2021). Muman (modern Munster) was the most south-westerly and largest of the Five Kingdoms of Éireann. For those interested in the story about the kidnapping of Fidelma's baby son, Alchú, it is found in *The Leper's Bell* (2004) and in *Master of Souls* (2005). The story of Caol's resignation as commander of the élite bodyguards of the Kings of Cashel, will be found in *Atonement of Blood* (2013).

For the reader it is essential to remember that, in ancient Irish law, the concept of inheritance by primogeniture did not exist. A family council, the *derbhfine*, was usually a family group of four generations from a common great-grandfather. Succession to property, to head of the family, therefore to kingship or any office passed through the family, was a decision of this council, which was supposed to choose the person best fitted as a just leader. Therefore the role might not necessarily pass to a son, but to an uncle, brother, nephew and also among the female side, for there was an equality of rights.

As ever, it is my practice to use the original Irish places names with two Anglicised exceptions to help non-Irish readers with modern locations: Tara, instead of Teamhair, 'the conspicuous place', and Cashel, instead of Caiseal, 'stone fort'. Words in Old/Middle Irish (with explanation) are used in the text as some readers tend to question whether the ancient Irish could have had such concepts in the seventh century. Readers anxious about correct pronunciation are referred to www.sisterfidelma.com website of The International Sister Fidelma Society.

CHAPTER ONE

'The Island of Oaks is not far past the next bend of the river. You will soon see the landing stage and the abbey buildings beyond.'

Duach, the boatman, was pointing with his right hand towards the river bank. His smiling features were in contrast to the name he carried, which meant 'the melancholy one'. Not a moment passed without him making some humorous remark. Duach had been born and raised along this wide river, called An Abhainn Mór, the Great River. There was not an inlet, a salmon pool nor a trout run that he did not know. He recognised every area of the river's midge-infested banks. He knew where otters and water voles would watch his boat as it slid pass on the currents. Now and then, he would glimpse badgers standing briefly on hind legs like sentinels watching for danger.

Above, in the great dark oak branches on either bank, wild cats contended for space with pine martens, who would sit scanning the skies with wary eyes for dark golden eagles and the smaller white-tailed sea eagles. If the pine martens descended to the forest floor to escape the winged predators, then there would be danger from another predator, the solitary red fox.

On both sides of the river, ancient oaks vied with one another to line the temperate river banks. Blackthorns broke through in isolated groups, forming copses as if in defiant bastions against the oaks.

Only now and then did the river travellers catch a glimpse of the hills beyond both banks. Although none was more than sixty metres high, from the river they appeared to be the equal of mountains.

Sometimes the human travellers were reminded of the one danger that might concern them in this great natural beauty: a predator as powerful and cunning as themselves. The lonely howl of a grey wolf summoning the pack for the hunt was often heard, rising in eerie resonance. Even armed with weapons and wolfhounds, humans often went in awe of these carnivorous opportunists.

Duach, in his knowledge of the countryside and its inhabitants, was not much in reverence of it. Instead he concentrated his mind on the harsh, unforgiving river from which he made his living. He knew every curve and point along the thirty-five kilometres of the broad waters from the great abbey of Lios Mór to the port of Eochaill, the town of the yew wood, standing on the shore, marking the entrance to the great grey seas beyond.

Duach had risen in his long wooden craft – his *ethar* – in order to haul down its single sail while his silent companion maintained the craft in mid-river with the use of a single oar. The boat was negotiating a right-hand bend in the river, sweeping round a headland on the western bank.

Having fastened the sail, Duach smiled down at his three passengers seated in the well of the river-boat.

'We will soon be landing at the abbey. I trust you agree that it has not been a bad trip, lady?' He addressed the red-haired woman, who was the leader of the three. She glanced up at him with sharp eyes. He was unsure whether they were green or blue. It seemed to depend on how the sun reflected on them.

'Isn't it said that any trip without incident must be a good one?'

she replied solemnly. 'However, I'll be happier when we reach our destination.'

The boatman laughed with good nature. 'Do not the philosophers say that happiness is a way of travel and not a destination?' There was a moment of silence before the woman shrugged. 'It has been a good time to travel, master boatman,' she observed, raising her head to the sky for a moment. 'You have made our journey pleasant enough. Soon we will be entering the dark half of the year and then we will see changes that may not be good along this river.'

Duach, having folded the sail and secured it, sighed. 'It is good that you chose this time to make your journey. The dark half of the year is always bad for travel.'

He saw a frown cross her face.

'Unfortunately, events chose my time for me.' Her voice was resigned. 'It was not my choice that we take passage downriver.'

Duach was not certain how to respond. He knew that she was Fidelma, the legal adviser to her brother, Colgú, King of Muman, the largest and most south-westerly of the Five Kingdoms of Éireann. Duach also knew that the man who sat next to her was her husband, Eadulf, who came from the kingdom of the East Angles beyond the great seas. The third man, seated behind them, he did not know by name, but it was enough to see that he was young and had the build of a warrior. He wore the golden torc of the élite warrior bodyguard of the Eóghanacht kings around his neck. Astonishingly, this young warrior's right arm had been severed just below the elbow, although he carried his shield and sword as if they were natural appendages.

Duach was hesitant, wondering whether he should make any further comment concerning the lady Fidelma's trip. The Uí Liatháin and the Déisi territories stretched along both sides of the Great River, and only six months ago both clans were in alliance to march on Cashel in an attempt to overthrow the young Eóghanacht king. The attempt had failed and now the land was tense with an uneasy peace. Duach could not help feeling nervous with his passengers.

Apart from that, Duach had heard that Fidelma of Cashel was of a brittle temper, like most of the proud Eóghanacht nobles who had ruled the kingdom since time immemorial. Duach had his own pride; he was proud of being a free man; a ferryman, who had been boatman and guide to many distinguished nobles, abbots and churchmen. Such folk would often travel between Lios Mór and the seaport of Eochaill and vice versa, and would use his boat. He was proud that his honour price and reputation made him the confidant of many princes on their journeys.

'If events dictated your choice to travel, then you may ascribe the decision to the Fates, lady,' he ventured. 'That being so, you are lucky that this day, and the river, turned out to be so mild in its temper. However, I share your misfortune of not having a choice as to when I must turn out to ply my *ethar* for trade along the river. It is the Fates that dictate whether I must run before the winds and ride the current of the river or whether I have to defiantly battle both the winds and the current. I have little choice. Each of us has to accept what the Fates allot to us.'

Fidelma stared at the boatman for a moment, her look darkening as she considered his familiarity. Then, abruptly, humorous lines appeared at the corners of her mouth.

'You are right, Duach. We are all in the hands of destiny,' she acknowledged with a deep sigh. 'It is a nice autumnal day. The river is beautiful and there is always much to observe. So, it is a pleasant journey and we give thanks for your services in making it such.'

The long wooden craft was easing round the headland that marked the slow bend of the river, opening up to the stretch of water that reached to the island abbey. Here the river turned to the west, then sharply south. The current increased as it obeyed the dictates of the confining banks. The long narrow island of sturdy oaks, which Duach indicated, was almost overgrown so that the travellers could hardly spot the abbey buildings hidden among the trees. However, they could make out a broad landing stage, with a few small boats of light frames and hide skins bobbing up and down at their moorings. They became aware of a small group of men working on the quayside, unloading items from the small rivercraft.

Anchored in the river, a short distance from the landing stage, was a larger vessel. Its sails were furled and no one was watching from its stout decks. Duach noticed his passengers' inquisitive glances.

'That's a Déisi merchant ship.'

'And yet, it displays the battle standard of a war vessel.' It was the one-armed warrior who spoke.

Duach frowned, wondering what to reply.

'It is not unusual, whatever ship it is, Dego,' Fidelma intervened. 'We are almost in Déisi territory.'

Dego! Duach should have known the warrior, for who had not heard the name of the one-armed champion, who had recently become commander of the King of Cashel's élite bodyguard? The warrior had been caught in an ambush and badly wounded. It had been Brother Eadulf, the husband of Fidelma, who had performed the operation to severe the infected part of the limb, using the medical skills he had learnt in the great medical school of Tuaim-Drecon in the north. Rather than accept what the Fates had dealt him, which would have destroyed most warriors, Dego had fought not only to recover from his injury but, once fit, to retrain and learn the warrior's art again. Soon he could wield his sword with his left hand with the same dexterity as he had used his right. It was said he could still better an accomplished warrior with full use of his limbs. The stories about Dego were often told around the hearths of the river folk. Now Duach looked upon the warrior with an expression approaching reverence.

otatiootorittimeata=>1. tagitemsitinemisiitiaiotoitis

PETER TREMAYNE

Eadulf, however, was examining the larger ship with puzzlement on his features.

'You say the Déisi territory, a place called Eochaill, is on the western bank not far down from the abbey? But the abbey is in Uí Liatháin territory, isn't it?'

'The borders are not as simple as that,' Fidelma replied. 'There was a time when the Déisi were claiming this territory. The settlement of Eochaill became theirs, while the lands beyond the western bank remained Uí Liatháin territory.'

'So what is a Déisi warship, bearing a warlike emblem, doing here?' Eadulf asked.

Duach leant forward with a smile. 'You will see several Déisi merchant ships in these waters. They are entitled to use the river. Eochaill is a port.'

'What would they be trading with the abbey?' Eadulf pressed. 'Does the abbey produce anything?'

Duach shrugged. 'Nothing much that I know of. Of course, it might be just that ships are needed for movement of people between the centres like Árd Mór and Dún Garbháin and the abbey. Who knows? Anyway, it should be of little concern now that we are all at peace again. The conflict ended six months ago.'

Duach had raised a small stag's-head banner on the mast while he had been lowering the sail. The banner, no more than a pennant, was the emblem of the Eóghanacht dynasty and this proclaimed that a noble of the King's household was on board.

When the abbot of Lios Mór had requested Duach to take some distinguished passengers on his journey downriver, including King Colgú's sister, Fidelma, Duach felt he should find an Eóghanacht pennant to display on his vessel at the appropriate time. Someone on the wooden jetty must have spotted it, for a bell started to ring urgently. That the approaching vessel was seen as having no hostile intent was demonstrated by the men on the jetty continuing their tasks, unconcerned by its arrival.

6

'It looks like you are to be officially welcomed,' Eadulf smiled as he examined the people on the jetty. 'It seems even the abbot has turned out to welcome you.'

'That is not the abbot,' corrected Fidelma. 'I met Abbot Brocc and his steward when they attended the peace negotiations at Cashel six months ago.'

'Why was Abbot Brocc at the conference?' Eadulf asked, screwing up his eyes as he tried to recall the event.

'Remember when the woman Sister Ernmas tried to assassinate my brother?' Fidelma reminded him. 'She claimed that she had been educated here in this abbey. Furthermore, seven hostile warships were allowed to anchor in the shelter here. They were full of Uí Liatháin warriors ready to march on Cashel. After the death of the Prince of the Uí Liatháin in the last skirmish, the abbot came to claim innocence of being involved. He denied that Ernmas had links to his abbey.'

'Do you recognise this senior religieux?' Dego asked, turning to the boatman.

'I think that might be the *scriptor*, the librarian, of Dair Inis,' Duach replied. 'I don't know his name.'

Fidelma and Eadulf concentrated their gaze on the group on the jetty.

'There seem to be several women on the jetty, helping with the work,' Dego pointed out.

'I would be surprised if there were not,' Fidelma replied. 'The abbey is a *conhospitae*, a mixed house, although I am not sure in what proportions. The community consists of men and women wishing to dwell together in the service of the New Faith.'

'Well, the *scriptor* wears the robes of a senior member of the community,' Dego continued. 'But I can't see the abbot, or his *rechtaire*, his steward, coming to greet you, lady. That does you little honour.' He sniffed with disapproval.

'The stag rampant of my family might be thought inappropriate

to honour,' Fidelma returned dryly, indicating the pennant. 'Someone would doubtless recognise the symbol and remember that we
were in conflict six months ago.'

The current had accelerated them around the river bend. The
contrary winds did not help them edge close to the shore, and
Duach and his silent companion used their oars dexterously to
keep the craft heading towards the landing stage. They turned the
prow of the vessel slightly, so that it bobbed in a sideways motion
until it gently thudded against the jetty. Duach rose to throw a
mooring rope to those gathered there. In a moment or two the
vessel was secured, and Fidelma and her companions were being
helped out of the craft on to the wooden landing stage.

A thin, skeletal religieux, the one Eadulf had mistaken for the
abbot, barely allowed them time to regain their balance after the
long period seated in the boat before he hurried forward. He carried himself with an almost limping gait, one leg seeming longer
than the other.

'*Deus sit apud vos*,' he greeted formally, but with a smile. 'I am
Brother Cróebíne and I welcome you to the Island of Oaks.'

'*Et vobiscum Deus*,' Fidelma returned solemnly. She ignored
the curious gait of the *scriptor* and his emaciated appearance. 'I
am told you are the *scriptor* here.'

'I have been *scriptor* here several years. One of my companions noticed that Duach's boat was flying the standard of the
Eóghanacht of Cashel. So who am I greeting?'

'I am Fidelma of Cashel, travelling with my husband and
bodyguard.'

This seemed to surprise the librarian and his eyes widened
slightly.

'It is good to welcome you here, Fidelma of Cashel. Yet your
visit comes as a surprise to us, lady. How may we serve you?'

'A surprise visit?' It was Fidelma's turn to be puzzled. 'But I
thought that you were waiting for my arrival?'

'Why would that be?' frowned the librarian, glancing quickly towards Eadulf and Dego, who had followed her on to the wooden jetty. He moved forward to repeat the ceremonial greetings with a fixed smile before turning back to Fidelma. 'We have not been informed of your coming.'

Fidelma was perplexed. 'If you do not know, then we should be taken at once to see Abbot Brocc. It was he who sent for us.'

The expression on Brother Cróebíne's face had become a curious mixture of bewilderment and . . . Fidelma was not sure. Could it be fear? He seemed to have become inarticulate.

'Come, Brother Cróebíne,' she said, irritated. 'Take us to Abbot Brocc. The abbot should be informed that I have arrived. I received his message by the wagoner Eachdae when we were staying at Lios Mór, and it sounded urgent. We came by the fastest way.' She gestured to the river. 'So the sooner I see him, the sooner I shall know what he expects of me.'

It seemed Brother Cróebíne was rooted to the spot with indecision, in spite of Fidelma's growing exasperation. His mouth opened and closed wordlessly a few times before he muttered an apology.

'Forgive me, lady. I know nothing of this . . .'

It was Duach who broke this curious spell of indecision. The boatman came forward and touched his knuckled fist to his forehead.

'I hope all is well, lady? I have to move on to Eochaill. If you no longer have need of our services, then Docht and I shall depart.'

'We thank you for the transport from Lios Mór, Duach,' Fidelma replied, while she signalled to Eadulf, who came forward and handed the ferryman some coins. Moments later they were watching the vessel pull away from the jetty, catching the current south, moving into the centre of the river as Duach and Docht hauled up the single sail. Fidelma smiled as she noticed

Duach already taking down the Eóghanacht pennant from the mast.

'And now?' she said, turning to Brother Cróebíne.

The librarian hesitated a moment before giving a sigh. 'I shall take you to the *rechtaire* of the abbey, Brother Guala.' There was reluctance in the man's tone.

Eadulf immediately took up their bags.

Fidelma was about to point out once again that she had asked to see the abbot and not the steward, but Brother Cróebíne had turned and was walking away. With a shrug, she followed as he led them from the wooden jetty, through the tree-screened bank of the island. Beyond this wall of oaks were the wooden buildings of the abbey. Dair Inis was built entirely from local material. The interior of the Island of Oaks had been cut to make a large clearing and the wood used to build a chapel, various living quarters and outbuildings. Some of the early abbeys built in such form were now being rebuilt in stone as their princes and abbots reflected on more lasting expressions of their roles. Eadulf noticed that there looked to be another entrance on the western bank, across the small rivulet that created the island. There was a major trackway through the rising hills and forests on this side. The abbey and its inhabitants appeared fairly well protected, like a small fortress.

Eadulf remembered that manuscripts were preserved in these wooden buildings. This would be a fine place in the summer, but during the winter months, without stone walls and fires, the precious manuscripts would not last long.

His train of thought was interrupted when a tall, auburn-haired man of erect stature emerged from the door of one of the nearby buildings. He was youthful, with pleasant features, in Eadulf's opinion. He paused as he caught sight of the strangers and examined them curiously with dark brown eyes. He wore religious robes of even more refined quality than those of the *scriptor.* Even from a distance the visitors could see the silver chain around his neck from which was suspended a silver staurogram – the symbolic Tau-Rho – the earliest emblem of the Christian movement. The young man seemed to be in authority.

Brother Cróebíne turned towards him and almost bowed.

'*Salvete, Frater Guala.*'

Brother Guala seemed to tower over the thin librarian as he stood carefully examining the group. There was a look of curiosity in his dark eyes. He first examined Dego, noting his golden torc, and also observing he had only one arm in spite of his warrior's accoutrements. Then he glanced at Eadulf, noticing his Roman tonsure. Finally his gaze came to rest on Fidelma. His eyes hardened in recognition. He pressed his lips together as if he found difficulty in making up his mind how to proceed. Suddenly, he sighed, a deep, resonant sound that seemed to expel all the breath from his body.

Brother Cróebíne intervened before the man spoke.

'Brother Guala, this is Fidelma of Cashel, newly arrived here with her husband, Eadulf, of the kingdom of the East Angles. I believe that you and Abbot Brocc met them when you were summoned to Cashel, following the end of the brief conflict that—'

Brother Guala made a quick dismissive gesture with his hand.

'Fidelma, sister of King Colgú,' he said quietly, in a modulated and pleasing baritone. '*Excipium te cum tuis partibus, domina.*'

'I thank you for your welcome,' Fidelma replied, forgoing the Latin ritual. 'I remember you, Brother Guala. Those were bad days; days that should not have been.'

A flicker of annoyance showed on his features, but disappeared almost before she had registered it.

'Hopefully those bad times have vanished,' he agreed.

'So, perhaps you will be good enough to take us immediately to Abbot Brocc? Brother Cróebíne seems reluctant to fulfil this request.'

For a moment it seemed as if a cold wind had sudden immobilised the steward. Then he glanced swiftly at the thin, anxious face of the librarian. Fidelma, observing, tried to reason what signal was passing between them.

'Is there something amiss?' she queried sharply.

The steward shifted his balance and then tried to form a smile.

'Perhaps we should arrange some accommodation for you first. Some rest and refreshment after your long journey? You came by boat along the Great River?'

'Perhaps it would be better to announce our arrival first to the abbot,' Fidelma countered. 'Abbot Brocc urged us to come to see him at the earliest opportunity. It sounded urgent.'

It was clear from the steward's expression that the abbot's request was news to him.

'If we could see the Abbot Brocc,' Fidelma pressed with emphasised patience, 'I am sure that he would then explain to us, and also to you, why he needed us to come here.' By now she was finding her temper hard to control.

But the steward was stubborn. 'Did Abbot Brocc explain anything in his message?' he asked.

'As the abbot did not confide in you, then I demand that we should be taken directly to him so that he might explain,' she replied, raising her voice to meet her exasperation.

'He explained nothing else to you?' insisted Brother Guala.

Fidelma drew a heavy breath and mentally counted a few seconds. 'He said only that he had urgent need of my services as a *dálaigh* and advocate of—'

'He said no more?' The steward cut her off sharply. 'He said nothing about a *deogaire*?'

Fidelma stared bewilderedly at Brother Guala. 'Why would he mention a soothsayer when he requested my visit?'

Eadulf had flushed with indignation, misinterpreting what the steward meant.

'My wife, the lady, is not a soothsayer. She is a respected advocate of the law; she is a *dálaigh*, not some fortune-teller. There are plenty of people that travel with fairs who claim to tell fortunes for the price of a meal.'

Brother Guala shifted uncomfortably. 'I did not mean to imply that the lady Fidelma was sent for because she was considered to be a mystic. Perhaps I should have said "prophet".'

'You should explain what you mean.' Fidelma now realised there was something serious behind the remark.

'Abbot Brocc told me that he had encountered a woman who had made a prophecy,' Brother Guala explained. 'It caused him much concern and I wondered if it were the reason why he sent for you.'

Fidelma was not amused. 'I have dealt with enough prophets and fortune-tellers to say that, if it was a reason, then it must be some sort of witticism of Abbot Brocc. No one takes them seriously. So, finally, let us go and see him and find out what really troubles him.'

The steward's gaze once more rested on his librarian for a moment as if trying to get support for a decision. Fidelma saw his troubled expression.

Then he went on, 'This female prophet was encountered by Abbot Brocc over a week ago. The prophecy caused the abbot much stress.'

'I fail to see what you are talking about,' Fidelma finally snapped. 'Your abbot requested my presence to consult with me. He said nothing about a soothsayer or prophetess, or that she had caused him any distress.'

'The woman foretold the death of Abbot Brocc.' The steward's words were cold and without emotion.

Fidelma's eyes widened. 'Someone has threatened the life of Abbot Brocc? Is that why he sent for us to advise him?'

'The prophetess was specific. She said that he would be dead before the celebration of the feast of the Blessed Monessa was ended.'

'Monessa?' Eadulf looked puzzled. 'Who was Monessa?'

The steward looked almost pityingly at him, but it was Dego who replied. He had been standing so quietly that they had almost forgotten his presence.

'I heard the story of Monessa when I was escorting the Chief Brehon to a town near Loch Aininn. Monessa was the beautiful daughter of a northern Uí Néill noble. Her father had been converted by Patricius the Briton. He persuaded the girl that she should also be baptised into the New Faith. The story was that Monessa was so pure that, when she rose from the baptismal waters, she fell dead.'

'That does not sound like a nice story,' Fidelma said.

'Why not?' Brother Cróebíne replied. 'Her spirit had been summoned by God because of its intense purity. That is why the women of this abbey celebrate her feast day this very month.'

'I see.' Fidelma exhaled impatiently. 'Are you saying that this so-called prophetess told Abbot Brocc that he would be dead before the end of your feast of Monessa, and the abbot sent for us because he felt it was a specific physical threat?'

'It is certainly an unusual request,' Eadulf pointed out. 'If the abbot feels threatened then there are surely enough strong lads in your abbey to provide protection. They would be more useful in that task than seeking help from a lawyer. Similarly, if the threat was just some curse, I would have thought the abbot's own religious faith was strong enough armour against that.'

Fidelma uttered a disparaging sniff. 'It is not seemly to talk of matters involving the abbot here in his absence. We should go now and speak with him of this matter and not stand gossiping.'

'I overestimated your knowledge, lady,' said Brother Guala. 'The feast of the Blessed Monessa was two days ago.' His voice was cold.

'Then, surely, the threat is over? So let us go to discuss with the abbot.'

'The threat is over but the evil remains,' Brother Guala replied in a hollow tone.

'How so?'

'Abbot Brocc was found dead on the morning of the day of the feast. We buried him last night at midnight, as the tradition stipulates. The prophecy was a true one in all respects.'

chapter two

Shortly afterwards, Fidelma, Eadulf and Dego were escorted into the late Abbot Brocc's chamber, having been shown to their quarters and allowed to have the ritual wash after their travels.

It was from this chamber that the abbot had run the business of his mixed community. Brother Guala had taken it on himself to sit in the abbot's chair. Brother Cróebíne was seated to the steward's right, while an elderly woman sat to the left. She was introduced as Sister Cáemóc, the *chomairlid* or the chief counsellor for the female religious in the abbey. Fidelma and Eadulf took the two remaining chairs facing them. Dego stood respectfully by the door.

Brother Guala broke the uneasy silence of the subdued gathering moments after they had seated themselves.

'I am not sure how these proceedings are run, not being in any way conversant with legal matters. In what manner should we begin? I shall follow your lead, Fidelma. What do you wish to know?'

'Having met Abbot Brocc when he came to Cashel with you, Brother Guala, I presume that was the reason why he sent for me to attend him. After the would-be uprising among the Uí Liatháin, you both came to make the case that this abbey did not have any involvement. At the time of the insurrection, I recall that the conspirator Selbach, Prince of the Eóghanacht Raithlinn, and his women retainers, stayed at this abbey and that the principal mind behind the plot, the vengeful Princess Esnad, claimed that she had even studied here.'

'That was not true.' It was Sister Cáemóc who answered sharply. 'The woman Esnad did not study here.'

'However,' Fidelma continued mildly, 'that is what she claimed. Seven warships of the Uí Liatháin rebels remained anchored in the river by the abbey, apparently waiting for the signal to begin their attack.'

'All the Uí Liatháin were accused of being part of the plan to overthrow your brother,' Brother Guala admitted. 'But this was not true. It is unfortunate that our prince, Tigerna Cosraigib of Dún Guairne, was a leader of the insurrection and died in the fighting. Many of our nobles felt it their duty to follow him. Abbot Brocc and I went to Cashel, to the peace talks, to give evidence and give assurance that we played no part in the uprising. Although we were found innocent of involvement by the Chief Brehon of Muman, many of the nobles of the Uí Liatháin were ordered to pay reparation to Cashel.'

Fidelma's features displayed a faint cynical smile. 'You do not have to remind me, Brother Guala. I only mention meeting you and the abbot in Cashel at that time to indicate a reason why he might choose me to come to give him advice.'

There was an awkward pause.

'I think we should start with the simple facts,' Fidelma continued. 'You have already implied that Abbot Brocc died an unnatural death. You have said that someone foretold his death and that death came about exactly so. We will deal with this prophecy later. First, the facts. In what manner did the abbot meet his death?'

Brother Guala shifted uneasily and glanced at the librarian. It seemed to be a habit that he sought the librarian's approval before he answered any questions.

'He was scalded to death.'

There was a moment's silence as Fidelma and Eadulf considered this surprise answer. Then Eadulf asked: 'You mean he was consumed in a fire?'

'I meant he was scalded, scorched, not burnt by the heat,' Brother Guala replied, enunciating the words slowly and carefully.

'You use the word "scalded", but that could have the same meaning as one who dies in a fire,' Fidelma pointed out. 'Are you saying that death was not in a conflagration?'

'My words should be clear.' Brother Guala was defensive. 'Scalded. I did not mean incinerated.'

Fidelma considered this thoughtfully. 'Then where was the body found?'

'In the *tigh 'n alluis*, the sweat house.'

'You have a sweat house here?' she asked, surprised.

'The abbot was a great advocate of the sweat bath,' the steward replied. 'I am not, but Brother Cróebíne and some others of the community liked to partake of such a means of cleanliness. The abbot's body was found in the sweat house and, in some way, he had scalded himself to death.'

Fidelma caught Eadulf's cynical glance. From their knowledge of sweat houses in other parts of the kingdom, they both knew that such an event would be highly unlikely.

'Then let us start with who discovered the body,' she continued.

'I did,' Brother Cróebíne responded. 'I was with Brother Scatánach at the time.'

'Brother Scatánach? A member of this community? Is he available as a witness and will confirm your story?'

'He is and he will,' the librarian confirmed.

'Then let him be sent for.'

Brother Guala paused to wet his dry lips before inclining his head in confirmation.

Fidelma now turned back to the librarian. 'Tell me briefly how your discovery of the body happened? We shall go into details when we all go to the site of this sweat house tomorrow, when there is light enough.'

Brother Cróebíne paused as if to gather his thoughts. 'It was mid-morning and it was my turn to use the sweat house. Like the abbot, I favoured this method of a healthy cleansing of the body. I had arranged to use it at midday; that is, after the abbot had used it. Brother Scatánach came with me, as I am not as adept as he is at raking out the coals and rekindling the fire.'

'I am surprised to hear that there is a sweat house here,' Eadulf intervened with a frown. 'Is it not dangerous to have it in a wooded area, especially in an abbey where I have seen only buildings of wood?'

'It is not constructed here exactly,' Brother Cróebíne explained quickly. 'You are right that our small island is crowded with trees and combustible wood. Our abbey is built entirely of local trees. The sweat house is built on a hill beyond the small western river that delineates this as an island, above the tree line, in a rocky area. It is situated by a rising stream and pool. It was easy for the community to build it there because it is surrounded by limestone rocks.'

Fidelma had seen many sweat houses across the country and understood the description. They were usually small stone buildings, usually about three metres long, two metres wide and just over two metres in height. They were entered by a small narrow opening through which one usually had to crouch or crawl. Wood or turf was initially piled inside and ignited. The fire continued to be fed until the interior stone walls were almost oven hot. Then the embers were raked out. The person who was to have the sweat bath crawled in naked and sat until a profuse perspiration was engendered. Then they would crawl out and take a plunge in the nearest pool of cold water. This was often a nearby river or lake.

Eadulf had also seen several constructions in his travels

through the Five Kingdoms, especially in the red limestone areas of the land. They were popular among those practising the healing arts, who added various curative herbs to perfume the fire inside. By this method, healers effected a cure for chills and fevers. However, it was usually only nobles and the richer abbeys who had such sweat houses built.

Brother Guala interrupted with a sniff, as though the subject was of no consequence. 'One of our early abbots, a prince of the Uí Liatháin, had the sweat house built. He had seen such constructions in various rocky parts of the kingdom. Some senior members of the abbey use the sweat house when the mood takes them. Personally, I have no liking for it and question its contribution to healthiness. This little island provides us with many more natural places for swimming.'

'But Abbot Brocc used this sweat house regularly?' Eadulf queried.

Before Brother Guala could reply there was a tap on the door and a young religieux entered.

'Ah, this is Brother Scatánach,' Brother Guala said, sounding relieved. 'Now we can get on with more pertinent matters.'

Fidelma turned her attention on the newcomer.

Brother Scatánach, a muscular youth with rich auburn hair, could only just have reached the age of choice, which was seventeen years.

'It is my understanding that you were present when Brother Cróebíne found the body of Abbot Brocc?'

The youth glanced nervously about before realising the steward and librarian were giving him permission to speak.

'I was.'

'And you will witness the veracity of the librarian's evidence about finding the body?' When the youth confirmed this Fidelma said, 'I shall want Brother Cróebíne and you, Brother Scatánach, to take us to this sweat house. There you can both explain in detail exactly how the body was found. For the moment, Brother Scatánach, you can tell me how long you have been a member of the community.'

'I have been here one year, lady,' the youth confirmed. 'But I ran errands for Abbot Brocc to his relatives now and then. I entered service here when I reached the age of choice and became a novitiate.'

'You are of the Uí Liatháin?'

'I am from a village that is a short walk south from here, along the river bank. My father was a fisherman there.'

'I suppose I should have guessed that you were of a fishing family by your name,' Fidelma smiled. It was part of her method to put young ones at ease when questioning them. 'But the name is not associated with river fish?'

'Our family were sea fishermen.'

'And they went out to sea in search of herring?'

The young man smiled. 'That is the meaning of my name, lady.'

'Did you fish with your father and hence you have developed a strong physique?'

The youth looked uncomfortable. 'Often there are hard tasks to be done in the abbey and items to be carried,' he confirmed.

'Like preparing the sweat house fire, stocking it, and emptying the ashes? Do you help with raking the ashes and building the fires in the sweat house?'

'It is one of the tasks I perform,' Scatánach admitted.

'And you did so on the day the abbot's body was discovered?'

Brother Scatánach glanced again at Brother Cróebíne, seeking his permission before replying.

'I did not do so for the abbot, but I did so for Brother Cróebíne. That was how we discovered the body.'

'You did not prepare and clean the sweat house for the abbot?' Fidelma frowned.

'I did not,' denied the youth.

'Then who did that task for him?' she pressed.

'He did it himself,' Brother Scatánach replied.

'It was an obsession of the abbot that he liked to prepare his own sweat bath and clean it afterwards,' Brother Cróebíne explained.

'As I have said,' Brother Guala interrupted with emphasis, 'Abbot Brocc was an advocate of the healing qualities of the sweat house. He used it often.'

'He would do so especially before the full moon,' added Brother Cróebíne. 'I consider more than once a week was weakening to the body. But the abbot had different ideas on the matter.'

'So did the abbot have his bath regularly?' Eadulf repeated. Fidelma noted from his tone he had something in mind.

'Just so.'

'Then it would have been known in advance what days he went to the sweat house?' Eadulf reflected.

'He had a ritual, it is true,' Brother Guala admitted. 'He always went to have his sweat bath on the morning of *Dardoin*.'

Eadulf knew this was the day that in his own language was called *Thor's daeg* – Thursday.

'I find it difficult to understand. How could the abbot have been scalded, resulting in his death? I know how these sweat baths work. You would not enter it until the embers were raked out and the stones would not be hot enough to inflict any injury. Did no one ever attend him to prepare the fire or to take the coals out when ready?'

'We have said as much.' It was Brother Cróebíne who responded firmly. 'The abbot always insisted on preparing his bath alone. He was a strong man. It was a sacred ritual for him.'

'So another question,' Eadulf continued with a frown. 'Who was the physician who examined the body? Who recorded how the abbot came by his death?'

The librarian now glanced appealingly to Brother Guala.

The steward shifted nervously in his chair. 'Our physician, Brother Fisecda, was called away three days ago to the homestead of Conmhaol, a local prince. A messenger had been sent here asking for the assistance of our physician as the prince was suffering with some ague. He always preferred to be treated by Brother Fisecda. The physician had not returned when the body was found and so he was not able to examine it.'

'Brother Fisecda, you say?' Eadulf asked. 'Is that his true name and not just his rank?'

Eadulf remembered from his own time studying the healing arts that the term *fisecda* indicated that a physician was of high qualification.

'It is his true name,' Brother Guala confirmed. 'Brother Fisecda joined us having studied the healing arts elsewhere. He was well known for his knowledge in these parts.'

It was clear by now that Fidelma was longing to intervene.

'You say that the body was not examined by your own physician, in spite of the fact that you suspect foul play. Is this local prince so important that he has a prior claim to be attended by your physician over the needs of his own abbot?'

'Prince Conmhaol would be ruler of the Uí Liatháin if had he accepted the decision of the *derbhfine*, the family council, after Tigerna Cosraigib was killed. He refused the office. But Brother Fisecda has a duty to the princes to whom the abbey pays tribute. Prince Conmhaol dwells on the Hill of the Magic Mist, which is the—'

Fidelma made a silencing motion with one hand. 'What you are saying is that Prince Conmhaol still retains such authority that the physician of this abbey would prefer not to antagonise him? I presume that you sent to his fortress to inform your physician that the abbot was dead, and in mysterious circumstances? The law states that a competent physician must examine the body and bear witness to the cause of death in such event.'

PETER TREMAYNE

'What point would there be in that?' demanded the steward. 'Anyone could see Abbot Brocc was dead. We did not need a qualified physician to tell us that much.'

'The need is that the law demands it, especially if, as you imply, foul play is claimed. I understood from the first that you claimed this was murder from the unusual circumstances. Or am I mistaken?'

'I have told you of the mysterious prophecy of Abbot Brocc's death and that it was fulfilled on the very day foretold,' Brother Guala replied hotly.

'Which we will shortly deal with. It is all the more reason that the law must be followed precisely. Did anyone examine and prepare the body prior to burial?'

Brother Guala grimaced almost in a dismissive manner. 'As I say, we could see the abbot was dead. There was little need of an examination. We needed to follow the religious custom and bury his body at midnight of the same day or, at latest, the next day.'

Eadulf was surprised at this defence, having learnt from Fidelma the important laws of medical procedure relating to crime.

'The abbot was therefore buried, and yet no physician examined the body, even though you claim that his death was unnatural?' he asked with more than a little irony in his tone.

'There was no reason to hold up custom to find a physician,' Brother Guala insisted. 'The leading members of the community all agreed on that.'

'I presume that the body was washed and wrapped in accordance with tradition before it was buried?' Fidelma asked. 'If so, then someone must have performed those tasks.'

Brother Guala remained silent but his whole manner was belligerent.

It was Sister Cáemóc who responded. 'I believe Sister Damnat

24

took charge of that. She helps our physician and looks after the minor ailments of the community.'

'Then I shall want to see her immediately.' Fidelma's voice mirrored her exasperation.

The order was clear. Sister Cáemóc rose, went to the door of the chamber and had a whispered exchange with someone beyond. She then returned and resumed her seat.

'Sister Damnat will be here shortly. I have sent for her,' she announced unnecessarily and in an almost challenging tone.

'While we wait, can we consider the prophecy that Brother Guala makes much of?' Eadulf asked. 'As we were talking about the abbot's bathing habits, a point occurred to me that I would not wish to ignore.'

'That point being?' Fidelma asked.

'The steward said that some fortune-teller had told the abbot that he would not live beyond the end of the feast day of Monessa,' Eadulf said. 'Prophecy is one thing, but a threat is another. The abbot must have seen it as a threat otherwise why did he send for us to come urgently to give him advice? And having done that, why did the abbot disregard the threat?'

'You think he disregarded the threat?' Fidelma asked, wondering what was in his mind.

'On the very day he had been told that he would die, he went alone to this sweat house. We are now told that the sweat house is secluded and away from your abbey buildings. Away from witnesses. Is that not so, Brother Cróebíne?'

'As you will see for yourself tomorrow,' the librarian confirmed. 'There is a wooden bridge to the Uí Liatháin bank and, from there, a track through the oak wood. One climbs a hillock to the rocky level where the sheltered sweat house was built.'

'That is the very point,' Eadulf said. 'Surely on that day of all days he would take attendants? Yet he goes alone to make the fire, rake the embers and so on. Even if he had the peculiar obsession to perform his toilet ritual alone, that day he would have been conscious of the prophecy's threat.'

'But that is what he did,' Brother Cróebíne declared.

'I was raised with the maxim that if it doesn't sound true, it is not true,' Eadulf remarked.

'It is what he did,' the librarian echoed flatly.

'Was he not reminded and forewarned of the dangers of going alone?' Fidelma demanded. 'If this was regarded as a threat, it would have been the logical thing to do.'

'It was a matter that was not known to me until after we found the body,' the librarian declared. 'The only person that the abbot had confided in was Brother Guala. It was only when the body was found that the steward told the rest of the community.'

Fidelma swung round to the steward. 'I have the impression that you considered it more serious than most. Why did you not remind your abbot of this?'

Brother Guala's jaw jutted pugnaciously. 'Do you imply that I am responsible for the abbot's death?' he snapped.

'How did I suggest that? You told us that the abbot confided in you that he had met with some sort of soothsayer,' Fidelma replied. 'There are plenty of fortune-tellers about these days. Usually they are present at the great fairs. There you pay to hear their tales of future happenings, but these are rarely as specific as a time of death.'

'Abbot Brocc told me in confidence,' replied Brother Guala.

'Then we must know more. You make a point of the fact that this prophecy came true. That alone is why you considered the death suspicious, as would anyone. You have also implied that it was a reason why the abbot must have sent for us, although you admit that he did not tell you that he had.'

'I am not a gullible attendee at a fair.' The steward stirred uncomfortably in his chair. 'I took the prophecy seriously. The abbot confided to me that the prophetess did not come to the abbey, but he encountered her while he was walking alone in the woods coming back from the sweat house. This was about a week before the fatal day. That was when he received the prophecy.'

Fidelma frowned. 'It sounds a dramatic encounter.'

'You know what time of year this is?' Brother Guala's tone was suddenly softer and almost fearful.

Fidelma glanced irritably at Eadulf. She just wanted to deal with the practical facts of the death of the abbot, but it was too late to divert back. She felt that she might as well indulge the steward into explaining something he obviously felt important.

'It is the month of *fochmuine*, the end of the harvest and the sharing of it,' she replied. 'The time of bringing the horses and cattle herds into shelter before the onset of the cold days.'

'*Haerfest,*' confirmed Eadulf, giving the season's name in his own language. 'The harvest is the second point of the year when the day and night are of equal length.'

'That may be,' Brother Guala replied with gritted teeth. 'I speak of ceremonies connected with the beliefs that we have maintained even after the adoption of the New Faith. It is a time of great spiritual danger with the growing darkness that soon will encompass the skies. It is the time of year when we believe the Otherworld will soon come into conjunction with this world. Then bad things can happen. Shades of the departed can cross into our world, exacting vengeance.'

'We are trying to assemble the facts as they apply to this world,' Fidelma replied icily. 'Although Abbot Brocc dismissed the prophecy – whether it was a supernatural or a physical threat – it should have been treated more seriously. His death was stipulated for a certain day, that day being the feast of Monessa. When you told us of this, Brother Guala, it seemed that *you* took it very seriously.'

The steward's expression tightened.

'It would therefore be logical to have reminded Abbot Brocc

that threats of death are often physical, even if the abbot dismissed it as some ranting of a fortune-teller. He was going to a place isolated from the abbey and on the very day the threat was said to happen. Why did you not remind him of it? Why was no one designated to accompany him to his bath? You could have sent someone after him as a guard without his knowledge if he was so adamant he wanted no one with him.'

There was a silence. Then Brother Guala exhaled and spread his arms helplessly. It seemed one of his favourite expressions of communication.

'You did not know Abbot Brocc. He did not believe in threats or prophecies.'

'Therefore I expect you now to tell me all the details surrounding this prophecy or threat, and why he would send for me, as a *dálaigh*, if he did not take it seriously.'

Brother Guala flushed and, for a moment, seemed unable to a response. There was a knock at the door, and Dego, standing patiently by, attended to it. A woman of tall stature entered.

'Sister Damnat,' Sister Cáemóc announced, waving the newcomer forward.

The physician's assistant halted before Sister Cáemóc and Brother Guala, hands folded underneath her robes. Her headdress almost disguised her dark rusty-auburn hair. She was quite young, with oval features, and her bright, grey eyes were both intelligent and attractive. Her darting gaze showed that those bright eyes missed nothing.

'Fidelma of Cashel is a *dálaigh*, an attorney of the law, who needs to ask you some questions relating to the death of Abbot Brocc,' Sister Cáemóc told her.

The girl turned towards Fidelma and then hesitated and looked back to Brother Guala. Her question to him astonished both Fidelma and Eadulf.

'What am I allowed to say to the *dálaigh*?'

chapter three

'You are allowed to say the truth and only the truth.' Fidelma's voice was sharp but her scowl was reserved for Brother Guala.

The steward's face had reddened and, for a moment, he found speech difficult.

'A misunderstanding, lady,' he finally said. 'Because of the peculiar circumstances surrounding the abbot's death, everyone was told not to speculate about it.'

When the young girl turned to face Fidelma there was a ghost of a smile on her features. It was as if the young religieuse had little respect for Brother Guala's authority.

'Brother Guala informs us that you prepared the body of Abbot Brocc for burial,' Fidelma stated without further preamble.

'That is so.'

'I understand that you usually perform this task with the physician.'

'Brother Fisecda is absent from the abbey. I am usually called to help him in some medical matters, and to perform some tasks whether he is here or not.'

'That means that you have some medical knowledge?'

'I was trained by my father to look after the sick. When some-one dies, after the physician examines them, I merely wash and prepare the corpses and wrap them in the linen winding sheet. Little medical knowledge is needed for that, but my father was known and respected for his skill in this territory. I would like to think I have inherited a little of his good training.'

Fidelma could see that Eadulf was holding back a desire to continue the questions. She looked at him and nodded assent.

'If the death was suspicious, as we are now told it was in Abbot Brocc's case, you must have some competency in expressing an opinion as to the cause,' he asked. 'When you first examined the corpse, what did you see? Presumably it was brought to you in the abbey as it had been found in the sweat house?'

'It was not brought to me,' Sister Damnat replied. 'I was called to go to the sweat house. I examined the body there in the presence of Brother Guala, who accompanied me.'

'How did this come about?' demanded Fidelma irritably, looking sharply at Brother Guala. 'I thought only Brother Cróebíne and Brother Scatánach went to the sweat house?'

'Brother Cróebíne sent Brother Scatánach to fetch me and Sister Damnat when the body was discovered. The librarian knew our physician was not here so he asked me to accompany Sister Damnat. It was in my presence that the body was removed from the sweat house and examined.'

'You all saw the body before it was removed from the sweat house?' Fidelma interposed quickly, thinking that extracting correct information was like fishing for a particular fish in a pool. She looked back to Sister Damnat. 'Did you spot anything about the corpse that would have led you to understand how the abbot came by his death?'

'I had no immediate thoughts, lady. Nor did I enter the sweat house. Anyway, it would be too dark inside for me to see anything. The body was brought out to me.'

The librarian shifted his weight nervously.

'I would say—' he began, but Fidelma motioned him to silence with a hand gesture.

'Describe your exact role in this matter,' she instructed Sister Damnat.

The young religieuse shrugged. 'When I and the steward arrived with Brother Scatánach, Brother Cróebíne showed us the body of the abbot. From what we could see, the abbot was lying among the heap of ashes inside the sweat house. This was strange as all the ashes have to be raked out before the one who is taking the sweat bath climbs in. It was as if the ashes had been piled over his body. He was, of course, naked. So, having observed this, I suggested that the abbot's body be taken out and laid on the grass before the entrance, where I could examine it in the daylight.'

'Did that not shock you? That the naked body had been put inside and the fire built over him?' Eadulf asked.

'Death comes in many forms,' Sister Damnat observed philosophically, almost without emotion. 'I have seen worse deaths in combat. It was scarcely six months since there were skirmishes around here at the time the Prince of the Uí Liatháin called for his warriors to march on Cashel.'

'In what state was the abbot's body?' Eadulf pressed.

'We poured water over it to rid it of the ashes so that its condition could be observed. In doing so, I noticed that, while certain small areas were scalded, it was not burnt.'

'Would that be unusual?' Eadulf asked.

'It was clear that the strength of fire was insufficient to inflict any significant burns.'

'You drew no conclusions from the state of the corpse?' Fidelma asked sharply.

Sister Damnat almost jumped nervously at her sudden intervention.

'Conclusions?' She seemed confused.

'So far we have been told that the abbot was scalded to death in the sweat house. Now you say that you saw nothing to confirm this.'

'The body was not burnt or badly scalded, the skin reddened, discoloured or blistered,' Sister Damnat confirmed. 'At the time, the body was dirty. It was as if it had been covered with a heap of ashes. As I said, we washed it as best we could to check on the condition of the skin. I further examined it after we transported the body back here, where it could be washed properly.'

It was Eadulf who pressed the point. 'Surely, if you cleansed the body, ready to wrap it in the winding sheet, you must have seen some indication of how the abbot came by his death. You drew no conclusion from what you observed?'

The woman paused a moment. 'I would say that the abbot died outside the sweat house and that his body was then pushed inside and covered with the ashes from the fire to make it look as if he had died inside.'

When the girl appeared to hesitate, Eadulf asked, 'You were confronted with the dead body of Abbot Brocc. The question would surely have come to you immediately: how did he die?'

The woman glanced nervously at Brother Guala before answering. 'I saw no major wounds, if that is what you mean?'

Brother Guala shifted uneasily and cleared his throat. 'This is why I did not want any speculation. If Abbot Brocc were subject to a prophetic curse, then it would be consistent with the shadow of death passing by, leaving no clue.'

Fidelma's sigh was audible. 'We are back to this curse again . . . You are of the New Faith – how do you reconcile your faith with such a prophecy? Do you believe in some supernatural curse being placed on the abbot? Are you saying that you believe in shadows of evil?'

Brother Guala's expression tightened, his skin pale. 'I believe in the New Faith. That does not mean I can deny the evil spirits of the Holy Scriptures. Should I deny what is clear? Are not Beelzebul and Beliar named as we take the Greek words from the Hebrew – *satanas* and *diaboles*? They are the enemies of God and of the True Faith. The New Faith tells me to recognise the shadows of evil and acknowledge their curses. They are servants of the great Daimon, the one who attempts to destroy our souls and our flesh. They have surely destroyed Abbot Brocc.'

Fidelma stayed thoughtfully silent a moment.

'I do not intend to question your beliefs, Brother Guala,' she said quietly. 'My intention is to discover who is responsible for the death of your abbot. Whether the culprit is human or supernatural, I have duties, as an advocate of the law, to follow the paths prescribed by law. We must take each step in order. It seems that Sister Damnat saw no wounds on the body when she washed and prepared the corpse for burial. Is that correct?'

The young nurse regarded her nervously, jerking her head in affirmative fashion.

'Neither were there any marks of burns or discolouration of the flesh that would be consistent with contact with fire or hot stones?' Fidelma continued.

'Only that the body was covered in ashes, as I said.'

'When the ashes were washed away, it was obvious that it was not the fire that was a cause of death and the body had been placed where a fire had been. After the fire had died, ashes were spread over the body. Why?'

'Not to hide it, but to mislead us about the cause,' Eadulf suggested.

'That would be logical,' Sister Damnat agreed.

'It also means that we are no further along the road of knowing how the abbot died,' Fidelma said. 'We have nowhere to go from here.'

'There is one possible solution in law,' Eadulf offered quietly.

'Which is?' Fidelma frowned.

'I think it is what is called the act of uncovering. We would call it exhumation.'

Fidelma was astonished the idea had not come to her mind.

'In law, we sometimes also call it *fochlaid*, or uprooting,' she confided. 'It is rarely done.'

'Whatever way,' Eadulf muttered, 'it means digging up the body for examination by a qualified physician to confirm the cause of death.'

'That is sacrilege!' Brother Guala was staggered.

'Yet it is still law,' Fidelma added coldly.

Brother Cróebíne was shaking his head in amazement.

'I have encountered the idea,' he confessed. 'What you say is basically true, but my understanding was that there has to be agreement on this matter. There must be the permission of the next of kin. They can prevent such a thing.'

'The abbot assumed authority to represent the Uí Liatháin during the peace talks. That means he is a member of the family council, the *derbhfine*. He must have kin to appeal to.'

This almost brought a smirk to the librarian's face.

'You should know by now, Brother Saxon, that in the abbey we are the *fine*. We are the kin, and the abbot is regarded as the father of the kin.'

Eadulf was about to point out that he was an Angle and not a Saxon when he realised the librarian was right. He had forgotten that the abbots and abbesses were often former secular nobles who established their religious communities, which controlled a great deal of tribal land and wealth. An abbot's honour price was often the equivalent of that of a territorial prince. He made a sudden guess.

'Then if the inhabitants of the abbey are the *fine*, I presume the leading members are considered the *derbhfine*, who can approve or disapprove the policies of an abbot in running the abbey and so can appoint a successor.'

'The curse of the Evil One,' Brother Guala muttered dramatically.

'Can you give us an alternative speculation?' Fidelma went on, ignoring the steward.

'There is, of course, a condition when the heart seems to stop beating, caused by *anordaighech,* as the physicians used to call it.'

'Irregular beating of the heart, or heart trembling,' Eadulf explained quickly to the others. There was suddenly an excited look in his eyes. 'It is condition that occurs with many people so that it is not considered suspicious. Just that some people are unfortunate in their physical condition. I learnt that when I was studying the healing arts.'

'Is that what you believe, Sister Damnat?'

'Abbot Brocc was a strong man. I merely mention it to show there are other alternatives. However, he could have been suffocated.'

'The word you use, *múchach,* implies suffocation,' Eadulf immediately interpreted. 'That is usually achieved by pressing down so that the victim cannot breathe and thus chokes to death. I am no expert, but the words *múch* or *tachd* can equally apply to suffocation or strangling.'

'But if it were strangulation there would be marks around the throat,' Fidelma pointed out.

'Not necessarily,' Eadulf answered before the girl did. 'Marks on the throat would only mean the victim was manually strangled. Squeezing the throat and preventing the air flow always leaves marks. The same purpose would be obtained by covering the mouth and nose by other means. Say, a pillow pressed over the face.'

'There is an argument that cancels such a theory.' It was the librarian, Brother Cróebíne, who spoke.

Fidelma turned to him with a questioning expression.

'The body of the abbott was found naked in the sweat house,' the librarian said simply.

Fidelma caught the meaning at once.

'You are saying that no one would have had the room to crawl inside with the abbot. No one could have room to apply enough exertion to suffocate him in such a confined space, even if the abbot was already entirely unconscious,' Eadulf summed up.

'Sister Damnat confirms that there were no marks on the throat that would indicate strangulation. Therefore he was not strangled. That leaves us with . . .?' Fidelma let the question hang in the air.

'I only made the suggestions for consideration.' Eadulf apologised. 'My personal thought would be that the abbot was more likely to have had a condition of his heart . . . the heart trembling, as you said.'

'It is possible.' Brother Cróebíne sounded a little too enthusiastic. 'Abbot Brocc was inclined to indulge himself in many ways.'

'Indulge himself? In what manner?' Fidelma asked, disappointed as she thought Sister Damnat had been about to reveal something more conclusive.

The librarian looked uncomfortable when he realised Fidelma was asking him a direct question. 'I mean that he was fond of the fermentation of apples made by Sister Cáemóc. She is distiller in the abbey and our cider is held in high regard in the surrounding country.'

This brought forth a snort from the elderly religieuse. 'No one has ever died from my cider,' she muttered.

'It is a logical explanation,' Eadulf commented. 'If he drank too much, ate too much and then went off to a sweat bath, and he had been following this course for some time, then he could easily have suffered from such an irregularity of his heart. Conditions that day could have caused such a trembling that the heart ceased to resume its regular motion and the life would be taken out of him.'

'And that would have left no outward mark upon him. His untimely death would have been by natural causes,' the librarian added in satisfaction.

'Except that there is an argument against this,' Fidelma pointed out.

'Which is?' Brother Cróebíne demanded.

'We have been told that Abbot Brocc was a strong man. He went to the sweat house alone, preferring to do all the heavy chores, such as collecting the wood, preparing the fire, raking the ashes and so on. Younger men, apparently less fit, would take a friend or colleague with them to help with the heavy tasks. Abbot Brocc does not appear to have been a weak man.'

'That is so,' Eadulf agreed. 'I say that the best means of reaching a conclusion would be to exhume the body for an examination. That should be done by agreement so no one would be offended.'

Brother Guala turned to Fidelma with a clenched jaw and stared inarticulately at her for a moment or two before composing himself.

'As the steward, and now acting abbot of this community, I say again that I refuse to give authority to such a sacrilegious undertaking.'

'I agree,' the librarian said firmly.

'Your decision can be overridden,' Fidelma pointed out.

'Only by the Chief Bishop, as you acknowledge,' Brother Guala replied. 'And we are a long way from Cashel or from Imleach. Even if we were ordered to undertake the exhumation so that cause of death may be accertained, I would still refuse such a procedure.'

'On what grounds?' Fidelma requested firmly.

'By my authority as the acting head of the ecclesiastic *derbh-fine* of this abbey. It is my right to do so.'

Fidelma shook her head. 'I think you know that the only advantage that you have is that Abbot Cuán, Chief Bishop of this kingdom, would not be able to reach here in time to make a difference. Putrefaction would have destroyed the evidence needed.'

'My concern is to prevent sacrilege. Nothing else.'

'That is your opinion, but it is contrary to your law,' Eadulf muttered. 'Our concern is to find out how Abbot Brocc was killed and, if he met with such an unnatural death as you claim, to discover who was responsible. That is – to make sure that the law is not ignored.'

'The law is your concern. The happenings in this abbey are now mine. Had Brocc been more concerned about not offending the phantoms of this place, then he might have assuaged their vengeance.'

'You speak in strong terms about the Old Faith, Brother Guala. How long have you been in this abbey?' Fidelma asked softly.

'I have served here a full decade. I am of the Uí Liatháin. I fail to see—'

'But you did not train here?' she said quickly, then turned to the *scriptor.* 'And you, Brother Cróebíne, are you of the Uí Liatháin?'

'I am, but was sent to study the New Faith at the school of Garbháin, son of Luigir. That is in the territory of the Déisi.'

'At the seaport called Dún Garbháin? I know it well,' Fidelma replied. 'Did you serve in any other community?'

'I did spend a period studying at Lios Mór. Why do you ask these questions?'

'I am well aware that the Uí Liatháin are not fully accepting of the New Faith and, indeed, most of your people are defensive of the Old Faith. What is your position on that?'

'We are aware that Dair Inis is an island of the New Faith in a territory where the Old Faith is still strong.'

'But it is said your archives are achieving a growing reputation. I believe you even train copyists here. You must be very proficient at your work.'

'It is not for me to assess the standard of my own work, lady.'

'Yet you have trained others here?'

'A few,' admitted Brother Cróebíne. 'I have a very promising young student in Brother Reuben mac Connadh. He has a fascination for collecting and examining the laws of Rome, which have been adopted by some who now advocate that Christians follow the new philosophies and rules of the Faith approved in Rome.'

'Interesting . . .' Fidelma paused.

'What has this to do with the matter we were discussing?' Brother Guala demanded.

'Frankly, I was left wondering why the steward of a Christian abbey is so defensive of the stories and rituals of the Old Faith.'

'We are an island, an isolated speck in a sea of the old culture. To survive we must respect the beliefs of those who live around us.'

'Come now, Brother Guala. You are a learned man and, moreover, you say you are of the New Faith. Yet you sound as though you have placed belief not only in the prophetess who foretold Abbot Brocc's death, if she exists, but also in such entities as emissaries from the world beyond; people with supernatural powers that are beyond our understanding.'

Brother Guala drew himself up with flushed features. He spoke in anger. 'Where is it written that being Christian, one of the New Faith, means you must not hold such beliefs in spirits and the intervention of beings from the world beyond? Is it not shown that the New Faith is founded on belief in the supernatural? We believe people can walk on water, can change the shape and nature of objects, can talk with beings others cannot see, can be cured of diseases, blindness and others maledictions by the touch or word of another.'

'They were miracles of the Christ,' rebuked Sister Cáemóc. 'And of those we designate as saints and martyrs, and we are told to entreat their intervention to help us with their miracles.'

'Then the same can be attributed to the old gods. It is not only the New Faith in which we accept that death has no dominion. We accept that our souls are constant. When we died in this world, we were reborn in the Otherworld. Death in the Otherworld allowed us to be reborn in this one.'

Fidelma was regarding him in some surprise.

'For a steward of a Christian community, Brother Guala, it sounds as if you have not yet lost the Old Faith.'

'I am trying to point out that there are things we must understand before we discard the old for the new. The Old Faith of our people accepted concepts that are claimed by some as teachings of the New Faith. The New Faith acclaims many that are blessed to have supernatural powers, while the Old Faith did exactly the same. We evoke the names of Blessed Ones in the New Faith and ascribe to them functions that we once attributed to the old gods. Now we call upon a Holy Spirit, believe in archangels, angels and saints – are these beings not supernatural according to the Faith?'

For a moment Fidelma was silent, staring at the man in surprise. Here was an intellectual argument that she had not encountered. The man was certainly erudite. She realised that Brother Cróebíne was looking at him with an indefinable expression, while Sister Cáemóc seemed horrified.

'Brother Guala,' Fidelma said slowly, 'let me concede that there are supernatural beings in whatever Faith people follow. It is clear that you are a student of theology and, as such, an expert in your field. Obviously we must return to this matter of the prophesy. I say that if a prophet is so accurate, they must have been involved in the deed. I doubt phantoms suffocate their victims, as Sister Damnat suggested might have been the abbot's fate, in preference to destroying them with lightning bolts.'

Fidelma looked round at Sister Damnat, who had been silent during the arguments, and smiled encouragingly.

'I have a feeling that you were interrupted when you were

about to put forward your speculation, Sister. You started by saying that there were no marks on the throat . . .'

Sister Damnat straightened and moved forward.

'I would have said that the contusion on the temple would not have killed him. It could have rendered him insensible before he was placed in the sweat house. Insensible long enough to smother him. That might imply that a person of strength could have attacked him, suffocated him and placed him in the sweat house.'

Brother Guala, glowering with anger, suddenly lost his self-control.

'I tell you clearly' – his voice was raised almost to the level of a screech – 'not only was Brocc cursed, he was told what day he would die. The prophecy was fulfilled. On that very day that he was told that he would meet his fate, he was dead by the sun's zenith. He was unwise enough to anger the Grey One, to ignore the curse. He sought no projection against the unholy spirits that were threatening him. He was struck down by them. He died by the hand of the Evil One.'

CHAPTER FOUR

A bell was ringing in a deep summoning tone, indicating that the time was approaching for the main meal of the day.

Warm water had been placed in the guests' washroom. It seemed that rules of the community were similar to the traditions maintained by the richer classes in which the main wash was made before the evening meal. Fidelma and Eadulf were offered their own sleeping quarters in a chamber next to the washroom area. Dego was offered a bed in the main dormitories, sharing the bathing facilities with the general members of the community.

When Fidelma came to rejoin Eadulf in their chamber she was anxious to tell him that she had found several surprise items in the washroom.

'It seemed the sisters of the abbey have not entirely abandoned the sin of vanity,' she announced with a characteristic grin. 'I have never seen such a choice of *boltanas* on the shelf of an abbey washroom.'

Eadulf looked perplexed; he had not encountered the word before.

'Fragrances,' Fidelma explained, having thought for an alternative expression.

'*Vanitas vanitatum dixit Ecclesiastes; vanitas vanitatum et omnia vanitas,*' Eadulf returned solemnly.

Eadulf knew that Fidelma often used a fragrance made from rose petals. Sometimes sandalwood was mixed with it as a base. Most people used the scents from a variety of plants, from honeysuckle to an apple, often distilled with rosemary.

'But so many,' Fidelma repeated.

'Well,' Eadulf replied, 'men use such fragrances as well as women.'

'But it is unusual in such a place. There were apple-scented soap bars. There was even a variety of sweet-smelling herbs on the face and wrists. But I have never known females in communities such as this to use such a variety of sweet-smelling fragrances. Certainly women of noble birth carry their comb bag, in which you will often find some favourite perfume among their toiletries, but the number here is surprising. Among the fragrances I found in the jars on the shelves were some quite valuable ones. I even found a jar of Nard.'

'What is that?' Eadulf demanded, totally lost.

'*Ungentum nordum,*' Fidelma declared. 'That was what it was called in Rome where I first encountered it.'

'I have no recollection of this Nard, nor do I even know the word.'

'It is a perfume that carries an aroma of early spring. *Ungentum nordum* is an amber-coloured liquid that has a heavy sweet smell of woodland. It is a fragrance used mainly by elderly women, but expensive. I have never seen it so far west, so it is doubly surprising to find it in a religious community.'

'I have never heard you talking about perfumes so fervently before,' Eadulf with humour. 'I didn't think they interested you to that extent.'

'The point that I am making is: here we are, in an abbey, not large and not endowed by the favours of a king. This is not some major abbey such as Imleach, Árd Magh or Fearna,' Fidelma explained. 'Who can afford such an array of perfumes for its female members? Yet the place reminds me of certain abbeys gifted by nobles of wealth.'

'Shouldn't we be concentrating on the murder of Abbot Brocc?'

'It is just an observation of something unusual,' she replied, annoyed at his reaction. 'Anything unusual is worthy of observation.'

It was then that the final bell summoned them to the evening meal.

If they had thought that they would be shown into a traditional refectory they were mistaken. Instead they were led to a separate screened area, which was apparently where the abbot and senior members of the community had their meals. The meal was presided over by Brother Guala, who led the *Grasta* or *Gratias*, as it was called in Latin. It had taken Eadulf a long time to accept the word *Grasta* was not adopted from the Latin for 'thanks', but an ancient native word, *grádh*, meaning love and, used as *grás*, expressing favour and benefit.

'O Lord, bless the food and drink of Thy servants always, now and forever and through the Ages of Ages.'

It was delivered in the traditional singing fashion, which Eadulf realised indicated that the steward was a cultural traditionalist. What interested him now was, as Fidelma had previously observed, the signs of wealth in the abbey. This part of the refectory was like a nobleman's feasting room where each table had a cupbearer, a young novitiate, to ensure each cup was filled. He recognised Brother Scatánach among them. Each table also had a traditional carver, whose duty it was to serve the diners with whatever dishes they preferred. Each diner was handed a newly washed linen napkin and a spoon. It was the custom that everyone brought his or her own knife to the table.

As well as water, the cupbearers poured mugs of *brocait*, an ale sweetened with honey and seasoned with spices. Fidelma found the drink too rich to go with the dishes placed before her.

She much preferred *meodh cuill* or hazel mead. The dinner started with cold hard-boiled goose eggs, sausages, which had a taste of pork in them, sweet woodcocks cooked in honey, and, with the abbey being so close to the sea, a variety of fish prepared in different ways, some seasoned with wild garlic. The main dishes were accompanied by leeks or *braisech*, a type of cabbage. Desserts consisted of little honey cakes, presented with dishes of various berries and, inevitably, apples.

Fidelma and Eadulf exchanged looks of incredulity at the variety and presentation of the food. Fidelma remembered her previous remark about the perfumes in the washroom. This was a wealthy place and it was clear the senior members of the abbey were of local nobility.

While the evening meal was taking place, no conversations were exchanged. Then, when the meal was finished, instead of dispersing, many of the diners moved into a space clear of tables. Here little groups of the brethren and sisterhood were allowed to come together to exchange news and gossip. Fidelma and Eadulf saw Dego making his way towards them through the gathering. They had been separated during the meal, Dego being placed with the main community. Now he was accompanied by a young man of short stature. Had he not been wearing religious robes, he could have passed for one of Dego's warrior companions.

'I trust that I don't intrude, lady.' The newcomer spoke before Dego had an opportunity to introduce him. 'I am Brother Echen, the son of Eachdae the wagoner, with whom you are acquainted.'

'Your father has been of service from time to time,' Fidelma acknowledged with surprise. 'I did not realise that Eachdae had a son in this abbey. It was your father who gave me the message from Abbot Brocc that brought us here. How may I serve you?'

The man seemed disconcerted at the question. 'You would serve me? Such a thought is far from my mind, lady. I thought I might serve you, especially when I found by chance that my old antagonist, Dego, was your companion and seated before me at the evening meal. It was fate.'

'Old antagonist?' Fidelma was looking puzzled when Dego moved forward nervously.

'Years ago, Echen attended the military college where I was instructing. I was then a captain of one hundred men, and drilling warriors in the duties of bodyguards.'

Fidelma turned thoughtfully to the young man. 'So you are . . . or once were . . . a warrior of the Uí Liatháin?'

'I was, lady. I will confess, when Prince Tigerna Cosraigib raised the shield of battle for the clan to march, I was among the first to answer with enthusiasm.'

'You hated the Eóghanacht that much?'

'Hate? Not hate, lady. However, they seemed to be behind all our misfortunes. You will know the duty and law is that everyone who holds land of any sort under his prince, is obliged to take part in military service for his prince and the defence of his people.'

Fidelma inclined her head slightly. 'You did not question the right or wrong of Prince Tigerna Cosraigib's decision?'

'I was obliged to serve my prince,' the young man replied. 'I felt he was justified in trying to recover the lands that the Eóghanacht confiscated from us. He was right to seek alliances. Yes, even with the Déisi across the Great River. True, they were the source of our ills for several centuries, but only because they had the support of the Eóghanacht. They, too, became discontented and rose up. Doesn't it run that the enemy of my enemy is my friend?'

'I have heard that said,' Fidelma relied distantly. 'A short-sighted attitude.'

'*Amicus meus, inimicus inimici mei*,' Eadulf echoed.

'It certainly didn't help us. Your brother, King Colgú, placed a heavy burden on us in terms of reparation. I was immediately reduced to seeking service in this abbey just for want of sustenance. The demands for restitution were crippling.' He seemed to drift off in thought for a few moments. 'I do not blame your brother, lady,' he added. 'After all, your New Faith is replete with exhortations to vengeance.'

'The law is only harsh against the instigators,' Fidelma told him, frowning slightly. 'It should have been sufficient to allow you to claim back enough of your land and to give work to your workers. I do not think the law was disregarded to the extent of punitive punishments.'

'You said "your New Faith".' Eadulf had followed Brother Echen's words carefully. 'You are here in this abbey – are you not of that Faith?'

Echen smiled whimsically. 'I was a tenant of Prince Tigerna Cosraigib. After he was killed, the *derbhfine* disputed as to who was most suitable to replace him. No one felt they wanted to take the oath of allegiance demanded by your brother and his council to seal a peace, so no successor has come forward to negotiate an agreement. I could not await the outcome of who next should acquire the legal claim of Prince of the Uí Liatháin. The matter is still debated. I did not want to starve and therefore chose to serve in this community for my security.'

'It is strange to see a warrior join a religious community for the sake of financial security,' Dego intervened.

Brother Echen looked at Fidelma with a knowing smile but said nothing.

Fidelma felt uncomfortable. That had been the very reason that she had joined the community of Cill Dara at the behest of her cousin Abbot Lauren of Dare. When her father, Faille Flann, had died, his successors, as Kings of Cashel, had mainly ignored Fidelma and her brothers, Fogartach and Colgú. They had to take charity from friendlier members of their families for support and education. When Fidelma had left Brehon Morann's law school with high qualifications, she had been told the community of Cill Dara needed a legal adviser. So she had joined them until the behaviour of the abbess, Abbess Ita, disillusioned her. She had never been a religieuse but simply a believer in law, truth and justice. So she had left to join her brother who, when Fidelma was twenty-five, had become *tánaiste,* the heir apparent, to a cousin, King Cathal Cú-cen-máthair of Cashel. Cathal had died of the Yellow Plague, and when Fidelma was twenty-seven, her brother succeeded as King.

'But, lady, would you agree it is not strange?' Echen asked.

She hear the teasing quality in his tone.

'Depending on the circumstances,' she replied shortly.

'I presume that you have come here because of the death of Abbot Brocc?' the former warrior said when she did not amplify her response.

'You know something of this matter?'

'If you mean could I give evidence leading to the identification of the culprit, I cannot say that I could do that. There is a rumour that a prophecy was delivered by the Grey One . . . I would not reject the ancient legends.'

Brother Echen's eyes focused beyond her shoulder and widened a little. He seemed to be staring at someone.

'It was good to see Dego again,' he said quickly. 'I wish you and your companion success, lady.'

He turned abruptly away, pushing his way through the gathering, disappearing into it.

Fidelma turned in the direction he had been staring and found that Brother Guala with Brother Cróebíne were almost on top of them.

'I trust that the food was to your taste, lady, and all was adequate?' the steward opened. He seemed more reasonable now than he had been before the meal.

'The abbey seems to have a fine cook, Brother Guala,' she replied a little stiffly. 'We found the choice of dishes excellent. You do not share the view of some in the New Faith who insist that frugality of food and choice of beverages is the way to sanctity?'

Brother Guala actually smiled, which Fidelma guessed was, for him, an unusual expression.

'The text of Ecclesiastes says: *Vade ergo et comede in laetitia panem tuum et bibe cum gaudio vinum tuum quia Deo placent opera tua.*'

Eadulf listened hard and translated: '"Go your way, eat your bread with joy and drink your wine with a merry heart because it is now that God favours your works."'

'Why then do some communities enforce starvation and claim justification for it?' Fidelma asked.

'Misreading of a couple of texts, particularly the epistle of Paul of Tarsus to Corinthians. A careful reading shows it is gluttony that is condemned, and overindulgence in wine. The New Faith has never advocated abstinence. Did not Isaiah say there would be a feast for all peoples – rich food and choice of pure and excellent wine?'

'It would certainly make sense of the tables in many abbeys I saw when I was in Rome,' Fidelma reflected. 'There was hardly ever a poor table among the abbots and bishops, nor even the priests.'

'For my part, I am pleased that you follow that scripture,' Eadulf replied solemnly, although there was no disguising his irony.

Fidelma decided to seize the opportunity to return to the contentious subject.

'I was considering the curious prophecy that Abbot Brocc had apparently ignored. It is a matter that we should continue. Is now an appropriate time? Of course, I would have preferred to wait until I had examined the place where the abbot met his death before I did anything else. We will expect to be taken to the site where he perished immediately after the first meal tomorrow. But it is best to gather this information first.'

'As you wish,' said the steward without hesitation, surprising her. 'Let us go to my . . . to the abbot's chamber.'

The five of them were soon returned to the chamber.

'Let me clarify one thing before you speak of this prophecy. Do you say that you first learnt of the prophecy directly from the abbot before his death?' Fidelma asked Brother Guala.

'I do.'

'Apart from you, he told no one else in the community?'

'So far as I know, he told no one else,' Brother Guala confirmed. 'It was only after the body was discovered that I shared the information with Brother Cróebíne.'

The librarian nodded.

'Abbot Brocc was concerned, and that must be why he sent for you,' Brother Guala went on. 'He knew that I had some knowledge of these things. I was also perturbed about it but he asked me to pledge not to say a word. I kept my promise to him until the news came that he was found dead on the very day the prophecy had declared.'

'You say that you knew something of such things?' Fidelma prompted. 'Meaning such prophecies?'

'The New Faith has only spread in the Five Kingdoms during these last two centuries. The Old Faith has been here since time immemorial. You must realise that the New Faith is only a thin veil over the Old Faith and in the places like this abbey, its hold is so weak as to be non-existent. The majority of the Uí Liatháin retain the Old Faith.'

'So you mean that most people still believe in omens and prophecies? Very well. Describe to me how Abbot Brocc told you of the prophecy.'

'I remember I was arranging things in the chapel. Abbot Brocc came in. He was flustered, which was unusual. He told me that he had just finished his sweat bath and had begun to walk back through the woods to the abbey. Then a voice called his name.'

'Male or female?'

'The voice? He said it was curiously high pitched, and so he identified it as female. He turned and saw a figure standing on the rocks slightly above him.'

'How did she appear? Did he describe her?'

'He described her as being clad from head to toe in long grey robes. Even the head was covered with a grey veil.'

'Grey robes and a veil, like religious robes?' Fidelma asked.

'Something like them.'

'That sounds very dramatic.' Eadulf suppressed a snort. 'What did this woman in grey do? What words did this apparition say to Abbot Brocc?'

'The abbot spoke first and asked her to identify herself. She did not respond to the question but began to intone in a high-pitched voice. She told him that she brought him the truth of the *imbas forosnai* . . . truth from the inner vision granted by the ancient ones of his people.'

'I have heard of the *imbas forosnai*,' Eadulf commented, trying to conjure the memory. 'Isn't that the highest achievement of inner wisdom? Wasn't it forbidden by Patricius?'

'Indeed, it was forbidden by the Briton Patricius when he preached the New Faith in the north of the Five Kingdoms,' Fidelma confirmed. 'There was a time when poets used to make themselves go into a mystic trance or ecstasy, so that they might achieve the *imbas forosnai* . . . the inner wisdom. What did Abbot Brocc do?'

'Naturally he challenged her,' Brother Guala replied. 'Then the young woman declared that she spoke in the name of Brigit, the High One, goddess of prophecy and divination, daughter of the highest of the old gods, the Dagda.'

Eadulf's immediate image was of the Blessed Brigit, founder of the abbey of Cill Dara. Then he had to remind himself that the Christian Brigit was named after the pagan goddess because her father had been a Chief Druid.

'What did the abbot do when she said that?' Eadulf asked.

'He said and did nothing. I think he was shocked. He told me that she said he would achieve wisdom when the sun rose to its zenith on the day of the feast of Monessa. On that day and time, he would meet with Donn, god of death and collector of souls. Donn would take his soul to the House of Donn, an island to the west—'

'I am well aware of these ancient legends about the rituals of death,' Fidelma interrupted tersely. 'Perhaps we had better hear more about this prophetess.'

Brother Guala shifted his weight uncomfortably.

'There is little more to be said about her. Abbot Brocc was dead on the very day and time, just as she pronounced that he would be. What else do you wish to know?'

'There is a lot more that you have implied, including that this prophetess has more to do with the abbot's death than just guessing at the time of it. The abbot gave you a description of her – is there anything to be gathered from that description?'

'I can tell you that stories have circulated in many areas of the Uí Liatháin territory about the ancient prophetess Líadan – "the Grey One". Doubtless you know that the founder of our kinfolk was named Liatháin – so we are named the Children of the Grey One. Some claimed to have seen a figure exactly as Abbot Brocc described her to me. She is always said to have dressed in grey robes, dark grey, the colour of mourning.'

'But have *you* ever seen her?' Fidelma asked with a slightly cynical smile.

'Never! Nor do I wish to look on the face of the Evil One.'

'But have any others, that you know of, ever seen such a figure as the Abbot Brocc described?'

Brother Guala looked uncomfortable.

'There are traditional stories that have been known over the ages,' Brother Cróebíne intervened.

'As librarian, you would have access to the folktales of this area. Have you read or heard of such a prophetess as the Grey One?'

'Obviously,' Brother Cróebíne said with a tired shrug. 'It is almost a founding legend of the Uí Liatháin – Children of the Grey One. We all hear such tales. Merchants come to the abbey with stories as well as their goods to bargain. Merchants are fond of telling stories and there has recently been a rise in popularity of such tales.'

'These stories feature a soothsayer dressed in grey making prophecies?'

'Exactly,' the librarian confirmed. 'They tell of the Grey One, who has appeared here and there with claims that the Uí Liatháin will once again rise and be led into battle by the warrior god, Nuada of the Silver Hand. It was Nuada whose descendant had been ordained to lead our people. The ancient stories tell that our people would rise to control their promised lands bestowed on them by the gods. This is why the Uí Liatháin hold their name, and this is their covenant with the mighty Nuada.'

Dego seemed to experience a sudden fit of coughing. Fidelma realised he was trying to choke back his amusement.

'I was just thinking that if anyone should have a covenant with Nuada of the Silver Hand it should be me! My right arm was severed just as Sreng, the warrior of the Fir Bolg, severed Nuada's arm with one blow of his sword. But while Nuada had the god of medicine, Dian Cecht, make him a silver arm, I had Eadulf here take my arm off in such a way that I found the use of it in my other limbs. My covenant with Nuada should be just as strong.'

Brother Cróebíne was defensive. 'I do not put the stories of the Grey One forward with any belief in them. I am merely recounting the stories that circulate among the people. The prophecies of the Grey One have naturally garnered a formidable reputation across the Uí Liatháin territories.'

'It is claimed that she is somehow a messenger of the goddess Brigit?' Eadulf asked.

'As she represents herself to be a prophetess, people think she is actually the goddess of prophecy and divination, in person.'

Brother Guala looked at the visitors disapprovingly.

'If the prophecy related to Abbot Brocc's death, then it must be spoken of,' Fidelma replied sharply. 'Abbot Brocc claimed that a woman in grey pronounced the time of his death. The prophecy, so you have testified, Brother Guala, was accurate. So it is natural to discover more about it. Were tales of this Grey One handed down over the years, or did they recently emerge? When did the merchants start claiming this prophetess was appearing, or was she always manifest?'

Brother Guala appeared uneasy again. 'Our folklore says that she comes to prophesy at the time of our people's needs because the Uí Liatháin are literally the Children of the Grey One. We are her progeny. When I related the story that Abbot Brocc told me to Brother Cróebíne, it was he who informed me about these stories of visiting merchants.'

'What do these merchants say about the prophecies of the destiny of the Uí Liatháin?' Fidelma's tone was sarcastic but the interrogative was still sharp.

Brother Cróebíne had a ghost of a smile. 'They said that the most recent reports of the apparition first appeared from the high hills to the north-west of this territory. There was talk she first appeared at Cnoc an Cheo, the Mountain of Mist. That was less than six months ago.'

Fidelma was thoughtful. 'So, after the Uí Liatháin conspirators submitted to Cashel?'

Dego decided to interrupt, missing the point that Fidelma had picked up.

'Cnoc an Cheo? It's a group of high forested hills in the north-west of Uí Liatháin territory. I have never been in those hills, nor do I wish to go. I have heard that those people still look towards the Druids for spiritual guidance.'

'That is reason enough not to go near them,' Brother Guala said. 'One of those hills is Cnoc an Fiagh, the Hill of the Magic Mist, where the River Dísorche rises. It is a place that should be avoided.'

Fidelma tried to suppress a cynical smile. 'Doesn't that name mean something like "river of twilight"? At least it sounds a suitable place for this apparition to emerge from with prognostications of the future.'

'The Grey One has made only one accurate prophecy we have been told of,' Eadulf pointed out, realising that she wanted to return to the main point. 'That is the death of Abbot Brocc. Her other prophecies seem to be unconnected with the matter we are investigating. The rest is understandable for a people who were misled into a conflict for which they have to pay retribution and who want some encouragement for a positive future.'

'Let me be sure about this,' Fidelma sighed. 'Do I understand that the prophecy that Abbot Brocc told you was not her first prophecy? I thought that Abbot Brocc had taken the prophecy seriously. He was concerned enough to send for me on the very day that he was stopped and the prophecy uttered.'

'If it was the same prophetess, it would be the first of her prophecies to come true,' Brother Cróebíne confirmed. 'Also, it was the first one aimed at an individual and nothing to do with the rise of the Uí Liatháin.'

'Then we might be dealing with two different matters,' Eadulf said thoughtfully after a moment. 'We might also be dealing with two different soothsayers.'

'In what way?' Brother Guala asked. 'The travellers, merchants and even fairground people all claim to know something of this Grey One.'

'But the prophecies have all been about the Uí Liatháin and

located in their territory,' Brother Cróebíne pointed out. 'The appearance that Abbot Brocc related to you is not in keeping with those.'

The librarian grimaced in disapproval. 'Let us pray we are protected by the Christ, and this Grey One is confined to the twilight waters and the dark mountain valleys; the places of the mists; places shrouded in ethereal fogs.'

'If the Grey One was responsible for an accurate prophecy of the abbot's death, then she is already here, among us, and we are unprotected,' Brother Guala said, his voice rising to a higher pitch, reminding Fidelma of his previous temper.

'Whoever gave the prophesy, whether we ascribe it to this Grey One or not, why was Abbot Brocc, a Christian, singled out for the prophecy of his death?' It was Eadulf who posed the pertinent question. 'Why was his death foretold and became a truth? Has anyone else had a death prophesised in such a way? Why here and why now?'

'Time and place would have no meanings to a seer of the Otherworld,' muttered Brother Guala.

Fidelma struggled to hide her derision.

'Who knows how and when the evil ones enact their revenge?' Brother Guala responded.

'That is what we are trying to discover and would have been served quicker and more efficiently if we had been allowed to examine the physical remains,' Eadulf added dryly.

'I have ruled on that matter,' snapped Brother Guala.

'Sister Damnat has put forward an interesting speculation about the cause of death,' Eadulf countered quietly. 'I would have thought it was in the interest of the Abbey that the speculation be confirmed or dismissed.'

There was an embarrassed silence before Fidelma gave an almost imperceptible shrug. 'We may have to come back to that decision later. I want to know a little more about this prophetess.

Abbot Brocc, in telling his steward the story, believed that she was a tangible apparition. She seemed real in the eyes of the abbot to the point that Brother Guala now accepts her presence to be the truth. Whether she is of this world or the Otherworld, it seems that she has her origin in the legends of the Uí Liatháin people. That is interesting.'

Eadulf could not disguise a look of cynicism. 'It seems most important names in this princedom are associated with greyness and dark perceptions.'

'Why so?' Brother Guala demanded belligerently. 'The legends originate in the culture of past generations, before the New Faith taught the people to forget the past so they had little understanding of it.'

'Many retain their understanding because they have retained their Old Faith,' Brother Cróebíne added. 'We are in the most southern part of the kingdom – its southern border being the boundless sea; its northern and eastern borders, the beautiful Great River. To the west, the hills climb into mountains and the entire area is criss-crossed by a number of streams and rivers and, surrounding them, great luxuriant forests replete with every type of beast, bird and fish. The colours of this place are almost blinding in their variety. Your grey perception is a contrast with the colourfulness of this country.'

'How people perceive things is not due to how they are in reality but how people's minds want to view them,' Fidelma suggested. 'There are feelings of loss and acceptance of death among the people, for grey has a negative connotation much associated with those feelings.'

Brother Guala was still disapproving. 'Grey is also associated with the mysterious as well as having the meaning of things hidden and not confronted. It is a symbol of compromise.'

'A compromise?' Fidelma echoed curiously.

'The Déisi have been famous for not compromising on any

matter,' the steward said. 'You are probably too young to recall the Battle of Carn Conaill?'

'I was about eight years old when it was said to have been fought. I was already in my schooling on Inis Celta. But I heard stories about it. So what point are you making?'

'Then you will know that the Uí Liatháin joined Guaire, the King of Connacht, to fight the King of Munster, who was supported by the High King Diarmait. Our king, or prince, as you prefer to call him, Tolomnach, was slain in that battle along with his heir apparent. As a retribution, the High King confirmed the territory of the Uí Liatháin was given as reparation to Cashel.'

Fidelma gave a sigh. 'I suppose you are going to say that that was another time the Grey One appeared with prophecies of the Uí Liatháin rising up to regain their rights. I do not see this conversation is progressing with the matter of our investigation,' she said. 'My object is to find out who killed Abbot Brocc and why.'

'That is true,' Brother Guala agreed. 'Forgive me. I was trying to show that there is a tradition that this prophetess in grey appears in times following an Uí Liatháin defeat by the Eóghanacht. There might be little connection, but that is your task as a *dálaigh* to work out.'

Eadulf realised there might indeed be a connection. What if some insurrection was being stirred up by the prophetess among the Uí Liatháin? It would be worth knowing.

'Who is the leader of the Uí Liatháin now?' he asked.

'There is none,' replied Brother Guala.

'Since Tigerna Cosraigib of Dún Guairne was killed, no one has accepted the office,' confirmed the librarian.

'Tigerna Cosraigib, Lord of the Slaughter,' Fidelma mused thoughtfully. 'I know he never came to Cashel to pay tribute, nor to take a seat on the advisory council. Even in death everyone talks about him.'

'But his *derbhfine* would have chosen a successor from his

family by now?' Eadulf pressed, for he had finally accepted how succession worked in this culture.

'Oh yes, the *derbhfine* met and chose Tigerna Cosraigib's second child as prince of our people.' It was Brother Cróebíne who startled them. His voice was harsh.

'And the name of their choice was . . .?' Fidelma prompted, seeking confirmation of the name she had been told.

It was Brother Cróebíne who answered her. 'We have mentioned him before. Prince Conmhaol. It was to him that our physician was called. We heard it was not a unanimous decision of the *derbhfine*, but Conmhaol held the majority. And he refused them. Conmhaol is regarded as a weak man who takes little interest in his people, preferring to have only concerns for his cattle herds and his horses.'

'So you knew members of the *derbhfine*?' Fidelma queried.

'With respect,' the steward spoke with heavy emphasis, 'we should not be repeating the gossip relating to the family decision.'

'Gossip or not,' snapped the librarian, 'no successor has been confirmed.'

'Why not?' Fidelma demanded. 'If it was Conmhaol who was chosen, why did he refuse to accept the position?'

'Can that happen?' Eadulf asked. 'If you are chosen under the laws of succession, can you refuse?'

'Oh, yes. It happens many times. Even a king can abdicate during his reign, and many have,' Brother Cróebíne answered.

'But the *derbhfine* must then choose someone else.'

'Except the *derbhfine* is reported to be in stalemate. Neither side appears to be in the ascendant,' the librarian said.

Fidelma suddenly drew herself up. 'We have spent enough time on this and now must return to our main concern.' She turned to the librarian. 'You have another task to perform shortly, Brother Cróebíne. It was you who discovered the body of Abbot

Brocc at the sweat house. You can take us to this place after the first meal and show us exactly how you found the body.'

The librarian hesitated. 'Brother Guala is steward and must now be acting abbot, so his is the decision as to how we should proceed.'

'There is no need for Brother Guala to decide anything,' Fidelma snapped. 'He did not discover the body. You did. When I request something, legally it must obeyed and any refusal may result in a hearing before the Chief Brehon of this kingdom. As a *scriptor* in this abbey, you surely know that?'

Brother Cróebíne looked tense for a moment, as if he would argue.

It was Brother Guala who intervened almost in a conciliatory fashion. 'You do not have to remind us of our legal obligations, lady. We have already agreed it. Of course Brother Cróebíne will take you to the location of the sweat house and show you how he discovered Abbot Brocc's body. Brother Scatánach and Sister Damnat will be in the party to answer your questions. We apologise for any hesitation. Our excuse is that we have just lost our abbot and are unsure of our obligations. We have to wait nine days before the senior members of the abbey, our own *derbhfine*, gather to elect and confirm the new abbot.'

'That is understood. However, it does not detract from the Abbey recognising its duties under the laws of the Brehon, which, as it is often quoted in the written texts, were set down and are not in conflict with the laws of God. Now, you were also there when Sister Damnat examined the body when it was taken from the sweat house. Therefore you were a witness. So you will accompany us.'

Fildema had a feeling that an angry look crossed Brother Guala's features before he relaxed and seemed resigned.

'You are the *dálaigh* and your requests are commands that shall be fulfilled.'

chapter five

It was well after first light the next day that they left for the sweat house. Brother Cróebíne led Fidelma and Eadulf, with Brother Guala and Brother Scatánach, followed by Dego, bringing up the rear. They emerged from the abbey's complex of wooden buildings, crossing the strong oak bridge to the west bank over the small branch of the river that encircled Dair Inis, the Island of Oaks. It was a pleasant autumn morning and Fidelma had a strange feeling of being encompassed as they walked through the densely growing oaks and yews that sheltered the trackway as it led, rising slightly, towards the westward hilly country.

It was a time of changing colours, for most of the oaks had reached their maturity and the dark green leaves were changing to amber, red and yellow. Soon they would begin their inevitable fall. Indeed, there came the occasional sharp noise of falling acorns. Fidelma reflected that it would not be long before small groups from the community would be out with their baskets collecting the acorns, to boil and mash for traditional *bairgen*, or acorn loaves. That was a lengthy business, often taking a week or two to remove the bitterness from the fruit. But, in her estimation, it was worth the effort for the result was bread tasting almost like sweet chestnuts.

As they walked, Fidelma could detect changes in the fragrance of the forest as temperatures cooled slightly and the odour rose from the previous seasons' dead leaves, which had partially mulched along with other vegetable debris. Now and then, the flitting shadows of squirrels, the scurrying sounds of badgers, and even the occasional bark of a fox were audible and reminded her that the forest was alive. It was that time of year when one might hear the isolated cry of a stag, for the rutting season would soon begin.

Brother Cróebíne paused and pointed to the left, where the path turned and rose steeply.

'We follow this path to the top of the hill.'

It was a surprisingly steep climb, and they found themselves emerging above the forest on to a level area where among the bracken were crumbling red sandstone blocks. In a curious rock-walled gully they came across a building that was of familiar construction to Fidelma and Eadulf's eyes.

It was a long, low construction of sandstone blocks with a small central entrance, which one would have to crouch or crawl to enter. It was, as they had imagined, two metres high and three metres in length, and the design followed an ancient pattern. A stack of firewood was alongside, covered in such a way that the bulk of it remained dry.

Nearby, a pool was supplied with constant cold water from a small natural waterfall cascading from an overhanging thrust of rock. It was clear that someone had dug this pool, keeping it rock lined. From it, and into a lower gorse-covered area, a man-made gully was obviously meant to take any overflow.

Fidelma stood for a moment surveying the area carefully.

'You begin, Brother Cróebíne,' she said, turning to the librarian. 'You came up here – now tell me what you saw?'

The librarian began with a shrug. 'As I described yesterday, the first thing I saw was that the door was in place, meaning someone was inside using the sweat house.'

'Describe the process again for me.'

'To prepare the bath, first a great fire is lit inside the sweat house to heat the stonework. The entrance is blocked by the door, which you see leaning against the wall. This keeps in the heat. When it is felt that the heat is sufficient, the door is removed and the remains of the fire and the ashes are raked out. You will notice the rakes are there for that purpose.' He gestured towards them. 'Once the area is cleared of ashes, the bather enters, replacing the door behind him. He sits inside until a sweat is generated and then crawls out and goes to that pond and immerses himself in the cold water.'

'You told us that the abbot preferred to prepare the bath and his toiletry himself. Was this always the case?' Eadulf asked. 'Now that I have physically seen what is involved, I am amazed. Surely it is too much work for one man to prepare the fire and then scrape the remains away to be able to crawl inside and secure the door after he enters?'

Brother Cróebíne shook his head. 'As we have discussed, Abbot Brocc was always an active man. He was strong, as Sister Damnat has told you. He liked the ritual of performing the tasks himself. I could not follow his example and I needed the muscles of Brother Scatánach when I came to use the sweat house. That is why he accompanied me on that day.'

Fidelma carefully regarded the stone construction. 'So when you arrived you saw the door shut and presumed the abbot was still inside?'

The librarian pursed his lips in a thoughtful expression. 'The door was shut. I called a few times and, when there was no answer, I opened the door and peered inside.'

'Was the place still hot?'

'It was warm. At first, I thought the abbot had abandoned the bath because the ashes were still piled up inside. No one would enter the sweat house without raking out the ashes first. I did not realise until I took a brand torch to examine the interior that the abbot's body was there but covered with ashes and debris.'

'Under the ashes and debris?' Fidelma grimaced. 'Do we deduce that he had been inside when the pile of burning wood was placed there? He had not crawled out? Was he inside when the place was being heated?'

'I have already explained my view,' Sister Damnat interposed.

'I am trying to get first impressions,' Fidelma explained, then turned back to the librarian. 'What were your immediate thoughts?'

'I could not believe what I saw. The body lying there covered in ashes.'

'What did you think had happened?'

'At the time, I did not think anything. The body was in the sweat house. The ashes were spread over him. That was all.'

Sister Damnat made to speak again but Fidelma motioned her to silence.

'Sister Damnat has said that when she saw the body, the fire had not been hot enough to damage it, let alone incinerate it.'

Brother Cróebíne agreed. 'The place was only slightly warm when I opened the door. I think no strong fire was lit, which means there was no serious attempt to destroy the body. Brother Scatánach and I had no difficulty recognising the corpse.'

'Did you search this area?'

Brother Cróebíne frowned. 'Why?'

'An unexplained death might have caused you to consider doing that?'

'I saw nothing to search for.'

'Where were the abbot's clothes? I presume he would have taken them off to be ready to crawl into the sweat house.'

'They were in a pile by the side of the door. They had not been touched, so far as I could see.'

'What did you do next?'

'I determined Abbot Brocc was dead. That was when I sent Brother Scatánach for Brother Guala. Sometime later he returned with the steward and Sister Damnat. I realised that Brother Fisecda, our physician, was not in the abbey, so it was logical that Sister Damnat came with the steward.'

'You stayed here alone while Brother Scatánach went back to fetch Brother Guala? Were you not worried that the killer might still be lurking in the vicinity?'

'It did not occur to me to be worried.' The librarian seemed confused.

'An unusual death. You must have asked questions of yourself?'

Brother Guala intervened, 'At that point Brother Cróebíne had no knowledge of the prophecy. I did not mention what the abbot had told me until later.'

'It did not occur to me that the abbot could have died in a way other than a natural cause or an accident,' the librarian added.

Fidelma turned to the young Brother Scatánach. 'Do you wish to add anything?'

The young religieux shook his head. 'This is what happened. I returned to the abbey, as the librarian said, and informed Brother Guala, who asked Sister Damnat to come with us.'

Fidelma now turned to Sister Damnat.

'I have told you my thoughts,' Sister Damnat said.

'Tell me again. The body was still in the sweat house when you arrived?'

'It was obvious that I would not examine the body inside,' she replied. 'So I asked that it be brought outside. It was covered in ash and I could see there was no life nor hope of life there. I took water from that pool and cleansed enough of the ash from the body so that the abbot could be carried back to the abbey.'

'You saw nothing that would explain the death?'

'Only that he had apparently asphyxiated. There was a slight contusion at the temple, as I mentioned earlier.'

'Would I be right in saying, Sister Damnat, that you thought, from that contusion, that the abbot might have been knocked unconscious, suffocated and then put back into the sweat house? Then the ashes were placed inside over him. Perhaps the fire was rekindled.'

'Brother Cróebíne believes the abbot could have knocked himself on the stone lintel while crawling in, causing the contusion, and then he passed out.'

Fidelma lips parted sceptically. 'That he continued to crawl inside, place the ashes over himself and, moreover, shut the door behind him, before conveniently dying?'

Brother Cróebíne was defensive. 'I was trying to find a reasonable explanation. As has been said, I knew nothing of that prophecy at the time.'

'You doubtless disabused the librarian of that idea?' asked Fidelma of Sister Damnat.

'I dismissed it, but it was not until I examined the body after it had been taken back to the abbey that I realised the blow must have rendered the abbot totally unconscious. An important point was there were no signs of his hands or feet being bound and, if they were not, surely he would have struggled if he was choking to death even though he was unconscious.'

'You have said that you do not think the blow on the head could have killed him?'

'I tell you what I found and did, that is all. It would not be right for me to speculate, as I mentioned last night.'

'But you have suggested that he was asphyxiated by something being held over his mouth and nose? And that must have been outside the sweat bath, otherwise it would have been impossible to exert the necessary pressure inside the cramped space?'

'That was my final conclusion.'

Fidelma turned to Brother Guala. 'Do you have anything to add at this stage?'

'I stood as a witness and agree this was what I saw,' the steward replied.

'I presume the corpse was then returned to the abbey, was properly washed and prepared for the funeral ceremonies. It was then that Sister Damnat was able to see more clearly the contusion on the temple. But when did anyone suggest murder had taken place?'

There were a few moments of silence.

'It is our task to try to reconstruct the means of death,' Sister Damnat said.

'We have shown you the facts,' Brother Guala added dryly. 'How you interpret them is your guesswork.'

'Usually one has to start with guesswork,' Fidelma returned. 'As things appear at this moment, I am prepared to go with the idea that the abbot was suffocated and not strangled.'

'Not strangled,' confirmed Sister Damnat quickly. 'No marks were apparent around the throat. I explained this yesterday.'

'The abbot came here alone,' Fidelma began reflectively, trying to clarify things. 'We are told that he liked to prepare the sweat bath himself. That raises many unusual points. Abbot Brocc was not a young man, but we are told he was of good health and strength. Even so, it is unusual for a person of status not to have an attendant to help with such chores.'

'That is one unusual point,' Eadulf agreed. 'People of status do not so easily drop their entitlements. But the major curiosity is that, even though he had been threatened that he would die on that very day, he came here alone and almost to where this prophetess foretold of his death. It almost seems as if he were challenging this augury. Even for someone imbued in the New Faith as a Christian, Abbot Brocc would not have entirely dismissed such a warning. We know he did not, at first, because he told Brother Guala and he also sent for Fidelma, presumably to advise him.'

Brother Cróebíne heaved an impatient sigh. 'You are overlooking that it was Abbot Brocc's habit to come alone for his bath here.'

'Habit would not account for the fact that he subsequently dismissed the warning,' Fidelma said.

'Some people's customs become obsessions,' Brother Cróebíne pointed out.

'Yet, if we accept what the abbot told Brother Guala, he was concerned with the threat. Call it a prophecy, if you like. He came alone here even on the very day that it was predicted that he would die. He prepared the fire inside the sweat house and waited while the stones were warmed up, undressed and was ready to enter. Are we agreed thus far?'

No one demurred.

'I agree with Sister Damnat that it was at this point that he was attacked. A blow on the head knocked him unconscious. While he was unconscious, he was smothered. Not strangled, but was held down with something over his mouth and nose to suffocate him. Then he was pushed into the sweat house. The ashes and remains of the fire had not been raked out, of course, thus his flesh was mildly scalded. The body was left until Brother Cróebíne came along . . . which was what time of day? Remind me.'

'It would be not long after midday,' the librarian said. 'That was the usual time I came for my own sweat bath.'

Fidelma was quiet for a moment as she gazed around.

'I do not think we will be able to gain much more here. It was clear the abbot was at his weakest in terms of being able to defend himself. It was almost as if he were a willing victim. Well, we cannot go much further yet in discovering any motive, nor why he changed his mind about the veracity of the threat.'

Brother Guala now spoke. 'It was as if he were inviting death, daring death to seek him out. Perhaps he had sublime faith that God would protect him.'

'Which he did not have initially,' Fidelma added. 'Why was that?'

'Surely that is self-evident,' Brother Guala said.

'Self-evident?'

'The prophecy of the Grey One was the reason. He was Abbot of Dair Inis and the prophetess appeared in the guise of Brigit, the goddess of divination.'

'Are you saying that the reason for his death was an act of hatred for the New Faith . . . he was killed because he was an advocate of the New Faith, which has spread across our land in the last two centuries?'

'There are plenty of fanatics defensive of the Old Faith, as well you know, lady,' the librarian replied.

'But there are plenty of more powerful advocates of the New Faith who could easily be attacked . . . and many more prominent. Why pick out Abbot Brocc to take vengeance on?'

'All we hear are questions. I thought a *dálaigh* was supposed to provide answers,' sniffed the steward.

'Our very next move is to return to the abbey to find out more about Abbot Brocc and his background to see if any other reason might present itself,' she said, glancing towards Brother Cróebíne. 'Are there records at the abbey? You have a library with many valuable texts, as I understand.'

'I should not think they would say much about personal matters.' The librarian was diffident.

'I am sure the abbey records will provide us with what we want.' She noticed a faint scowl on the librarian's features. 'I know all this is keeping you from your real work in the library. Let us go there. As I say, I do not think that we can learn much more from continuing to examine this site.'

'Except one thing more.' Surprisingly it was Dego, who had been so quiet since their arrival that Fidelma had almost forgotten the warrior was there. She turned to him with a look of query.

'I have heard much about Abbot Brocc being foretold his fate by this prophetess. Well, now we have seen where and how the abbot met his death. It was no lightning bolt from the goddess. He was killed by someone physically, a person of flesh and muscle. Whoever killed him could not be a young girl in a grey robe, if that apparition was a reality. There must have been a person of equal strength to the abbot involved, or even several others.'

'We should make enquiries about strangers in the area of the abbey,' Eadulf agreed. 'That is, if the idea that this might be an attack by some fanatics of the Old Faith leads us anywhere.'

'There were no strangers visiting the abbey at the time,' Brother Cróebíne replied.

'There was that *seanchaidh* from the territory of the Déisi,' Sister Damnat corrected.

'An historian? Who was he?' Fidelma demanded.

'He was a scholar who came to look at some of our texts. He left the abbey before we found the body of the abbot.'

Fidelma caught a look of disapproval at the steward.

'Strangers?' Brother Guala was dismissive. 'We are an island surrounded by a rebellious sea of pagans.'

With that he turned and began to lead the way back down the hill through the forest. Fidelma and Eadulf paused for a moment before trailing after the others, with Dego bringing up the rear.

It was Eadulf who quietly raised the point.

'If we accept the veracity of that prophecy, then that allows us to follow various interpretations.'

'I know,' Fidelma agreed. 'One of which is that the prophetess could also be part of some group whose assassination of the abbot was meant to create dissension between the Old and New Faiths.'

'Part of a conspiracy to mislead everyone based on their natural fears of the ancient deities and their spirits?' Dego observed quietly, following behind them.

Eadulf frowned, glancing back over his shoulder to the

warrior. He had been raised with the old pagan deities of his people and was not converted until he was in his late teens. There were times when he felt the ancient deities were still lurking in the shadows and were still as powerful as ever they were; powerful and all-seeing.

'You don't believe in the power of the old gods and goddesses?' he asked Dego.

'I am a practical man. If a warrior lived in fear of the Otherworld, of supernatural shades with greater powers than he has, then he would not even bother to take up arms in defence of this world. That fear is what these so-called soothsayers and prophets rely on to fulfil their purpose. Well, I have been close to being transported to the Otherworld.' He made a movement with the stump of his right arm and grinned at Eadulf. 'Thankfully, you did not believe in inevitability, otherwise I would have perished. We must seek the future in ourselves and not in fortune-tellers.'

'What of the fact that the abbot died on the very day he claimed it would happen to him?' Eadulf pointed out.

'To a practical man, it could mean that the prophetess was a person who was involved in making their prophecy come true.'

Fidelma smiled; Dego had confirmed her thinking. 'I agree, Dego, the abbot's death was encompassed by someone of this world and that is where we should start looking.'

'So, we just go out into these forests looking for this woman in grey?' Eadulf was not enthusiastic. 'That sounds an impossible task.'

'You have forgotten what our next move is, as I told Brother Cróebíne. We will see what information we can get from the abbey's archives.'

'What are we looking for?'

'If an abbot is murdered, then there must be a reason why. This business of a prophecy must hide some reality. Maybe that motive lies in the abbot's past. We will find out what we can about the man.'

It was not long before they arrived back at the abbey buildings on the island. Brother Guala immediately left them, followed by the youth, Brother Scatánach, and Sister Damnat.

'Which is your library, Brother Cróebíne? We will not delay, but go straight there,' Fidelma said. 'We will look at any record about Abbot Brocc's life.'

'I don't think you will find much to help you. I know the archives. Abbot Brocc seemed a very secretive person.'

'Which might be a pointer to the fact there was something to hide,' Fidelma reflected with a thin smile.

The librarian frowned at the suggestion but he said nothing. He was clearly not enthusiastic about the visitors searching the archives. He glanced up at the sky.

'It will not be long before the bell sounds for the midday meal,' he observed. 'Would it not be better to wait until afterwards?'

'We will not die of malnutrition if we miss one meal,' Fidelma assured him. 'It will not take long to see what sort of relevant archives you have.'

Reluctantly, the librarian led the way to a thick-beamed wooden building not far from what was obviously the chapel in the centre of the island. It was a heavy log-built construction in which they saw rows of wooden beams with pegs from which hung numerous ancient *tiag liubhair* or leather book satchels.

'We have little in the way of original texts. We do have several copies of scriptures,' Brother Cróebíne explained, standing to one side and waving his hand towards the rows of satchels. 'I suppose our most valuable assets are the poems of Colmán mac Lénine. He was a great innovator as a poet.'

'He is known, even in Cashel,' Fidelma acknowledged with irony. 'Moreover, he was the abbot of the community at Cluain-Uama, the field of the caves, which is in Uí Liatháin territory to the north. That was one of the first communities of the New Faith here.'

'It is the annals relating to this abbey that we came to see,' Eadulf pointed out in a falsely patient tone. The librarian's prevarication had begun to annoy him.

Observing his expression, Brother Cróebíne turned and walked down the row of satchels, peering at the names burnt on to the leather. He took one down, moving over to a nearby table where there was light, and opened it.

'These are the only annals we have,' he said, placing the contents of the satchel on the table. 'We have concentrated on borrowing and copying texts, but we have only two copyists so we still have much to do and preserve.'

Fidelma and Eadulf began to examine the few small loose pages that were not within the leather-bound book that had been placed before them.

'Unlike the larger communities – those with great libraries – our small community has little to boast of,' pointed out Brother Cróebíne, indicating the slim book.

'And are these loose pages also from the abbey's annals?' Fidelma picked up the unbound pages and read the title. 'This is unusual. *Cogadh Anfóill Oirne* – "The Terrible War Against Us"?' she queried. 'What is this about?'

Brother Cróebíne seemed embarrassed. 'It seems they are misfiled. It is an account of an old battle campaign of the Uí Liatháin.'

He took the pages from her and returned them to the book satchel.

'There is not much here,' Fidelma sighed, as she glanced through the volume. 'I see you record the dates here in the old method of *Aois Domhain,* the Age of the World. It is listed here that five thousand two hundred *Aois Domhain* was the eighth year of the reign of the High King, Crimthann Nia Náir, which is the first year of the accepted Christian period. Who did these computations?'

'Brother Rímid. He was one of the first to join with the Mael An Faidh in founding this abbey, which was back in—'

'I understand the old dating,' Fidelma interrupted. 'Did this Brother Rímid have a reputation for his computing skills?'

'He did.'

'He certainly had the right name for it,' Fidelma commented with momentary humour. 'The name means the one who counts,' she added to Eadulf. 'But now let us look down at the dates of the abbots and what is said about them . . .'

Her expression suddenly changed to one of concentration as she examined the text. Finally she frowned.

'What is it?' asked Eadulf.

'I see that a few years ago, the reckoning by *Aois Domhain* changed to the concept of the calendar of the New Faith of *Anno Domini* . . .'

'That was when I started to make the entries,' Brother Cróebíne said in a tone of self-satisfaction. 'Although we use a system that Eusebius of Caesarea approved, it was not as accurate as the one compiled by order of Julius Caesar and based on the year of the foundation of Rome.'

'You appear to have started this dating less than a year ago. But I see that you have crossed out some of the previous entries with *Aois Domhain* and changed them to fit in with the Roman calendar and the year of the start of the New Faith. Why was that done in retrospect?'

'I found the annals had been neglected so I wanted to bring them to a standard form.'

Fidelma continued to look through the entries and then she raised her eyes to the librarian.

'This is curious,' she said.

'In what way?' Brother Cróebíne seemed defensive of any criticism of his work.

'I see the entry for *Aois Domhain* five thousand eight hundred and sixty-four says that Brocc of Dún Guairne was given the abbey of Dair Inis. But you have not added the Christian date.'

'I wanted to put everything in the new form of *Anno Domini,* but there is much work to be done; a lot of calculating to standardise the dates.'

'But I find this very remarkable.'

'I am not sure I understand.' Brother Cróebíne was confused.

'Surely abbots are elected by the *derbhfine* of the abbey? Even your steward used this as a reason not to allow the exhumation of Abbot Brocc. The senior clerics of the community are those who stand for the community family in place of a blood family. They are not appointed from outside the community. What intrigues me is the phrase that Abbot Brocc was "given" or "presented" with the abbey. This word, *láithirsit,* means he was *presented* with.' She said the word with emphasis.

'I have not worked fully on that section,' the librarian replied in a defensive tone again.

'It is unusual,' Fidelma assured him. 'I think there is more written on the next pages . . .' Her words died, as she turned the pages and stood staring down in bewilderment.

'What is it?' Eadulf asked, watching her expression.

'This page has been cut out. Someone has taken a knife and deliberately cut the page from its binding.'

CHAPTER SIX

It was not until after the midday meal that Fidelma and Eadulf were able to obtain another private word with Brother Guala. He had taken over what had been Abbot Brocc's study. They found him alone and sorting out some of the late abbot's papers. This allowed Fidelma an easy excuse to raise the matter of the missing page from the abbey's annals which, according to previous notations, gave information on the appointment of Abbot Brocc.

Brother Cróebíne had continued to maintain a lack of knowledge about the disappearance of the page. He told Fidelma and Eadulf that he had not looked at the annals since he had been appointed to the library. When Eadulf said that this was surprising, for surely he would have taken the papers to make the entry about Abbot Brocc's death, the librarian became irritable and pointed out that he had many other duties to fulfil before he could spend time recording recent matters. He admitted that, apart from the two young copyists, the only recent visitor to the library had been a Déisi scholar, Sárán, who had been given permission by the steward, Brother Guala, to research in the library.

This had been Fidelma's opening question to Brother Guala.

'I believe the man Sárán was a secular scholar,' he said, almost defensively. 'Our library is open to all scholars and not just those

78

from the religious communities. I hardly spoke with him and he was only in the abbey a few days.'

'What was he researching?'

Brother Guala grimaced, almost a sneer. 'I was not particularly interested. It was something to do with how the Déisi obtained sections of our land, supported by the Eóghanacht.'

'Was it a text entitled *Cogadh Anfóill Oirne* – "The Terrible War Against Us"?'

The expression on Brother Guala's face was enough to confirm that it was.

'I see,' Fidelma sighed. 'We found that text, some loose pages, misfiled with the abbey's annals in the same satchel bag. What was it about?'

Brother Guala hesitated. 'Brother Cróebíne ought to know it better than I.' The steward decided to continue when she did not respond. 'It was a text relating to the war after Conall Corc, the Eóghanacht King of Cashel, gave Uí Liatháin territory to the Déisi to settle on. The Déisi were exiled from Midhe, the Middle Kingdom, for some misdeed. That was two centuries ago.'

'They were given Uí Liatháin territory?' Eadulf asked with interest. 'Did the Uí Liatháin then live east of the river as well?'

'All the land the Déisi now hold was ours. It was Conall Corc, the first of the New Faith rulers, who gave away our lands to appease his new wife, a princess of the Déisi. The Uí Liatháin were driven out, their farms and homesteads given away or destroyed in the conflict that followed. We were forced to dwell on this side of the river. The Déisi even tried to take lands this side of the river. The last was the settlement of Eochaill.' There was bitterness in Brother Guala's voice.

It was a subject that Fidelma had no knowledge of. She had often wondered why the Uí Liatháin were so vehemently antagonistic towards Cashel. She tried to bring her thoughts back to the present.

'Do you find it interesting that that very text was found misplaced in the book satchel? The same one that contained the annals of this abbey from which an essential missing page had been cut.'

'Obviously it was a mistake in replacing it in the wrong book satchel,' dismissed the steward.

'A mistake made when hastening to disguise an action and trying not to be seen,' Eadulf commented dryly.

'More important for us is the fact of it being replaced in the book satchel containing the annals of the abbey from where details of Abbot Brocc have been purposefully cut out. So, tell us something about this Sárán. You say he was not from a religious community?'

'He told me that he was a reciter of lore and history; a *seanchaidh*.'

'A Déisi historian?' Fidelma asked for confirmation.

'He was from Dún Garbháin and had come to consult some texts that our library held. As steward I gave permission, for I try to follow the teachings of the Faith I have chosen.'

'So you also converted? The Déisi are of the New Faith,' pointed out Eadulf.

'When Conall Corc granted them the lands, his condition was that they all converted, as he had, to the New Faith.'

'Is that why the vast majority of the Uí Liatháin have clung to the Old Faith?' Eadulf was thoughtful.

Fidelma felt they were losing the line she wanted to follow and interrupted before Brother Guala replied.

'You say Sárán came from Dún Garbháin? That is the principal fortress of Prince Cummasach of the Déisi. Where is this Sárán now? I would question him.'

'He is no longer in the abbey. He had already left the abbey when you arrived.'

'Exactly when did he do so?'

'He left later on the day that the body of the abbot was found.'

Fidelma stared at the steward in disbelief. 'After the body was found?' She did not wait for the confirmation. 'You mean you did not confine everyone to the abbey until a proper investigation was made as to who might be responsible?'

Brother Guala shifted uncomfortably. 'There was no reason—'

'Where did Sárán go? Back to the territory of the Déisi?'

'I was told that he was asking the route to Dún Guairne.'

'To the main fortress of *your* prince?' Eadulf questioned.

'We have had no officially appointed prince since the death of Tigerna Cosraigib, six months ago. The *derbhfine* of Tigerna Cosraigib would not agree on a successor,' he reminded them, then added: 'at least, not one that your brother, King Colgú, would recognise.'

There was a silence. Fidelma was thinking. Brother Guala eventually coughed nervously to disturb her.

'Is there something else I could help you with?' he asked.

'There is,' Fidelma replied. 'With the mysterious disappearance of the page relating to the background of Abbot Brocc, we shall have to ask you about his background and appointment. As steward you must know something of him.'

'He shared with me little about himself,' the steward replied sullenly.

'I think you may have already answered the mystery. The sentence before the missing page in the annals ends with the line that Abbot Brocc was presented with the abbey, Dair Inis. It would be unusual that Brocc was appointed abbot here or, to interpret, he was given control of Dair Inis, without ever serving in any religious role in the abbey or being appointed by the community itself. I do not have to remind you, Brother Guala, that an abbot cannot be appointed from outside the abbey. The community, the abbey's *derbhfine*, which you have invoked already, using the same rights and arguments as a blood family, would have had to approve. Did this happen?'

Once again the steward was reticent before responding. 'It is not so unusual. I was at Cluain Uamha when I was appointed as steward here.'

'And if we spoke to the community, or maybe your records survive, I am sure we will find you were elected by the community as steward and asked to return here with their approval?'

This time the silence was long. He did not correct her.

'So now, the question is . . . instead of being elected by the community in the usual manner, how was Brocc given the abbey of Dair Inis and by whom? He had, so far as we know, spent no time in this abbey. So who had the right to give him this abbey?'

Brother Guala lips twisted in a cold smile. 'Much power in that word "give",' he muttered.

'Can it be explained?'

'You disappoint me, *dálaigh*. I would have thought that you would have spotted the simple explanation.'

'So illuminate me.'

'You tell me that this text says that the abbey was given to Brocc of Dún Guairne.'

It was Eadulf who spotted the connection.

'Dún Guairne was the principal fortress of the last Prince of the Uí Liatháin. Then Abbot Brocc was . . .?'

'A son of Tigerna Cosraigib,' Fidelma concluded. 'Let me get this clear. You were already steward here when Brocc was appointed?'

Brother Guala blinked, perhaps realising for the first time that Fidelma's will was as strong as his own and her questioning meticulous. His features seemed to tighten as he replied.

'I was here five years before Brocc came. I returned to this community after some years at Cluain Uamha. That was a community near the caves, as the name suggests, in the west of Uí Liatháin territory. The Blessed Colmán mac Lénine established the community over a century ago. Our library holds copies of

Colmán's poems. I studied for a while at Colmán's abbey at Cluain Uamha and achieved the Fourth Order of Wisdom, the *Staruidhe,* there. I became master of the thirty lessons of divinity – the sacred lessons. Having achieved that, I was told this community was in need of a steward and they had asked me to return and fulfil that office. I did so in approval of the wishes of the community.'

'Did you know Brocc before he became abbot?'

'I knew of him. It was only a year ago that he came here as abbot.'

'So before the uprising?' Eadulf looked to Fidelma. 'In the entry above, the mention of Brocc is inscribed in the *Aois Domhain* reckoning – the year of the age of the world. It is difficult to be precise as there are variations in converting it, but from my knowledge, it would accord with what you say.'

'At least six months before Tigerna Cosraigib decided to join the alliance with Selbach against Cashel,' agreed Brother Guala.

'So we come to the question yet again. He did not serve here so who decided to make him abbot?' Fidelma repeated.

Brother Guala gave an expressive gesture. 'I surely do not have to point out that practically every abbey in the Five Kingdoms has been established by princely families. Every abbot is usually related to the king or prince of the territory. They had the education, authority and wealth to establish the foundations of the New Faith. It is because of that very fact that the New Faith has spread in this island with such remarkable speed. Once the High King accepted it, the nobles did so, except where local conditions prevailed.'

'So Brocc was appointed simply because he was related to the prince of this territory?' Fidelma asked. 'And he was appointed by the Chief Bishop of Muman, which would have been the Bishop of Cashel?'

'I do not think I could have been clearer,' Brother Guala said.

Fidelma grimaced as if resigned. 'So the point is that Brocc was appointed not because he was trained as a religieux but because he was of the noble ruling family. But again, you say the nobles were mostly of the Old Faith. Surely Tigerna Cosraigib would have been outraged at Brocc's appointment? And surely members of the community in the abbey would have felt resentment?'

'Resentment? Do you imply that is the reason why he was murdered?'

'It's as good a reason as any other. You were already steward here. Did this noble family not consult with the community about this relative being placed in charge of them?'

'Consult? A nice word. The family of Tigerna Cosraigib were not ones to consult about anything. Yet it was strange that there was no conflict between father and son over the matter of faith.'

Fidelma was mystified. 'I have not known nobles of whichever faith who do not make some observance to the law of the Brehons. I suppose, in truth, I know very little about the cultural belief of this territory . . . You mentioned that Tigerna Cosraigib's son Conmhaol was approved as Prince of the Uí Liatháin, to succeed his father. He had been brother to Brocc.' Fidelma was thoughtful. 'But before we follow that track, let us confirm that Brocc was never endorsed by the election, by the abbey community at any time. Was he accepted as abbot after he had been here some time? He came here a year ago and that was six months before his father joined the attack on Cashel.'

'That is so,' Brother Guala confirmed.

'You are telling us that you really know nothing of his training in the New Faith before he became abbot? If he had studied at a monastic school he would have been expected to acquire the Seventh Order of Wisdom, achieving the status of *Druim Clí*. That degree would have allowed him to achieve qualification as abbot that no one would argue about.'

Fidelma did not really trust what Brother Guala was telling them. Although she knew he was right that many nobles were self appointed as abbots and bishops, they were educated in ecclesiastical colleges.

Brother Guala was watching her expression and could see her scepticism.

'I will resort to gossip. As a young prince of his people, Brocc achieved his education with a sword rather than a pen. I heard that he had minimal learning in a bardic college. Oh, once here he did try to get Sister Cáemóc to teach him much of the Holy Canon, the main scriptures, but he was more interested in the retribution tales in the scriptures and not the Gospels. The abbey's hound had more chance of reaching the level of *Sai* than he did.'

Eadulf knew a *Sai* was a degree of an ecclesiastical college.

'Surely the community here realised that Brocc was doing them more harm than good in the role of abbot?'

'Lack of scholarship was not a concern,' replied the steward. 'He was someone who had authority to govern and that is what he did in the abbey. He was a protector of the community.'

'It strikes me that you were the educationalist in the abbey,' Eadulf observed. 'Was there any conflict between you and Abbot Brocc?'

Brother Guala shook his head. 'I was happy to be in charge of scholastic instruction and Abbot Brocc was happy making sure the abbey remained well funded, free from tribute after the attempted uprising, and secure and influential. At the surrender of the Uí Liatháin six months ago, we went to Cashel to plead our innocence before your brother, King Colgú.'

'I remember it well,' replied Fidelma. 'I suppose there is one question I should ask you: what sort of man was Brocc?'

'*De mortuis nil nisi bonum.* Should I speak ill of the dead when they cannot defend themselves?'

'You should speak exactly as it was *because* he is dead.

We need such information *because* he is dead. You seem to indicate that you will say something that would need defending if he were still alive.'

The steward merely shrugged. 'Then I must confess . . . and be honest in my confession . . . I disliked Brocc as the shepherd dislikes the wolf.'

'Yet you were his steward? You have just said you were happy fulfilling different roles in this abbey. Are you now withdrawing that testimony?'

'I just wanted to emphasise there was nothing in common between the abbot and me. Not even the Faith we are supposed to practise. If he spent any time studying, even secular works, then he displayed little profit by it. That is my personal opinion.'

'Yet he spent a year in this abbey. Did no one challenge his lack of knowledge? Indeed, you imply that you did not challenge it.'

'Do you think that I wanted to shorten my life?'

'You mean that he threatened you physically? Or are you suggesting that his family were a threat?'

'No one made threats. Knowing the reputation of that family, it is just a foregone conclusion. It is not without significance that their emblem is the sign of the grey wolf, or that his father was known as "Lord of the Slaughter", often interpreted as "Lord of Carnage".'

'You were not the only one of intelligence here – so how was he regarded by the rest of the community? Did no one challenge and dispute with him?'

'It depends whom you speak with.'

'Explain.'

'Some feared him. Some tolerated him. It depended on what you wanted in life.'

'I don't understand,' interposed Eadulf.

'Say nothing and enjoy what life you could. Challenge his authority and accept the consequences.'

Eadulf was shocked. 'And this man a bastion of the New Faith! What consequences? Did he chastise his critics or inflict harsh disciplines on them?'

Eadulf was well aware of how some nobles behaved in his own territories. Some appointed themselves as abbots and bishops, looking upon the offices simply as an extension of their own princely authority and power, treating their communities almost as serfs to do their bidding. However, he could not accept an abbot – prince or not – could rule through fear, as did many temporal princes in other lands he had been to. He had lived too long with Fidelma, learning about the incredible egalitarian law system of the Five Kingdoms, where even a king could be challenged by his people. Yet now he was being told that not all the noble families respected the law of the Brehons.

Brother Guala considered for a moment.

'I knew his family, or some of them. His brother, Conmhaol, as I mentioned, still uses our physician, Fisecda, and sends for him when he wants him. They are still a power in this land. The darkness that emanated from Brocc's person was the same darkness that I saw in others of his family. Brocc was a brooding man as if he was not of this world. I do not know how to describe him further.'

'You have already presented a strange description of someone who was supposed to be a leader of the New Faith in this territory.'

'Let me put it this way, when he entered a chamber it was as if coldness suddenly entered with him. There was an aura of the grave about him. Talking would cease as if people were afraid of expressing their thoughts before him. A few argued in the early days. They are no longer in our community and we were told that they had decided suddenly to go on pilgrimage. We do not expect their return.'

'Again, to sum up, contrary to the impression we were first

given, it seems that there were plenty of people with motive to kill the abbot.'

'Motive, yes, but not the courage. I have had my say. All I want now is to continue here with my studies and pupils. I wish you well, but perhaps I should add this. Don't confine yourself to the community in this abbey when you seek suspects. Even among the abbot's own family you may well find those who hated him.'

The afternoon was warm when Fidelma and Eadulf made their way to the empty refectory for somewhere to sit alone and discuss what they had learnt. There was hardly anyone else at the tables in the large chamber, but as they entered Fidelma saw a familiar figure. It was the muscular young religieux who had accompanied them that morning, Brother Scatánach. He was busy polishing the tables after the midday meal.

Fidelma led the way to where the youth was and seated herself with a greeting to the boy.

'Good afternoon, Brother Scatánach. Do not let us disturb anything urgent,' she added quickly, as the young man began to move away, which she put down to his nervousness.

'I was told at last night's meal that this abbey is famous for its cider, brewed from crab apples.'

'That is so, lady,' the young man replied.

'Is it allowed that you bring us a jug?'

When a jug and two mugs had been placed on the table and Eadulf had poured the liquid, he and Fidelma saw that Brother Scatánach was standing watching them suspiciously.

'If you can spare a moment, we would like a word with you,' Fidelma said in invitation.

The young man glanced around quickly and looked nervously from one to the other. Fidelma motioned him to take a seat.

'I am only a noviciate and not allowed to sit,' he returned. 'I can tell you little more than I did yesterday,' he went on before Fidelma could pose a question.

'I understand, but what do you make of all this?' queried Fidelma in a friendly fashion. 'I mean of the death of the abbot.'

'Make of it?' The young man frowned.

'You must have some opinion of this strange event. Some prophetess foretelling the death of your abbot, which has now turned out to be correct. There must be a lot of talk among the community about the fact, and speculation on the culprit.'

'I am sure you have spoken to those with better knowledge than I. We novices have to be guided by the wiser and more senior members of the abbey,' the youth replied almost in a wooden voice, as if reciting a lesson.

'Brother Guala, your steward, seems to give credence to the prophecy,' Eadulf observed. 'Brother Cróebíne, your librarian, seems to regard his story with little credence.'

'Each to his own opinion.'

'And rightly so,' Fidelma agreed. 'That is what I am interested in. What are the opinions of the community here?'

'We were shocked,' the boy replied.

'That is natural,' Eadulf sympathised.

'While no one initially suggested a motive, it appears there might be many,' Fidelma said then.

'I do not understand. Many reasons why someone would kill the abbot?' The boy seemed mystified.

'Then put it this way: many people willing to kill for the same reason.'

The youth shrugged. 'It is too complicated for me.'

'Let's make it easier. The abbot was from a family of a local prince, is that not so?'

Brother Scatánach nodded.

'It is interesting that, on the morning of the murder, your

physician was called away from the abbey to attend to Prince Conmhaol, who is brother to the abbot.'

The relationship did not seem to be news to the youth.

'Everyone knew that the abbot was of the princely family of our people. Perhaps you should take this up with our wise leaders.'

Fidelma sighed heavily. Brother Scatánach shifted in his position as if he had grown uncomfortable.

'I seem to remember you are a local boy,' Fidelma said, as if changing the subject.

'All my life I have lived under the shadow and influence of Dair Inis,' he replied. 'I determined that, when I was old enough, I would come here to improve my reading and writing, and to study further, even if it meant accepting the New Faith.'

Eadulf picked up on the nuance of the words.

'So you were raised nearby, and in the Old Faith?'

'The small fishing settlement by the Great River, where it meets the confluence of another called the river of Gleann-Doimhin.'

'At the mouth of the deep valley,' nodded Fidelma. 'You say it is a small settlement?'

'Apart from the native fishermen and their families, it has several who sell their wares and talents to the abbey. It attracts various artisans and traders who come and settle, and earn their livings there.'

'Does the settlement come under the control of the abbey?'

'No, the village is of the Old Faith and has its own *bean-tiarna*. The abbey has a good relationship with the village. It governs itself. It was said that it was here long before the Island of Oaks became a Christian abbey.'

'A *bean-tiarna* – a princess?'

'Her name is Lalóg.'

'I know it is allowed in law, but it is not often one comes across female nobles in control of territories in these southern lands,'

Fidelma answered. 'We have already learnt that the princes of these southern territories are warlike, arrogant, boastfully virile and jealous of each other. From what I have seen, it is they who control the *derbhfine* and manage to exclude women from office. If what Brother Guala says is right, Abbot Brocc would surely be exerting his authority over his small neighbour.'

To their surprise, Brother Scatánach protested.

'Abbot Brocc was not like that. Princess Lalóg was also a *banchomarbae*, inheriting in her own right. They were brother and sister, and close friends. She would visit the abbey and I have often seen him in her settlement.'

Fidelma and Eadulf exchanged meaningful glances.

'Perhaps the fault lies not with the *derbhfine* but in the historians who write down their preferences in histories to exclude such female rulers. Remember history is the prejudice of the historian and not some great unquestionable truth set down without bias,' said Eadulf.

Fidelma had already turned to the young religieux.

'Tell me of this noble lady, Princess Lalóg.'

'She was daughter of Tigerna Cosraigib, and is also sister of Conmhaol – the wolf warrior. I know Conmhaol well for I used to accompany a merchant to his homestead, delivering goods, before I joined the abbey.'

'Did this princess attend the obsequies of her brother Abbot Brocc?'

'She and her daughter were both there.'

Fidelma uttered a little sigh. 'So which is the best way to this village of your birth?'

'You want to go there?' The young man seemed surprised.

'That is my intention,' she assured him solemnly.

'Well, if the sun remains shining without rain, it is a pleasant walk along the west bank of the river. If you are averse to walking, and can handle an oar in a small *noí,* then it is but a few strokes between us and the settlement – that is, keeping to the right bank of the river.'

'You had better carry on with your work,' Fidelma suddenly advised him, observing a senior member of the community standing staring at them across the far side of the refectory.

The youth seized his cloths and hurriedly left to continue his polishing.

'We are going to pay our respects to this princess now?' Eadulf raised his brows in query at Fidelma.

'There is plenty of daylight left and if the village is as close as the boy says it is then we have time to go at once and make ourselves known to this Princess Lalóg,' she assured him. 'Let's find Dego to come with us.'

'Perhaps we had better inform Brother Guala that we are leaving the abbey and going downriver to visit the little township.'

Fidelma shook her head.

'There is no reason to bother the poor man,' she said with a curious smile.

CHAPTER SEVEN

Fidelma and Eadulf found Dego, informed him of their intentions, and the three of them left the island. The path along the shoreline south to the area where Brother Scatánach had indicated the settlement lay was easy to find. Dego insisted on leading the way, shield attached to the stump of his severed right arm, his left hand brushing his sheathed sword. Eadulf was still amazed at the refusal of the warrior to let his amputation become a disability. He had trained himself to fight with as much dexterity with his left hand as he had with his right. He had once again established the prowess that had earned him his reputation in the élite bodyguard of the King of Cashel. He still proudly wore the golden torc symbol of office and carried himself with a slight attitude of conceit as he walked ahead. He had much to be proud of, but Eadulf knew that Dego merely affected the attitude when acting as bodyguard to Fidelma or, indeed, her brother Colgú.

The southward track that ran alongside the broad river was bound to their west by the tall oak forest and underbrush. It was a pleasant enough walk. The day was warm and the air filled with a myriad of bird and animal calls.

Eadulf suddenly turned to his companion. 'Does this remind you of anything, Fidelma?'

She was puzzled and said so.

'I am reminded of walking along a similar track nearly a year ago when we were journeying from the abbey of Fionn Bharr on that mission for your brother. We had to cross marshy ground. That journey eventually took us to the western territory of the Uí Liatháin.'

'What made you think of that? This is an entirely different terrain.'

'I don't know,' Eadulf confessed. 'Perhaps it is that Dego is ahead of us, as a guard, as was Enda at that time. There was thick undergrowth on both sides. It was almost the same circumstances when we were attacked.'

'But that was marshy land and we were on horseback – different circumstances.'

'Maybe I was just thinking about Enda. I miss him.'

'I know he felt deeply for that poor girl Cera, but to simply sacrifice his life after she was murdered is beyond my comprehension. Is that what you were thinking, Eadulf?'

'I suppose so,' he replied hesitantly. 'Yet there is something else; something familiar about this path. I have a feeling that . . .'

Fidelma cast him a disapproving frown. 'A feeling? That journey was not as comfortable as we are now, walking in the pleasant sunshine on this dry and warm afternoon. Your perceptions are playing you tricks.'

Eadulf hunched and then relaxed his shoulders as a gesture of indifference. 'Even so, I feel an atmosphere, a presentiment, if you like . . .'

Fidelma was chuckling softly. 'Don't say that you are letting Brother Guala's notions of curses and soothsayers affect you?'

For a moment, Eadulf looked offended. Then he returned her smile.

'Atmospheres are real.'

'You'll be seeing this prophetess in grey shortly.'

'I am just experiencing an aura . . .'

It happened so quickly that they were not sure what it was that had taken place. They were aware of a cry of warning coming from Dego. There was a ring of metal striking metal. It was followed immediately by a cacophony of alarmed animal and bird cries around them.

The next thing they knew was that Dego had his shield raised while his good left hand was wielding his sword in a defensive mode. He had fallen back to protect them, shouting to Eadulf to get closer so that he could adequately cover them both. Then the noise abated as they stood waiting for something more to happen. A few moments later and the regular sounds of the forest inhabitants returned.

For some time the three of them crouched huddled together, watching and waiting, senses alert for something to happen next.

'What was it, Dego?' Fidelma finally asked softly.

'We were shot at,' the warrior responded dryly. 'A single archer, one arrow. I saw a flash of sunlight on something in the bushes and raised my shield just in time to deflect the arrow.'

'A single arrow?' Eadulf queried. 'It must have been aimed at you, for we were walking a short distance behind and unprotected. Had the attacker wanted to kill either of us, they would have been able to.'

'Perhaps it was just meant as a warning?' Fidelma suggested.

'A lethal warning,' Dego muttered. 'That was an arrow from a longbow, and you heard the ring on my shield. That has a metal-tipped barb.'

Eadulf was aware that Dego was now moving forward and motioning them to keep behind him and his raised shield. The noise of the forest had completely settled now. No unusual movement could be detected in the bordering woodland. It seemed that their assailant had vanished.

Eadulf bent forward, picked something up and handed it to Dego. It was the broken arrow. It had snapped in two parts on encountering Dego's shield and the pieces had ricocheted off into the undergrowth. Dego quickly examined it, playing particular attention to the flights, which indicated a lot about the arrow's origin.

'This is the weapon of a professional bowman,' Dego announced. 'It's professionally made and with a metal arrowhead. Maybe that was what the sun reflected off. The flights are made from goose feathers. It's not a rural hunting weapon. But there is no marking, which is unusual if it belongs to a noble or his retinue, although the metal arrowhead shows that it was meant for a noble. Poorer people use flints or fire-hardened wood.'

'Was it meant for us, or was it a mistake?' Eadulf queried.

'If it was a mistake, it could have been a costly one,' Dego replied. 'Such people who use this type of weapon are not given to mistakes. We must find a maker of arrows – a fletcher – for perhaps the attacker might be traced.'

'This is true, but perhaps the provenance of this arrow is the very place where its maker, and the bowman who used it, do not want us to go.'

Dego did not quite understand.

'I'll make it clearer,' Fidelma explained. 'Maybe the fletcher is from the settlement that we are making for. Remember what Brother Scatánach said? The settlement houses many artisans, professionals whose craftsmen are employed by the Abbey. Maybe the man who fired it is from the settlement.'

'And maybe they are employed at the abbey,' Eadulf pointed out. 'Employed by certain people who do not want us to reach the settlement.'

'Another possibility,' Dego muttered. 'There was a Déisi ship at anchor and maybe it was someone from that ship who recognised you and was bent on vengeance after the Déisi surrendered.'

There was silence while they considered the possibilities.

'I suggest we continue our walk to this settlement to see what we can learn,' said Fidelma. 'But let us walk carefully and keep our eyes open.'

'I believe the assailant has gone,' Dego said. 'But we should take care and keep to the shelter as much as possible. Those trees on the river bank will make good cover, if we continue.'

As they moved towards the trees that Dego indicated, the warrior went ahead, keeping his sword unsheathed. His eyes flickered this way and that, scanning the woods and undergrowth. Once or twice, he entered the undergrowth itself. It was obvious he was trying to find some trace of the archer. Finally he rejoined Fidelma and Eadulf with sword sheathed and shield adjusted on his shoulder.

'Our archer friend has definitely gone,' he confirmed. 'Back there,' he jerked the thumb of his good hand, 'I found the spot where he stood waiting.'

The Warriors of the Golden Collar were expert trackers and able to read signs that many would miss.

'So, whoever fired was definitely waiting for us?' Fidelma asked.

'Luckily, the spot was slightly damp, and whoever it was had stood there a while. The earth and moss were depressed as he shifted his weight, and he had made the mistake of leaning against a tree trunk to steady his arm as he sighted the bow. Some marks of lichen, yellow patches on the tree, will have stained his upper tunic. They might be a way of identifying our friend.'

'Did you get any idea of which way he went?' Fidelma asked.

'Westerly, of course, but he could have turned in any direction once in the cover of the darkness of the trees,' Dego said.

'It was a warning shot to prevent us going to this village?' Eadulf queried.

'I think it was, otherwise one of us would be dead.'

'If that was the intention, it failed. Anyway, only one person knew of our intention,' Eadulf said.

Fidelma did not respond.

A short distance later they began to see the outskirts of the port settlement. Wooden barns and storehouses, as well as stockades for horses and cows, stretched along the river bank. There were groups of *currachs* and one or two larger river boats. Fidelma and her companions, hearing people shouting and calling and even applauding, exchanged glances of surprise, hesitating as they tried to identify the sounds.

They turned a corner to find an elderly man was securing the gate of a wooden compound nearby in which some goats were incarcerated. Fidelma greeted him.

'What is happening in the village?' she asked. 'It sounds as if there is some festivity.'

The old man levered himself up from his task and examined her and then her companions. His skin was wrinkled and weathered, his eyes deep set and mouth sunken. Then his facial muscles moved in a toothless grin.

'Strangers, eh?'

'We have just come from Dair Inis,' Fidelma replied easily.

The old man cast his eyes over Dego, taking in his weapons and the golden torc around his neck.

'Since when has Dair Inis been populated by the élite warriors of the Eóghanacht?' he wheezed in sarcastic humour.

'I am a *dálaigh* and this is my personal bodyguard,' Fidelma felt obliged to respond.

Just then there was another roar of enthusiasm from the village, followed by applause. The old man seemed to notice the concern in Fidelma's eyes and chuckled.

'Have no fear, lady. It is only an entertainment.'

'An entertainment?'

'This morning, Scannail the Contentious arrived, and doubtless he has been persuaded to perform some of his verses.'

'Scannail the Contentious?' The name meant nothing to Fidelma. 'Who is he?'

The old man regarded her with astonishment. 'You must truly

be strangers to the lands of the Uí Liatháin. Scannail is a bard of great reputation. He was once *seanchaidh* to Lord Tigerna Cosraigib. Now he is known for his wandering, his teachings, his stories and poems of our people. Wherever he goes, he is welcomed by men, women and children alike. He is especially welcome to this village.'

'He bears an interesting name – is he an argumentative person?' Eadulf asked.

'We are not often responsible for the names that we are given, Saxon.'

Eadulf was surprised that the old man had spoken to him in Saxon. Before he could ask how he knew, the old one continued, 'I was once a guest of a Saxon raiding vessel for a while. Time enough to gain some knowledge of your harsh tongue.'

Eadulf flushed. 'I am an Angle, not a Saxon,' he replied defensively.

'It sounds the same roughness to me. What does your name mean?'

'I was told it means the lucky wolf,' Eadulf found himself responding.

'Does that not prove my point, Saxon?' the old man chuckled. 'Sometimes we do not merit the names that we are given by parents, but are better for the names that we earn. However, I admit Scannail's is an apt name for there is belligerency in his verse.'

'How contentious is he?' Fidelma intervened, not wishing Eadulf to launch forth about being called a Saxon instead of an Angle, for to her ears the languages were all one and the same. In fact, her people had developed no separate name other than 'Saxon' for all the tribes of Jutes, Angles and Saxons.

'Truly, you are a stranger in this territory,' repeated the old man. 'Scannail is placed highly among the bards of the Uí Liatháin. It is best to know that, if you speak with him. He holds the eighth highest grade of bards, a *sóerbaird*. Even the high born tremble at his satires. How contentious?' the old man repeated with a grin. 'I would explain that his verse would be especially contentious in the ears of the Eóghanacht, who are the source of all our troubles.'

'Then is this Scannail a bard of the old schools?' Fidelma asked. 'There should be no conflict, as the bardic colleges are still regarded as equal to the ecclesiastic ones. I, myself, attended a secular college, which was the law school of Morann, near Tara.'

'It is whispered that Scannail is more than just a bard: he is a repository of all the wisdom and crafts of the ancient ones.'

'I suppose Scannail is a priest of your Old Faith?' Eadulf probed.

The old man gave another wheezy chuckle. 'You must have realised that you are in the territory of the Uí Liatháin, Saxon?'

'I *know* we are in the territory of the Uí Liatháin,' Eadulf snapped, irritated. 'We come on official business under the laws of the Five Kingdoms, of which, may I remind you, that this is part? I know many of you still do not accept this.'

Fidelma glanced disapprovingly at him. She wished Eadulf was a little more diplomatic at times.

'If this Scannail is a Druid, then he might be the very person that I should have words with,' she reminded Eadulf.

'You think that he might know something of the attack on the Abbot Brocc?' Eadulf asked. 'You think he might know something of this Grey One and the prophecy?'

The name seemed to have a remarkable effect on the old man, who let out a rasping gasp and moved off with a speed that astonished them. He vanished between the nearby wooden sheds, hobbling quickly as if being pursued.

Fidelma scowled at Eadulf. 'A stupid thing to mention names. There is a time to keep one's thoughts to oneself.'

'I wasn't thinking,' Eadulf confessed, his cheeks colouring. 'But—'

'Too late now, but be careful what you say about the Druids. Druids still have rights in law and are acknowledged as an independent professional class in our society, in spite of what certain members of the New Faith say,' she snapped. 'Even the Blessed Colm Cille wrote, in his poem about the changing Faith – "My Druid is Christ . . .", which means he acknowledged the wisdom of the Old Faith being transferred to the New Faith.'

Fidelma was looking at the spot among the sheds where the old man had vanished.

'He will soon be whispering the news of our coming, so we might as well go into the village without subterfuge. I would want to see if this Scannail can provide us with information. If he is a wandering bard in this territory, even a bard with Druidic bias, then who better to inform me about this curse of the Grey One and why Abbot Brocc received it?'

'Well, from the way the old man reacted, it seems this Grey One is certainly known in these parts,' Eadulf replied firmly.

They moved in the direction of the clamour, but then the noise grew quiet as the strong timbre of a baritone became prominent. The voice was melodious in its rise and fall, with careful enunciation of the meter and tonal element. It was clearly a voice well practised in the songster's art. Soon the visitors could clearly make out the words, so distinct and vibrant were their enunciation.

> Lofty Cashel; Cashel of the Kings
> Praiseworthy scene of mighty deeds
> No seer knows its destiny
> But the unblinking eye of the Grey One.

Eadulf cast a worried look at Fidelma. 'It's as if someone knew of our coming. A song about your family combined with mention of the very prophet that we need to learn about.'

Fidelma did not reply. She, too, had registered the words. They had entered a space at what appeared to be the centre of the settlement, one side open to the sea and constituting a small harbour where a few ships were bobbing on the waters. There were many people with their backs towards them; all were focused towards a central wooden stage on which stood an almost shapeless figure with arms raised as if to emphasise his words. Not at all in keeping with the strong baritone notes that emanated from his mouth, the figure they beheld was short and corpulent, with fleshy features surrounded by long, white straggling hair on which the red-yellow gleam of the lowering sun seemed to dance.

The people watching him were now still and quiet, as if mesmerised by the rhythms of the chanter.

> Eóghan Mór begat children in Cashel
> Here the haughty Eóghanacht rule
> So to them is paid all honour
> And no one questions the burden of tribute.

> The wise Druid compares them to other princes
> But all are found wanting, all unworthy,
> Uí Liatháin decay on the *fidchell* board of life
> And try to will it otherwise.

> One day it shall be otherwise, says the Grey One
> In the infinite eyes is the vision—

He stopped abruptly as he caught sight of Fidelma and her companions at the edge of the audience. It was as if he had recognised them. That moment of silence was swiftly broken by a dozen whispers from the surrounding gathering as heads were turning in the direction of his gaze.

It was then that Fidelma noticed a seated person to one side of

the platform on which the poet stood. Even seated and with indis-
tinguishable features, there was something commanding about the
poise of this person – clearly a woman. Standing on her right was a
tall man. On her left was an equally tall woman, apparently an
attendant. The three presented a commanding group. The man was
still for a moment, examining the newcomers, as had the bard.
Then he bent to the seated figure and whispered quickly. Fidelma
saw the seated woman was well dressed, but her attire was unlike
the dresses worn by the women of the settlement. She wore a circlet
of beaten silver around her head. Beaver skin trimmed her cloak,
which, though fastened at her shoulders, parted to reveal a dress of
silk that would not have put any princess to shame. This could only
be Lalóg, the noble who ruled this territory.

Fidelma seized the moment to step forward towards the foot of
the platform on which the woman was seated.

'I did not mean to interrupt your entertainment. I am—'

'Fidelma, sister of Colgú, the Eóghanacht King at Cashel,' interrupted the man, taking a step forward to the edge of the platform as
if to shield the seated woman. Fidelma noticed he had the build of a
warrior. He was dressed without weapons except for a dagger and
short knife in sheaths at his belt. He was dark of skin, with dark
brown hair and beard, and what seemed piercing black eyes under a
lowering brow. Both he and the attendant woman were unusually
dressed for members of the small fishing village. Fidelma reminded
herself that the woman was one of the ruling nobility of the
territory.

Before Fidelma could reply to his recognition, the man added,
'Your reputation as a *dálaigh,* one of the legal advocates of the
Eóghanacht king, precedes you.'

Fidelma looked to the seated woman and found herself staring
into the face of someone not very much older than she was. Her
hair was a curious golden brown with little dancing highlights as
the sun caught it. The heart-shaped features were not really soft;

there was something aggressive about the jaw and the lips. There was also something quite challenging in her stare. The eyes, so ice-cold grey, and defiant in an almost unblinking stare, appeared sinister. The aquiline nose, the prominent bridge of which made the face of the woman less attractive, exuded a sense of power.

'I am Fidelma of Cashel,' Fidelma confirmed. 'And my companions are Eadulf of—'

'We know who you are,' replied the aggressive man. 'I am Cathbarr, steward to Princess Lalóg of the Uí Liatháin. What do you seek here with your foreign husband and your Eóghanacht bloodhound?'

Fidelma swallowed a little at the confrontation. She decided to ignore the belligerent young man and continue addressing the woman Lalóg.

'I come seeking information.' She tried to keep her voice sharp but not too confrontational.

It was still Cathbarr who replied.

'It does not require intelligence to assume that when a *dálaigh* appears unbidden they always want information,' he sneered.

'I am told you are aware of the murder of your brother, Abbot Brocc of the community in Dair Inis. Abbot Brocc sent for me as he had some premonition of death. I am therefore investigating the circumstances.'

Not by the slightest movement of her features did Lalóg betray any change of emotion.

'There are better places and times to speak of that matter,' her steward replied.

'You will be aware that a *dálaigh*, and one with the degree of *anruth,* can dictate both time and place when in pursuit of answers in an investigation.' Fidelma's voice was now raised above the murmuring of the people. Her eyes remained fixed on the seated woman.

At that moment, Scannail, who had taken advantage of the

interruption to take a drink, put down his mug and came forward. He had a curious gait. Now he was close Fidelma could see his grey-white hair was long, without curls, like smooth silk. His skin was weather beaten, his pale eyes were cold and pebbly, like crystal washed on a seashore. His features were disfigured by a purplish scar running from the corner of his mouth, across his right cheek to his right ear. It was difficult to be sure of his true expression under both his bushy beard and disfigurement of the scar, but his tone was one of amusement.

'Remember, Cathbarr, such a *dálaigh* can even sit themselves in the presence of the High King without asking permission. So beware of entering verbal combat on the subject of etiquette with such a one who holds the degree of *anruth*.'

The woman Lalóg suddenly spoke for the first time.

'I am not in need of legal tuition.' Her voice was cold, with a crisp quality to it.

'Perhaps the legal adherents of the New Faith have changed that law, as they have been wont to do,' Scannail added in a mocking tone.

'Try no legal tricks here, Eóghanacht lawyer,' Cathbarr sneered.

Fidelma turned her gaze to Lalóg's arrogant steward. 'I presume I address someone who adheres to the Old Faith? However, as a *rechtaire*, you should know something of the laws, which were revised by the special commission of the High King Lóeguire. That was two centuries ago when it was decided that both Faiths were to be accepted equally into the new law unless they were totally and violently in conflict. Thus, after nine years of patient research by lawyers, the laws of the Brehons were approved by the convention and by the High King, Laoghaire, by King Conall Corc of Muman, and by King Daire of Ulaidh. In support of them were the Chief Brehons Dubhtach, Rossa and Fearghus. Thirdly, the new Chief Bishops of the kingdoms,

Patricius, Benignus and Cairneach, signed off the new laws. The rights of the people were agreed, as they have since remained. Those of the New Faith will not break the principles agreed nor should those of the Old Faith.'

'Do not think you can use your Eóghanacht arrogance in this land . . .' began Cathbarr.

Lalóg scowled with disapproval. Her look alone caused her steward to hesitate and then she turned back to Fidelma, lowering her tone but still defensive. She climbed from the platform in an almost languid motion. 'I shall leave Scannail to finish his entertainment. He should not disappoint the people who came here in order to listen to him rather than to discussions about law; or questions about the death of my brother. If it is acceptable, Fidelma of Cashel, we will go to my poor *bothán* to discuss the reason for your coming here.'

'That will be agreeable to me.' Fidelma inclined her head in acknowledgement. 'I apologise to Scannail. My regrets that time does not allow me to relax to hear a bard of your reputation singing about my family, the Eóghanacht.'

The old man smiled thinly at Fidelma's sharp reminder about the contents of the song that he had been singing.

'I sing songs of people that I learn about on my travels, lady. Yet I am truly honoured that a distinguished advocate of the Eóghanacht wants to hear of what I sing.'

'Reputations grow and spread, as I am sure yours will,' Fidelma replied, leaving him to decipher the hidden meaning.

Princess Lalóg's tall female attendant had joined her from the platform. As Cathbarr was about to follow, Lalóg said sharply: 'I shall not need you for this discussion.'

Cathbarr was both annoyed and surprised. 'My advice might be required when you speak of the Abbot of Dair Inis. The fact that he sent for this Eóghanacht lawyer before his death might be of importance.'

'I will not need you, Cathbarr,' Lalóg repeated firmly.

Fidelma turned to him with a smile. 'Have no concern. You must surely be aware that my oath is of allegiance, as *dálaigh*, to the law, which must be obeyed by all, from kings, bishops and even Druids.'

Scannail interrupted to reply for the steward. 'Is it not an axiom that many nobles, like the Eóghanacht, forget the law once they obtain power, if it becomes inconvenient for them?'

'If the saying is true, perhaps it is why lawyers exist: to remind the kings and nobles and their stewards of their duties,' Fidelma replied.

Princess Lalóg was obviously controlling her impatience.

'I feel the text of the *Crith Gabhlach* is forgotten where it clearly states that a people are stronger than a king or a lord. It is the people who ordain the king. The king does not ordain the people. I am a servant of my people.'

'That is the principle under which nobles should govern,' Fidelma conceded.

'Then explain,' the steward replied with a triumphal expression, 'why do the Eóghanacht rule over certain clans who do not want them to be their overlords?'

'If you refer to the peace that was made with the Uí Liatháin six months ago' – Fidelma realised where the man's argument was going and felt unsure of the history she had been hearing – 'agreements are made by the wise. But often there are those protesting against such agreements who would argue that force is a more persuasive argument than negotiation and argument.'

Cathbarr was still angry. 'Such as the attempt against Eóghanacht rule six months ago, which was met with force and therefore force was instrumental in causing our surrender.'

'As I recall, little force was used.' Fidelma knew she was facing a fervent Uí Liatháin and tried to get back on familiar grounds.

'Conspirators were uncovered and the facts laid before the King's Council. The facts were accepted. There were no major clashes of armies. But reparation had to be made.'

'That is not how it is seen among my people.' The steward was stubborn.

'The agreement to desist from conflict after only a few lives were lost was a wise decision. Preventing the Uí Liatháin taking to the battlefield after your Prince Tigerna Cosraigib was killed was a wise one. If such a battle had taken place, more lives would have been lost.'

'It caused the Abbot of Dair Inis to go running to plead with your brother that the Uí Liatháin were innocent of involvement.'

'Is that why the abbot had to die?' Eadulf snapped.

'You accuse me . . .?' Cathbarr stepped forward, hands on hips.

Dego took an involuntary counter-movement forward, his hand sliding to his sword sheath.

'Cathbarr, enough!' Lalóg's voice was no longer modulated but a sharp ice-cold command to her steward. 'I will have you speak no more of my brother Brocc.'

Cathbarr hesitated and then seemed to relax a little. 'I apologise, Lalóg. I felt my honour, and the honour of our people, was challenged,' the steward protested.

'You provoked the challenge. Unless there is calmness in your manner, I suggest you retire. Take Tóchell with you.' She nodded to the tall woman attendant. 'I have said I will go to my *bothán* to discuss matters with the *dálaigh* and her companions. This I intend to do. These words should not have been spoken here. Nor will further words of insult be given by anyone.'

The steward looked as if he was going to disobey her, his body tense, his hands, at his sides, clasping and unclasping as if seeking a weapon. Then the tall female attendant reached forward and put her hand on his arm. A familiar action, but one which surprised Fidelma. Cathbarr twisted on his heel and strode aggressively towards some nearby buildings followed by the woman Tóchell.

Lalóg turned to the visitors with a stony expression on her features and motioned for them to follow her.

Fidelma glanced quickly to Dego.

'I suggest when Eadulf and I go inside to discuss with Lalóg, you remain outside and keep watch,' she said quietly.

'Are you sure, lady?' Dego queried.

'That young man is an arrogant puppy but he could be dangerous.'

'I understand,' Dego replied. 'I will keep a careful watch.'

CHAPTER EIGHT

The building that Princess Lalóg led them to was surprisingly modest for one of her apparent status. But then she had referred to it as her *bothán*, the word applying more of a little hut or cabin than any larger construction. It was a square timber building, mainly of oak but with a lot of red yew panels for the interior. The door posts and lintel through which they passed were ornamented in bronze embellished with semi-precious stones. Fidelma recalled the fines that could be imposed on delinquents for scratching or disfiguring these posts or lintels. She wondered how such a construction was even accepted in a small rural fishing village.

Inside was one main room and what appeared to be a side room. The walls were held together with mortise and tenon joints. Several lanterns were hanging from the beams. Even so, Fidelma and Eadulf were surprised to see a *forles*, or skylight, in the flat, planked roof, totally unlike the conical thatched roofs of the local villagers. To one side was a *seinistir*, a window with a square thick glass covering that gave extra light. The floor was soft under their feet, and Fidelma realised that there were rugs laid across the wooden planks of the floor. There was a small table on which jugs and baked clay mugs stood together with a plate of simple bannocks or pastries. Around this were chairs. Lalóg waved to them to be seated. An elderly attendant appeared, took a jug and poured three measures, which she handed to them. Eadulf was about to refuse after their icy welcome but realised that this was a belated gesture of hospitality to visitors. It would be an insult to refuse.

'I apologise for my steward's belligerence,' Lalóg began as she settled herself before them.

'We understand that there are strong feelings in the aftermath of the Uí Liatháin clashes with Cashel,' Fidelma acknowledged. 'There is no need to apologise.'

Eadulf decided to follow her lead by not reflecting on the past. 'Your little port seems busy. I saw a merchant ship near Dair Inis when we arrived.'

'Merchant ships ply their trade along the southern coast of our territory. The captain of that ship you saw at anchor is a guest this evening. Tóla often trades with us.'

'Tóla? I thought this was a fishing settlement?'

Lalóg seemed relaxed at the question. 'We have expanded, thanks to Tóla, who owns his own vessel. Our port is a good collection point for the goods he trades in. Sometimes the workers bring their goods here and he does business with them. Other times he sails west along the southern coast to a few good harbours.'

'What goods does he trade in?' Eadulf asked.

'Tóla's main trade is in tanned leather. We have several centres where our tanners turn out tanned leather or themselves make excellent goods from it. Our *pattaire* are famous, for example.'

'Makers of *pai,* leather bottles?' Eadulf guessed, for they were a popular form of water carrier that he had seen used in several places in the Five Kingdoms.

'Our tanned-leather workers make shoes, bags, bottles, and jackets that warriors, like your one-armed companion, wear. Such leather jackets are often made for use in battle. The leather

PETER TREMAYNE

can be made quite strong. We were once famous for this trade, but these days . . .' Lalóg turned her gaze directly to Fidelma. 'I am sure you are not particularly interested in the trades between our territories, which have declined after the reparation payments. You say that you have come to see me about the death of my brother Brocc. Why?'

Fidelma tried not to show her surprise. 'Because he was murdered,' she replied.

'We are a small, isolated community. I meant, why would a lawyer from Cashel come here to investigate? On whose authority do you act as *dálaigh*?'

'Brocc himself sent word that he wanted to consult me. We arrived on the day after his burial. We found he died in mysterious circumstances and unlawfully.'

'And why come to me?'

Fidelma was puzzled at her tone. 'I am told that you are his sister and were a frequent visitor to the abbey.'

'I did visit. He was my brother.'

'You visited him in the abbey?'

'When need arose,' Lalóg replied. 'Is there a law against people of different religious ideas knowing one another or being related?'

'Of course there is not. How did you view your relationship with Brocc?'

'How should I view the relationship between brother and sister?'

'Did you argue over religion?'

'Is that a crime?'

'I presume you did not approve of his conversion?'

'Many of the family did not.'

'I am told you are sister to Conmhaol. I understand he refused to succeed his father as senior Prince of the Uí Liatháin. Was that because he did not believe in the Old Faith?'

Lalóg smiled cynically. 'Rather it was because he believed in the Old Faith. Brocc opted to follow the New Faith. Many families are being divided by this new religion from the east.'

'We are told the New Faith is still a minority in this territory and that it is even associated with the rule from Cashel. Dair Inis stands as the only Christian community in this territory and is regarded with suspicion. That must have placed Abbot Brocc under great stress with his family?'

Lalóg answered with a shrug. 'Many feel it was irrelevant.'

'But many must feel like your steward, Cathbarr?' Eadulf interrupted.

'Cathbarr is not skilled in verbal diplomacy.' Her eyes seemed to rest a moment on Eadulf. 'Cathbarr is a loyal steward and his skills lie in other realms. Not everyone is blessed with tact. You probably believe that when the world changes, one must change also. Here, we of the Uí Liatháin are slow to change. Dair Inis is, as you intimate, a bastion of the New Faith. Across the river to the south of us is Eochaill, the town of the yew wood. It was the last of our territory annexed by the Déisi several years ago. Árd Mór stands to the east across the river. To the north-west of our territory is the abbey in the Field of Caves – Cluain Uamha. Not all the kingdoms and territories of the Five Kingdoms have made the complete change to the New Faith in the last two centuries. The Uí Liatháin are one of the last bulwarks of the Old Faith, unless one counts isolated communities in the far west. We are also the original people of these territories. We held this land even before the Déisi were exiled and arrived here to be allowed to settle and displace our people.'

'That was several centuries ago,' Fidelma pointed out. 'Even so, the lack of conflict generally in the changing religions has been remarkable. Yet there is still a conflict here. So how is it that your brother took the path to Christianity?'

'It was a personal choice. A few others of our people accepted the New Faith because it was a way of obtaining rights and property. As I say, I did not approve of his choice. But it made him no less a member of the family.'

'Did he explain his reasons to you?'

'He would argue that your New Faith had spread due to the power of the nobles, like the Eóghanacht. They had adopted the New Faith because it made them powerful. At least the earliest converts had more sympathy with the philosophies of our Old Faith. Did you know Pelagius was one of our people?'

Fidelma and Eadulf were both surprised at her knowledge.

'You know of Pelagius?' Fidelma asked.

'Why should I not know of him and his works?' Lalóg demanded. 'He was one of us. It is said he was a noble from this very coast three centuries ago. His real name was Murchadh, one born of the sea. When he left here for Rome, he took the Greek name, meaning the same: Pelagius. In Rome he explained that our Old Faith was not so different from their new concepts. He was jeered at and they called him "full of Irish porridge" and claimed he was trying to make Christianity a part of Druidism.'

Fidelma was impressed at the princess's knowledge.

'So you know that the insular churches still adhere to the philosophies of Pelagius? It is those in the eastern lands that condemn him as a heretic,' she asked.

'Brocc argued for Pelagius,' Lalóg sighed. 'He told me that Pelagius and his works were ignored in Rome or that they decided to adopt philosophies devised by someone called Augustine of a place called Hippo. This man made the claim that everything is pre-ordained. Whether we live badly or well, we are already condemned to this new Christian Heaven or Hell. So, on this basis, what is the point of trying to live a good life if we are already condemned? That is why we still follow the Old Faith.'

'You seem well informed for . . . for . . .' Eadulf hesitated.

Lalóg smiled thinly. 'Well informed for someone who rejects

this New Faith of yours? Do you think we of the Old Faith have neither education nor understanding, my pious Saxon?'

Eadulf's protest that he was an Angle was smothered by Fidelma before he could enunciate it.

'What were the results of these discussions with your brother Brocc? I was under the impression from Brother Guala that your brother was not well educated in ecclesiastical matters?'

'Brocc relied for much of his knowledge on the librarian as well as his steward. Brocc was of our people and did not convert to the New Faith until after the battle of Cnoc Áine. He was then a young warrior in our father's army, which was defeated, as you know. He saw that power for him might lie in being a leader of the New Faith, so he gained what knowledge he could. I have also discussed many subjects with Brother Cróebíne. He, too, is a supporter of the teachings of Pelagius. We each agree that men and women are responsible for all their actions; that nothing is pre-ordained.'

Fidelma frowned at Eadulf, hoping he would not attempt to enter the argument. She wanted to know more about this autocratic *bean-tiarna*.

'It is not for a discussion on theology that we came,' she said firmly. 'But it raises a point. Could Brocc have been murdered because of his Christian role? Several days before he was killed, he encountered a soothsayer who foretold the very day that he would die. Brocc seemed so concerned with this that he sent for me to come to discuss matters. According to Brother Guala, his steward, when the day arrived, Brocc seemed to have dismissed the idea and ignored the warning. He died just as it had been predicted.'

Lalóg's face was sad.

'I attended the obsequies. My brother deserved that. My other brother, Conmhaol, was too ill to attend. Fisecda, who is the physician at the abbey, was attending him at that time. Oh, yes, we were of different religious beliefs, but we are family and that is stronger. My young daughter was staying with me and she also attended.'

'We were told that the abbot's physician, Brother Fisecda, had left the abbey to treat Conmhaol, your brother. Was that at the fortress, Dún Guairne?'

'Not there. My brother dwells at his *crannóg,* his lake house, on the River of Omens.'

'As Prince of the Uí Liatháin, I would expect his fortress to be at Dún Guairne,' Eadulf remarked curiously.

'Dún Guairne was the fortress of our late father. Dún Guairne was where we all grew up when our father, Tigerna Cosraigib, was Prince of the Uí Liatháin. When Conmhaol refused the endorsement of our family council, the *derbhfine,* to succeed our father, he refused to dwell in his father's fortress. He chose to take up residence in a small *crannóg.*'

'So he is like you, who dwells in this small village and not in . . .?' Eadulf hesitated.

'Why do I not dwell in some great lonely fortress?' Lalóg continued. 'That is because I prefer it here. Being daughter of a prince does not mean that you are condemned to spend the rest of your life in a palace unless you desire to do so.'

'Let me hear more about Abbot Brocc,' Fidelma invited. 'Do you have any ideas who killed him?'

'Brocc was an Uí Liatháin. He was of the ruling noble family. Many felt that he had abandoned his people by becoming one of the New Faith. As I have said, he converted when life changed for many after the defeat at Cnoc Áine. But he could not neglect his cultural upbringing. When this prophetess appeared he was concerned. That's obviously why he sent for you. He knew the symbol of the Grey One.'

'But if he believed in the prophecy, he would not have invited its fulfilment by going alone into the hills,' Eadulf pointed out.

'What do you think your brother Brocc was thinking when he did not heed the prophesy?' asked Fidelma.

'Maybe he was trying to prove something to himself. Prove he no longer believed in the power of prophets of the Old Faith. He was a man of deep thought and individuality, although he was stubborn. I cannot answer for him.'

'But did he really believe in the prophecy?'

'I only know what details he told his steward, Brother Guala, and the story that Brother Guala passed to me. Such a prophetess is known in the popular folklore of the Uí Liatháin.'

'And such prophecies are believed among your people?' Fidelma asked.

'Even the children here are brought up on such stories,' Lalóg said in a tired tone, as if bored with the subject. 'The idea of the grey-robed one, able to read portents, is not unusual. Even my daughter could recite a hundred such tales before she reached the age of maturity. Among our people, whose very name, Uí Liatháin, means "The Grey Ones", there are many such grey symbols and countless such grey-clad spectres.'

'Spectres? If we trust Brother Guala's account of what Brocc told him, this seemed to be a person who was very much of flesh and blood. He believed it was a young female.'

'It would take a person of flesh and blood to kill Brocc. If, as you say, he was murdered.' Lalóg was silent, seeming to consider Fidelma's meaning. 'Are you saying that the prophetess and the murderer were one and the same?'

'That is the position I am taking,' Fidelma agreed solemnly. 'I am not saying, however, that the prophetess was some supernatural entity. But there are many questions that need to be answered. If Abbot Brocc was truly concerned about the prophecy, why did he go alone to the sweat bath on the very day he was told he would die? And if he was not concerned, why send for me?'

'All I can say is that it was what it was,' replied the princess.

'He followed his custom and it was his nature to maintain rituals. That is what he did. Tradition outweighed supernatural threats.'

'He paid the price with the fulfilment of the prophecy,' Eadulf pointed out quietly. 'The fact is, Lalóg, we believe that Brocc was murdered and the only link we have is that his murderer, or the accomplice to the murderer, foretold it. That foretelling was presented in the form of prophesy, which is in the tradition of your Old Faith here. The prophetess was dressed as a familiar cultural figure to people of that faith – the Grey One.'

It seemed for a moment that Lalóg was not going to comment. Then she sighed. 'I believe, with his upbringing, he did take the prophecy seriously, but there was something that made him abandon caution when he went to the sweat house.'

'People in the abbey knew the location of the sweat house,' Eadulf said. 'Did your people, the people of this village, know about it?'

'Why should they not know of it? It was masons here who built it for a previous abbot. Of course they knew of it, but I think you can be assured that no one here ever went up in the hills to use it. Everyone knew it was used by certain members of the abbey. They felt it polluted. We have the confluence of two great rivers to bathe in. Brocc was an individualist and became an advocate of sweat baths.'

'Let us consider other points,' Fidelma suggested. 'Who would wish to see Brocc dead? We can accept there might be enmity between the Old and the New religions. Were there any prominent conflicts involving personalities?'

Lalóg smiled thinly. 'We all have enemies, Fidelma. But we do not win arguments about theology by murdering each other.'

'Then I speak of enemies who would benefit from Brocc's death, either substantially or emotionally.'

'The abbey will require a new abbot now,' pointed out Lalóg.

'You mean Brother Guala?' said Eadulf. 'Very well. And those expressing physical animosity to the abbot – I suppose your steward, Cathbarr, would be a suspect?'

'My steward? Why would he want to murder my brother?'

'Probably for the same reasons that he showed violence to us,' Eadulf replied. 'It is obvious that he loathes the community at Dair Inis.'

'Cathbarr is his own person, as are all the people of this settlement. However, the abbey provides the artisans of this village with much of their work. Whether they believe in the Old Faith or New, their views are their own and it is of little importance so long as they are content and keep to the laws. Some of the local people have even seen the benefits afforded them by joining the community of Dair Inis itself. Young Scatánach is an example. His father was a local fisherman, but the boy decided he wanted to read and write and my brother allowed him to became a novitiate at the abbey. That meant him adopting the New Faith . . . at least outwardly.'

'That surely does not meet with the approval of Cathbarr?' Eadulf queried cynically.

'Cathbarr is my steward; one of my family but a distant one. It is what I approve of that counts. It is my views that are more important,' returned the princess with a tone of annoyance.

'However, it is clear that your steward does not approve of your neighbours at Dair Inis. Very well. That is something to be considered.'

'So long as he abides by the law. Fidelma, what united us – those of the Old and those of the New Faith – is the law. Cathbarr was related to Brocc, distantly, as I say. He would not consider killing him over theology any more than I would. That you will surely understand.'

'Is Cathbarr a bowman?' Eadulf suddenly demanded.

Lalóg looked astonished at the unexpected question.

'Why would you ask that? He prides himself on being a swordsman, and he served my father.'

'But he is your steward and had some training?'

'He is of our family. I can't say that I understand what you are implying.'

Fidelma gave Eadulf a warning look.

'He is not implying any specific point,' she said to Lalóg. 'But we have observed that your steward seems quite belligerent to outsiders. It is reasonable to assume where his sympathies lay six months ago.'

'Everyone had their opinions. But that attempted rising failed. Once again, we now pay tribute to Cashel and that has doubled with reparation and fines.'

'Any legal appeal and alleviation of the reparation will be confirmed once you have appointed your new prince. Perhaps we may talk of why your brother Conmhaol refused the office when the *derbhfine* supported him.'

'You would have to ask him.'

'Can you tell us why anyone would try to stop us coming to talk to you?' Eadulf suddenly asked.

'Did someone stop you?' she countered with a frown.

'Someone tried,' Fidelma admitted. 'An archer.'

'Ah, that is why you asked about Cathbarr being a bowman? And asking, means you did not capture or identify your assailant. If it helps you,' Lalóg added, 'Cathbarr has been with me all afternoon. We were on the platform listening to Scannail and his ponderous recitations and songs.' She smiled quickly 'Oh, yes, even I get tired of repeated recitations.'

'How long were you listening to Scannail?' Fidelma asked.

'Most of the afternoon. To be accurate, I usually sit in council to hear any complaints or problems of my people. Having finished with those matters, we were being entertained by Scannail, who had arrived this morning with his latest verse, when you arrived. He plans to travel on tomorrow at first light. Does that satisfy you?'

'As far as Cathbarr is concerned. But someone did shoot at us along the path. So it falls to me to discover the cause and the culprit.'

Lalóg shook her head. She was clearly troubled. 'I can tell you nothing else. But you should do more before you make specific accusations. There is no denying that there are tensions among our people.'

'It is by questions we pursue our task, not with accusations,' Fidelma protested.

'May I suggest that such questions should be carefully thought out. Start with why anyone should try to stop you coming to the settlement to raise these questions with me. And consider, if they were serious, why would they shoot a solitary arrow at you and then flee?'

'Did I say it was a solitary arrow?'

There was a silence. 'From the way you mentioned it, I felt it was no more than that,' the woman replied hurriedly.

'As you say,' Fidelma said after a thoughtful pause. 'There are mysteries but no reasonable answers. We are still a long way from even considering why Brocc should have been killed or even why he seemed to invite death.'

Lalóg resumed her troubled look. 'I do not think he invited death. He was too much of an arrogant man to do so.'

'Yet you cannot deny on the day the prophetess said he would die, he went up into the hills, to that sweat bath, alone and unprotected.'

Lalóg mulled over this before replying. 'My brother was conceited, have I not admitted so? Maybe it was to lure his enemy into the open,' she suggested.

'If so, surely he would have made sure that he had the means to confront and constrain the enemy rather than just allowing himself to be presented as an unprotected victim. Why not take one of the brethren for protection?'

'If the enemy knew Brocc – and one would presume the person who killed him did know him – then the killer would have been warned by the fact that Brocc was not alone. It was his custom to be alone and prepare the bath himself.'

Eadulf nodded, appreciating the point Lalóg made, but an idea occurred to him. 'We have asked about enemies. It is suggested that anyone could be an enemy. Maybe a single name or two might be useful.'

'We all have people who dislike us. Anyone who gains a position of office has enemies. It depends on their character as to how far they take their enmity. I am sure my brother had many, but for specific names I would not be able to be fair by mentioning them.'

'You are right,' Eadulf agreed. 'I was suggesting any person who might stand out with more intense hatred, fuelling the flames that are needed to destroy a man in such a precise and cold-blooded way. I find it odd that he did not confide in you about this prophetess. It was only Brother Guala who told you? Guala did not confide this until after the death?'

Lalóg was silent for a moment or two. Then: 'I was naturally shocked when I heard the details.'

'You did not ascribe it, as Brother Guala did, to a being of supernatural intent? You regarded it of the real world and a threat to Brocc from a real enemy?'

Lalóg hesitantly shook her head. 'As I have said, Brocc described the prophetess as a young girl. The ancient culture of our people holds that such stories about prophecies are possible, especially with the tales and legends that we have of the Grey One. But I would dismiss matters, as Brocc did, that it was some real enemy, trying to use prophesy as a form of intimidation. When I learnt of Brocc's death from Brother Guala, I could not believe he took the prophecy seriously. I tried instead to consider the questions of motive and who might be responsible.'

'But no answers have obviously come?'

Lalóg shrugged but made no verbal response.

Fidelma waited a moment or two and then rose from her seat.

'We have pursued our questions long enough for the time being,' she announced. 'We thank you for your help, Lalóg. If you can think of anyone or anything that may help resolve these matters, someone who held even some petty grudge against your brother, we would appreciate if you would share that with us.'

'You will be staying at the abbey?'

'For the time being, unless some new path emerges.'

After formal salutations were exchanged, Fidelma and Eadulf left Lalóg's *bothán*. They found Dego waiting for them a little way beyond the cabin. The warrior had news to impart.

'That bard, Scannail, appeared while you were inside.' Dego assumed an almost theatrical whisper. 'He said that he wanted to meet with you before you left the village.'

'Where is he?' Fidelma asked.

'He did not want to be seen with us so he gave me directions to a place along the river . . . the tributary called the River of the Deep Glen.'

Fidelma glanced up at the on-coming dark clouds.

'It will be twilight soon. Have you secured a lantern and know the way?'

'I have. But his words were for you to go alone and tell no one. He said it was a matter of life or death.'

chapter nine

'Life or death?' Fidelma repeated in surprise.

'There is no way you will meet him alone,' Eadulf intervened brusquely.

'I agree and I told him so,' Dego affirmed. 'He said that he will meet you across at the jetty where the village fishermen fasten their boats. There is an oak grove behind it and, on the other side, a secluded place to talk. I warn you against the secluded area if he has evil in mind.'

'I do not want to miss the opportunity of putting some questions to him,' Fidelma said thoughtfully. 'We will go there together, but be alert. How did he suggest this meeting to you, Dego?'

'When he saw me waiting for you, he came straight to me with his request. He simply said that he had things to talk to you about, but this was not the place to be seen openly. He had to wait to negotiate with Cathbarr his recompense for his poetry, and would be available afterwards.'

Eadulf was only slightly aware that a fee was a serious matter agreed and received for a poet's *imchúairt*, reciting his work at various locations.

'He agreed to wait until we had finished with Lalóg?'

'You were longer than expected. It is approaching early evening, but he is probably still at the jetty.'

'Then let us join him,' she said firmly.

It was a short walk through the now almost deserted village. It seemed that, following the entertainment, people returned to their homes to prepare the evening meal.

Fidelma and her companions walked, keeping mostly to the shadows of buildings, to the river front. They could see that the little river port was in frequent use and several small boats had been dragged to positions on the bank close by. There was already movement from fishermen, arranging nets and preparing for the next morning's work.

The visitors did not attract attention as they made their way towards the jetty. At this point they saw that this part of the village was on a headland and that the river of Gleann-Doimhin, the Deep Glen, flowed into An Abhainn Mór, the Great River. The joining of the waters was noisy, like rapids, but the headland protected the little port. There were no buildings close by. The headland seemed to be a border without human habitation, except for the jetty.

Scannail had given Dego very precise instructions of where he would be waiting. The day had changed much, the sun had lowered in the sky, but the day was still pleasant and not cold. Although he didn't express it, Eadulf was worried not only about their vulnerability, but that they were not leaving time enough to get back to the abbey before nightfall.

'For someone who suggested meeting you alone, this bard has certainly chosen a place to give us little confidence of his not having ill intent,' Eadulf finally muttered.

Dego had taken his sword from its sheath and was holding it loosely in his hand, his shield hooked to the shoulder of his severed arm. His alert eyes were constantly sweeping the area.

Near the jetty, on an old log, sat the still figure of the elderly bard. He did not turn in their direction as they approached him but seemed to be entirely aware of their presence.

'*Slán-seiss*, Fidelma,' he called in the ancient greeting. 'May you sit safely.'

'Health to you, Scannail,' she replied solemnly.

He turned and looked from Fidelma to Eadulf with a frown.

'I know you wanted to see me alone, Scannail,' she explained before he said anything, 'but I never move far without my husband nor my bodyguard. It is my custom.'

'I can understand it, lady,' Scannail replied, not rising. 'I regret the seating has limitations.' He moved along the log and motioned her to be seated. 'You need have no fear of harm coming to you. My concern was that secrets shared by three are no longer secrets. Well, no matter.' He glanced at Eadulf. 'There are some logs by those *currachs* behind you. You can bring one here and make yourselves comfortable.'

Only Eadulf brought over a nearby small log to sit facing the bard. Dego preferred to stand by, watching, his eyes constantly surveying the area.

Scannail took the lead in opening the conversation.

'You sought the answer to a question earlier, Fidelma. You still wish an answer?'

'Earlier?' Fidelma tried to recall what he meant. 'You speak of Abbot Brocc's death? I thought you had only arrived here this morning. Do you know anything about it?'

'I still have ears and people still have tongues. Your question is obvious.'

'It is why I came. To find out who killed Abbot Brocc.'

'I cannot name you a specific suspect, but I can tell you where responsibility lies.'

'That sounds like a contradiction,' Eadulf frowned.

Fidelma agreed with him. 'Can you explain what you mean?'

The elderly poet's tone was mocking. 'Your first question should have been: what action of Brocc's would make him merit death? I might say that when a leader has grown apart from his people, it presents a root for antagonism that can turn into hatred. Difference sows seeds for hatred, and the fruits of hatred are turbulence.'

'Are you saying that since Brocc became an abbot of the New Faith he has grown apart from his people, those people of the Old Faith?'

'Once a prince is no longer respected by his people, disrespect can turn to hatred.'

'I know Brocc was the son of Tigerna Cosraigib, but his father was still alive when Brocc converted. Neither was he elected as Prince of the Uí Liatháin. I understand it was his brother, Conmhaol, who was.'

'You believe Brocc was killed because he adopted the New Faith,' affirmed the elderly man.

'Yet if that is so then why was he not attacked over a year ago, when he became Abbot of Dair Inis?'

'Events change lives and therefore the motivations of people.'

'Yet I would like more explanation,' Fidelma told Scannail. 'When someone in a position of authority is killed, the first question is the one the ancient Roman jurist Cicero always asked – *Cui bono?* – To whom is it a benefit? In other words, who stands to gain?'

Scannail chuckled softly. 'Are you thinking that the obvious choice is Brother Guala?'

'So obvious that I am inclined to dismiss it.'

'But it is possible?'

'I am impressed that a wandering bard of the Old Faith apparently knows what goes on inside the minds of those in the abbey of the New Faith.'

'I am of the Uí Liatháin,' Scannail returned simply.

'I take it that you have some knowledge that you wish to pass to me? You told Dego it was a matter of life or death. I am waiting to hear whose.'

'Do not worry, Fidelma. I am a *seanchaidh* and bard of my people. It is even correct to talk of me as a Druid – that is, one immersed in knowledge. While some of us are possessed of the foresight, many of us are not all-seeing as people claim.'

'Let us not play with innuendos of clairvoyance or other abilities. Tell me what you mean plainly.'

Scannail gave a motion of his head that seemed to be a bow of acknowledgement.

'I know you well enough, lady. You are of the practical world, although I suggest you, Fidelma, probably also know more of the world beyond than most. I am not trying to mislead or claim knowledge I do not have. I know you have given your life to the service of the law, the law that we share together in both the Old Faith and New Faith. I have also heard that when you were young, Fidelma, you began your reputation by joining the abbey of Cill Dara. You were then known as Sister Fidelma, a religieuse. Is this not so?'

'It is true that when I was younger I served at the abbey of Cill Dara, but as adviser on law and not as a religieuse under vows.' She did not know why she bothered explaining this, but there was something about the way the old man encouraged confidences. 'I left the religious some time ago,' she found herself saying, 'but not the religion, although I have to admit that I am not entirely in accord with its many recent philosophies and its practices that now come from Rome.'

'I have heard of your reputation, Fidelma – as an interpreter of law. So it is purely the law that brings you to the isolation of Dair Inis?'

'It is the death of Abbot Brocc,' she replied. 'No more, no less. So what is it you wish to tell me? A matter of life or death, you told Dego.'

There was a humorous quality about the old man's voice when he replied. 'It was a phrase to catch your attention, but there is a truth in it. When we speak of matters of life and of death, we have Brocc's death as example. The majority of our people would find that good news,' the poet stated.

'Good news? Why should the death of Brocc be deemed good news? Is it because the news of the death of one of the New Faith is good to you?'

Scannail shook his head. 'To answer that, I would have to enter into specifics.'

'Then it is specifics that I am looking for,' Fidelma replied sharply.

Scannail was quiet for the moment, sitting with eyes closed. Fidelma thought the old poet was falling asleep. Then he stirred suddenly and exhaled deeply.

'Certain cultural ideas are hard to eradicate. One of the matters that should not be abused is the hospitality granted to a travelling poet or musician when they are on *imchúairt*, the performance circuit. A rule applied especially after they have accepted a fee and the hospitality of a princess. You have surely come across the rights of the poet's circuit before?'

Fidelma was not sure why he had brought this up and she thought he was changing the subject. She said so.

'I have said I am a *seanchaidh*,' he replied.

'As such in law you are considered of noble status and your honour is as much respected as any other. Usually, a *seanchaidh* is attached to a noble house. Is there a question about this matter?'

Scannail made an indifferent gesture. 'I was so attached when Tigerna Cosraigib was alive and am now called to advise his *derbhfine*, the family council.'

'So I am waiting for you to expand on the matter of life or death.'

'And to why I felt Brocc's death good, and I shed no tears at his passing?'

'Then consider these questions asked,' Fidelma replied irritably. 'Remember, as a *dálaigh* I am considering if Brocc had adversaries and, if so, whether that was reason enough for him to be slain in such a fashion.'

'From the little I have heard of your reputation, Fidelma, it is known that you are an expert on the meanings of names. Do you know what the meaning of Brocc's name is?'

'That's not hard,' she replied. 'It means one who is sharp faced.'

'There is another meaning,' Scannail pointed out.

'You mean Brocc being a name meaning a badger? It's unusual as a name, although the diminutive, Broccán, is much used in this area. But I know that to be called a badger is thought to be an insult.'

Scannail chuckled again. It seemed to Fidelma that the old man was always in a state of amusement with the world.

'For us the badger is a symbol for persistence, determination and endurance. Those are the qualities that the lowly badger taught us. Some of the warriors of the Uí Liatháin carried the name of the badger as a matter of pride. Do we not also have a saying, "as grey as a badger"?'

Fidelma was not impressed, missing the inflexion that he put on the saying. 'I admit that it is unusual for a leader of a Christian community, as it is not a worthy name in the New Faith. But some continue to bear a name if it is birth given.'

'Ah, the New Faith and names.' There was a slight sneer from Scannail. 'So many of the leaders of the New Faith have cast aside their given names to adopt ones more suitable, in their minds, for the claims of the new Christian philosophy.'

'Let us get back to talking more of Brocc,' Fidelma insisted. 'I suppose he did not change his name when he converted. Is that what you are saying?'

'Perhaps Brocc kept to his birth-given name for a reason,' suggested the old man.

'All I want to know is why you praised his death. Did you not think his soul worthy to lament on its journey to the Otherworld, as you of the Old Faith would see it?'

Scannail sniffed deprecatingly. 'That is, if his soul was noticed by the collector of souls and ever reached the House of Donn.'

'I still need an explanation,' Eadulf pressed. 'I think Scannail has implied that it was religious differences that led to the abbot's murder? Can I be clear on my understanding?'

'Some among the Uí Liatháin claim there was once a prince who dwelt in the hills. The New Faith had not achieved much success among them, but this prince determined that it would never take hold. He burnt those communities of the New Faith seeking to establish themselves. He slaughtered their inhabitants. That was no hardship, as most advocates of the New Faith at the time were the Déisi who were settling our lands, supported by the Eóghanacht.'

Dego was uneasy and moved closer to them.

'The day is growing darker,' he called softly. 'Perhaps it is time to commence our return to the abbey.'

'I heard similar stories when I was younger,' Fidelma conceded, ignoring Dego.

'The prince had been driven from his main citadel at Caislean Uí Liatháin, the fortress of the Uí Liatháin, and had to retreat south to the more secluded banks of the Guairne. That prince was killed six months ago in a skirmish during the last contention with your brother, Colgú.'

Fidelma was shaking her head. 'All this seems irrelevant to me. I now know that the prince was Brocc's father. I am told, however, he did not condemn Brocc for abandoning the Old Faith.'

Scannail sighed heavily. 'Tigerna Cosraigib actually forgave Brocc for deserting the religion. You have spoken with Lalóg, who spent time trying to get her brother to return to the Old Faith. Brocc's father sought independence of the Uí Liatháin and even allied himself to the Déisi, the enemies of our blood, during the attempt on Cashel six months ago.'

'From what I know about the dislike by your people of the Déisi, that was not a popular move,' Fidelma said.

'Tigerna Cosraigib asserted that whoever was the enemy of the Eóghanacht was his friend. And he was the fiercest defender of the Uí Liatháin,' the old poet continued.

Fidelma regarded the *seanchaidh* thoughtfully. 'I have heard that even the surviving council of Druids became horrified at Tigerna Cosraigib's brutality and senseless slaughter. Do you suggest that his own son, Brocc, was killed out of revenge for what might have been seen as a betrayal of his father?'

'It is possible,' acknowledged the old man.

'Are you saying that six months after his death, some follower of his father or even a relative killed him?'

'It is possible. However, you are still not making the connection.'

'Are you pointing out that Brocc has a brother as well as a sister, Lalóg?'

'It is so,' said the poet.

Fidelma closed her eyes for a second.

'Brocc was brother to Lalóg, so brother to Conmhaol . . . and they were of this family of this . . .?'

The old man said nothing.

'Brocc's father was trying to wipe out the New Faith?' Eadulf said. 'How did he let his son convert? How did Brocc break loose of his father?'

'Brocc's father was a man with excessive self-admiration and self-centredness. One might expect him to enact vengeance on his sons. He did not. He never raised his hand against Brocc, even when Brocc took over the community at Dair Inis.'

Fidelma was trying to see a hidden message in the old man's words.

'Are you saying that power over the Uí Liatháin mattered more than religion? When Conmhaol refused the nomination to be leader, Brocc was claiming it and when he came to Cashel it was not with support of . . .'

'I merely place the idea before you. His father was a prince and defender of the Old Faith, which Brocc rejected. So that Brocc should become the new leader of the Uí Liatháin was untenable.'

'Conmhaol refused the approval of his *derbhfine* to fulfil the office of his father and become Prince of the Uí Liatháin,' Fidelma said slowly. 'Why?'

'Conmhaol is a strange person who prefers a reclusive life. He deserted his father's fortress at Guairne and went to live in an inaccessible place – a lake dwelling away from any main tracks.'

'Being a recluse, then, was that why he refused to succeed as Prince of the Uí Liatháin after his father was killed?' Fidelma queried.

'I merely tell you a story. You may interpret it as you would wish.'

'Does your story give credence to the prophetess appearing to foretell that Brocc would die on a certain day and that it happened just as she said?'

'I just recount things I hear,' Scannail replied. 'There was talk in the village about it. You may even hear talk of the prophetess who was named Líadan, the Grey One, although she is an ancient folk memory among our people.'

'The folk memory seems to have come alive,' Eadulf muttered.

The *seanchaidh* stroked his beard thoughtfully. 'It all fits the drama. I have heard stories of a new soothsayer who appears from the very territory where Tigerna Cosraigib was raised. So it is not beyond possibility. A voice seeking vengeance and urging our people to rise once again to right the wrongs that have been inflicted on us. Retribution on Brocc for betrayal. Revenge on a son of Tigerna Cosraigib, Lord of the Slaughter. I leave you with these thoughts and mysteries for they are for you to resolve. That is all I can say.'

'You have set many thoughts in motion, Scannail,' Fidelma sighed. 'It is scarcely a wink of an eye since the New Faith swept our land and we must realise that change is not welcomed overnight. But why are you sharing your thoughts with us when you are clearly an adherent of the Old Faith?'

The *seanchaidh* rose without warning and seemed to be smiling down at them behind his unkempt beard.

'I have imparted what was in my mind. I must continue on my circuit of recitation at sun-up. I suggest there is little need for further investigation. You could easily get a ferry to take you upriver to Lios Mór. Little need for you to enter deeply into the Uí Liatháin territory and examine its internal conflicts. Doing so could be dangerous, as there are many who have lost family and property during the bad times. Wiser to stay safe. Stay safe in your own culture, Fidelma of Cashel.'

They rose and stood watching Scannail moving with surprising dexterity back towards the village until the tall, dark trees obscured him from sight. Fidelma stood still, frowning as if fixed in her thoughts. Eadulf's voice finally brought her back to present consciousness.

'It's almost twilight now,' he pointed out. 'We should start back to the abbey.'

She shook herself as if trying to shed the atmosphere of the place. She realised he was right. The sky was darkening almost as much as the atmosphere that had been created.

'What now?' Eadulf was saying as the three of them began to walk back through the village to find the river path back to the abbey. 'Can we believe what he says? That the son of a former slaughterer of Christians would suddenly convert to the New Faith and became an abbot? And then was slaughtered himself to prevent him become the leader of his people . . . a people intent on keeping their faith. It sounds impossible. It sounds confusing. Why didn't Lalóg tell us this?'

'It's not so impossible,' Fidelma replied thoughtfully. 'Is it not said that Saul of Tarsus persecuted the first followers of Christ? When he was converted to the New Faith he changed his name to Paul. It is this same Paul who wrote most of the original texts on which the New Faith is based; from him and his letters most of the teachings of the New Faith are attributed.'

'How did you learn so much?' Eadulf was truly amazed.

'I did not waste my time at Cill Dara, but spent much of those years in the library,' she smiled. 'Anyway, your question was "What now?". I think we must find Brocc's surviving brother, Conmhaol. Didn't Lalóg say that he dwelt on a *crannóg*, an artificial island in the River of Omens. We must find out where that is and go to see him. The librarian should be able to help us, or understand those who produce charts and maps.'

'We should also find a local guide. The journey might be complicated even if we can get a chart to show us. It depends on the hills and river crossings between here and that place, wherever it is. At least most of the hills in this territory are small, rounded affairs, not very high. We also need horses. I haven't seen many horses here and we might need to purchase three good ones to make the journey.'

Eadulf was inwardly groaning. He was hoping for once that no extensive travel on horseback would be needed. He had, in recent years, grown to dislike horse travel less, but he only undertook long journeys by horse when necessary.

'Do you think we must go to this place?' he asked Fidelma. 'The old poet seems to advise us that it is not worthwhile to proceed further because we would never find the killer.'

'Which is the reason I want to go there,' Fidelma said in a firm tone. 'I want to speak to Conmhaol and see what he has to say about the murder of his brother. If nothing else, we should remember Brocc would know of threats to his brother.' She pursed her lips for a few moments. 'Scannail's suggestion was that we accept his story and cease further investigation. Perhaps he was hoping we would conclude that Brocc was probably killed by those seeking revenge for his change of religion. Perhaps Brocc's own brother is a suspect. I found Scannail's intervention more confusing than helpful. It was almost as if he were attempting to confuse us on purpose. There is a deeper mystery here than I at first thought, Eadulf.'

'Scannail is like Brother Guala in that he seems to talk in half-forgotten stories of his people,' Eadulf pointed out. 'Can we waste time in finding out whether Brocc was really a target because of this princely family? Lalóg, his sister, showed him no animosity.'

'We should not leap to any conclusions. Don't dismiss anything. I will say that it is an interesting point. Brother Guala seems to be a believer in these ancient curses and Druid soothsayers. He is not quite what is to be expected of a steward of a Christian community.'

'But more typical than the librarian,' Eadulf replied. 'The abbey librarian who claims he does not hold records of anything pertaining to the abbot who has governed Dair Inis for the last six years, and did not even bother to tell us that Lalóg was his sister or that his father had been the prince of his people. That is more inexplicable than a steward still believing in the ways of the Old Faith.'

'Perhaps.' Fidelma was reluctant in her agreement. 'Anyway, it does not sound unlikely that Brocc was trying to escape being associated with a father like Tigerna Cosraigib, a destroyer of villages and people in the name of the Old Faith and in ways that even shocked the Druids and others of his own Faith. I can understand a son's rebellion to the point where he would suddenly convert to the New Faith.'

'Another way of looking at it could indicate that the man had no moral religion but his own self-interest,' Eadulf continued to his theme. 'If he was an evil man, it explains why Scannail felt his death was not worthy for any lamentation.'

'All that is speculation. It leaves so many questions unanswered, and to get answers we must question Conmhaol.' She turned to Dego. 'I'll leave it to you to discover where this lake homestead is and how we may get there. We will ask the same of Brother Cróebíne and meet afterwards to make plans.'

When they returned to the abbey Fidelma and Eadulf went straight to the library, where they found Brother Cróebíne hunched over some papers and engaged in cataloguing.

'Can I help you, lady?' he asked, glancing up nervously as they entered.

'There are some matters now that I have met Princess Lalóg. From that you may guess she has told us much about the background of Brocc. I am sure you would have known this all along.'

'Lady, it was not my place to say. The abbot's family is his family and that is a personal affair.'

'You did not even tell us about Princess Lalóg and her relationship to Brocc. Was there an objection at her visiting here so regularly from the abbey community?'

The librarian was unabashed. 'I am a mere *scriptor*. I was a minor in the council of decision making in this abbey.'

'Not important enough to explain that the abbot's brother, Conmhaol, the same prince whom your physician, Brother Fisecda, attended, was the choice to be Prince of the Uí Liatháin? You told us that Fisecda was attending Conmhaol and did not return when Brocc was found murdered. He has still not returned?'

Brother Cróebíne blinked. 'He has not. But would such information of his family have helped you?'

'That should be left to me, as a *dálaigh*, to decide,' Fidelma snapped. 'By the way, I gather Princess Lalóg is quite scholarly and often spent time in your library. I also learnt that she had discussions with you and Abbot Brocc. Yet according to Brother Guala, Brocc was, by comparison, not educated enough. Why am I being told such distortions? For what reason?'

'We have tried our best to supply the information that you would require as an advocate.'

'It is not your place to decide what I would require. When I have the information, then I will decide what I require. And did that missing page turn up?'

Brother Cróebíne looked blank. 'Missing page?'

'The one that was cut from your annals,' Fidelma replied patiently. 'The one that you were going to search the library for?'

The librarian tried to hide his embarrassment.

'Oh, I have not made a proper examination yet. There has been much on my mind.'

'I would have thought that was a matter of priority.' Suddenly an idea occurred to her. 'If Lalóg was a visitor to the abbey, perhaps she felt that she should remove the information about her brother?'

Brother Cróebíne looked confused. 'That would be illogical. She would know her brother well enough and not need to look in the records of the abbots. She had no cause to cut that page from the ledger.'

'I did think she would know him.' Fidelma was sardonic.

'Perhaps I could look for the missing page tomorrow . . .?'

'Tomorrow it is our intention to go to visit this Prince Conmhaol to complete some inquiries. We intend to travel to his *crannóg* on the River of Omens.'

Brother Cróebíne was clearly astonished. 'You want to go to An Tuairigh? But . . .'

'We will start early,' Fidelma ignored him. 'I don't know how long this will take. I understand his *crannóg* might be a horse-back ride from here. Therefore we need to find some horses. I have sent Dego to make inquiries.'

'To the River of Omens?' The librarian still seemed confused. 'Conmhaol's *crannóg* is to the west of Uí Liatháin territory. It is a place where there is no liking for Eóghanacht. How is there a connection with the killing of Abbot Brocc? It is a place that is usually shunned.'

'So apart from horses,' Fidelma said, continuing to ignore him, 'we would also need a guide to take us there.'

'It would be impossible to find without a guide. Brother Fisecda goes there frequently but he has not returned to the abbey yet.'

'I am sure you know someone who can take us. I am asking this with the authority of my office. I had presumed that you were the best person to consult. I see the abbey has only two mules for use for moving goods or timbers. So I am hoping that Dego will be able to find better horses. Wasn't there a smithy in the village? If horses cannot be found we will requisition the mules.'

Brother Cróebíne flushed in astonishment. 'You would take the abbey's only mules?'

'I have the authority.'

'I did not mean to question you, lady. It was just an unusual request. Much of the transportation we need on this island is conducted along the rivers. But we have the mules to fetch and carry. And we need them for transporting any heavy equipment when we are in the process of building.'

'Are you telling me there is nowhere to purchase horses?'

'Forgive me, lady.' Brother Cróebíne paused a moment as if considering the matter. 'You said that you noticed the smithy in the village. Echrí, the smith, might help, for he has access to horses.'

'Then we shall make a deal, if that is possible. Echrí, you say? Lord of horses? An appropriate name. Now, as to a guide . . . a pity your physician has not returned if he has so frequently travelled to Conmhaol's island.'

'Finding a guide to the River of Omens will not be easy. It is a dark and evil place.'

'If it is in a river, I imagine that it is possible to reach it along one of the rivers if it crosses Uí Liatháin territory?'

'Not directly,' the librarian conceded. 'Horseback is the only way to negotiate most of the territory, which is criss-crossed by many rivers and high hills.'

'So *can* you recommend a guide?' Fidelma insisted.

Brother Cróebíne was reluctant for a moment before his face lightened.

'There is one young man who has such knowledge. He used to travel with traders and their carts across country as a means to help his family, who were poor. That was before he came to this abbey. He is still a noviciate here so you would have to seek special permission from Brother Guala for him to escort you.'

'What is his name?'

'It is the young man that you have already met, Brother Scatánach.'

'The same youth who accompanied you when you found the body of the abbot? He told us that he had accompanied traders to such parts.'

The librarian looked momentarily ill tempered.

'He should not have been telling you anything without approval of the Abbey.'

'On the contrary, he would be in far more trouble if he had refused to truthfully answer a *dalaigh*'s questions. So, it is that young man who might be our best guide?'

'Being one born and raised in this area and well travelled with traders, I would say he would be the best choice. However, as I say, you will have to obtain the permission of Brother Guala. As steward, he is now an aspirant for the position of abbot when the council of the abbey meets to elect the office. He has to give permission in the absence of the abbot. That is, of course, if Brother Scatánach is willing in the first place. There are the dangers to be considered.'

'What dangers?' Eadulf demanded.

'You are proposing to go westward into the hills with only a one-armed warrior. I intend no disrespect. You know the history of the Uí Liatháin. Their traditions are of a fighting people. One warrior will not deter them if they object to your presence. You are Eóghanacht and of the New Faith. So on both counts it is a dangerous journey.'

'It is not my intention to invade the territory. A peace was agreed earlier this year over the last matter in which the Uí Liatháin were misled into supporting the conspirators who sought to overthrow my brother as king,' Fidelma pointed out. 'Those factions who tried to overthrow Cashel have either come to terms or been eliminated. The only conflict I know of in this territory is that between those who refuse to accept the New Faith and maintain the Old Faith and those who have embraced the New. That does not involve me. I am inquiring about a murder.'

Brother Cróebíne snorted. 'Even one enemy is more than enough to be worried about.'

'Enemy? Do you regard the adjoining village as an enemy? I thought your co-existence was quite amicable. I would have considered they were people who hold on to the past, trying to retain the old culture. When the Roman emperor Constantine accepted the New Faith, he felt that the Old Faith had to be tolerated. Afterwards, other emperors used their legions to spread the faith. Likewise, here in the Five Kingdoms, we do not usually find martyrs for the New Faith or for the Old Faith. We have a common culture and from that we have been able to exchange ideas. Like the Greeks and Romans who married their ideas with the New Faith, thus shaping it, we have found our culture has much to contribute.'

'But it has not been accepted by many of the Uí Liatháin,' pointed out Brother Cróebíne. 'Factions of the Uí Liatháin and their princes have been in conflict on this very point.'

'Let us hope that is now all in the past,' Fidelma said.

'When blood is shed, nothing is ever in the past,' Brother Cróebíne replied sourly. 'It is part of a librarian's task to look after the chronicles and maintain the histories so that none forgets.'

'So what are you suggesting? That in this territory people have long memories, in spite of treaties and the law, and that people of the New Faith are not welcome? If that is so, how is it that this abbey has survived?' Fidelma asked.

'It was an Uí Liatháin prince who set up this abbey less than a century ago. We have survived long enough to have begun to build up a reputation for scholarship. We now have many ancient works housed here, including some of the works of Pelagius, who—'

Fidelma held up her hand. 'Spare us the lecture on Pelagius and his works. Your reputation will not keep even the abbey safe in a hostile population. You are in a good location in this sheltered bend of the river. It is a natural harbour, as we knew earlier, when Selbach moved his warriors ready to attack Cashel in the overthrow of my brother. Seven warships were anchored off this island ready to answer his call to aid the renegade prince Elodach.'

'I cannot deny it,' Brother Cróebíne agreed. 'While we do not threaten certain princes in this area, they usually let us alone. I know Brocc went to plead our innocence of the conspiracy to the King of Cashel. With regard to the killing of Brocc, I would have thought it worth considering in whose interest such a death would be.'

'That is why we think it is worthwhile heading to the River of Omens to pursue our inquiries.'

'I have told you what I know and can say no more,' the librarian conceded.

'I thank you for the information,' Fidelma said. 'We will find Brother Scatánach and see if he is interested in joining us and then obtain the steward's approval. Then let us hope Dego can find us some horses.'

chapter ten

It was just after first light when the group of four pony riders left the abbey, crossing the wooden bridge from the Island of Oaks to make their way west along the track through the tall, dark oak forest. There was just room for two horses to go abreast. Brother Scatánach, as guide, rode alongside Fidelma, while Dego and Eadulf came close behind them. They were mounted on small mountain and moorland breeds. Fidelma, who was a more than competent equestrian, actually felt uncomfortable as their movements and mannerisms were unlike the Gaulish pony she was used to. However, these were the only breeds that Echrí, the smith and horse breeder, had to offer.

As Echrí had pointed out to Dego, apart from mules, there was no market in the area for the type of breeds that nobles and warriors might aspire to own. Princess Lalóg and her steward had their own mounts. Fidelma had encountered these breeds before, but only as working horses. In spite of their smallness they were often used for transporting heavy items and hauling carts. Their low weight compared to their height of twelve to fourteen hands, also gave them an unusual footfall, meaning they could move easily on soft marshy ground. So they were renowned for surviving in harsh conditions, even as a feral breed. Echrí admitted he had purchased them from Uí Fidgente traders as he was intrigued by the fact that the breed seemed to thrive on heather and sphagnum moss. While the ponies would not have been the choice of either Fidelma or Dego, the small steady animals actually suited Eadulf's idea of equine transport.

As they headed at an easy pace through the forest, Fidelma recalled how easily Brother Guala had agreed to allow Brother Scatánach to guide them to the River of Omens where Prince Conmhaol dwelt. It seemed that the librarian had been overpessimistic about their seeking permission from the steward. The only caution the steward had raised was to point out once more that they were heading to a wild, isolated area. Other than that, he returned to his favourite theme.

'It is a place where the battles between the ancient gods and goddesses were said to have been fought in the time of legends. Now the battles are fought between the believers and unbelievers and will continue to be so until the annihilation of one side or the other. It is called Cnoic an Taibhsí – the Hills of the Phantoms. It is a cursed place.'

'You do not sound optimistic that this will be a worthwhile trip,' Fidelma had commented. 'Nevertheless, it is important that we go.'

'I cannot stop you doing so. You are of the Eóghanacht and a *dálaigh* of reputation. All I can do is warn you that you will probably not be welcomed and many might not respect your status.'

It seemed everyone had the same warnings to impart when it was known in what direction they were going.

As she had told Brother Guala: 'I am not only under the protection of the King but of the Chief Brehon of Muman. If harm fell upon me, then the consequences would not be good. I hope that is understood.'

'It is none of my affair,' Brother Guala had said dismissively. 'I have warned you. At least Brother Scatánach knows the route. He is acquainted with Conmhaol, which might help, and is a strong lad, and withal a fair bowman if you need protection. You must act as you think fit. Yet I fail to see how visiting Conmhaol would help to solve the death of Abbot Brocc.'

'That is for me to find out,' Fidelma had responded.

Brother Scatánach had surprised them, by accepting the idea of acting as their guide with alacrity.

Now, as he led the way to the river in the Deep Glen, which rose somewhere in the west, Fidelma was thinking whether the youth had accepted with too much eagerness. She was uneasy about the reference to his being a bowman after the incident on the way to Lalóg's village. Then she realised that the young man was addressing her and she set aside her thoughts.

'We will go upriver a way until we come to a ford. The river rises in the north, but we don't want to follow it as it will take us out of our way. We will cross and move a little way among the high hills where the tops emerge above the forests,' he told her enthusiastically.

'I see it is quite hilly countryside ahead,' Eadulf observed, overhearing from behind. He was obviously thinking of his limitations as an equestrian.

'It is not a difficult terrain to follow,' the young guide replied. 'However, it is good that we are riding these bog ponies, otherwise I do not think we would be able to move so easily through it.'

'How is it that you know this track so well?' Eadulf asked.

'Although I grew up at Lalóg's settlement, the son of a fisherman, it does not mean I spent all my time there. To earn my way, I used to help transport goods from merchants that were landed at the harbour.'

'Why didn't you follow your father to sea? Didn't you say that you joined the abbey to learn how to read and write? But did you really want to be a religieux?'

'I had a thirst to read and write, so I went to talk with Abbot

Brocc,' Brother Scatánach admitted. 'Believing in this New Faith
is difficult. I have to say, I do not understand it. It seems to me little
different from most stories of the gods and goddesses that people
are taught. Usually the god is born of a mortal who is a woman
impregnated by a god. Eventually this god goes forth with his followers. He says that when we die, we will be born again in the
Otherworld, or go to Heaven in the New Faith. In the New Faith
some say the souls have to await in purgatory. I am told that comes
from the Latin for a place of cleansing. The Old Faith call it Teach
Donn, an island south-west where souls wait before being transported to the Otherworld. In the Old Faith we call the Otherworld
Magh Mel, the Plain of Joy, or Tír na nÓg, where people are Ever
Young. We continue life there until we die there and are then
reborn in this world. So the cycle of life and death continues. What
is the difference?'

'Did Abbot Brocc or Brother Guala not explain the differences
to you?' Eadulf was genuinely curious. 'Or did they merely criti-
cise your belief?'

'Why would they? They believed the same things when they
were my age. They are converts to this New Faith. There are
really no boundaries restricting the two beliefs, only what people
build for themselves.'

Eadulf sunk back into his thoughts, surprised at the simple
philosophy of the youth.

It was just after midday when Fidelma suggested a halt to rest
the ponies and for them to take something to eat. They had
climbed up along easy tracks into the hills and were about to start
descending into the entrance to a valley still leading directly
north.

'Is that the way we go now?' Fidelma asked, pointing. It looked
more like a ravine than a valley: a pass covered in numerous trees
and bushes.

Brother Scatánach nodded. 'Once on the far side of the valley the countryside barely changes – low hills and rivers and streams – but they are all easily fordable.'

'This ravine looks like a really dark narrow passage,' she said. 'There's not even a stream running through it.'

'It's called Gleann Dubh, the Dark Glen, although it is hardly a valley. As you said, it is a dark passage. But there is room for the horses to go through in single file. It would be another matter if we were travelling by cart.'

Eadulf was puzzled. 'I thought you said you came this way with merchants and their goods?'

'Not this precise way,' admitted the boy. 'We would skirt these hills in a semi-circle, which is a much longer journey. Without a cart to impede us, this is a quicker path.'

'Well, let us find a place to take our rest,' Fidelma interrupted. 'If there is no stream through the ravine, where do you propose we find water for the animals?'

Brother Scatánach grinned. 'I do know the way,' he assured her, and pointed to an area of trees just a little way off.

Had they been travelling without the youth's knowledge they would have ridden by the place without much thought. Brother Scatánach led them among the tall, close-growing oaks and brambles until they came abruptly to a small area blocked to one side by a tall red sandstone wall, which formed one of the walls of the ravine. Here they heard the sounds of splashing water. It was a curious gush, which seemed to come out of the rock face some way up and spurted down to feed a pool. It looked almost manmade, yet close inspection showed that it was an aberration of nature, for the water filled the pool but it did not overflow. Neither was it stagnant. Somehow the water exited underground and the pool remained cool and clean.

The travellers let the four ponies drink while they sat nearby and had their midday meal. Obviously, the original estimate of how long it would take to reach the mountains was going to be unrealistic. The small mountain ponies did not possess much speed, even if the countryside had allowed it. It was while thinking of the journey that their young guide had suggested a place where they could stop for the night.

'I did not think this River of Omens was so far from the abbey?' Fidelma said.

'The territory of the Uí Liatháin is a confused network of rivers and streams,' the youth replied. 'It's difficult to cross without knowing certain paths. I was twelve years old when I first worked with merchants. I was a strong lad and found a merchant who took me on, carrying goods for him as he journeyed from one market to another. From him I learnt to track and know the paths that have proved useful. I know a lot of the fords.'

'How long did you do that job with the merchant?'

'For two years.'

'So you have been several times to Conmhaol's homestead? You know him?'

'Conmhaol was a warrior before he became a recluse,' the boy replied. 'He was well respected. His family wanted him to lead our people after his father was killed.'

'He was a warrior?' Fidelma was surprised. That was not what Scannail had indicated.

'Both sons of Tigerna Cosraigib were warriors. One became the abbot and the other a recluse. Each follows his own path.'

'Did you ever meet Tigerna Cosraigib?' Eadulf asked.

'I never met him, but I saw him,' the boy replied. 'One of the traders did business at his fortress at Dún Guairne. The merchant dealt with the *fedmannach* there.'

Seeing Eadulf's blank look, Fidelma explained. 'That's a steward but one of lower status than a *rechtaire*. It's the person who runs the domestic side of a household.' She turned back to the youth. 'And do you recall the name of this steward? Is he still alive?'

'His name was Cetliatha. I was told he was killed alongside Tigerna.'

Eadulf sighed in resignation. 'Cetliatha? Yet another name meaning "one turning grey". I wonder why there is the fascination with the colour grey.'

'It is part of our culture,' the boy answered immediately. 'After all, we are the Uí Liatháin – "the grey people".'

Eadulf was not impressed. 'Are you saying it is all tradition that there is such a prevalence of people and places ascribing to the colour grey?'

'People like to follow tradition,' the boy insisted. 'It gives them comfort.'

'So you must have stayed at Dún Guairne during the trade visits?'

'Often we would be given overnight rest at the fortress.'

'Was that when you saw the prince and his family?'

'Yes, but not closely. Only Conmhaol was friendly. And I did make friends with a girl who lived there.'

'You never heard any interesting talk among the family? Was anything said about Brocc and his conversion?'

'There was much talk about the possibility to overthrow the Eóghanacht, begging your pardon, lady. It was said that foreign princes called Elodach and Selbach were going to lead a rebellion. Then there were stories that they had called on Tigerna to help defeat the Eóghanacht and whether they could rely on Brocc to support them.'

'That was only six months ago,' Fidelma pointed out. 'But what did you know of Conmhaol, who you say was a warrior?'

'He treated me kindly, but he was not happy with those who had joined the New Faith. I think he shared his father's views on that. My sweetheart, who works on the farmstead at the fortress, said that there were quarrels in the family. Especially between Conmhaol's sister, Lalóg, and the abbot.'

Fidelma frowned. 'I thought Lalóg had a good relationship with her brother Abbot Brocc?'

'Maybe she was ashamed to mention their arguments,' the youth replied. He did not seem concerned. 'I think it is why Conmhaol dwells in his *crannóg* on an islet in the marshes of the River of Omens. He sought to escape the quarrels within the family.'

'What do you know of this artificial island in Tuairigh River?' Eadulf recalled. 'I thought that it was closer to Dún Guairne?'

'Not close by,' replied Brother Scatánach. 'The River of Omens is north of that place.'

Fidelma smiled grimly. 'The River of Omens. It sounds ominous.'

The youth nodded eagerly. 'It is a river of portents and foretelling. It is thought to be a place where soothsayers bathe by moonlight to enhance their knowledge of predictions.'

'From what I have seen,' Eadulf sighed, 'it might have been better to make our entire journey by small boats along the rivers.'

'It would be long and exhausting. These rivers twist and turn, and I don't think anyone has truly negotiated all of them,' Brother Scatánach commented, taking him seriously. 'Some of the rivers are so narrow they end in springs; others suddenly become broad torrents. Then there are shallows, rapids and waterfalls. One would probably spend twice as long carrying a *currach* up mountains or hills as paddling it on the broader safer waters.'

They ate and drank sparsely so that they could continue their journey in as short a time as possible. It was not long before they were making their way through the dark ravine along the narrowest of paths. They walked down from the bare higher ground on which the ravine had emptied and crossed the rounded hill before entering the woodlands that followed a snaking line through the valley. This turned out to be a very marshy river and the line of trees showed its course.

Fidelma was quite surprised when the dark greenery of the sombre forests and undergrowth spread out into an area devoid of trees where it was obvious herds of sheep and goats had kept growth to a minimal. The contrast between the primeval forests and these areas was amazing. Here and there it was as if the fields had been manicured and mown to such a level as could only be achieved by careful cultivating. Eadulf remarked on it.

Brother Scatánach was still philosophical. 'Nature has a way of looking after its own, sometimes to better advantage than we do. Now our way lies west through the marshlands to join the River Tuairigh. There is not much human settlement.'

'Why is that? This looks pleasant enough country,' Eadulf remarked.

'I think that question has been answered,' Brother Scatánach smiled knowingly. 'A river of ill omen, through marshlands. People have shunned this area since the time before time.'

'But you say that Conmhaol has his home in marshland along this river,' Eadulf pointed out. 'That means he is not afraid of ill omens.'

The youth tapped his forehead with two fingers. 'Insanity,' he said with a dismissive grimace. 'We are not all of the same mind. If we were, then I suppose there would be little to quarrel about.'

'You are young to have started to learn philosophy,' Eadulf chuckled.

'I speak from my own observations. I have listened many times to old Scannail when he has visited my village to recite and talk.'

'Ah, that is why you seem advanced in such observations.' Eadulf uttered a sigh. 'I thought you had a depth of understanding there unusual in your years.'

'This is hardy country to traverse, even with these moorland ponies,' Fidelma observed, realising just how marshy the area was. Since coming through the ravine, she had grown more uneasy at her surroundings. Now they had crossed through mud strewn round with the smell of rotting vegetation before coming to a river bank that was equally unpleasant.

'Did you usually come this way when you came to trade?' Eadulf pressed again. 'I would have thought trade paths would be more beaten and hardened and so easier to follow?'

'This is the quickest way to Conmhaol's *cránnog*, and I presume you wanted to go the quickest way,' the boy replied dryly.

They were not sure whether he was being sarcastic.

'We presumed that we would be going the safest way,' Eadulf replied, matching the sarcasm.

Then he started to wave a hand in front of his face as if trying to drive off some irritation.

It was soon obvious why.

Clouds of midges or gnats were moving here and there as if in one body. The little ponies began to twitch and shake their heads, tossing them nervously, thrusting their noses upwards and stamping their feet.

'This is ridiculous,' Fidelma finally snapped. 'Let us get away from the river and these marshy banks.'

Brother Scatánach did not reply, but immediately nudged his pony to quicken its pace through the muddy waters and up the far river bank. Here the river was tree lined and plunged through the closely growing trees and undergrowth. The way seemed to rise a little and they followed to a more elevated ground than the midge-infested marshy banks.

'I feel I have been bitten so badly, I can't feel my skin for itching,' muttered Dego. He had been quiet as usual during the entire trip, speaking only when necessary. But now he felt compelled to express his scratchy indisposition. The midges were as painful as they were populous.

'You are the healer, Eadulf,' Fidelma complained, as they

halted, trying to examine their bites and brush off the insects. 'Name something quickly to get us out of our misery.'

'I can't,' Eadulf admitted, glancing around to try to spot any wild herbs that might assist. 'I don't even have a small jar of honey in my bag.'

'Honey?' Dego queried perplexed. 'What do we need with honey?'

'A small smear of honey on the bites would ease the itching and calm the skin.'

Brother Scatánach smiled thinly. 'I think I know where we might get some relief. Meantime, I have a little balm in my bag, but there is not enough for all of us.'

'Is it honey?' Eadulf asked.

'It is a herb whose leaves are boiled down with water. We call it *corrchopóc*.'

'Almost the same as the word for midge or gnat – *corrmilóc*?' queried Eadulf.

'Almost.'

The boy took a leather water bag from his bag and told Eadulf to proffer his arm where the bites were numerous. Then he poured the liquid on it. Eadulf sniffed at it and smiled. 'It is a distillation of something familiar . . . it's something called *Plantain* . . .'

'We did not go to a school of healing, as you did, Eadulf.' Fidelma was irritable, turning to the youth. 'You say that you know where we might obtain some more of this liquid?'

'There is a place, just a little out of our way, where a healer mixes this liquid,' Brother Scatánach said.

'Then I suggest you lead us there as quickly as possible,' Eadulf instructed. 'Meanwhile,' he turned to the others, 'try not to scratch the itches, as they could turn septic.'

They were not long making their way through the forest and out on to a heather-covered hillside. Then Dego raised a shout.

'There is a building not far ahead,' he called.

It was not one building but several conical-shaped constructions of the ancient round style. A thick pall of smoke hung over one of them and a curious smell hung in the air. The travellers rode up to the first one, which seemed to be the main round house. A tall man came out to greet them as they came close. He had a curiously long face with penetrating black eyes and very thin, almost blood-red lips. His eyebrows seemed to cross over the sharp ridge of his nose. The eyes that surveyed his visitors were dark, almost without pupils and without emotion. His gaze fell on Brother Scatánach and widened a little. The thin red lips parted in a gash, which was apparently a smile of welcome.

'Ah, greetings, young Scatánach. It is some time since you have passed this way. How may we serve you?'

'We have been attacked by midges and must ask for your services,' the youth explained.

The tall man stepped forward, examining them with a sweeping glance.

'Get off your ponies,' he instructed, then turned and gave a shout. Another man appeared from one of the outbuildings. He was immediately attended by another and together they took the reins of the horses. The man who had greeted the youth spoke again.

'Go into that round house.' He pointed to a nearby building. 'In there, remove your clothes. You will find two *dabach* or bathing tubs with warm *corrchopóc* all ready. We keep them warmed and mixed for just such emergencies. Bathe as long as you wish or can. When you emerge, do not dry yourselves. I will send someone to place healing medicine on your skin. Let it be absorbed. You will find robes hanging nearby. Then, you must drink of a medication I will send to you. Do not be concerned; it is a mixture of herbs that will keep you from the ravages of the *corrmilóc.*'

By this time Fidelma and her companions' bodies were painful with the bites, and the desire to scratch was almost unbearable. They felt no desire to question this strange man and there was no time for false modesty. Inside the round house they found the bathing tubs separated by curtains. Fidelma and Eadulf stripped off their clothes and plunged into one of the tubs. They sunk, holding their breaths and totally immersing themselves in the curious-smelling waters. Each tub contained a small ledge to sit on while the magical, warm waters came up to their necks. Dego and Scatánach settled into the other tub. In spite of the strong odour of the herbal concoction, the liquid was refreshing and soothing to their skins. The medication was a little different from the small amount of the liquid that Brother Scatánach had made them splash on their faces.

For a while they sat in their tubs, eyes closed, feeling the irritation slowly subside, and it was almost as if their bodies were returning to normal. After some time, just when Fidelma was thinking of moving, there was a movement at the entrance. A plump woman with a kindly face and friendly smile entered. She was carrying an earthenware jug and four beakers. She proceeded to fill these from the jug and handed one to each of them.

'There now, drink this and you will soon be better,' she ordered as she went to hand the drinks to Dego and Scatánach in the other tub.

The beverage was also strangely comforting.

'How do you feel?' the woman said, returning to them and addressing Fidelma.

'How are our ponies?' Fidelma's first concern was as an equestrian. 'Have they been damaged by the midges?'

'Rest easy, lady. They are better protected than you are,' the woman assured her. 'With such thick manes and coats it is only around the eyes and muzzles they need attention. They are being well looked after by our master of the stables.'

Fidelma climbed out of the tub and was helped into the robe that the woman had taken from one of the pegs.

'We will attend to your clothes. They need washing, as midges tend to lodge in them. Do not worry about them,' the plump woman assured her.

'What sort of place is this?' Fidelma asked, pushing her hair back. 'Who runs it? Are you the hosteller? Is this a tavern?'

The plump woman chuckled and shook her head. 'This the *Bróinbherg*, the House of Sorrow of Íccaid the Healer.'

Eadulf realised that 'House of Sorrow' was the name often given to a hospital, a place where sick folk came to be healed. But this was not one maintained by the local noble for the clan, in accordance to the law. Each clan was supposed to maintain a *forus tuaithe* – the house of the territory – where a physician was always in residence. This was different.

'Íccaid the Healer?' Fidelma echoed the name.

'I am his wife, Suaibsech,' the woman smiled.

'A healer, in this god-forsaken country?' Eadulf could not help but sound astounded.

The plump woman did not seem offended by the remark.

'It is certainly not forsaken by my gods, nor the healing goddesses,' she replied. 'If it had been, then you would not be feeling as well as you now do. Nor would Íccaid had been given the foresight to set up his special hospital here to treat the devastation of the gnats and midges that prey among those who are unwise enough to use this river route through these marshlands below. Where else would Dian Cécht, the great god of healing, have decided to place such a house in order to help his people if they fall into illness? Did you not know that the marshlands alongside the river are best avoided?'

'We had warnings of the territory although not specifically of the river,' Eadulf said in irritation. He was thinking that Brother Scatánach, as their guide, would have much to answer for. If he had come this way before, he would have known the dangers of this marshland. He had not climbed out of his bath yet so he could be remonstrated with later.

'You should have stuck to the main traders' track, which runs parallel but in higher country. It's enough above the marshland so that travellers are not troubled by these flying gnats or midges. This marshland and its unwelcome denizens are well known. So we are not entirely deserted by the gods,' Suaibsech added reprovingly.

Just then the tall figure who had greeted them entered and looked round.

'I trust you are all feeling better after your misfortunes? I am Íccaid the Healer and head of this house. I trust each of you is feeling relaxed and better for your experiences with the *corrmilóc*? Have you been well looked after by my wife, who also serves as stewardess? Do you have other urgent needs?'

'It is well that you have set up your house of healing at this spot. We were much in need of it,' Fidelma said.

'I did not even have to consult Dian Cécht, the god of medicine and divination, before I chose this site.' Íccaid smiled thinly. 'Come, follow me to the main house where I may make you more comfortable.' He paused and glanced to where Dego was climbing out of the tub. Scatánach had clearly not finished. 'Come when you are ready,' he called. 'My wife will attend you.'

Fidelma and Eadulf followed the healer into an adjoining building, which was clearly living quarters, with a warm central fire. Their host bade them be seated.

'So who is the physician among you?'

The question was unexpected and it was a moment before Eadulf realised that the man had seen his *lés,* the medical bag he always carried. It was something he had grown used to on his travels and had often been a help to Fidelma in dealing with medical matters in her investigations.

'It is my bag,' he admitted. 'But while I attended Tuaim Drecon, I left before my final qualifications.'

The eyes of Íccaid widened. 'Tuaim Drecon is regarded as the leading medical school of the Five Kingdoms.' He paused. 'Then I am guessing that you must be Eadulf the Saxon, husband to . . .' he turned to Fidelma, '. . . the sister to King Colgú of Cashel? Fidelma the famous *dálaigh*?'

'You are correct on both accounts,' Fidelma replied, glancing quickly towards Eadulf, hoping he would not make his inevitable correction about not being Saxon.

Íccaid's features were welcoming.

'It is unexpected to find Eóghanacht of your rank in this territory, lady. Yet I extend a welcome to my unworthy establishment, my House of Sorrow. I offer my hospitality to you and your companions on behalf of myself and Suaibsech.'

'For that we are in your debt, Íccaid. We gather that this is not the hospital under the guidance of the local lord of the territory?'

The man's smile broadened. 'It is not, lady. That does not exist. Conmhaol is the local lord and one who claims control of this area, but he does not like to exert authority. He dwells in his *crannóg* at Cnoc an Fiagh, the Hill of the Magic Mist, which is a short distance along the river. Although the same river, it is thankfully a place midges do not inhabit.'

'It is there that Brother Scatánach was guiding us.'

'He should have taken a better route. He has sometimes accompanied the physician of Dair Inis who attends Conmhaol. Conmhaol does not trust many of the healing arts.'

'Do you refer to Brother Fisecda?' Fidelma asked.

'Fisecda is a worthy physician. I know he has a reputation as he studied in Fachtna's abbey at Ros Ailithir before he joined Dair Inis.'

'Why does this Conmhaol refuse your services? You are closer to his fortress than Dair Inis. And already I am impressed with what I see.'

'For which we thank you,' Suaibsech answered, suddenly

appearing with Dego. 'Conmhaol is of a family that has drawn praise and hate in equal proportion. We are, in fact, cousins, and we maintain the Old Faith and the old ways. Importantly, our family rules the Uí Liatháin. Now our family council cannot agree who should be our prince.'

'I am told Conmhaol has refused the leadership.'

'There is still much confusion among the family council.'

'He is definitely of the Old Faith yet, in illness, he sends for a physician of the New Faith from Dair Inis? That is extraordinary.'

Íccaid twisted his lips in amusement. 'A Christian robe does not make the wearer a Christian. There will come a day when people will demand to know whether they believe in this god or that god before they then ask whether the healer is worthy or not. That is sad. People's bodies do not change depending on their religious beliefs. The faith in one god or another does not make their skeletons change in shape or structure, nor their muscles alter in form, nor make their lungs change the air necessary for breathing, nor their eyes focus differently.'

'You are saying that Brother Fisecda attends him because Conmhaol has a personal preference for him, and not for any other reason?'

'I believe that Brother Fisecda is close to Conmhaol in spite of their differences. Also bear in mind that it was an ancestor of Fisecda, Prince Mael Anfaid, who built that abbey, becoming its first abbot, before he was made abbot at Lios Mór. Now, you and your party must dine with me and be my guests for the night. You are under my protection.'

'That is much to ask of you,' Fidelma replied gravely.

'Not at all,' the physician smiled thinly. 'There is no tavern this side of Conmhaol's homestead. You would not get there before dark, and there is much bog land between here and there. You need good eyes to keep to the track.'

'In which case, your hospitality is warmly accepted. It seems,

Íccaid, that Dian Cécht placed your "House of Sorrow" in a good position. Do you get many travellers along this route?'

'A fair number, for there is much trade along the Great River, and often travellers leave it and join the confluences of rivers that cross the territories of the Uí Liatháin.'

'So how is that old badger who claims to be abbot?' asked Suaibsech.

Fidelma stared at her a moment to gather her thoughts.

'Abbot Brocc?'

'My cousin,' confirmed the physician.

Fidelma decided to be direct. 'You have not heard that he has been dead three days since?'

It was clear from their responses that Suaibsech and Íccaid had not been informed. Íccaid's mouth tightened into an expression of sorrow.

'I have not heard,' he answered softly. 'I am truly saddened for the death of a kinsman. How did he come by his death?'

'He was found dead in a sweat house. He was suffocated.'

There was a few moments' silence.

'I don't think there will be much grieving for our cousin in this part of the territory,' Suaibsech finally remarked, as if stifling a soft moan.

'Do I gather that Brocc was not liked in this territory?' Fidelma asked. The question was superfluous because she had already deduced, especially from the old bard, Scannail, that Brocc had not been liked here at all.

'He was not best loved by everyone,' the physician replied tightly. 'However, we will talk of this later. You and your companions have not finished your cure.'

Fidelma was not happy.

'You know my name, Íccaid, and you know I am a *dálaigh*. Know also that I am investigating Brocc's death, for it was an unnatural one.'

'I am afraid his enemies would be beyond counting,' the physician replied cynically.

'Except that this enemy appears to have foretold his death a week before it happened.'

'The prophetess dressed in grey?' The physician's expression did not alter as he asked the question.

'How did you know that?'

'It is part of our folklore and legends. Recently, word has passed through the territories that the prophetess has appeared making more predictions on the fortunes of our people.'

Fidelma's expression was closed as questions came into her mind.

Íccaid, clearly perceptive, stood up abruptly.

'Let us leave things until our guests have relaxed a little. We cannot offer you food and drink for a short while until the medications have taken effect. After that we invite you to share our hospitality. But now I suggest you finish the application of the liniments, otherwise you may succumb to infections.'

Suaibsech peered round as if puzzled. 'Where is young Scatánach? He was following us when we left the bath house.'

CHAPTER ELEVEN

It soon became obvious that Brother Scatánach had disappeared from the *Bróinbherg* complex. Íccaid sent for a man who was the master of the stables.

'Scatánach?' The man looked worried at the sharp tone of the physician. 'But he left the *Bróinbherg* immediately after his bath. He took the pony he came on and departed.'

'He was supposed to be guiding us,' Fidelma said, quietly angry. 'When did he leave here? Why were we not informed?'

'I thought this had been arranged with you,' the man replied with a worried look. 'I did think it strange as darkness was descending when he set off.'

'Did he say where he was going?' Íccaid asked angrily.

'I did not ask and he did not say. When he left, he was certainly taking the western track towards the Hill of the Magic Mist. But he surely would not be idiotic enough to travel in darkness.'

The physician turned to Fidelma apologetically. 'I should have been more attentive. We thought Brother Scatánach was acting in agreement with you, yet you say he was supposed to be your guide?'

'He was our guide from Dair Inis,' Eadulf replied bitterly. 'In fact, he was the youth who helped recover the body of Abbot Brocc.'

'Where was he taking you to?' Íccaid asked.

'To the *crannóg* of Conmhaol.'

'But you don't need a guide to get to Conmhaol's *crannóg*. You just follow along the north bank of the river. In fact, from Dair Inis you need not have come this way at all.' Íccaid was puzzled.

'I had a feeling that boy was misleading us,' Eadulf muttered.

'Why would he want to do that?' asked Suaibsech.

'A question that I was hoping to put to him,' Eadulf returned dryly. 'I think he purposely led us into that midge-infected marshland. After we had managed to get out of it, he said he knew of your place and that he had called here before. That much was confirmed when you recognised him and greeted him by name.'

Íccaid grimaced. 'Indeed. We did not know he had joined Brocc's abbey as a novitiate. Which means he must have converted to the New Faith.'

The physician looked towards Suaibsech, who spread her hands in a gesture of bewilderment.

Fidelma turned to the master of the stables, who was standing looking uncomfortable.

'You say he was riding west?' she asked. 'Would that be towards Conmhaol's place?'

'More or less. As I say, due west along the River of Omens. If you follow the river, keeping to the northern bank, you would avoid the gnat-infested areas. Conmhaol's homestead is on this river, although it is a place where the waters run wildly as the flow turns from its southerly route almost at right angles to the east.'

Dego suddenly cleared his throat and spoke. 'Can I ask your master of stables whether our ponies have remained or did the young man take them? His intention might have been to strand us here,' he added.

'The ponies of the three guests remain here,' the master of stables immediately responded.

Suaibsech pointed out that there was little purpose in trying to go after Scatántach.

'Food and a bed for the night is the best idea for the moment. You can start after him in the morning. But for now, rest. I will call you when it is time for the evening meal,' she said.

Suaibsech conducted Fidelma and Eadulf to one of the round huts where they could rest. She then brought their saddle bags to them and informed them that a bell would be sounded when it was time to eat. She advised them that, having had the medicinal bath, they should not take the traditional evening baths before going into the meal, but allow the medicinal bath time to work against the bites. She then asked Dego to follow her to his accommodation.

As Fidelma and Eadulf lay down, Eadulf could not help articulating the thought that had been bothering him.

'We should have a word with young Brother Scatánach when we catch up with him.'

Fidelma smothered a yawn. '*If* we catch up. Why? To what purpose?'

'You must agree that the boy led us into that midge-infested marsh on purpose?' he asked in a lowered voice. 'He knew that area and must have been aware of the virulence of those midges and that they would inflict pain on us, if not worse.'

'It is logical.'

'I noticed the smaller pests did not harm him,' Eadulf replied. 'He must have planned beforehand where he would lead us because he had that medication with him.'

'If he led us into the marshland deliberately, what was the point?' Fidelma was perplexed. 'Why would he then bring us here so that we could be treated? Did he mean to bring us here all along? Maybe it was just to delay our journey rather than stop us.'

'That may have been his objective,' Eadulf agreed. 'But why this curious delaying tactic?'

'Let's wait until we catch up with him. Meanwhile, it seems that we will have to stay here for tonight. At least we may find out some more general information from this physician and his wife now we know they are part of the *derbhfine*, the family council of Brocc and his siblings.'

It seemed they had just closed their eyes when a bell started to sound. To their amazement they found, during their short sleep, a change of clothing had been brought, ready for them to dress. Eadulf excused himself as he wanted to find the *fúaltech*, or urinal, and it was there that he bumped into Dego.

The warrior was looking distracted. 'I was thinking about that young Scatánach,' he said.

'You are not alone,' Eadulf answered.

'And we are not the only guests seeking medical treatment in this place.'

'Is that so strange?' Eadulf replied. 'After all, Íccaid seems to be the only physician in the area, and this is a healing centre.'

'I overheard one of the attendants speaking to Suaibsech about a patient. He referred to the man as "the old Déisi".'

Eadulf shrugged. 'The Déisi country is just across the Great River so it would be natural for them to be in this territory. Why do you think it is worth noting?'

'I do not speak lightly, friend Eadulf,' Dego returned in annoyance. 'The complete phrase was "the old Déisi from Dair Inis".'

Eadulf's eyes widened. 'That would be . . .?'

'Suaibsech was asking the attendant if he thought there was any sign that the "old man" would live. The attendant replied that the "Déisi scholar might not last the night". That was the phrase he used.'

'Was there mention of his name?'

'No, but I knew that you and Fidelma had been interested in the Déisi scholar who had spent time in the library at Dair Inis. Also, the fact he had left the abbey on the day the abbot was murdered.'

Eadulf was about to reply when a louder, more urgent note resounded from the dinner bell.

'We'll speak of this later. Meanwhile, if you can find out more, let me know.'

When Eadulf rejoined Fidelma he found an attendant with her, ready to lead them to the main meal of the day. They were conducted to a large refectory, where both attendants and guests apparently had their meals.

There were half a dozen male and female attendants ready at separate tables. Fidelma and Eadulf were shown to another table accommodating several places and told to take seats. A moment later Íccaid and Suaibsech entered and the company fell silent as they moved to the seats. Íccaid raised his right palm and everyone stood in silence.

'Good food, good drink – may good health proceed from them,' he intoned. Then he motioned everyone to be seated.

Once seated, he smiled at his latest guests. 'I trust you have rested well and the irritations are subsiding?'

'We have rested and the inflammation is already subsiding, thanks to your treatments.'

Fidelma expressed surprise at the size of the physician's household. It was Suaibsech who told her that the hospital had an apothecary, a female assistant, some students learning the healing arts under the physician and his assistant. There was a gardener and two assistants, a master of stables and his assistant, and a general worker. When the centre was full, they took chosen times to eat with the physician so they were not altogether in one place and hindering the running of the complex.

There was no server or cup bearer. Everything was already placed on the tables. Water or cider stood in jugs. Each person was expected to use his or her own knife, as was the custom. The knife, to cut meat, was held in the right hand, while the fingers of the left hand were used to pick up items or transfer food to the mouth. For anything more liquid, spoons were provided.

The food was taken from the centre table where a gridiron stood on which two types of meat had been broiled: ox-meat and mutton. The meats had been cooked in honey and salt. The diners placed their choice of meat on platters and then helped themselves to vegetables, the main choice being leeks, onions or wild garlic. Herbs of various sorts, even watercress, were already on the table. Hazelnuts were in dishes, as well as hard-boiled eggs, always served as a cold dish.

Fidelma was quite impressed when, on another side table, she spotted dishes of apples, whortleberry, strawberries and even a baked custard tart made of honey, eggs and a sweet pastry.

Íccaid smiled apologetically as he saw her examining the dishes.

'I am afraid that you join us on a "meat-eating only" day. We divide our meals in accordance with the availability of the day.'

'Sometimes the ill cannot partake of meat,' pointed out Eadulf.

'In that case, the needs of our patients are paramount and our attendants provide accordingly.'

As they fell to serving themselves, it was Íccaid who brought up the matter weighing on Eadulf's mind.

'I have given thought to the disappearance of your guide.'

Eadulf glanced at Fidelma before saying: 'Did you come to any conclusion?'

'Perhaps he thought that you had come to harm Conmhaol.'

'Why would we, and why would he think it? We are investigating Brocc's death.'

'He's a youth. He probably imagines he is a friend of Conmhaol.'

'You are of the family council. Can I ask if you wanted Conmhaol to become leader of the Uí Liatháin?' Fidelma asked.

'It is no secret that I did.'

'But when Conmhaol refused, would that not have placed

Brocc in contention, or was the fact that he had converted to the New Faith an impediment?'

'You should know the law, Fidelma. Faith is not considered an inability. One elects the best person for the task.'

'But when Conmhaol stood down, Brocc might have been in contention?'

'Brocc would not have found favour. He had the same ruthlessness as his father. It was not for nothing that Tigerna Cosraigib had the name "Lord of the Slaughter".'

'But Brocc was of the New Faith,' Eadulf argued.

The physician regarded him with sadness. 'I am sure that you have heard the expression that you may drive the brambles from your barley field but be sure the brambles will return.'

'You think Brocc would be like his father?' asked Fidelma. 'Brocc was, by all accounts, very strong in his advocacy of the New Christian Faith.'

'A man may put on a new robe, but that does not mean he becomes a new man.'

Fidelma realised that she had heard a similar saying before about Brocc.

'Neither does it mean that his death was not received with sadness within his family,' Suaibsech confirmed.

Eadulf regarded the physician with interest.

'I thought this place was of the Old Faith. Yet the death of one of the New Faith makes your family sad?'

'The death of any member of our family is a matter of sadness,' Íccaid replied.

'Even so, you did not support Brocc to become the leader when Conmhaol declined the position?'

'The answer to that is obvious. I am even surprised that you find it so unusual that you remark on it. During these days when the two Faiths are vying with one another for domination, it is still usual that people meet and discuss family matters.'

Íccaid seemed to hesitate about something.

'You want to speak of some aspect of the death of Abbot Brocc?' Eadulf asked encouragingly.

'Not exactly,' Íccaid replied. 'There was another matter which, on reflection, might be connected, but I would like to consult you about it.'

'Other matters? How connected?' Fidelma demanded.

'I said – might be. We have a patient who arrived in the same bad way that you did, having suffered the same infections that you nearly succumbed to. I was going to ask Brother Eadulf to examine him because he said that you might have something to add, with your training at Tuaim Drecon . . .'

'I left without a final qualification,' Eadulf reminded them, realising they might be talking about the Déisi patient that Dego had told him of.

'No matter,' Íccaid replied. 'Your reputation is sound enough, Eadulf. I thought it was a case that you might be interested in, having gone through a near-similar experience. This poor person did not find us as quickly as you did. Therefore, we could not treat him with such speedy results. It is taking longer to fight the infections. You will see what would have happened had you been as unfortunate.'

'You want me to examine this man?'

'Come, I will take you there. He is still unconscious.'

'You go with the physician, Eadulf,' Fidelma said. 'I would not be of help in this matter.'

'Who is he? What is his name?' Eadulf pretended to be ignorant and hoped Dego would not say they had already spoken about the Déisi scholar.

'He has been almost unconscious since he arrived. But from the few words he has spoken we have learned he is from Déisi territory and that his name is Sárán.'

'Sárán?' Fidelma pretended surprise. 'There was a scholar at

Dair Inis who left the day Brocc was murdered. When did Sárán arrive here?'

'Two days ago. We did not learn much about him before unconsciousness overtook him . . .'

'How did he arrive here? Was he alone?'

'He was alone and on foot,' Suaibsech replied. 'He was hardly conscious when he arrived. He swiftly slipped into unconsciousness so infected was he by the midge bites. I think he may have come part of the way on horseback and perhaps fell, for he had abrasions on the head and shoulder. Our stable master did a search but found no sign of the animal. The man carried a personal bag, a satchel.'

'You have examined it?'

Íccaid pursed his lips for a moment. 'Is it correct to examine the personal items of a man who cannot maintain his rights? Under the law, is it permissible? The man should be recovered and certainly able to travel by the end of the week.'

'It is permissible to search his bag by my authority,' Fidelma assured him. 'We will examine the bag and find out more. Eadulf, you go with Íccaid and check the condition of this man. If he wakes and is able to talk, let me know.'

The physician looked to his wife, who went to a cupboard and returned with a leather bag, laying it on the table before Fidelma. Then he and Eadulf left the room.

Fidelma opened the satchel and glanced through the contents. She could ignore most of the items except for one group. There were some pages of treated vellum and a notebook. There was a name written of the first page of the notebook which confirmed the identity of the man: Sárán of Dún Garbháin.

'That is the main fortress of Prince Cummasach of the Déisi,' Fidelma confirmed, trying to remember what Brother Cróebíne had told her.

'Look at the title that he has written on the first page . . . *Tairired na nDéisi*.' Suaibsech pointed.

'That means "Journey of the Déisi",' Fidelma translated. 'That just confirms he was a scholar searching for material for some history of his people, the Déisi.'

'What is this "Journey of the Déisi" then?' Suaibsech asked. 'Is it to do with when they came and took our land?'

'It happened a long time ago. They were a prosperous people living in Midhe, the Middle Kingdom.'

'That's the High King's personal domain. It is where Tara is located.'

'Just so. It was the days of Cormac mac Art, when he was High King. One of Cormac's sons was named Cellach. He desired the daughter of Oengus, who was then Prince of the Déisi. When she rejected him, to his shame he raped her. Cellach then refused to pay compensation and kept the girl a prisoner in his fortress. Oengus demanded compensation of blood. In casting his spear, he not only killed Cellach but the spear somehow took out the eye of the High King, Cormac mac Art, himself. Under law, such a physical deformity prohibited Cormac from remaining High King. No High King can have a disability. Cormac's other son, Eochaid Gunnat, became High King and took revenge on Oengus and the Déisi, driving them from Midhe to become wanderers without land. Some of the clan went to the land of the Britons, where they established the kingdom called Dyfed. We know that, for Eadulf and I were once shipwrecked there.'

Fidelma remembered only too well the strange adventurers they encountered there.

'Others of the Déisi fled with Oengus, who brought them south to Muman. They were given permission to settle in the south-east of the kingdom. Hence the Déisi settled across the river in the territory that now bears their name. They are supposed to pay tribute each year to Cashel. I did not know it was previously the land of the Uí Liatháin.'

Eadulf and Íccaid returned. Eadulf was shaking his head as he caught Fidelma's eye.

'The old man is in a deep sleep. Just a little fever, and he will probably come out of it tomorrow. There is nothing I could advise that Íccaid has not already done. I am afraid the only thing that remains is patience. I am impressed. I have learnt several things about the herb mixtures used here to treat the insect bites.'

'We just have to continue with the liniments and salves as well as liquids,' Íccaid agreed. 'That, and hope that Dian Cécht, the god of healing, is watching over the old man.'

'Did you find out anything further from the man's belongings?' Eadulf asked Fidelma, looking at the leather bag on the table.

'There is nothing in it that helps us. A few curious notes in the papers, which presumably were helping his research. He seemed to be researching the history of his people. There is one note that might indicate some reason for Sárán's journey. He writes the names "Conmhaol" and "Abbot Brocc", and the words "Is the garland weaker?" and then "no unity in the family", and finally, "no longer an alliance".'

'And does he explain why the Déisi are so resentful to Cashel; why they are always trying to create insurrection and seek revenge on the Eóghanacht?' Eadulf asked.

'I was just explaining to Suaibsech that the Déisi wandered without land until they came and settled across the Great River,' Fidelma said. 'It is why the very name Déisi, after all these centuries, has come to mean, among our people, "vassals".'

'You leave out an important fact,' Íccaid said sharply. 'That land was once all part of the Uí Liatháin territory, but we were forced to give up our farms and lands and flee across the Great River to these lands. Our legends tell the story of our former greatness and how we fell under the thrall of the Déisi through the intervention of the Eóghanacht. That is why we are so easily led when our princes call for us to rise against Cashel.'

'It doesn't really help us in seeking the murderer of Brocc, or the motive for his death,' Eadulf commented.

'There is no connection with your journey through our territory except that Sárán was a visitor to the library at Dair Inis,' Suaibsech pointed out. 'And yet . . .'

'Yet it is curious why a Déisi scholar should be searching for material there. I suppose, when motives are lost in the mists of history, it helps to consider what people believe,' Eadulf finished.

Fidelma was frowning and reached again for the manuscript they had been examining. She looked at the notes, which she had noticed on a loose page. Then she tapped with her forefinger on the entry.

'Rhun, a prince of the Uí Liatháin, was descendant of the Eóghanacht of the Valley of Yew Trees. Maybe the old man was travelling to ask Conmhaol about him?' suggested Suaibsech, reading where Fidelma pointed.

'A strange name, that,' Eadulf commented. 'Rhun is the name for a Briton.'

'So the Déisi historian was looking for Conmhaol to talk about this?' mused Fidelma. 'It looks like some legend.'

Suaibsech shook her head in bewilderment. 'Even if they are considered myths and legends, sources are sources. One has to consider what people believe. Often people become determined to give their lives for a mythology that their minds have made into a reality. Is the old historian not to be praised for wandering the country in search of myths?'

Fidelma had a ghost of a smile around her mouth. 'I spoke with a bard of your people, one Scannail, who seemed to imply that some people in the west of the Uí Liatháin territory might be able to tell us more of such legends and myths. He did not want us to pursue that.'

'You met Scannail?' The physician's wife's brows rose a little in surprise. 'He had no liking for Abbot Brocc.'

'So I gathered. I felt that Scannail knew of something in Brocc's background that might provide the motive for his being killed.'

'Motive is often an easy route to the murderer,' Suaibsech agreed. 'Certainly someone hated him. As I recall, old Scannail had more reason than most.'

Fidelma stared at the physician's wife for a moment. 'Why Scannail? I know he seemed indifferent to the news of Brocc's death and had no liking for him. Are you saying that he had a reason to murder him? Yet he was friendly with Brocc's sister, Lalóg, and popular in the little village nearby the abbey.'

'He never mentioned to you that he was once flogged by Brocc?' Suaibsech asked.

Fidelma's eyes widened. 'Flogged?'

'In the time before time, the legend says, a curse had been put on the Great River by seven evil Druids. The river was then called the Daurona. It ran dry. The people were in despair. King Fiach of the Two Sorrows called upon the great Druid-God Mug Roth, who would ride across the sky in his glittering chariot. He immediately uttered a prayer to the goddess Mór, the great protector of Muman. She conjured the seven great hounds representing the seven deities of the seven tributaries of the river. The hounds sprang forth and destroyed the evil magicians. Mug Roth said the waters would return so long as people never returned to calling the river the Daurona. That is why it is simply called the Great River, An Abhainn Mór. So the waters soon flowed back along the parched river bed from Mullach an Radhirc, where it rose, and down to the open sea.'

Eadulf groaned openly. 'Why can nothing happen in this country without recalling some legends or piece of mythology that are regarded as reality?'

'So why did Brocc flog the old bard Scannail? I find ancient stories relevant only when they have meaning. I don't see—' began Fidelma.

'There was a day when Scannail was heard outside the abbey, singing praises to the oracle of the river goddess, Mór. It enraged Brocc. Although he was raised in the Old Faith, he had newly converted to the New Faith, and converts are always fanatics. He ordered the bard to be brought before him and had him thrashed for what he called blasphemy. It was when many of the Uí Liatháin nobles and warriors had decided to march with Tigerna Cosraigib. Brocc wanted to persuade those of the New Faith that he was loyal.'

'Was it a bad flogging?'

'Scannail was badly lacerated. His followers took him to some place – I think a place called the Valley of the Phantoms – where he was nursed for several days by the Grey One. It took some time before he recovered, but recover he did.'

'For this he hated Brocc and what he stood for?'

'It was not the first or last time that stories of Brocc, and his apparent pleasure in causing physical pain on those who stood against him, were talked about,' Suaibsech answered. 'That is why I said earlier that the family council would never have made Brocc the Prince of the Uí Liatháin after his father died.'

'He was known to be someone who gained satisfaction from inflicting physical pain on people,' Íccaid agreed softly.

'As was his father, Tigerna Cosraigib,' added Suaibsech. 'He, too, was known to be a cruel man. Did you know that Brocc had once been a warrior who had fought at the Battle of Cnoc Áine? Only after the defeat there did he convert to the New Faith.'

'That was six years ago.' Fidelma was thoughtful. 'My brother had just become King of Cashel.'

'It was your brother's victory over the Uí Fidgente and their allies. And we were of that number,' the physician added. 'Tigerna

Cosraigib, Brocc and Conmhaol retreated into this territory. According to the stories, Brocc eventually converted to the New Faith and then emerged as the abbot at Dair Inis. Conmhaol became estranged from his father.'

Fidelma was reflective. 'I understand that some people do change their faith,' she said. 'Indeed, have not the majority of people in the Five Kingdoms changed their religion during the last two centuries? But when you say Brocc changed his allegiance, was it a practical change? Or was it a change of true belief?'

'He was one of the leading warriors of the Uí Liatháin until the defeat at Cnoc Áine,' Suaibsech said, leaving Fidelma to draw her own conclusion.

'What you are telling us is that Brocc probably had too many enemies to enumerate,' Fidelma sighed. 'Therefore, we probably would not find it worthwhile to investigate his closer family to identify his killer, as he was so well hated throughout the Uí Liatháin territory?'

Suaibsech shrugged indifferently. 'I would say that it would be as if I were searching a nest of gnats to find out which one caused the death of a fever patient.'

'A good comparison,' Fidelma approved. 'Even so, we have not much else to go on. Scannail, the bard, more or less said the same thing. He had felt it useless to attempt to see Conmhaol, as did Lalóg.'

'The River of Omens is a place strangers should stay away from,' the physician replied.

'When you sat on the *derbhfine,* did you support Conmhaol to be the new prince, or were you one of those that opposed him?'

'We supported Conmhaol,' Íccaid replied.

Suaibsech seemed to recall what the old scholar had written. 'Are you saying that the old historian was commenting in his notes on the current situation? When he wrote "no unity in the family", "no longer an alliance" and "is the garland weakened", was he implying Conmhaol is like some weak flower? The family cannot decide a leader since Conmhaol refused, and the alliance Tigerna Cosraigib formed with Cummasach of the Déisi was finished? Do you think these notes mean that?'

Fidelma paused and then said slowly: 'We were told Conmhaol refused to accept the title that his *derbhfine* wanted to bestow on him. We are told the family council of the last recognised prince, slain in the conspiracy six months ago, disagree about a successor. Could it be that this Déisi scholar is some agent, come to try to negotiate a new conspiracy between one of the *derbhfine* and Cummasach of the Déisi? As a member of this family council, you can tell us what is relevant.'

'There is little we know for certain, and our people are reticent about sharing even that information with the Eóghanacht,' Íccaid said bluntly.

Fidelma was suddenly finding difficulty in disguising her annoyance.

'If that is so, then I would have to report to my brother, the King, and to his Chief Brehon that I am unable to reach any conclusions or resolve any mysteries until the Uí Liatháin have renegotiated their recognition of the kingdom of Muman and taken their ritual oath of allegiance. That means your people have retracted their allegiance to Cashel on two occasions. An agreement is put at absolutely no worth and further action has to be taken.'

The physician stared at her, the shock apparent on his features.

'Are you saying that if you are not respected your brother would be prepared to march an army into our territory?' he asked finally.

'I am saying that the Uí Liatháin should respect the laws and the treaties they have made. When such laws and treaties are ignored or broken, then there are consequences.'

'Lady, if it seems that some in our territory do not respect you, especially your rank as a *dálaigh* and legal adviser to your brother, then there is no denying it. But let me hasten to say you are wrong in making the entire people of this territory responsible,' Íccaid said firmly. 'No matter what we believe about Abbot Brocc, right or wrong, he was Abbot of Dair Inis and, until declared otherwise, he was under the protection of the law of which you are judge and administrator. I know nothing about secret ambitions. My role in the family council is negligible. I have tried to answer your questions as far as I am able to.'

'Brocc was a member of the *derbhfine*, as are you,' replied Fidelma with a grim smile. 'Remember, I do not speak for the King but for the law as administered by the council of Brehons.'

Sometimes Eadulf was surprised at how far Fidelma would go in verbal terms to exert authority and get what she wanted. Often, he wondered what she would do if she came across someone of stronger will, who would face down her implied threats.

'It is as it should be, lady. As long as I know the answer, I will answer. What would you know?'

'Is Dún Guairne entirely deserted or does it still hold members of Tigerna Cosraigib's family who might come forward before the *derbhfine*?'

'To my knowledge, there are no warriors there. There are no members of our family there. The family council has not managed to form any agreement as to succession. If anything was different, then I would know.'

'Suaibsech, you have intimated that I would gain nothing by going to Dún Guairne. Do you still maintain that?'

'I agree it is as my husband says. I regret I can give you no other facts.'

'There is no Uí Liatháin noble dwelling at Dún Guairne and plotting further attacks on Cashel,' the physician insisted.

'Has a family council been recalled to consider a successor?'

'Our choice was Conmhaol. He was chosen and he rejected the family choice.'

'And there is much unrest in this territory until a new leader is chosen,' Fidelma pointed out.

'The unrest is because people have seen warriors on grey stallions riding among the Hills of the Phantoms. Warriors dressed in the grey of those that always attended the princes of our people in ancient times. They are reminded of the suffering of our people, which began when the Déisi arrived. It is said that the warriors are led by the Grey One, a female prophet who warns that a day is near when the Uí Liatháin shall come into their own again.'

'Grey stallions, warriors in grey – ah, this territory and its love of grey,' Eadulf muttered loudly. 'But now you are allies of the Déisi against the Eóghanacht instead of enemies.' Eadulf was bewildered.

'We made an alliance, joining against what Tigerna Cosraigib thought was the greater enemy.'

'Was Conmhaol against his father's alliance with the Déisi? Did Abbot Brocc share his brother's views?'

'Do you mean did Abbot Brocc and his brother become secret allies to lead the people in another insurrection?' Íccaid shook his head immediately. 'Would a sheep lie down with a wolf? There was no way they would form such an alliance.'

'So as Conmhaol stood aside from the leadership, he genuinely had no wish to be involved in such matters? Or did he stand aside thinking to allow his brother to become leader?'

'That is a bizarre suggestion.' Íccaid was astounded. 'Conmhaol preached peace and reconciliation. That is why he succeeded in obtaining the support of most of the family council. What are you implying?'

'To be clear, Tigerna's children, Brocc, Conmhaol and Princess Lalóg, all offered themselves to the *derbhfine* for one of them to become head of the family and therefore the leader of the Uí Liatháin? Only Conmhaol was approved?'

'We chose Conmhaol,' agreed the physician.

'And since then the family council has not met? There is no other member of the family worthy?' Fidelma pressed.

Íccaid grimaced impatiently. 'You know the rules. Any member of the *derbhfine* can present themselves. The *derbhfine* are the family group of four generations descended from a common great-grandfather. Not just sons, but uncles, nephews and so on might be prevailed on to become head of the family, to bear the title of that head.' He glanced at Eadulf. 'Unlike with your people, eldest sons do not automatically inherit.'

'And often daughters inherit,' replied Eadulf. 'That much I know.'

'We have not met again and no one has come forward,' repeated the physician stubbornly. 'However, the family council should be summoned soon for the situation cannot be allowed to continue.'

Fidelma rose and stretched languidly. 'In that case, we thank you, Íccaid, and you, Suaibsech, for your help and hospitality. We will not forget it. We will continue our journey at sun-up.'

'Where will you go?' Suaibsech inquired, frowning.

'We will go westward in search of Conmhaol,' Fidelma replied firmly. 'To the Hill of the Magic Mist.'

chapter twelve

A t the crowing of a cockerel, Fidelma heaved a sigh before leaning forward to shake the still-sleeping Eadulf by the shoulder. The cockerel crowed loudly several times, accompanied by the loud clucking of several other birds. Fidelma smiled as it struck her that the noise was sometimes similar to her brother's councillors in heated session. Eadulf turned in the bed, groaning as he did so. The noise seemed to surround the house where they had been sleeping.

'Is it first light yet?' he muttered, blinking.

'What time do you think it is with a cockerel crowing outside?' Fidelma replied dryly.

'You know that you can't always tell,' he replied. 'Those damned birds can crow all day and not just at dawn, as some people think. They are a bit like kings: they crow when they feel threatened and they crow to demonstrate their power and assert their control of their tribe.'

'And talking of cockerels strutting around to announce their powers, Dego has been up some time, washed and eaten, and been to check on our ponies. He even went for a short ride in case he could obtain information from the tracks left by Brother Scatánach's pony.'

'How do you know that already?' Eadulf demanded, swinging out of bed, then noticing she was already dressed.

'I rose at first light and had a word with him before he went to Íccaid's stables,' she smiled. 'But I thought you could do with some extra sleep.'

There was little other movement among the buildings of the *Bróinbherg* as Eadulf took the customary morning wash of face, hands and feet. Then he dressed while Fidelma prepared their saddle bags. They went together to the building used as a refectory. They were surprised to find Suaibsech already there and ready to supervise their *cet-longud*, the first meal of the day.

At the tables there were a few of the attendants who looked after the medical centre having an early meal. The visitors were surprised, as they had heard no one moving about beforehand.

Fidelma always insisted on a frugal meal first thing, especially as they were to make what might be a long ride that morning. She maintained that it was best not to be overfed when riding. For Eadulf it was hard to ignore the table spread with plates of cold meats, cheeses, fruit, honey, oat cakes and jugs of cider and goat's milk, but Fidelma's look at him was enough for him not to succumb to temptation.

They were just finishing when Íccaid entered and came to sit with them. He leant across the table and helped himself to a beaker of cider, smacking his lips with relish at its taste.

'You have rested well?' he asked.

'Well enough,' Fidelma replied. 'How do you manage to keep such an opulent and luxuriant household when I heard so much about poverty due to reparation payments? Even nobles have complained they are reduced to poverty.'

'The hospitals and physicians are the last places our rulers want to impoverish,' Íccaid observed cynically. 'Are you sure that you intend to continue on to find Conmhaol?'

'That is our intention,' Fidelma replied resolutely. 'I am still pursuing the matter of the unnatural death of the abbot. As he was your cousin, I presume you want an answer to the question.'

'How is your unexpected visitor, Sárán, this morning?' Eadulf intervened.

'He is doing exceptionally well; perhaps still a little feverish, which is to be expected after a prolonged state of unconsciousness. In fact, he is wide awake and says he wants to leave immediately. I cannot allow that, but he might be fine tomorrow.'

'He plans to continue his journey to Conmhaol?' Fidelma was surprised.

'No.' Íccaid shook his head. 'A merchant wagon calls here tomorrow and heads for the Déisi settlement at Eochaill. He has wisely decided against tracking off to the Hill of the Magic Mist.'

'Ah, I will have a quick word with him,' Fidelma announced, rising. 'I will be back in a moment.'

The way she said it implied that she wanted to see the old scholar on her own. Eadulf felt a little frustrated as they were delaying their own journey. However, it was only a short time before Fidelma returned. There was almost a smile of satisfaction on her face.

'He is strong for one so elderly,' she announced. 'And, now, are we ready to continue our journey?'

'I did check with Dego at the stable that your ponies are well fed and safe,' Íccaid said. 'As regards this matter, you are our guests,' he added, as Eadulf fumbled with the purse at his waist. 'Let it not be said that an Eóghanacht did not receive a welcome here.'

'Then we must bid you and your wife farewell and be on our way. Once more, our gratitude for your hospitality and our thanks. I will advise my brother that your *Bróinbherg* deserves acknowledgement for its hospitality.'

It was a short and uncomfortable farewell, for Fidelma was nurturing a growing suspicion that the mystery of Brocc's death now centred on some matter connected with the decisions of the family council.

They found Dego waiting with their ponies outside the stables of this curious 'House of Sorrow'.

'I rode along the trackway a little way to the west,' he informed them as they were tightening their equipment, ready to mount. 'That young man must have eyes like a cat to have ridden off into the dark.'

'So Brother Scatánach was heading to Conmhaol, as we suspected?'

'The youth might be laying a false trail,' Eadulf suggested.

'Íccaid's stable master confirmed the route,' Dego assured him. 'No, that route takes him directly to Conmhaol's *crannóg*.'

'Well, as Íccaid said, there seems no logic to this unless the boy wanted to divert us from seeing Conmhaol or warn him of our coming,' Eadulf said. 'If either were his purpose, then why bring us as far as this place? I don't understand it.'

Fidelma tried to keep her exasperation to herself. 'As I have said many times, Eadulf, speculation—'

'Without information, it is a worthless pastime,' Eadulf interrupted and sighed. 'But surely when one encounters strange behaviour then speculation is allowable?'

'To a point. Rather let us wait until we can progress this with fact.'

'The only way to construe Brother Scatánach's behaviour is as one of intent,' Dego muttered. 'He leads us into a swamp where we are bitten and might have died without treatment. So then he miraculously leads us to a specialist physician. Was that a mistake on his part or his plan?'

'You may safely assume it was no mistake,' Fidelma confirmed. 'He claimed he knew that river and marsh, but led us among the insects. Then he knew the physician's abode and saved us by leading us there. And just when we were about to question him, he disappears.'

'What can we deduce from that?' Eadulf asked.

'Little else,' she confirmed, smiling at her husband. 'So there is no point in trying to devise explanations. We must wait until we have added to our tiny store of knowledge before we can make intelligent speculations.'

'I wonder what story he will tell those back at the abbey as to his failure to guide us to the Hill of the Magic Mist.' Eadulf could not help asking a rhetorical question and was not surprised to receive no response.

They had been riding west for some time, keeping on a track that was parallel but well on the north side and above of the dark river, when Dego, who had been leading, called back over his shoulder.

'There is a thick oak forest ahead. Best to keep a careful watch. I don't think we should count on this being friendly country.'

'Don't these people know that the person of a *dálaigh* is above politics?' moaned Eadulf. 'Lawyers are given neutral rights in all the Five Kingdoms.'

Fidelma clenched her jaw tightly for a moment: 'We will know if that is respected once we reached Conmhaol in safety.'

Dego glanced up at the sky, noting the position of the sun.

'The river seems to be turning more northerly ahead.'

'So long as this trackway docsn't descend into the marshland,' Eadulf replied. 'I am still feeling the ravages of the gnats on my skin.'

'Be assured,' Dego said, equally moody, 'I aim to keep well above those muddy river banks. Anyway, it seems the tracks that we have followed continue to keep us away from the midges.'

As Dego had said, they could see the track winding more northerly, still among the dark oak trees, which seemed to grow even closer together than before.

'Halt your mounts!' a voice cried from behind them. 'Don't try turning round!'

Even as the words were spoken, an arrow hissed over their heads from behind and embedded itself in a tree ahead of them. 'Keep looking forward!' continued the same voice. 'Hands stretched to the sides where they can be seen.'

Dego's mind was racing, trying to make an estimate of whether there was more than one person who had been hidden in ambush among the trees. He was contemplating action when the voice cried even in a harsher tone, 'If you want to die then it is your choice. You have but to continue moving as you are contemplating – just a fraction – and you will find it is your last movement in this life.'

Dego was shocked that the smallest twitch of his body was so quickly anticipated.

'Can I speak?' Fidelma called, keeping her body rigid.

'No,' snapped the voice.

There was movement behind them and it was clear that whoever was there was not alone. Quickly Fidelma began to reason whether she should cry for everyone to urge their mounts forward and try to outrun their ambushers. She immediately gave up the thought. Had she been on her own horse, she might have attempted it, but she did not know how fast these moorland ponies could move into a gallop. And there was Eadulf to consider, who was not an expert equestrian.

'I am a *dálaigh*,' Fidelma insisted on calling. 'My party is protected by law.'

'Did I not warn you to be silent?' came the voice. 'I know well who you are.'

Fidelma hesitated.

'Then you know well the punishment that is due for any harm coming to a legal—'

There was a movement and Fidelma actually found herself

tensing to receive an arrow. It was the sound of a bowstring being drawn that stopped her in mid-sentence. There was a moment of silence.

'A good choice!' The voice came from close behind her now. 'But we would rather carry corpses than let prisoners have freedom to create problems. So keep your silence and maintain your gaze forward. Then dismount. Stand by your horses, still looking forward.'

After a moment or two, when they had dismounted, the order was repeated to continue looking forward and not to try to examine their captors.

The first voice continued: 'One of my men will tie your hands.'

There was an immediate guffaw from another male voice.

'How do you expect me to tie the hands of this man behind his back when he has only one?' The man had apparently spotted Dego's one arm.

'I expect you to have some intelligence,' replied the first voice firmly. 'Secure the hand of the one-armed man behind his back so that he cannot use it. And make sure all their weapons are removed.'

Still staring ahead of her, Fidelma could not help saying: 'As a *dálaigh*, I do not carry weapons. Nor does Brother Eadulf, who is my husband.'

'But you have to eat, so you still carry a knife,' replied the voice. The knife was the one personal item that everyone carried by custom into meals.

'The law . . .' began Fidelma. The man next to her jerked her arms behind her back and tied a rope around her wrists with expert ease. Then her arms were jerked upwards, causing an involuntary cry of pain to break from her throat.

'You have been told to keep silent,' the male voice hissed.

She heard Eadulf let forth an exclamation of anger in his own language. There was another movement, a thud, and Eadulf seemed to have fallen to the ground.

'A sword thrust for the next one who thinks they can argue,' the first voice said heavily.

Fidelma realised they were in the hands of someone who did not care for the law. It did not signify that a Brehon or a *dálaigh*, even an *Aigne*, or any 'giver of judgements' stood neutral in these attackers' eyes. Lawyers were usually protected by their high *enech*, or honour price, and that honour price would be higher still in Fidelma's case, she being the sister to the King of Muman. Usually no one would dare to find themselves having to pay the lawgiver's honour price, on which they would also lose their own honour price. At worst they would become a *daer-fuidhir*, a non-freeman, losing all rights of society and ensuring descendants would also lose all rights for three generations. Truly, it seemed that these captors, whoever they were, did not care about risking such penalties.

'Stand perfectly still,' the leader's voice came again. 'We will put blindfolds on you to stop you being placed in harm's way. Do not try to remove them.'

Fidelma was about to ask how they could even attempt to do so when they had their hands pinioned behind them, but she thought better of it. Perhaps the best way forward was simply to be passive and compliant until they knew more about their captors and the reason for their abduction.

'Excellent,' came the voice after the blindfolds had been fixed. 'You will now be assisted back on your ponies. My men will lead your ponies so make no interference. We will be travelling only a short distance. Whether the journey is hard or easy obviously depends on your behaviour. I advise you to make the journey easy.'

There was a brief pause. The leader probably gave a signal because the ponies began to move forward. Fidelma had to move a little to adjust her weight on the animal and she uttered a silent prayer that Eadulf, with his lack of skill in horse riding, would not slip off. After the warnings they had been given, there was little need to postulate what would be their punishment.

Instead, Fidelma fell to spending her energies on seeing if she could estimate the direction and distance they were going. She had known they had been facing west when they started out along the track, but the track was now bending northward, ascending but still following the path of the river. She could still hear the faint murmuring of the waters as it moved downstream.

She wondered whether they were still on the path towards the homestead of Conmhaol until she remembered Conmhaol was said to dwell in a *crannóg* and that meant a lake or marsh. Could these be Conmhaol's men? But why would they suddenly abduct Fidelma and her companions, and with threats of violence? None of this made sense.

Prevented from examining the sky, they had no means of estimating the passing of the day. It seemed a long ride. Neither could they discern anything from their captors, whose silence was absolute. After a while Fidelma guessed that they had moved off the main track by a change in the sounds of the ponies' hoofs on what had been a stony surface to the soft thud on earth. Fidelma guessed that they were still moving in the north-north-westerly direction, and climbing, from the angle of their mounts. She thought they were nearing the source of the River of Omens, the Tuairigh, for the sound of the waters had become more like the splashing of waterfalls. She wished she knew more about the topography of the Uí Liatháin territory. When her old teacher and mentor, Brother Conchuir, had tried to teach her the hill lore, she had not thought it worth remembering much except how the five main highways linked the Five Kingdoms to the seat of the High King at Tara in the Middle Kingdom.

It helped her to pass the interminable journey by trying to remember all the seven classes of highways listed in the ancient laws. Then she tried to be practical. She realised that they had been travelling on what had become a small track, more for the use of farmers herding their stock, and that the way continued to rise upwards into the hills. She was just thinking it was no use giving herself a headache trying to work out the route when she felt their captors halting their mounts.

She sensed that they had pulled up in some enclosure. The smells reminded her of stables: the confined smell of horses, of wet straw that had not yet been cleared away, of the stink of animal dung and other odours.

'You will be helped to dismount,' came the voice of the leader. 'The same rules apply. Your blindfolds will stay fastened. Any attempt to see or speak will be met with serious consequences. You will then be taken from this place to a secure cell.'

Strong arms were tugging at Fidelma and she allowed herself to be almost dragged from her pony without resistance and set on her feet. Then she was being guided and propelled forward. Simply from the smells and the touch of her feet on the ground she realised that she was being led from the stable yard into a rocky outside courtyard. She was guided across this courtyard to a door and, at once, she found her footfall echoing on wooden boards.

'You will be guided down a flight of wooden steps,' the voice said close to her ear. 'They will be counted and there will be two sets of nine steps. Remember that so that you may descend safely.'

The hands guided her forward and a voice counted close by.

It seemed easier than she had thought. She was aware that as they descended, the air was becoming colder. They had descended into some underground chamber: some sort of cave or dungeon. They halted momentarily at the bottom of the steps. Then she knew she was being led from the steps into another area, which was colder still and which she imagined was a smaller cave.

'Sit here!' said the commanding voice, its owner almost pushing her down on to a wooden seat. 'Stay there.'

Her now attuned ear picked out footsteps crossing a stone floor, followed by a squeaky sound and a thud. It was a door being swung shut. Then there was silence – although not quite complete silence. Head to one side, she thought she heard the sounds of breathing, a deeper breath than usual as if the person was unused to breathing the colder air.

Fidelma decided to take a chance.

'Is there anyone here?' she demanded.

At once she heard the combined voices of Eadulf and Dego nearby.

'Lady, we are nearby, but blindfolded and tied. How about you?'

'I am here and in the same condition. I think our captors have left us for the moment.'

'Can anyone get these blindfolds off so that we can at least see?' came Eadulf's voice.

'Hard to reach with our hands tied behind our backs,' Fidelma replied.

'Could anyone work out where we are?' Eadulf asked.

'We are certainly in a dungeon,' Fidelma replied, trying to flex her wrists to see if there was any play of movement, but without success. 'I would guess that we are in some fortress. I think we followed the river for a while but north; north up into the hills.'

'I would agree,' Dego joined in. 'Had it not been suggested that Conmhaol's homestead was just a *crannóg* built on a raised section of land like an island in those marshy lands, I would have guessed this might be his fortress. Who else would want to abduct us and incarcerate us in a cave?'

Fidelma was more concerned with judging where Dego was in relation to her. The voice sounded suddenly close to her, almost making her jump at the unexpected proximity.

'Stay still, lady,' his voice sounded. 'I think I can judge enough to remove your blindfold.'

A moment later the cloth that was bound round her eyes was loosened and removed. She sat blinking in an attempt to adjust her sight. She finally peered round the semi-gloom of a large dark cavern in which a flickering lantern was burning to one side. It was on a shelf placed near a wooden door, which seemed reinforced with rusting metal.

'At least they have left us a lantern, even if they thought we would not benefit by it,' Fidelma smiled grimly. 'And the lantern is flickering. That shows us there is some air down here.'

She turned and noticed Dego's good hand was free.

'By what trick did you pull that off?' she wondered.

'No trick, lady,' the warrior replied with a smile. 'It is just that men used to tying hands or wrists together are not as expert at binding someone with one wrist rather than two. I could have taken off the blindfold while we were riding, but I thought it better to wait for the opportunity to release you both. All I had to do was snap my trouser clasp and use my teeth to unloose the knot on the rope.'

'You had a good strategy, except we still have both wrists tied tightly behind our backs,' Eadulf said. 'So can you get my blindfold off?'

Dego did so with a confident grin. Then he bent down, rolling up the leg of his trousers and extracting from a small sheath, strapped to his lower leg, a sharp little dagger. It was short work to sever their wrist bonds. Then they stood massaging their wrists, examining their prison. Dego was the first to check the single door into the cave, finding, as they had all suspected, that it was locked and strongly built.

While Fidelma was sitting rubbing the red welts on her wrists, where they had been too tightly bound, Dego began examining the darker corners of their prison.

'It is not some man-made chamber,' he observed.

'Is it a natural cave?' Eadulf said, peering around. 'Are there any other means of egress?'

'I have seen the *úama*, the natural caves in the north of this territory. This is of the same configuration,' Dego replied. 'It is said the Uí Liatháin territory is replete with cave systems. I saw one that some claimed the River Bríd flowed through. Some of the caves are amazing, holding the bones of ancient animals as well as signs that our long-ago ancestors dwelt in them.'

'Whatever the interest in this cave,' Fidelma announced coldly, 'I suggest our attention would be more happily engaged if we can discover a way out of it rather than admiring it.'

'True enough,' Eadulf agreed. 'We can admire the cave after we find a means of escaping from it.' He had made the comment with irony and regretted it after a moment. 'I meant that many of these caves have side chambers and passageways and we might find a way out of here,' he added.

Dego, noticing Fidelma's flush of annoyance, decided to smooth things over.

'I think we must be careful. Waters do flow through caves like this, although I expect this to be fairly dry if it has been used domestically. It depends what fort is built on top of us. At least we felt that we were led up a hill or a mountain so there should be little chance of flood water.'

In fact, from one corner of the cave Fidelma was sure she could hear a soft dripping sound. The limestone had a porosity and there were traces of where the underground waters had once run and maybe still were running. The main chamber in which they were imprisoned was fairly dry. She realised that whatever search they made would not be conclusive and that many cave groups had been hewn over centuries by water courses eating through the limestone.

'Then let us feel the walls first for any dampness,' Fidelma suggested. 'At the same time we can see if there are any hidden passages in the walls.'

'I would doubt it, as they meant to imprison us here,' Eadulf said with a pessimistic sigh.

Fidelma ignored him.

'If you find any tunnels, do not attempt to go along them until we have finished checking the walls for signs of water that might indicate contact with a river or stream.'

'At least we have had practice in escaping from caves,' Eadulf shrugged.

'This is probably not going to be so easy,' Fidelma replied irritably. 'So I suggest we get started now.'

By the time they had finished they were unsure how long they had been incarcerated in the dark and cold cave. All they had to show for their efforts were chilliness and utter exhaustion.

Eadulf sat back on his stool with his head resting against the rocky side of the cave.

'Do you think they will allow us food and drink?' he suddenly asked. 'Do they mean to starve us or are we to die of thirst?'

'Without knowing who they are, nor the purpose for which they have abducted us, I can make no prediction as to what they will do,' Fidelma sniffed.

'Maybe it is all a mistake,' Dego offered. 'I mean, maybe they were a group of brigands who were just looking for captives to collect ransom on and we just happened to be in the wrong place at the wrong time.'

'I am sorry to disappoint you, Dego,' she replied in a flat tone. 'You have obviously forgotten that when I tried to tell them who we were, their leader knew exactly. It was no mistake.'

'If it was Brother Scatánach's work, he must have warned them that we would be coming along that track,' Eadulf said.

'More likely than not.' Fidelma was feeling exasperated.

'This is a strange land, this territory of the Uí Liatháin,' Eadulf grunted. 'I can't make sense out of anything so far.'

Fidelma did not even bother to respond. Had she done so they might have missed the quiet movement outside and then the rasping of a metal key being thrust in the lock of the door. The moment it became obvious, Eadulf was on his feet, moving to the door in a crouch-like movement. He turned down the lantern by the door to give them the element of surprise.

A harsh voice sounded through a crack in the door.

'You inside! The first person who comes through the door will be the first who dies. Understood?'

Fidelma glanced to where Dego and Eadulf had positioned themselves on each side of the doorway, ready for action once it opened. Whoever these guards were, they were professionals. She waved her companions back.

'We understand,' she called.

'Then the three of you will stand in front of the door so that you will all be seen when it is opened.' There was a pause.

Fidelma glanced at her companions and then called to gain time. 'We will try, but you have left us with our hands tied . . .'

There came raucous laughter from behind the door.

'Do you really think we would not realise that people with your intelligence would have found a way to loosen and remove your bonds? Or found a way to extinguish the light of the lantern, which we left for your comfort? I suggest you find a way of reigniting it, otherwise we will simply shoot our arrows into the darkness. We would not like to hurt or kill anyone when it can be avoided. All three of you should then be standing in the place indicated.'

Fidelma was surprised at the efficiency of their captors. She had not thought the extinguishing of the lantern would be a warning sign to anyone outside. She had merely thought, as had Eadulf, that it would give them a good advantage over those not adjusted to the darkness.

'I am waiting for your compliance,' came the voice.

'It will be as you ask,' she called. 'The light was extinguished but we have no means to reignite it.'

'Very well. When we enter the cavern you will be standing as instructed, hands held up to the level of your shoulders.'

A moment later the door swung open. Three men were outside, where lanterns had been lit. One was kneeling, two were standing. Each of them held a strung bow in his hand. The points of the arrows never wavered. The men were clad like warriors but their faces were covered in what looked like dark masks. There was no insignia on their clothing as there was with most professional warriors.

Having identified that the prisoners had obeyed, one of the men set aside his strung bow, reached to the lantern and, crouching so as not to impede the aim of the others, used his lantern to relight the one Eadulf had extinguished. Light illuminated the cave again. Then the two archers entered quickly, still covering their prisoners. It was all done with the careful timing of professional warriors.

'Stay still,' came a voice Fidelma recognised as the person who had led their capture.

This time another warrior, similarly dressed, emerged with a tray on which were jugs, mugs and something in a small sack. He set the tray down on one side before moving back to the door. The archers backed to the door and the next moment it was slammed shut. The prisoners were left alone again but the lit lamp remained.

Fidelma peered at what had been brought to them.

'It looks as though they heard you, Eadulf. At least they plan to feed us, and there is water here.'

There were bannocks, cheeses, some cold meat and fruit with the jugs containing water and cider.

'So we are clearly prisoners of someone who wants to keep his captives healthy,' Dego observed cynically, regarding the food and drink.

'But for what purpose?' Fidelma asked moodily.

When they had eaten, they tried to arrange themselves with some comfort, but there were only a few stools to sit on. There was not even somewhere to stretch comfortably for a short sleep.

They did not know how much time had passed before there was a noise at the cave door and then a familiar male voice called: 'The door is about to open. As before, stand together in front of the door with the light upon you and the same distance away from the door. Once again, any deviation will result in injury.'

Reluctantly, Fidelma and her companions rose and moved to the appointed spot.

Fidelma raised her voice to announce their compliance.

As before, there came the grating sound of a key being turned and the door swung open to reveal the three bowmen, bows once more strung and aimed. A moment passed – presumably the prisoners were quickly inspected. Then the voice was raised again in command.

'Fidelma of Cashel, walk slowly towards us. Keep your hands held away from your sides.'

Fidelma began to do so.

'Slowly, now!' snapped the voice.

She reached the door. Then one of the bowmen, having laid aside his weapon, grabbed her arm and pulled her quickly into the passage. The door was slammed shut behind her and the key grated in the lock. She could hear Eadulf and Dego cry out in protest. Around her the dark shapes of the warriors, who had lowered their bows and replaced their arrows in their quivers, closed around her with swords unsheathed. She was aware, from the distortions of the lantern light, that her captors were clad in black or dark grey robes, with scarf-like masks over their faces. A fourth man, similarly clad, seemed in charge.

'You will follow me, Fidelma of Cashel.' Once again Fidelma recognised the voice of their captor from the encounter on the track. 'Try not to be troublesome, as I know you can be. You will be escorted by my men, who will not hesitate to inflict injury on you.'

'You know the consequences if harm befalls either my companions or myself,' she returned.

'We have already discussed this matter, Fidelma of Cashel, and I have told you that it is of no consequence.'

He turned and led the way up the flights of wooden stairs. When they reached the top of the steps she could also see through the half-open door that it was almost dark outside. She made a quick calculation. They had been taken prisoner before midday. Allowing for the ride to this place, they had been prisoners for well over a *cadar*. A day was divided by four *cadars*, the first being reckoned from midnight, while the third was from midday.

'We must be moving towards the middle of the fourth *cadar*,' she remarked.

It was warriors who usually split the day into such a measure. The man leading with the lantern paused, twisting his mouth in a smile.

'So you count the periods of the day as warriors do?' he asked. 'Well, as you have eyes, I can confirm we are not far from the end of the fourth *cadar*.'

'Where are you taking me?'

'You will see.'

'I understand you will not tell me where we are or who you are. It would be good if I knew why I and my companions are prisoners.'

There was still no response.

It was clear to her that she was wasting breath so she fell silent. Moonlight lit the stone-flagged courtyard, a bright moon having emerged from the shelter of the clouds. Parts of the walls of the surrounding buildings were stone blocked, including one tower, while most of the interior buildings and some of the perimeter walls were of thick oak. Fidelma wished it was fully daylight as she sensed that this fortress was built on the brow or summit of some hill or mountain. She would not know a name, of course, but the scenery might indicate where she was. Even as the wish occurred in her mind, they had crossed to a door on the far side of the courtyard. Her guide halted, raised the pommel of his sword and hammered three times on the wood. It was opened and Fidelma followed her guide inside. She was aware of two guards behind her and realised the other guard had remained outside.

Fidelma's guide put down his lantern on a nearby table. Fidelma found herself in an oblong stone room with a fire at one end. The room was also lit by a couple of lanterns. The interesting thing for her was that, apart from the central log fire built in a raised stone hearth, so that one could sit around it, the only furniture in the room was a stout carved wooden chair placed to one side of the fireplace. She had often seen even members of middle nobility using such carved chairs of office.

'Am I not to be seated?' she asked humorously, seeing she had no choice but to stand.

'You will stand,' returned the taciturn guide, who had taken up a position, standing with legs apart, keeping his sword held across his chest. His eyes watched her unblinkingly.

'For what are we waiting?' she asked, trying to sound bored to provoke him.

'For instruction to do otherwise,' he almost snarled.

It was not long before she felt a cold draught of air followed by the sound of a door opening and closing. For a moment or two the flickering flames of the fire blocked her vision as a figure entered on the far side of the fireplace. It was a lithe figure of no great height.

Fidelma frowned, trying to focus on the detail of the newcomer.

The person was dressed entirely in grey. Although the grey

robe distorted the outline of the wearer, it was obvious by the height, carriage and movement that the person could not have been more than a youth. Fidelma found the incongruous thought coming to her that, in spite of the distortions of the robes, the graceful movement showed the figure could excel as a dancer. She realised it could be equally a girl or a boy behind the robes. There was no clue as the figure sat in the chair.

Then she saw a second figure had emerged out of the shadows to stand in the light of the lanterns and flickering of the fire. This was an elderly male figure with long hair and a shaggy beard.

'You are welcome to this place, Fidelma of the Eóghanacht,' came the elderly man's cheerful voice. 'Even though I warned you against coming.'

Fidelma had been surprised by many things in her life so she was able to disguise her astonishment at the identity of the man that greeted her.

'Scannail the Contentious,' she acknowledged solemnly. 'We meet again.'

Chapter Thirteen

'We have been expecting you.' The amusement in the *sean-chaidh*'s voice was apparent.

'But you felt it necessary to have me and my companions forcibly abducted?' Fidelma replied cynically. 'I did not realise you were so keen to renew our acquaintance. I thought you were trying to dissuade us from coming here when I last saw you. You had only to invite us rather than abduct us.'

'There were special circumstances that required it,' Scannail responded, not changing his bantering tone.

'Special circumstances?' she asked sarcastically. 'There are special laws against harming a *dálaigh* and their party.'

'Not if it was to save your life,' the old man replied easily.

Fidelma was not expecting this and could not think of an adequate response for the moment.

'I was hoping my warning was enough for you to avoid these dark forests and hills. Perhaps I made it too subtle?'

'It was obvious that you did not want me to come looking for Conmhaol,' she replied, summoning her amused tone.

'I was hoping you would accept matters as they were and return to Cashel.'

'How could I do that?' she asked.

'I told you something about Brocc and of the animosity that

was felt in this territory. I was hoping that you would accept that and make no further inquiries.'

'If you thought that I would end matters there, you know little about me and much less about the duties of an advocate of the Brehon courts.'

'Probably not. I was hoping that it was sufficient for you to accept that Brocc made enemies, and anyone of the many he had antagonised could have killed him. You showed resilience in finding transport and a guide to this place . . . That silly boy Scatánach gave himself more importance than he merited in reality. We heard that you had reached the *Bróinbherg*. Íccaid is a good man but a worried man.'

'Worried? About what?'

'About you and the intentions of Cashel. He is of the family council of Brocc. Ironically, he is on your side, lady, if sides must be chosen.'

'I am confused. So what side have you chosen? From our last conversation, I gather you have little respect either for the Eóghanacht, who rule this territory, or for the New Faith. Where does your allegiance lie?'

'Always to the Uí Liatháin, my people. They, and they alone, should rule here.'

Fidelma looked around as if changing the subject. 'I have deduced that this is not the homestead of Conmhaol, where we were heading. So where is this?'

'You are at Cnoc an bhFúath, the Hill of the Malevolent Spirits. More particularly, you are in the sanctuary of the sacred order of the Grey One.'

'I presume that is not Cnoc an Fiagh, Hill of the Magic Mist? And this is the sanctuary of the Grey One?' She smiled towards the slim, seated, masked figure in grey. 'I should have guessed. So, I presume that you are called Líadan, the Grey One?'

The figure in grey did not move even a fraction.

'The order is sworn to silence except when making pronouncements of the *imbas forosnai*,' Scannail told her.

'Very convenient,' Fidelma replied cynically. 'Your lady in
grey can announce the prophecy of the death of Brocc but cannot
answer the simple questions of a *dálaigh*. In being so accurate
about foretelling his death, she places herself as first suspect in
his murder and you are an accomplice. Will she speak now?'

'You are the one to answer questions, lady,' Scannail responded
sharply. 'You are an Eóghanacht and came into our territory at
Brocc's invitation. Brocc betrayed his family and countrymen.
We are still wary of your purpose, in spite of your visit to Princess Lalóg. What did you expect of Conmhaol?'

'Our purpose, as you well know, is to find out by whom and
why Brocc was murdered. We are here to ask questions under the
law that prevails in all Five Kingdoms. Our questions have led us
to seek out Conmhaol. You find this dangerous? We are told that
he had no quarrel with Dair Inis and that he sends for Brother
Fisecda, their physician, to treat him when he is ill. This requires
answers to questions.'

'Perhaps, perhaps not. Conmhaol is one who would prefer to
spend most of his time playing *fidchell* – wooden wisdom –
hunting or feasting than undertaking statecraft.'

'Then who are we supposed to be in danger from that we need
you to abduct us?'

'We were hoping you would be in no danger at all. Had you
given up this quest, accepted my word and not decided to come
into this territory you might not have encountered any dangers.
But you are an Eóghanacht. By ignoring my warning, you could
encounter people who might want to prevent you from discovering who is responsible for Brocc's death. So we contrived your
abduction.'

'Contrived? This is the second time that you have intimated
that you took us prisoner to prevent us falling into others' hands.'

'To save you from danger,' repeated the old man.

'What seems real to us is that you are the one intent on endangering us. Are we locked in your dungeon or not? And this "sacred order" . . .?'

'They are real and they have existed since the time before time. From the time when people listened to and trembled at the voices of the Children of Dana. Under the blessing of the Mother of the Gods, they exist for good, not for evil. It was good that Brocc was slain, for he denied the blood of Tigerna Cosraigib, the great prince, which coursed in his veins.'

'That I cannot understand,' Fidelma declared, 'because all I have heard so far is riddles in answer to my questions.'

'Then let me say, we shall keep you safe but as prisoners. It will be temporarily until the immediate danger is past.'

'Once again your words raise more questions than answers.'

'Then it is my regret that they cannot be answered at this time.'

'Your regret is more than shared by me, Scannail. I believe in our law and in the basis of it. I have a rank as an attorney and my brother is King of Muman. I do not believe I am greater than the law. The law is greater than both of us. Greater than even a young girl disguised in grey robes.' She glanced to the seated figure. 'The law shows that, as I am a representative of it, I should be respected in accordance to it. You have committed a crime by incarcerating me, my husband and my bodyguard, Dego. Soon the Council of Brehons and the Warriors of the Golden Collar will be alerted to our disappearance. Several times I have warned of the consequences.'

The old man was shaking his head, still smiling.

'Then we must end this meeting with regrets, Fidelma of Cashel. The regrets are not for our parting, but for our inability to satisfy you with explanations on your misconceptions. Otherwise we might have been able to offer you a more comfortable accommodation. Be assured that you will be released at the moment a solution to our crisis is reached. Until then, your security is our paramount concern. So we must take care of you as best we can.'

Whether it was at some quick signal or other means, the silent figure in grey rose in one lithe movement. Scannail made a sign to the guard who had been standing behind Fidelma. A tap on the arm and she found herself being propelled forward out into the dark courtyard and across to the door that led down the steps to the cave-like dungeon.

As soon as the iron-studded door was closed and locked behind her, she was showered with questions by Eadulf, while Dego sat mostly in silence, trying to follow the account of her curious meeting with Scannail and 'the Grey One'.

'It sounds nonsensical,' Eadulf commented when she had finished. 'There is no logic in it. If Brocc was some sort of local warlord then one could accept some people had risen up against him. But he was Abbot of Dair Inis and one who outwardly accepted paying tribute to your brother and Cashel, unlike the views of that pagan Scannail. This so-called Grey Lady was there and Scannail seemed in service to her. We know she was the one who prophesied Brocc's death and, as you said, by being so accurate, it seems obvious she was in league with his killers. So how can he claim they want to protect us from those who killed Brocc by abducting us?'

Fidelma shrugged. 'The trouble is that Scannail has intimated various things but not made the story clear. He talks in conundrums that seem to have no answers. I don't believe anything he says. And what of young Brother Scatánach? Mention was made of him but not of his being captive. So where is he?'

'If we are to take Scannail's word, we are going to be prisoners here indefinitely.' Eadulf was shaking his head. 'What does he mean, that we can only be released when this crisis is cleared up? What crisis and how does it involve the murder of Brocc?'

'The questions seem to multiply instead of lessening,' Fidelma sighed.

PROPHET OF BLOOD

'How will the crisis be resolved?' Dego finally broke his silence. He had clearly been listening attentively. 'Didn't this Scannail say we would be kept prisoners temporarily until the immediate danger passed? What immediate danger is there?'

'The answer to that is the root of this mystery,' Fidelma replied. 'Whatever the mystery is. I have tried to push it to the back of my mind as it is pointless to speculate without facts. How have we not been able to gather sufficient facts? Usually, when I am asked to investigate, there is a mystery and questions are asked and answered. From that an explanation emerges. In this case, I don't know what the mystery is because it seems that Brocc's death is not it.'

Eadulf, too, sighed. 'Well, I thought the mystery was the murder of Brocc. So let us at least consider what we know about that.' He paused with a rueful smile. 'After all, we have the time to fill.'

'Very well,' Fidelma agreed. 'We were in Lios Mór when Eachdae the wagoner arrived and told us that Abbot Brocc wanted to consult with us. Why?'

'Because you had seen Brocc at the peace negotiations?' Eadulf suggested.

'Let's reconsider that. Six months ago, there was a combined conspiracy against my brother, Colgú,' Fidelma replied. 'The conspiracy collapsed. Aincride, widow of the Prince of the Áine, who was killed in the battle of Cnoc Áine, and her son, Elodach, plotted to overthrow my brother. Among the discontents they recruited was Selbach, Prince of Raithlinn, whose territory is on the northern border of the Uí Liatháin; Tigerna Cosraigib, Prince of the Uí Liatháin; and Prince Cummasach of the Déisi.

'The conspiracy was overthrown. Aincride and Elodach were killed. Selbach and Cummasach surrendered. Tigerna Cosraigib was killed in a last skirmish and there was no formal surrender of the Uí Liatháin as no successor became their leader. Only Brocc,

207

as Abbot of Dair Inis and one of the negotiators, came to make peace along with his steward, Brother Guala. I did not know he was a son of Prince Tigerna Cosraigib. I remember seven of the conspirators' warships were allowed to anchor off Dair Inis, waiting for the word to the attack Cashel. Abbot Brocc denied culpability. I supposed he sent to ask for my advice on treaties because he accepted my reputation as an advocate of the courts and legal adviser to Colgú.'

'But when we reached Dair Inis,' Eadulf continued, 'we found Brocc dead. He had told no one of our coming. Intriguingly, everyone said he had met with some local soothsayer a week before, who had foretold his death to the very day. The soothsayer is now identified to us as a prophetess called "the Grey One". We now appear to be her prisoners. In spite of what we have been told, we feel this is to prevent us discovering who killed Abbot Brocc.'

'It is intriguing that the Abbey seemed to hide that Brocc, as a son to Tigerna Cosraigib, was of a noble family, raised in the Old Faith. That he had converted to the New Faith; that his brother, Conmhaol, had refused to fulfil his father's role as leader of his people, and that Brocc's sister was Lalóg,' Eadulf said.

'There is something else,' Dego frowned. 'You spoke of Aincride and her family. When she took her own life at Cashel, do you remember, it was said she was an observer of omens. So she, too, was of the Old Faith and was hailed as a *celamine,* one who knows the prophecies. Doesn't that point to the fact she would have had an alliance here? Her allies might be plotting some revenge on your brother, Colgú.'

'That is a point,' Eadulf nodded thoughtfully. 'There might be a connection with the prophetess, this Grey One, who foretold Brocc's death. So, you saw this Grey Lady just now, with Scannail as her intermediary. That seems to solve the problem of Brocc's death. She was involved, if not the killer.'

PROPbET OF BLOOD

'From my perspective, however, it is not irrefutable evidence that this Grey One, or even Scannail, were the actual killers of Brocc.'

'But the circumstances are—' Eadulf began to protest.

'*Ainfiadnaise!*' Fidelma interrupted, using the legal word that meant 'unproven'. 'Contentions have to be proved by evidence that cannot be challenged. From what we have learnt so far, what do we really know?'

'We could surmise that, in spite of the treaties, the acceptance of your brother Colgú as the King of all Muman, there is still some discontent among the nobles of the Uí Liatháin, who resent paying tribute to Cashel,' Eadulf said. 'That's nothing new. There is usually one person behind the discord. One or other of these nobles who are the *derbhfine*, who appoint the new leader of their people, did not want anyone seeking peace with Cashel.'

'I think we know who always seems to be the hidden instigator of such unrest,' Dego pointed out. 'There is someone who always seems to instigate discord among the peoples of this territory.'

'You mean the King of Laigin?' Eadulf gave a resigned grimace, acknowledging the many times the king of their eastern neighbours had been involved in trying to annex parts of Muman. 'Yet somehow I can't see Fianamail reaching this far into our kingdom. His efforts have usually been to try to seize Osraige or obtain a passage through it. I don't think he will do so now that the Chief Brehon has imposed the cattle tribute as punishment for Laigin's last attempt to interfere with Osraige, using that border-land to foment rebellion against Cashel.'

Fidelma was deep in thought for a moment. 'That seems logical. The fact that the High King intervened in support of the defence of Colgú's kingdom has left Fianamail and Laigin in a poor state. I think what is going on here is more internal to Muman. Yet there does seem something different to this mystery.'

'Different?' Dego queried.

'I can't put my finger on this feeling I have,' Fidelma admitted.

There was a silence and then Eadulf said: 'So what now? How can we tackle this mystery when we don't know what it is?'

'Scannail and his so-called Grey One have confused us. If we can find a way out of here, I think we should continue to find this Conmhaol. I have a feeling that the solution to the mystery lies with the family council.'

'Do you think that Abbot Brocc was killed because he was brother to Conmhaol?' Dego suggested.

'All I am suggesting is that we could find out more by confronting Conmhaol. But, remember, he refused to take the role of Prince of the Uí Liatháin and that decision in itself seems to play an important part in whatever is happening here.'

'I agree with the idea to progress the inquiry in this fashion except for one minor problem,' Eadulf said.

'Which is . . . what?' Fidelma asked. 'You have an objection to the plan?'

'An easy objection,' Eadulf replied drily. 'Before we pursue our journey in search of Conmhaol, we have to find a way out of this dungeon.'

There was a moment of silence before Fidelma chuckled.

'I can accept that as a valid objection.'

'Nonetheless, it is a fact,' Dego agreed. 'We have already searched the walls of this cave and the only way out is through the door.'

'We searched the walls in semi-darkness and by hand,' Fidelma pointed out. 'The guards left us a second lantern when they brought the food. Maybe using both lanterns we could search again and have more luck?'

'But the oil in one of them is almost gone and I doubt if the other would last much longer,' Dego objected.

'Then we must get the guards to replenish the lanterns.'

Before they answered, she moved to the door and shouted, 'Is anyone there?'

To her surprise a male voice answered immediately.

'What is it?'

Fidelma looked at her companions and pulled a face.

'We need blankets for the cold and oil for the lamp,' she shouted back.

There was a suppressed exclamation.

'Why?'

'Because, if we are spending a night in this cave, it will be very cold and we don't want to be plunged into darkness.'

There was a silence, then the voice shouted: 'Stand back from the door, as you did before. Stand in the light.'

It was lucky they decided to obey as the open door revealed the same order of bowmen covering them with strung weapons. As before, they were all clad in grey with veils across their faces. The centre bowman put down his weapon and turned to pick up a bundle of blankets from behind him, which he pushed into their prison.

'I was told to bring you some blankets as the temperatures sink at night,' the man said shortly. 'Oh, I am also instructed to remind you that the length of your stay here is in your hands. You have only to give Scannail the sacred *rattadh focal* and you can be allowed to go to more comfortable accommodation.'

'We are very willing to go to more comfortable accommodation,' Eadulf replied, not really understanding the term that meant giving one's word.

The guard smiled thinly. 'The conditions are known to the lady Fidelma. Are you saying that she agrees to those?'

'Scannail already knows that I will not betray my office for the sake of a comfortable bed,' Fidelma snapped.

'So be it.' The guard was about to turn away.

'One moment,' she called him back. 'It is cold and dark in this cave and the oil in the two lanterns we have is all but gone. We would appreciate it if the oil in the lanterns could be replenished.'

The guard hesitated.

'What harm would it do?' Fidelma asked persuasively. 'We will stay in this dark cave, but it would be better if we had light for . . . well, domestic matters.'

'For what?' The guard sounded bewildered.

Dego explained. 'We are, as you can see, two men and a woman. I do not believe you will have to think hard about the problems that might occur?'

The response was an irritable expletive in an effort to hide his embarrassment.

The man left the oak door with the bowmen still blocking the entrance, bows strung and aimed. He returned shortly with two lanterns, already lit, and, to their surprise, he reached in his waist bag, drew out a few candles and placed them together. Then he picked up the two old lamps.

Fidelma thanked him.

'In case, you have need of them,' he said almost indifferently, then: 'If you were wise, you would agree to Scannail's terms so that you could be accommodated as guests rather than as prisoners. Then you would have no need to rely on the goodwill of the guards. It needs only your surety.'

Fidelma paused for a moment, thinking there was something familiar about the voice of the man.

'Each person has to decide the price of the moral issues that confront them,' she replied. 'You obviously know well who I am, and that I have no choice but to confront Scannail with the law that he is supposed to obey whether he is of the Old Faith or the New Faith. By not obeying the law, he has to make an accommodation with his own conscience.'

The guard sighed, then turned and left. His companions pushed the door shut and the prisoners heard the rasp of the key again.

'So what now that we have light?' Eadulf asked. 'What was this *rattadh focal* – I have not heard of it – a surety or a promise?'

'More solemn,' Dego answered. 'It is from the word *rathaigecht* – parole.'

Fidelma interrupted. 'The first thing is to make doubly sure that this cave has no exits we may have missed previously in the dark. We each take a candle and see if we can find an opening.'

'Well, at least one of our captors seems to have compassion for our situation,' Eadulf said, taking one of the candles from Fidelma.

'What makes you think we have missed some opening?' Dego regarded the candle he was offered dubiously.

'You see that door, which we think is the only way in or out? It is fairly tight shut. You would think that it would exclude all fresh air.'

'I suppose it would,' Dego conceded.

'Do you remember how many steps we had to take going down the stairs to this level?'

'One of our captors said there were two sets of nine steps apiece, when he warned us to be careful.'

'That is correct and I counted them when I was taken up to the courtyard. This means we are probably ten metres below ground level. With that door closed there must be some other way of obtaining breathable air down here.'

'Perhaps there is only a short air passage or just a way that a small amount of air can recycle into the cave?' Eadulf was pessimistic.

'The flame flickers and dances this way and that. I would say that a substantial amount of air must feed it to keep the flame moving,' Dego replied, realising what she was suggesting.

'We take a flickering candle and follow it to the source of the air current,' Eadulf agreed.

'So our first task is a close examination of the cave to check the location of any passages of air,' she confirmed.

They dispersed to various points of the cave. If nothing else their efforts confirmed that this was a curious, almost oblong cave with only one very small chamber, so low there was hardly room for anyone to stand upright. A sniff and intake of breath gave them a clue as to what it had been used for. Dego held the candle up but there was no significant change to the dancing of the flame to indicate an air current. After a long period of search, in which they came across two or three places where it seemed air permeated into the cave, they realised none of these places would constitute an exit. Obviously, when this fortress had first been erected, the cave had been purposely chosen as the ideal prison. Once they realised this, they moved to the warmer area near the door and sat down. There was little else to do.

'What's the plan now?' Dego's voice sounded morose.

'We probably are not able to do anything unless our guards make a slip, and even if we get by them, we have to climb up those steps into the courtyard,' Eadulf sighed. 'There will be guards there, no doubt. We don't know how many and whether we can access our ponies. It looks pretty hopeless.'

Faced with the inevitable, they took the blankets the guard had brought and they made themselves as comfortable as possible. It was not long before sleep came unwillingly to them.

When Fidelma heard the door being unlocked she thought she had been asleep for ages but she could only have been dozing. She blinked and focused on the solitary figure in the doorway. He was masked, as the guards before him, and dressed in the grey robes of a warrior.

'What is it?' she demanded, quite forgetting that here was an opportunity because the man did not have the usual back-up of archers. Nor did there appear to be anyone with him.

'Keep calm. I mean you no harm,' the figure replied. 'You must come with me immediately.'

By now Eadulf and Dego were stirring.

'Keep calm, I say!' the figure hissed. 'I have fed and saddled your ponies. Your saddle bags are ready, even with Brother Eadulf's doctor's bag. The ponies are in the stables at the back of the courtyard. The other guards are still asleep. If you are quiet, you should be able to lead the ponies away before you mount so that you are not heard. Judge your distance before you mount and you can be well free of this place by the time the sun has risen.'

'Where are your comrades and their bows and arrows?' demanded Fidelma, suspiciously. 'Are they waiting outside for us to walk into a trap?'

'They are not. I am placed on watch during the night. They are all asleep. I had to wait until now before I could move.'

'Who are you and why are you doing this?' she demanded again.

'There is no time to discuss my motivations now. You must move quickly before things are discovered.'

'If we are now placing our lives and freedom in your hands then we must know who you are and your motivation.'

The masked man made a noise expressing frustration.

'I am merely taking you to the stables where you will find the ponies and your bags. After that, your welfare is up to you. You need not know any more.'

Dego had risen and been listening with his head to one side in an attitude of concentration.

'I have heard your voice before,' he said in slow reflection.

'We do not have time for this,' the mysterious guard replied in anger. 'It will soon be daylight and time for others to come on duty. The opportunity will be lost. You must be away from this fortress by then.'

Fidelma, like Dego, had been listening to the familiar resonance of the voice, including the particularly strong note of command in the man's tone. Recognition came flooding into her mind.

'You don't have to disguise yourself any longer, unless it is by choice that you hide among these Grey Ones, or whatever they call themselves. We recognise you, Caol, son of Cóelub, one time commander of the Warriors of the Golden Collar.'

Chapter fourteen

The grey-clad man's shoulders sank and he let out a long low breath.

'I am he, lady,' he acknowledged.

'I thought I recognised your voice,' Fidelma said. 'What are you doing here?'

'A long story, lady. Too long to keep us here. You should leave now while you have time before the other guards are awakened.'

'Caol, you resigned from the King's bodyguard two years ago, at the time of Cet Gaimrid, the first month of winter.' Dego was examining his former commander in astonishment.

'You resigned, as I recall, for what you felt was a moral issue,' Fidelma declared. 'When Colgú was attacked and badly wounded, you killed the would-be assassin. But there was something additional, some other reason you felt you had to resign your command of the bodyguard.'

Eadulf was also looking at the masked figure as he tried to remember the details.

'The assassin rushed on Colgú with a knife yelling, "Remember Liamun!" Liamun was a girl whom the assassin had been in love with. He was a confused man who thought that Colgú had been Liamun's secret lover and that he had been responsible for her death. But he was neither her lover nor responsible for her death. It was all confusing.'

There was an astonished silence as Caol removed the grey mask from his face.

'I killed the assassin to protect Colgú. I also thought he was her lover,' the tall warrior said bitterly. 'The assassination was not as simple as an act by someone seeking revenge against the lover of a relative. It was Fidelma who discovered this. Fidelma had that uncanny ability to untie that twisted skein. Fidelma claimed that I had done nothing legally wrong. I felt otherwise, I acted for the wrong reason. I had committed a moral wrong and that's why I resigned and let Gorman be promoted to commander of the Warriors of the Golden Collar.'

'But what are you doing here?' Fidelma repeated.

'When I realised that you were the prisoners of the Grey One, I had to act. I suggest we move quickly before the other guards return and we are all discovered. For the sake of all you believe in, let us hurry to escape. Come with me to get your ponies.'

There was still some hesitation before Eadulf advised briskly: 'He is right, Fidelma. There are a million questions in the air, but I feel we must now avail ourselves of the route that Caol offers to escape.'

As Fidelma still hesitated, Caol's voice was almost pleading. 'Lady, I act in repayment of the kindness you showed me then. This is why I release you now.'

'I don't know what brings you into this company, Caol, but I know you. Your companions will know that you have released us. So you must come with us away from this place. We will find somewhere to halt and then you can tell us why you joined this group. Perhaps you will be able to explain something of what is happening in this strange territory.'

'That is my wish also, Caol,' Dego urged when the tall man

hesitated. 'We served well together over the years. We fought side by side at Cnoc Áine and so I trust you.'

Caol paused a moment with a look of appreciation at his former comrade.

'Having been disloyal to the Grey One, I will not be welcome here. I will have to leave anyway. I shall ride with you.'

With as little noise as possible, they moved out of the cave, Caol behind them carrying one of the lanterns. He halted to secure the iron-studied oak door and turn the key to lock it.

'It may take a while for them to open it and realise you are gone,' he explained. Then gesturing them to follow him, he went quietly up the wooden stairway. As he did so he unsheathed his sword in case they encountered his former comrades.

The courtyard was dark, although there were the flickering flames of a few torches attached to the walls of the far side. Without pause, Caol pressed into the shadows, moving along the nearside walls of the flagged courtyard, signalling them by hand to keep in a single file after him. Caol led them through a small stone archway, which was clearly connected with the place where many animals were kept. The distinct aroma of mules, goats, sheep and other livestock was evident. There were even several pigs somewhere. They could smell the animals long before the growing half-light of pre-dawn illuminated them as shadows.

'Be as quiet as possible,' Caol whispered, 'and try not to disturb the animals. Your ponies are tethered beyond that fence.'

'You are coming with us, remember?' Fidelma insisted, picking up on his exact words.

'Do not be concerned,' the warrior assured her. 'My horse is with yours anyway, as I did plan to leave.'

Carefully, they picked their way through the animal enclosure until they came to a wicker gate and silently passed through it. Beyond that, their ponies were tied, their saddle bags secured. Nearby was a stallion, obviously Caol's warhorse.

'Follow me in single file,' he told them. 'I know a track where we will not leave the signs of our passing and we can make it to a small place atop one of the hills. It would be the right place to hide out for a few days while a decision is made about what you want to do.'

When they had mounted, Caol led the way from the dark shadows of the fortress walls and along what felt like a muddy track down into the surrounding forests. After a distance, they picked up a small stream, which Caol turned along. Fidelma uttered silent thanks for the moorland ponies, which were sure footed in the muddy-bottomed stream, although Caol's warhorse was finding it difficult to keep its balance. However, she knew him to be a talented horseman and tracker as well as a skilled warrior, and that he was taking this difficult path to avoid any trackers and hounds finding out the route.

She had faith in and respect for Caol. She remembered well the day he had been promoted to the command of her brother's body-guard. He had replaced Capa at the time that the evil Uaman the Leper, Lord of the Passes, had kidnapped her baby son, and killed her nurse, Sárait who was Caol's wife. Poor Sárait had been sister to Capa's wife, Gobnait. After that tragedy, Capa had felt he should leave the bodyguard. Caol had become the steady hand, commanding the bodyguard until the incident of Liamun. During those years he had been a strong and steady leader of his élite warriors. She felt a curious sense of security to be riding once again behind his now grey-robed figure.

As the sun rose, they came to more level ground, and encoun-tered a spread of rocks over which the waters chattered. Caol halted his horse and swung round towards them. In the sunrise everything seemed bright and clean. Caol's features, devoid of the grey mask, were as relaxed and humorous as Fidelma remem-bered them to be. It seemed that he had not aged at all.

'We'll leave the stream here, cross by those rocks down into that other valley and then climb again through the woodlands on that far hill. It's a height surrounded by woods and one where I know we should be safe if the Grey Ones try to follow us.'

Fidelma knew that only Eadulf was feeling discomfiture with the ride through the stony hills, but his features were firmly set. He became more relaxed as they entered a terrain where their pathway led through woods. She could see that even Dego looked content, riding once again under the guidance of his old commander.

The descent down the rocky path was not so easy and Eadulf had the good sense to allow his pony its head so that the sure-footed animal relied on itself, which was better in the circumstances than a nervous rider.

It was mid-morning when they reached the forest-covered hill that Caol had pointed out. Fidelma realised that they must all be feeling hunger as they had not had anything to eat since the previous evening and the journey had been very tiring. Now it was way beyond time of the *longud,* or first meal.

'Any chance of pausing for a meal, Caol?' she called. 'That is, if we can find something.'

'Just over the brow of this hill, lady,' he replied confidently. 'Just through those woods in front of us, and I promise you one of the best meals that you'll taste.'

It seemed quite a time before they noticed the woods thinning and they realised they were on the brow of a hill looking across a series of small hills and valleys that stretched away in the distance. Caol abruptly halted and took out a small carved wooden whistle. He blew a short series of notes on it – a shrill *kee-kee-kee.* Fidelma knew it as the warning cry of a small bird of prey, the *pocaire gaoithe*, 'the wind frolicker', as it was called. It was usually a silent bird but now and then it gave a warning when possible danger approached its nest. This was the sound that Caol was making now. He sounded it only three times; but to whom was it a warning?

Suddenly an answering bird call came from further down the hill. Caol put his whistle away with a smile and then he was moving on at a slow amble down the slope through the trees. Fidelma caught Eadulf's puzzled gaze and allowed herself a slight shrug of bewilderment.

It was not very long before Caol led them out of the trees into a small clearing, like a large flat shelf. They immediately saw a wooden *bothán,* a hut, with an entire area fenced off by the side of it. In this enclosure were a number of cows, sheep, two goats and some chicken runs. At the back of this was a strong-looking colt that seemed by stature and colouring to have been bred from the stallion that Caol was riding. Nearby stood a stone drinking trough fed by waters that ran naturally down the hill. The astonishing thing to Fidelma's eyes was that smoke arose from a fire. The aroma of cooking food was inviting.

Suddenly they realised that a youth was standing nonchalantly at the door of the cabin. He was holding a longbow in his left hand and, in the same grasp, an arrow. A quiver of arrows hung from a leather strap over one shoulder.

'Cadan!' Caol greeted, swinging off his horse. The boy had dropped his bow and arrow and ran forward quickly to be embraced by Caol.

After a moment's hug, Caol pushed the boy gently back and shook his head sternly.

'Have I not taught you never to discard your weapons until you have made sure of the identity of those who accompany your father?'

The youth's cheeks coloured but he did not lose his broad grin. He looked swiftly round at them before bending to retrieve his dropped bow and discarded arrow.

'Sorry, Father. I observed the way you led them down the hill, and I heard your warning whistle. I saw your companions presented no danger. But I kept my bow ready until I made sure there was no danger. Anyway, I recognised your companions from the time when you were commander of the guard at Cashel.'

'It is still not a good thing to drop your weapons,' Caol admonished. He turned to his companions, who were now dismounting. 'This is my young son, Cadan. When I left the guards, we had purchased a farmstead near the banks of the Fruinseann, the ash river, in Gleann Iubhair. It's good for salmon and trout – so you can guess what plans I had.'

'Isn't that the territory of Finguine, my brother's heir apparent?' Fidelma asked as they dismounted. 'So what are you doing here in Uí Liatháin territory?'

At that moment an elderly woman appeared abruptly in the doorway of the *bothán*. Caol waved her forward. She was a small motherly figure with wrinkled features but a welcoming smile and bright blue eyes.

'This is Finnat, my cousin, and this is her *bothán*. She allows me and my son to stay here. While there are duties to perform, she keeps my son in food and drink.' Caol grinned and sniffed the air appreciatively. 'Didn't I promise a great meal? I smell it already.'

'You are all welcome.' The woman called Finnat encompassed them with a smile. 'The meal will not be long. You are welcome to sit and take cider while you wait.'

Caol glanced to his son. 'We will take the horses and unsaddle them. We'll bring the bags inside.' He turned to Fidelma and Eadulf. 'I must help with the beasts; they will not feed and water themselves. You go and help yourself to cider, for you will be dry after our ride. You are my guests and it would be a dishonour if I did not perform this service in welcoming you here.'

At once Dego drew himself up. 'I might have only one hand but I am not helpless, Caol. I did not become commander of the Golden Collar because of my good looks.'

Caol smiled and seemed to understand the attitude that incited Dego's offer.

'I simply thought you might not be rested enough after your adventures with the Grey Ones.'

'Which is what we must talk about,' Fidelma assured him.

Dego insisted on going with Cadan to help with the horses, rejecting even Eadulf's offer of help.

Finnat had bought out jugs of cider and water and some mugs to place on a table outside the *bothán*.

'I trust you will have an appetite,' she smiled at them.

'From the aromas from your *bothán*, Finnat,' Eadulf said, 'you will not need to concern yourself about our appetites.'

The woman left in a good mood.

'Finnat was a cousin to Sárait, my wife,' Caol explained as he poured the drinks. 'Since her death, she has helped me rear young Cadan.' He raised his drink, as if avoiding something he did not wish to remember. 'To the renewal of our friendship.'

Fidelma showed appreciation after taking a sip of the surprisingly cold liquid.

'Finnat keeps the jugs cold in the mountain stream,' Caol explained.

'You seem to imply that your grey-robed companions do not know of this place, nor would you wish them to do so. Is that so?' Fidelma asked after another sip.

'This is a special hidden place where only I come to meet my son when I have information for him to pass on. No one comes up this hill, and the homestead is concealed by woodland.'

'Information to pass on?' Eadulf frowned.

Caol held up his hand. 'I will explain, but in my own way.'

'Do your grey companions know who you are or were?' Eadulf pressed. 'I am sorry but I can't keep my thoughts to myself.'

'I will tell you this. They know that I was once commander of the guard at Cashel. That would have been hard for me to conceal. I have used the fact that I resigned from the bodyguard to enable me to join their fraternity. Other than that, they know little about me.'

'Then the next question is why have you joined them?' Fidelma asked. 'You are no Uí Liatháin.'

'It is a long story but it will be told,' Caol admitted with a sigh. 'If you say that we are safe here for the time being, then we will wait for the others to return. We will eat and then ask the questions.'

At that moment, Finnat reappeared from the *bothán*, wiping her hands on a cloth.

'The meal is ready. Call young Cadan and tell him to bring your other companion to the table,' she instructed, before returning inside.

Caol shouted for his son to bring Dego for the meal. A moment passed before the boy arrived, followed by Dego. He took a mug of cider and handed it to Dego before accepting one for himself.

Fidelma smiled as a memory struck her.

'I have just remembered how your son received his name,' she told Caol.

'I don't think I have told Cadan that story,' admitted the warrior.

'The name was chosen by your mother,' Fidelma confided to the boy. 'I knew her very well when she served as my attendant when I had my own little boy. She chose the name because of your father's profession.'

'Why so?' demanded the boy with interest.

'The name is ancient, meaning "a wild goose" – one that wanders around, giving alarms and attacking any predators,' Fidelma explained. 'It is oft times the name for wandering warriors.'

Caol was chuckling. 'You have an excellent memory, Fidelma.'

Dego nodded in approval. 'It is a good name to have. But I am interested in the strange, grey cult you have joined.'

'There are many stories to be told,' Caol returned shortly. 'We have agreed to talk of this when we go inside to eat. Ah, and there is Finnat, impatiently waving us to the table again.'

As they entered, they found themselves looking around the interior of the *bothán* in approval. It was larger than it appeared from the outside. They sat round a fair-sized table. There were dishes of preserved meats, such as salted venison; the traditional hard-boiled goose eggs; various cheeses, predominately goat's cheese; and toasted bannocks baked from acorn-nut flour. There were dishes of hazelnuts and berries and, inevitably, apples. But the main dish was the cooked venison whose aroma was infused with herbs.

'The venison is excellent,' Cadan pointed out. 'The lower forests are replete with deer herds.'

'Are you the bowman that brought it down?' Fidelma responded to the boy's enthusiasm.

'I had good luck that day,' Cadan replied modestly.

Some time later, after some prompting from Caol, Fidelma felt she had to tell the story of their capture in order to encourage him to tell his story. Caol responded with expressions of surprise: first at the news that Abbot Brocc had been murdered, then at the story of the prophecy by the woman in grey, and finally at Scannail's explanation as to why Fidelma and her companions had been captured and imprisoned.

'Now we come to your story, Caol. How did you come to be among those pagan warriors serving the Grey One and that curious bard Scannail the Contentious?' Eadulf asked when Fidelma had finished.

Caol sat back, took a deep draught of his cider and grimaced.

'I should make clear that I was not among the raiding party that abducted you. I did not know that you were the prisoners until I was sent last night to do guard duty and brought you extra blankets and light.'

'Caol, I know your values,' Fidelma replied. 'It doesn't make sense that you are serving as a mercenary with this strange group. Tell us how you came to serve this Grey One. What made you come into Uí Liatháin territory? I believe their hatred of the Eóghanacht is intense.'

There was a pause and then Caol replied: 'You are right, lady. There was always conflict between the princes of the five territories of Muman. After the battle at Cnoc Áine we thought all had been settled. Yet are rival ambitions ever settled? There is no need for me to conjure memories of Elodach, of Selbach and others engaged in one conspiracy after another. The Uí Fidgente were once our enemies but they have come to terms. The Déisi and the Uí Liatháin have shown they would seize any chance to break apart this kingdom. And they have been encouraged by the King of Laigin, who has often demonstrated that he would like to take over the princedom of the Osraige. All have tried to march on Cashel at one time or another.'

Fidelma made an impatient gesture with her hand. 'We know our history, Caol. But what has that to do with you serving in this strange group?'

'I have mentioned that when I left Cashel as a bodyguard, I returned with the idea of farming in Gleannúir, the Glen of the Yew. That is the territory of the heir apparent to your brother, Prince Finguine. Finguine feels guilty that he did not suspect his own cousin, Selbach, was acting in a conspiracy and encouraging insurrection among the Uí Liatháin.'

'That was discovered and dealt with. Finguine was absolved of complicity by my brother and the Brehon Council, so why does he feel guilty?' Fidelma asked.

'Finguine felt there were other matters still to be uncovered. He knew I had settled with my son in his territory. I just wanted to farm, but he made me an offer.'

Fidelma's brows rose a fraction. 'An offer for what?'

'Finguine knew my service well, and that I had served you in some of your inquiries. He also knew that I was acquainted with some of this area. As I said, my cousin, Finnat, dwells here. After the conspiracy six months ago, Finguine heard alarming stories from merchants. The arrogant prince Tigerna Cosraigib had been killed, but stories of plots and new conspiracies were being told. Finguine's proposition was that I should come into Uí Liatháin territory and begin to make inquiries. Finguine wanted to know if a continuing conspiracy was a reality and a threat to Cashel. There was much talk of prophecies to try to encourage the people with their hatred against Cashel.'

'Are you telling me that you are here serving the interests of Finguine? That you are some sort of informer for him?'

'I believe the heir apparent acts in the interests of your brother, the King, lady. I serve the interests of all Muman. I find the term "informer" distasteful.'

'I apologise,' Fidelma said. 'I was trying to seek the right term.'

'Perhaps *fer focsi,* a scout, might be appropriate.' The suggestion came from young Cadan, who had been listening with a frown.

Fidelma gave the boy an appreciative look. 'An appropriate word,' she agreed. 'And so?'

'I came with Cadan,' Caol continued. 'Finnat was once married to a man of the Uí Liatháin, who was now dead. This place in these mountains was ideal to have as a base. I settled here with Cadan and soon began to pick up on the stories of the Grey One, who made pronouncements on the coming freedom and greatness of the people. You have probably heard how popular these legends are among the Uí Liatháin, who seem so concerned about their destiny and ancient deities. Soon I learnt there was actually a group of Uí Liatháin nobles trying to raise the battle fever of their people by claiming to be the embodiment of the Grey Ones, who were destined to free their people and be as great as they had been before King Conall Corc gave half their territory to the Déisi.'

'So you joined these Grey Ones to find out more?'

'Just so,' Caol agreed. 'I confess that the prophecies were not something I took seriously. However, I pretended I belonged to some magical Druid order among my own people. As you know, this is a land of folklore, prophecies and all manner of mysticisms. I kept in touch with Finguine through my son, who takes reports back across the Great River to the Glen of the Yews – to Finguine's fortress at Gleannúir.'

'I cannot see you as a Druid, Caol,' Dego chuckled.

Fidelma silenced him with a motion of her hand.

'It was not soothsayers the Grey One wanted,' Caol replied seriously. 'They were satisfied with old Scannail the *seanchaidh* spreading his ancient nonsense. He visited them from time to time, mostly at the place where you were imprisoned. He seemed to be their spiritual adviser, if you could call it that. What I found surprising was they were trying to hire professional warriors as a bodyguard.'

'Why would you find that surprising?'

'You would think that such a movement would find many volunteers among the Uí Liatháin, although it was only a few months ago that their army was defeated and were forced to pay retribution to Cashel.'

'You have a point,' Fidelma agreed. 'So why recruit outsiders?'

'I think it was to force a change of power among the nobles and make another attack on Cashel. That's what Finguine suspected, but I found only a dozen men in the group. It seemed absurd.'

'It's certainly curious. But why did they let you into their midst?'

'They wanted me to train the few warriors they did have. I was able to entrench my position by saying that I had been forced to resign as commander of the King's bodyguard for some infringement. In my bitterness, I was looking for a way to put my talent as a mercenary to good use. I succeeded.'

'Until last night,' Eadulf reminded them.

'I would have left anyway. There was not much news to pass

back to Finguine. I did not think there was anything serious to report. It seemed all just a drama to try to encourage the people.'

'So what else did you find out about them?' Fidelma queried. 'Who is this Grey One, their leader? I was not even sure last night if it was a youth or a female, although Abbot Brocc described her as a girl.'

'That I did not know,' Caol confessed. 'Whenever there was a need to speak seriously to the followers, it was Scannail who acted as the main voice . . .'

'But Scannail could not always be there,' Fidelma pointed out.

'He was never far away. The main commander, the one who made you prisoners, was the one who gave military orders. The Grey One never spoke if she attended meetings.'

'Never?' Fidelma was surprised.

'Never.'

'Something must have been said about the purpose of the group.'

'The main message was repetitive and that was usually delivered by Scannail. It was a reiteration of some ancient prophecy: that the Uí Liatháin would rise up to claim their old territory again. Of course, this was often dressed up with stories of the origins of Liatháin, who was the eponymous founder of the people. There was much criticism of Prince Tigerna Cosraigib, killed in the conspiracy against your brother.'

'They criticised him?' Fidelma frowned.

'For his alliance with the Déisi, whom they called the old enemy.'

Fidelma was puzzled; it changed the pattern she thought had been emerging. She continued, 'But I have heard they did not support a successor.'

'That is the strange thing, lady. They seem to regard the Grey One as the leader of the people.'

'Yet from the silent leader, Scannail is the one who takes a lead. Who is the commander? The one who abducted us?'

'We just called him the *Cend Fedna* – the commander.'

'He seemed to be a professional warrior,' Dego muttered.

'I think he must have been a commander in the days of Tigerna Cosraigib. But he was only one.'

Fidelma glanced at Caol. 'It takes only one pair of hands to kill,' she said.

'That is true, lady,' Caol sighed. 'I made a point of identifying local leaders and nobles, and even tried to visit their forts to assess their fighting men. I pretended to be looking for work as a shield bearer or armed attendant. Most nobles had been reduced to poverty as punishment for Tigerna Cosraigib's ravages.'

The company was silent for a while. Finally Fidelma spoke.

'So the Grey One is not a force to be worried about? They were not working for any ambitious warlord?'

'Not that I could discover,' Caol agreed. 'In fact, the most violent thing that happened was when I discovered they had abducted you and I realised that I had to organise your escape.'

'Do you think Scannail is really the head of this mystic organisation? That the figure of the Grey One is only there as a threat or distraction.'

'Personally, I think Scannail likes the sound of his own voice. He is the storyteller who reminds people of the greatness of their semi-mythical ancestor Eochaidh Liatháin. Scannail is no military leader. Mind you, you don't need to be a military leader to command a score of ill-disciplined men. I confess I and the *Cend Fedna* were the best trained warriors there.'

'What of this *Cend Fedna*? Could he be the hidden power?'

'True, he has training, but as for being a noble with ambition for his people . . .' Caol grimaced, dismissing the idea. 'He was a follower, not a leader.'

'Did you ever visit Conmhaol?' Fidelma asked. 'We were on our way to see him when we were abducted. The stories about him are somewhat mixed.'

'I have encountered him once,' Caol acknowledged. 'Conmhaol is a man without ego or ambition. He runs a small homestead. It is a *crannóg* with a couple of attendants only. I know he says he rejected the Grey Ones. I think he just wants to be left alone. He has good relations with a physician called Fisecda, who is of the New Faith and I believe is related to him.'

'I would still like to meet him.' Fidelma was thoughtful. 'People who want to be left alone usually have something that they want to conceal.'

Eadulf grimaced. 'If I had a father like Tigerna Cosraigib, the notorious Lord of the Slaughter, I would not want to acknowledge him.'

ChAPTER FIFTEEN

They had all moved outside to sit in the afternoon sun, while Finnat cleared the remains of the meal. Fidelma was locked in thought for a time and it was left to Eadulf to reopen the conversation.

'You are thoroughly satisfied that the Grey Ones are not in a conspiracy against Cashel?'

'I don't see them constituting a serious threat with few poorly trained men,' Caol replied. 'They seem concerned with the Old Faith and their ancient past. They speak in terms of their supernatural beliefs and how they were once a strong people. Scannail, of course, would like people here to walk in fear and trembling of the ancient gods, but times are changing.'

'Yet there must be some specific purpose to them?'

'I think they are a limited threat. But now you tell me about the death of Abbot Brocc of Dair Inis and the Grey One appearing to foretell it. I cannot understand that. It is the first time I have heard of reality mixing with their supernatural confusion of teachings.'

'Would you say their aim was simply to discredit Tigerna Cosraigib's family from continuing as princes of the Uí Liatháin and to set up their own leaders, or are they working to empower a member of that family?'

Fidelma sat up abruptly.

'Now there is an idea and one that makes sense,' she commented. 'When we came to find Conmhaol, we met with resistance. Conmhaol was offered the princedom but refused to accept it. Could Lalóg now demand to be considered for election by the *derbhfine*? There is something she said that makes me suspicious.'

'Could Princess Lalóg be this Grey One?' Caol asked speculatively. 'I know that Conmhaol, in recent times, has often had visits from Brocc, Lalóg and other members of the family. When Conmhaol refused to take the leadership there was much talk of Brocc assuming the role. He went to Cashel immediately to negotiate and accept the demands for restitution that the people had to pay. He was certainly hated for that.'

'Lalóg is not the Grey One,' Fidelma demurred. 'She has entirely the wrong physique, for a start. Don't forget I saw this prophetess last night,'

'But could Lalóg have so callously contemplated the murder of her brother?' Eadulf asked.

'Such things have been known. But I am sure the physician Íccaid would have mentioned if Lalóg had presented herself to their *derbhfine* to be considered as head of the family. He was one of the council.'

'If Abbot Brocc was killed to prevent him becoming leader, then Conmhaol was the only other likely candidate.'

'And had already rejected it. Also, Abbot Brocc did not represent himself as speaking as a prince of the Uí Liatháin. He simply wanted the Abbey of Dair Inis to be absolved of complicity in the conspiracy, especially over the matter of the seven Uí Liatháin warships that were anchored there during the insurrection.'

'I am truly confused,' Eadulf admitted. 'Surely that means that if Brocc had the authority to negotiate representing the Uí Liatháin he could not do that unless he spoke with authority as Prince?'

'Let us try to straighten out some matters,' Fidelma suggested. 'After Conmhaol refused the role as Prince, would you say the family saw Abbot Brocc as the new head of the family, as Prince of the Uí Liatháin? Was he killed by those of his family who rejected him taking the role?'

'It is a logical explanation,' Eadulf said. 'But, Caol, you think Scannail and his Grey One do not have any influence.'

'Influence on what?'

'To reject the traditional selection from within Tigerna Cosraigib's immediate descendants. What if they wanted to set up an alternative family line? Maybe a very distant cousin, who is able to be elected by your curious system? I still uphold my people's system of primogeniture is best.'

'It is a possibility,' Caol answered. 'But I had not heard of Brocc's murder before you arrived. I heard no whispers from the group.'

Eadulf suddenly saw the point. 'Brocc's death would have been good news to them if they were trying to create a new princely family!' he exclaimed. 'It would be another step closer to ridding themselves of Tigerna Cosraigib's family and also Brocc's New Faith approach.'

Caol sighed. 'I can tell you little more.'

'Are there any serious rivals to Tigerna Cosraigib's family among the Uí Liatháin?' Fidelma asked. 'Any strong enough to form an opposition that would then be supported by this Grey One? Or even be the Grey One?'

'There were only two rival families,' Caol replied. 'Both of them claimed their descent from the same Eochaidh Liatháin, the first Grey One, from whose name these people chose their own name. Uí Liatháin – "Descendants of the Grey One". Tigerna Cosraigib's family descend from the sons of Caille, while the second family descend from the sons of Thassaig. They gave up contending for power centuries ago and are now merchants.'

PETER TREMAYNE

'Which brings us back to suspecting the Grey Ones are something to do with one of the branches of Tigerna Cosraigib's family. We should have taken steps to identify all the *derbhfine*,' Fidelma sighed.

'The only link so far is the Grey One.' Eadulf shook his head. 'If it is the same person who accurately prophesied Brocc's death. We only have the description he gave before he died to follow.'

'So I was wrong in thinking the Grey Ones are a harmless mystic sect?' Caol asked.

'What if there are two different entities?' Eadulf interrupted. 'The Grey Ones you were allowed to infiltrate and the Grey One who murdered Brocc? It might make more sense.'

'It is all conjecture at the moment,' Fidelma summed up. 'To be honest, this experience has taught me a lot. I had not realised there remained so much antagonism between the peoples. I have been raised to believe Muman was joined as the five divisions of the Eóghanacht kingdom. Perhaps I have been self-delusional.'

'I have always said I find your system of inheritance too complicated,' Eadulf commented. 'I thought only Conmhaol and Lalóg were main contenders for the leadership, as surviving children of Tigerna Cosraigib. Now I understand any descendant of Tigerna Cosraigib's grandfather could challenge them.'

'Now I think of it,' Fidelma continued moodily, 'there was always antagonism. I knew there were problems in that some did not like the rule from Cashel, especially the Uí Fidgente. But we now have a good, peaceful existence with them. I knew, too, that the Uí Liatháin always allied themselves with the Uí Fidgente during those years of conflict. Then there was constant antagonism from the Déisi and, more recently, from the Osraige. Now I am beginning to realise dissension does not arise without deep-rooted discontent, and after conflicts we demand retribution without attempting to understand the origins of the conflict.'

Caol grimaced cynically. 'It is the nature of life. But I gained no real evidence for any impending uprising against Cashel. There were all the references to mythology and impending gloom, but there was nothing that amounted to anything specific. In fact, I was thinking it was high time that I returned home and told Prince Finguine that I could learn no more.'

'And we were on our way to see Prince Conmhaol,' Fidelma said. 'I think we should continue that journey, for we have mysteries to resolve.'

'Mysteries?' Caol frowned.

'The disappearance of our guide, young Brother Scatánach. Did he alert the Grey One to capture us? It is almost a pity that you were not involved in our capture, Caol, or you might have been able to find out how they knew who we were and how they could lie in wait for us if it was not Brother Scatánach who warned them.'

'That part might be explained by the involvement of Scannail,' Eadulf suggested. 'Although the youth is a good suspect.'

'Scannail did say he had thought he had dissuaded us from journeying to see Conmhaol,' Fidelma sighed.

They fell silent for a short period.

'It seems that a murder inquiry has changed into a more significant mystery,' Eadulf finally said. No one responded. 'Are we really convinced that it is a new conspiracy against the rule of the Eóghanacht?'

'I was happy to go back to Finguine and report that there was just rumour and talk but no evidence to argue a strong case of some armed uprising,' Caol admitted. 'Scannail is no figurehead for a new assault on Cashel.'

'But the Grey One is the important mystery figure,' Fidelma insisted.

'You feel that the young one is clad to disguise her true identity and, when revealed, would be a strong leader of such an insurrectionary movement?' Dego asked, emerging from his quiet listening.

'It makes sense,' Fidelma replied.

'Well, it doesn't to me,' Caol shook his head emphatically. 'People have to follow the law of succession to find even a charismatic leader.'

'Or bend the law to their purpose,' Dego muttered. 'As for Brother Scatánach, we must not forget he led us into that swampy river where we could have suffered bad injuries, even death from the infections. If that was his purpose, then why did he take us to the physician where we were treated? Why did he abandon us there? Why not lead us further on, if he were leading us into a trap?'

Caol was regarding him in bewilderment. 'He took you to Íccaid's place to be treated, but disappeared, leaving you there?'

'You know Íccaid?' Fidelma asked.

'He is related to Conmhaol. He is a member of the *derbhfine*.'

'He told us himself,' confirmed Eadulf. 'He was very open about matters.'

'He could claim leadership, if the *derbhfine* supported him,' Caol pointed out.

'There are a lot of currents and characters.' Fidelma's tone changed. 'We have made speculations enough. We are investigating the illegal killing of the Abbot of Dair Inis, whatever the motive. The first thing that makes this a mystery is that. It was the murder that was apparently foretold correctly to the day and time by a person clad in grey robes. The investigation hangs on that fact. If the prophecy was correct it means, in my mind, that the person who pronounced it is part of that murder, if not the actual murderer. Eadulf has already pointed this out. We do not believe in supernatural powers. So the first thing is to find the prophetess who has made that prediction.'

'It's hard to believe the group that I infiltrated are assassins,' Caol reiterated.

'That leads us into another area,' Fidelma said. 'The prophetess was dressed in the robes of this group. Caol says he is here to investigate them as they are suspected by Prince Finguine of involvement in stirring up some sort of plot against Cashel. Caol is happy to exonerate them after spending some months here.' She turned to Caol. 'Are you bound to return in person to report immediately to Finguine at Gleannúir?'

'I usually send messages by my son.'

'Would you be able to help us resolve this conundrum?'

'We seem to be after the same thing, more or less,' Caol agreed. 'It is always an honour to work with you, lady. Indeed, it will be like the old times.'

'Very well.' Fidelma glanced around at her companions. 'When we have decided our next step, I suggest young Cadan ride to Finguine and tell him what our intentions are.'

'Do you have an idea where you will start?' Caol asked.

'We will continue our journey to find Conmhaol and follow our first intentions.'

'You mean go the homestead of Conmhaol?'

'Yes. We know that it lies on marshland by the river where we encountered those midges,' Fidelma confirmed.

'I have been there and observed Conmhaol from afar. I know the river, An Tuairigh, well and the swamp areas where the midges can be avoided. You know the meaning of its name – "the River of Omens", in which it was said the ancient esoterica of the Old Faith used to bathe to increase their powers of prophecy?'

'We were told its name but could not foretell its gnats and midges,' Eadulf moaned. 'Do we have to return there?'

'The place of Conmhaol's homestead is presumably free of those insects, unless he is a masochist?' Fidelma said.

'Conmhaol lives in an area where the river flows rapidly so the marsh does not build until later. The homestead is on an island above the swamp,' pointed out young Cadan. 'I once went to the *crannóg* of Conmhaol.'

Caol chuckled. 'My son is above the age of choice and I have taught him those things he should know: tracking, hunting and the art of defence. He has made sure he knows the country around here. So, Cadan, tell our guests what keeps the midges clear of the island on which the *crannóg* was built.'

'Looking at the island, it does not seem to rise out of the river but from a flat dark green surface, which is created by a growth called *copóg uisce*.'

'Dock leaves?' Eadulf interpreted in surprise. 'A special kind, which is the water dock leaf. In its natural state you rub it on the body where you have been stung by insects or even by nettles. It is even known to halt bleeding, provided the wound is not deep.'

'Well, there is one called *glaisléna*, and you take and mix it with the root of the pepperwort and apply it as a paste,' the boy said, surprising them. 'My aunt taught me that. Anyway, I have heard from wandering merchants that these strange leaves, mixed with other herbs, seem to keep the occupants of the place from being bitten.'

'What you say is interesting,' Eadulf confirmed. 'Did you go into the *crannóg* and meet anyone?'

Cadan quickly shook his head. 'Not inside. I was just investigating the topography. It is a strange country, these lands.'

'I have to say, lady, my son is right,' said Caol. 'This is a country of folklore and magic. Even the hill overlooking the marshland is called the place of invisibility. The *féidh fiadh* was said to be a cloak that the ancient Druids put on to become invisible.'

'Is that why Conmhaol's *crannóg* takes that name? Hill of the Magic Mists?' Fidelma asked.

'It seems this entire area is full of followers of the ancient mystical beings who are determined to drive the New Faith from the shores of this land,' Eadulf observed.

'Exchanging one belief for an opposite one takes time, Friend Eadulf,' Caol said firmly. 'I even hear the kingdoms of the Angles and the Saxons worship both their gods Woden and Thunor alongside Christ? Did not your own King Raedwald of the East Angles have Woden and Christ placed side by side on his altars?'

Eadulf was embarrassed, having not converted to the New Faith until he was a young man.

'I just find it unnerving to be surrounded by places named after phantasms of ghosts, witches, goblins or whatever you call them . . .' he said quietly.

'We don't have to waste time on place names,' Fidelma interrupted caustically. 'We have much to discover.'

Caol glanced up at the sky. 'It is probably too late now to commence. We need the light with us if we are going to approach Cnoc an Fiagh.'

Fidelma hesitated for a moment before agreeing. 'Very well, we will make a start at first light. If agreeable, young Cadan should ride to Gleannúir and tell Prince Finguine what our intentions are. Then we will head to this *crannóg* and demand to speak with Conmhaol. Is that agreed?'

There was a chorus of assent.

'In the morning I shall tell Cadan what to report. Are you sure that we will be secure here, Caol?'

'Only if truly possessed with second sight will they find us here,' the warrior grinned. Then, seeing Fidelma's serious expression, he added: 'They have not found this place before now. They talked much about the old gods and their prophecies. I used to hear those tales of gods and goddesses when I was at my mother's knee. A lot of those tales were told for a reason.'

'A reason?' Dego asked.

'To control children. To make them obedient for fear of

creatures emerging from their lairs to devour them. I doubt if you could walk a few metres in any direction before you came across a spot that some ancient would be able to recount was associated with a tale of evil curses or fantastic beasts.'

'We are not children and not dealing with the supernatural,' Fidelma reminded them dryly. 'We are dealing with a murder.'

It was still early morning when they brought their horses to a small copse under the hills and dismounted. Finnat had prepared a good meal to start the day with, and Fidelma had spent time instructing Cadan in the message he was to take to Prince Finguine. Then, with goodbyes exchanged, Caol had led Fidelma and her companions back over the wooded hills.

It was surprisingly not a long journey this time and Caol knew the short cuts between the hills.

'Conmhaol's *crannóg* is on the far side of this hill,' Caol told them after a while. 'It is where the marshland and the river create a natural rise, which is basically an island. There is a small copse here, so best to leave the horses before we climb over the hill and you can then look down on the *crannóg*.'

'But we want to meet Conmhaol,' Fidelma insisted.

'It's wise to survey a place before you rush into it,' replied Caol. 'From what you say, it seems we are entering dangerous times. No one usually comes along this way so we can leave the horses in safety. Travellers to the homestead take one of three easy paths. The track is directly to the east . . . that's the one to Íccaid's apothecary. Then another track to the north. There is a small ford across the river, which takes one south towards Dún Guairne. So no reason for anyone to come through the forests here.'

'How do people cross on to this island?' Eadulf was still nervous about the river. 'Or are they taken by boat to it?

'There's a wooden planked causeway,' Caol replied. 'You'll see it from the hill.'

After a quick exchange it was decided that Dego would look after the ponies while Fidelma and Eadulf would be guided by Caol up to the vantage point of the hill, keeping low, and examine the *crannóg* first. They were warned to keep their heads down. Eventually, they lay on the brow of the hill and peered cautiously at the river island.

'Why,' Eadulf gasped, examining it, 'it's hardly a house for a noble at all.'

'It is as I said,' Caol replied patiently.

Eadulf had seen many such artificial islands in lakes. They were often built of stones and large logs, taking their name from the word for a tree – a *crann*.

'Instead of this *crannóg* being built on stilts it seems to rest just above the green slime of the river. As my son explained, dock leaves,' said Caol. 'It is surrounded by swamp and bog, and that is more dangerous to anyone wishing to attack it than the defences of an ordinary fortress. I think it was already in existence, an ancient construction, when Conmhaol restored and rebuilt it.'

Fidelma was examining the *crannóg*. She had to admit that she was disappointed when she saw a small stockade of oak-wood timbers, almost oblong in shape, with a square turret at each end. Rather than some threatening military construction it was no more than a small family homestead. It was certainly not something to be wary of, as Scannail had tried to represent it.

She lay looking down thoughtfully on the Hill of the Magic Mist. Everything looked so quiet. There was no movement in or about the homestead. It was so undisturbed that even the river birds were silent as they flew in inquisitive circles over this strange construction in the middle of the odourless marshland. It was as Fidelma considered this that a thought occurred to her. It was too quiet, too serene even for the habitation of a recluse.

'What is it, Fidelma?' Eadulf asked, wondering why she had fallen silent.

'I don't know,' she admitted, rising to her feet. 'Just that there is something strange down there.'

'What is it?' Caol frowned, leaning forward. 'You should stay under cover.'

'I think the place is deserted,' she declared.

'But it is Conmhaol's habitation,' Caol said. 'I have been here once and also observed it from this hill. There was nothing wrong then.'

'And is this how you saw it?'

'It was . . . well, there was a little more activity.'

'Think for a moment, Caol. Is there anything different from how you previously saw this *crannóg*?'

Caol was about to reply when he checked himself.

'It is rather quiet, I will grant you.'

'Let us recover our ponies and then pay a call on this *crannóg*,' Fidelma suggested.

It was not long before she and her companions had halted their horses on the embankment at the end of the causeway, which led across to the gates of the wooden construction. At the far end, the gate into the main building stood wide open but there were no signs of any guards. Fidelma suggested that they wait some moments to allow their presence to be noted. Then Caol, with a nod from Fidelma, dismounted, left his horse hitched to a rail and walked on to the wooden planking towards the gates. As he reached them, he turned and spread his arms to indicate there was no one about. Fidelma gestured for them all to dismount, tether their ponies and follow Caol across the spanning walkway.

They passed through the gate and emerged into a deserted yard surrounded by wooden stockade walls and frontages of buildings. They halted and looked round in the silence.

'What now, lady?' Caol demanded. 'Ah—'

He was abruptly silent. Fidelma followed his look and saw a

bundle of clothes. Not clothes . . . it was a body. She did not have to give it more than a cursory glance.

'It is Brother Scatánach,' she announced simply.

Eadulf moved forward and dropped to one knee to quickly examine the body.

'Expertly done,' he muttered. 'A single sword stroke.' He glanced at Fidelma, showing his perplexity.

'If he was trying to prevent you coming to this place, then this shows a curious form of gratitude for his service,' Dego muttered.

'Do you have any comments?' Fidelma addressed her question to Caol.

'I know nothing except what I see.' He glanced at their surroundings, eyes narrowing. 'I suggest you keep your hands on your weapons until we discover what has happened here.'

'I agree,' Fidelma said quickly. 'We start by a quick search of this place. Go back to the river bank, Dego, where there are stables. Check them and, if all clear, put our horses there so they are not in full sight. Then stand sentinel while we search. Make sure that no one is hiding. A blast on your horn will sound an alarm. We will make a search, starting with that building.' She indicated the first building. 'We will keep one another in sight and not wander off on our own.'

It soon became obvious that the *crannóg* was unoccupied with the exception of the body of Brother Scatánach. It occurred to her that it was odd that no attempt had been made to hide the body. The homestead was entirely deserted. There were no horses, cows or goats. Not even a chicken had been left behind. But there was some cooked food and unfinished plates, spilt cider, and heavy pitchers and other containers and vessels, ewers and milk jugs. It was as if someone had given an order and people had left aside whatever it was they had been doing, taken the animals and disappeared.

Eadulf was thankful when he returned to the courtyard and sunlight. He took some deep breaths of fresh air. He had been brought up with his own pagan gods and spectres before he converted to the New Faith and it did not take his imagination long to sink back into the twilight of evil shadows. He was looking around for his companions when Dego emerged across the causeway carrying a leather bag.

'I found this in the stables back there,' he called to Eadulf, jerking his head to the wooden construction on the river bank. 'I thought you might be interested in it as I have seen you carrying a similar one.'

Eadulf looked at the bag with a frown of surprise. 'It is a medical bag,' he said quickly. 'Where did you say you found it?'

'In the stables. It probably fell from one of the horses in the confusion of vacating the *crannóg*. It was dropped then or was abandoned. All the horses are gone,' he added unnecessarily.

'Nobles and warriors don't usually carry medical bags,' Eadulf began, and then he remembered that Brother Fisecda, the physician from Dair Inis, had been visiting Conmhaol. He turned as Fidelma came up and he showed her Dego's find.

'Go through the bag, Eadulf,' she said. 'It must belong to Brother Fisecda. So here is his bag but there is no sign of him.'

'Nor any sign of Conmhaol nor those of his household attendants, nor any that dwelt here,' Caol said, joining them.

'There are no animals in the stables or nearby,' added Dego. He was regarding Caol with an inquisitive look. 'Nothing is living in the pens and other enclosures along the bank that they must have raised and kept for food. It is almost as if they had been warned of our coming.'

It was not the first time Fidelma heard a tone of distrust in Dego's voice when he addressed the former commander of the bodyguard.

'Wherever they have gone, Brother Fisecda went as well,' Fidelma said quietly. 'Only Brother Scatánach is left dead. None of this makes any sense.'

'So what is our next step on this strange road that we have embarked upon?' Eadulf broke the silence.

They were all looking at Fidelma as if expecting an immediate answer.

'I have a question for Caol,' Dego suddenly said. 'At the fortress of the Grey One, we saw only one place for prisoners. That was the cave where we were incarcerated. Were there any other places where prisoners or others could be held?'

Caol shook his head. 'That the Grey One and her warriors could have descended on this place, killed Scatánach and taken off Conmhaol and his followers is beyond belief. I would say that the group was too weak to perpetrate this act. I have told you before that I do not think them a serious threat.'

'If Conmhaol left of his own volition, why kill the youth? Why leave everything in such a condition; why leave the physician's medical bag?' Dego sniffed. 'You seem keen on pointing out that you think the Grey One and her followers are just an innocent group of fanatics who believe in the old gods. They don't sound so innocent to me. You admitted that you were hired to join them as part of a small band of warriors.'

Fidelma examined Dego for a moment with a serious expression. 'What is on your mind, Dego?'

The warrior did not hesitate to answer. 'My thoughts are these: when we met Caol he did not deny he was serving the Grey One. The lady Fidelma was told that Scannail was their spokesperson. It was implied that they were adversaries to Conmhaol. Why were we abducted and imprisoned? To stop us meeting up with Conmhaol. When Caol appeared, we took the opportunity he offered to escape. We went with him without question. We accepted Caol's account that he had infiltrated the followers of the Grey One on orders from Prince Finguine. He was to investigate a possible coup against the Eóghanacht. We accepted Caol saying this group were more or less harmless esoterics, not capable of leading an insurrection. Why then were they training a small band of warriors? Now Caol joins us, leading us to Conmhaol. But we find his homestead deserted, apart from the body of our former guide. And there's an abandoned medical bag belonging to Brother Fisecda from Dair Inis, who had been attending Conmhaol. Have I summed up correctly, lady?'

'It is a fair summation, Dego.'

'There might be some suspicions among us,' Dego went on. 'Although we knew Caol, we have not seen him since he left Cashel and disappeared. If Caol was serving the Grey Ones, perhaps he might still be serving them. Conmhaol was their enemy, and anyone who was connected with him. Perhaps the Grey One devised a plot, knowing who Caol was and that we would know him: our release was purposely contrived and Caol misled us about assuring Prince Finguine that there was no conspiracy. However, we brought him here. Conmhaol has disappeared. Has the Grey One already attacked Conmhaol, either killed or imprisoned him and his attendants, as they killed Brother Scatánach? Perhaps the idea was to make us believe the story that Scannail told the lady Fidelma – that Conmhaol was plotting against Cashel. They had prophesied the death of Abbot Brocc and murdered him as part of the plot.'

Eadulf was deep in thought. 'I suppose I can see the logic of this thinking, yet Caol had a long and distinguished service among the Warriors of the Golden Collar. Fidelma has said that she accepted that he resigned as a matter of morality when he could have easily remained as commander. I would have thought, Dego, you would have known him better than that. Why do you accuse him now?'

'Dego is only providing the context for the legal position that must now be followed,' Fidelma told him. 'Suspicions do arise from the matter that has been outlined, but we have all known Caol. Therefore I propose our suspicions be dealt with. Caol, now is the time to meet these questions. In law you have the option of a denial by oath. It is not to be lightly taken, and if, later, an untruth is discovered then one's honour price is lost, and lost for ever without hope of retrieval in this world or in the Otherworld. So do you, Caol, now accept to swear to us plainly where your loyalties in this matter lie?'

CHAPTER SIXTEEN

'My thanks, lady.' Caol stood before them and regarded them each in turn. His eyes finally rested on his former comrade, Dego. His gaze was unflinching and serious. 'Dego has summed up where some people's thoughts might lead them to view the curious circumstances in which you found me as suspicious. There is a saying that suspicion must be answered before it grows like poisonous weeds and smothers truth. It is understandable that such thoughts arise. I would be sharing them if I were Dego. Therefore I must be grateful to Fidelma for suggesting the legal path of the *dithach,* or denial by oath.'

'It is a solemn undertaking, which, if abused, results in a life-long elimination of one's honour price,' Fidelma reminded him.

Caol drew himself up. 'So, in accordance with the law, I now swear, by the deities of the Old Faith and those of the New Faith, by all that is sacred to the people of the Five Kingdoms, that I have held nothing back from you. You are my friends and companions, and I swear that all I have told you is the truth, without subterfuge or duplicity, serving no other purpose than the truth because truth is great and will prevail.'

'You swear this freely in accordance with the laws handed down by the Chief Brehon and Council of Brehons, the judges of the Five Kingdoms?' asked Fidelma.

'I do so swear it.'

'So it is sworn. So it is witnessed. So the words are recorded, whispering on the four winds of this world and joining the sighing breeze of the Otherworld.' Fidelma proclaimed the legal ritual reverently.

There was a solemn moment of silence for the *dithach* was not taken likely. From that moment on, any transgression of the oath meant Caol would forfeit all rights under law, not only in the mortal world but also in the Otherworld. As one person the four of them each drew in a breath before letting it out in one great sigh. Even that breath was part of the ritual for it meant their breaths would join on the winds transmitting the oath to the Otherworld.

Solemnly each of them shook hands with Caol to show the clearance of suspicion and renewal of friendship and trust.

Uncertainly, they stood looking round the deserted *crannóg*.

'And now?' Eadulf prompted.

'Now we must see if we can continue our search for Conmhaol and, of course, discover what happened to Brother Fisecda,' said Fidelma. 'I don't suppose anyone can offer any suggestions.'

She made the point of asking everyone to show that suspicion of Caol was now put to rest.

'The only other thing I know about Conmhaol was he and his siblings were raised at Dún Guairne. It might be, if he left of his free will, that Conmhaol has gone there, for he might still have family in that area,' Caol said.

'Then logic dictates that Dún Guairne is our next stop to seek information,' Fidelma replied firmly.

'I am not sure that there is logic in any of this.' Eadulf was not convinced. 'This is unlike any previous investigation we have been on.'

'Not all investigations are alike. I am expecting that you will agree this is the logical path.' Fidelma sounded irritated.

'A logical path, but is it a wise one?' Eadulf replied. 'Dún Guairne is claimed to be deserted.'

'It is logical enough, lady,' Dego said, 'but I agree it may not be a wise move.'

'Not wise?' Fidelma raised her brows, but Dego was not intimidated.

'From what we have heard, none of Tigerna Cosraigib's descendants have any love for your brother, the King. The symbolism represented by that fortress might be best avoided.'

Fidelma considered their concerns for a moment. 'We are faced with an unknown enemy. I have been thinking that Conmhaol may be that enemy in spite of the stories that we have heard about him. Why? Because logically there is no one else of such stature. I know he rejected the family council's approval of him to succeed Tigerna Cosraigib, but what if he is playing some game and really means to have that power? If Brocc was his brother and rival, he could easily have had him eliminated. These Grey Ones were against Conmhaol for some reason. And now he is not here. It does not mean he has been captured, but it is probable.'

'But the followers of the Grey One wanted to overthrow all the descendants of Tigerna Cosraigib,' Caol pointed out.

'On that basis, it would be worth going to Dún Guairne to check on other family members,' Fidelma argued. 'Yet it is still all speculation.'

'We have searched this place and everything has disappeared without little sign of violence – horses, livestock – as if they took everything that was gathered and simply marched off,' Dego pointed out. 'What if Conmhaol has just taken his household to Dún Guairne to be ready?'

'You are weaving an interesting tale, Dego,' Fidelma commented. 'To be ready for what?'

'Ready to take over the leadership and prepare a new assault on Cashel. I am suggesting that this is what may have happened: that the leader of the Uí Liatháin would be symbolically centred at the ancient fortress. It would be logical . . .' He paused with a smile over the use of the word. 'It is where a new leader would first try to entrench his power over the Uí Liatháin before using it to form some new conspiracy against Cashel. If I am right, then it would be ridiculous to walk into that lair. We know there must be some conspiracy brewing. This is why Finguine, your brother's heir apparent, sent Caol here to infiltrate the Grey Ones. Caol, however, centred his investigation on Scannail's group, which might not be the same as Conmhaol's group.'

Fidelma did not respond immediately. Finally she shrugged. 'You certainly seem to be giving the matter a lot of thought, Dego.'

The warrior assumed a defensive expression.

'I have been watching you and Friend Eadulf pursue problems for some years now. I think I have learnt a little from you.'

'You may be right,' she acknowledged. 'But we still need more information and we won't get that information until we get near to Conmhaol. Anyway, it was not my intention to ride up to the gates of Dún Guairne and, if he is there, accuse him. We must find some way of posing some questions that will help us find a rational basis of fact.'

'Then what?' Dego prompted impatiently.

'It is true that I think Abbot Brocc's death is entwined with all these stories and rumours that have now been given substance by what we have discovered so far. My intention is to try to find out if we can expand our knowledge more before we confront Conmhaol.'

'Just as dangerous,' Caol muttered. 'Our presence is probably known already among our enemies and, if not, it soon will be. And who are those enemies? I think we will soon know if we make ourselves known at Dún Guairne. As the lady Fidelma used to quote from a favourite writer, Syrus – "news travels fast". Our enemies probably know what we are doing before we do.'

Fidelma had an indulgent smile as she replied. 'I am glad you recall Publilius Syrus, whose philosophy I often quote. However, the quote you want is from Publius Vergilius Maro. The exact quote is *fama volat* – "rumour travels fast", not "news".'

'Whether rumour or news, it is the same. If Conmhaol is our enemy then he will have known of your presence perhaps since your landing at Dair Inis.'

'Perhaps we should acknowledge that we have two different purposes,' Eadulf suggested. 'Fidelma approaches this matter as a lawyer faced with resolving the murder of a prelate of the church. Six months ago, there was unrest in this area and neighbouring areas against her brother's rule. Then a peace was agreed. We are now getting immersed in what appears to be family power wars.'

'Which could result in some new warfare against Cashel, that is obvious,' Dego interrupted.

Eadulf was impatient. 'We now seem involved in a second matter. We find Caol employed by Prince Finguine, acting as a . . . as a *brath* . . .'

Caol breathed in sharply, slapping his hand to his sword.

'If you were not of a foreign birth, I would challenge you to combat, Eadulf. The word *brath* means a betrayer or informer.'

'Wait,' Fidelma said, annoyed. 'It can also imply spying or reconnoitring. Let us not quibble over words. We have had enough suspicions and disputes. I would tend to use *mairntid* to imply a spy. Indeed, that is how Caol describes the task he was sent here to do. Let me remind you that we have just heard and agreed to Caol's *dithach*. So we will proceed from there. Continue, Eadulf.'

'I apologise for the choice of words. My point was we have been viewing this in different ways and we have merged them all, which has led to confusion. If the murder of Abbot Brocc was regarded as a civil crime then the suspects would be investigated by due process of the law and eliminated. Fidelma would be afforded that respect and cooperation as is stipulated by law. However, as we are now investigating the abbot's death as part of a plot, a conspiracy or an insurrection against the kingdom of Muman, we are proceeding in the belief there is a plot already in place. We are trying to proceed so that we do not provoke the very thing we seek to prevent.'

'In that, we agree,' Fidelma approved. 'Yet I say we must approach Dún Guairne with utmost caution. Caol, you are still our guide. Can you lead the way avoiding any main routes through the forest, just in case we are ambushed as we were previously?'

'I have not tried such a route before but I will do my best to get us there undetected,' Caol agreed. 'Let us start immediately.'

It was some time before Caol halted uncertainly on the brow of a hill. Below them the forest had started to thin. They were looking over a small valley that was more gorse covered than impenetrable woodland. Along it twisted a fair-sized stream.

'I think I might have come too far south-east,' Caol admitted, peering about. 'These thick oak forests in the valleys are deceptive unless you know the tracks.'

'Look!' Dego exclaimed, pointing. 'There's a place where we might find directions.'

There was no need to explain further. Caol led the way cautiously down the hill, crossing the stream and moving towards the spot that Dego had indicated. A little way ahead, on the edge of the stream, was a log cabin with black smoke billowing from its single chimney. Fidelma halted her mount and had signalled the others to do so before they reached the cabin when something caught her keen eyesight. Outside the door of the innocuous-looking cabin was a tall oak pole. From the way the sun enhanced the shadows on it, the pole was obviously carved.

But it was the metal attachment at the top of this pole that caught her attention. It was a circular emblem, which seemed to be worked in silver.

'One of those knot emblems,' Eadulf muttered. 'There is no beginning and no ending to the pattern. Isn't that a symbol of the Druids?'

'It is an ancient symbol of eternal life,' Fidelma agreed. 'From the time before time we have believed that when our souls die in this world they are reborn in Tír na nÓg, the Land of the Ever Young. The emblem also helped us to accept the teaching of the New Faith with its promise of eternal life. Many other faiths do not accept that idea.'

Caol edged his horse close to her and spoke quietly. 'Lady, it is also a symbol of the Grey One. Therefore I suggest caution.'

'That was what I was thinking, Caol,' she responded. 'Dego, you will scout the area behind the cabin before we reveal ourselves. The inhabitants may be friendly but we should make sure before we assume anything.'

In a short time Dego had circled the cabin. There were no signs of anyone being close by. He pointed out that at the back there was a single horse of a breed not unlike the moorland ponies they were riding.

'Then let us pay a call on its inhabitant,' Fidelma decided. 'However, because of the symbols outside, we won't give them the benefit of announcing ourselves before we enter.'

Caol went through the door first. He did so by kicking it open and entering with sword in hand. An elderly man had begun to rise from a chair by the fire with a surprised exclamation. He stood a moment, recognised the intruders, then sat down abruptly and began to chuckle.

'So this is where you have brought your friends, Caol?'

Fidelma, coming behind Caol, halted in surprise, as had the warrior. Eadulf and Dego, behind them, also froze in astonishment.

The tattered and bearded figure of Scannail the Contentious sat regarding them in amusement.

'Well, well, now I know for certain how you all escaped the cavern,' he said, calmly surveying them. 'My companions and I deduced that we had a traitor in our midst.'

'It's a strange word that you use, Scannail,' Caol replied coldly. 'You don't seem to believe that you hold allegiance to the King of Muman.'

'Caol, make sure he has no weapons on his person,' Fidelma interrupted. 'Dego, you stand at the door and keep your eyes alert just in case his grey-clad friends show up.'

'The only weapon I have is my tongue and my pen. I don't know how you tracked me down to this place, but I can assure you, your advantage will be a passing one.'

Scannail seemed totally relaxed as he allowed Caol to search him. Then he rested back in his chair.

Fidelma glanced to Caol, who shook his head as he met her eyes.

She turned her gaze on Scannail. 'I presume that this is your personal hideaway. Do you not prefer to live in a secret hideout with your friends in the ruins of their fortress?'

'I have no need to hide from anyone, Fidelma,' the old man responded, still with amusement in his voice. 'Yet I do prefer this place for contemplation rather than the opulent buildings that nobles prefer, even their ruined palaces.'

Fidelma decided to play along with his humour and seated herself in a chair opposite him.

'I cannot say I perceived any opulence where we last met. However, I was not viewing it from the best position.'

The old man chuckled again. 'My compliments on your sense of humour, lady.'

'Humour does not always have to be apparent. You should realise that moods are reflected in an appropriate time and place.

I think we will avail ourselves of your hospitality, Scannail. It will be much more appreciated this time. Oh, don't bother to rise,' she added quickly as the old man made a movement. 'Caol has already spotted some jugs on the table there, and I am sure he will find some beverage that is to all our likings. Something that will satisfy our thirst.'

Caol checked the contents of the jugs, sniffing each aroma, then tasting one.

'It's a good cider, lady.' He turned to look for some mugs, then poured the cider for everyone, although Scannail shook his head.

'I regret my hospitality is at fault,' he said. 'I do not have enough chairs to entertain all of my guests. Oh, I suppose it will be pronounced as a breach of the laws of hospitality? Does it come under the duties of *coible* that I am duty bound to be generous in providing for the needs of uninvited guests?'

'Do not feel stressed,' replied Fidelma with equal irony. 'I will not charge you for the crime of *esáin*, of driving away guests without providing adequate hospitality.'

Scannail seemed relaxed as he regarded them. 'I feel there is hostility between us, even if you overlook the etiquette lapses in hospitality. You did not believe what I told you, Fidelma?'

'Believe?' She frowned for the moment. 'Oh, you refer to the story that you had abducted me and my companions to protect me? *Did* you think we would believe such nonsense?'

'You will discover that the Grey One is really the protector of the rights and justice of the nobles of the Uí Liatháin.'

'You forget, Scannail, that I have been with the Grey One's men for these last few months,' Caol intervened. 'I came under the instructions of my lord Finguine to discover conspiracy.'

This caused the elderly *seanchaidh* to sit upright for a moment and then relax again.

'So, Caol, it was not just a last-minute decision to change sides that you released Fidelma? I presumed that, as you have served as bodyguard to Fidelma's brother, it might have been some idealistic decision to return to her service. Now I learn you were already acting on instruction from Finguine. Well, well, I understand much now.'

Fidelma hoped that Caol would not reveal that he had first thought Scannail's organisation was harmless and just disagreed with the ruling family of Tigerna Cosraigib.

'What is your real aim, Scannail? You want to overthrow the children of Tigerna Cosraigib? Make someone else leader and attack the Eóghanacht again?'

The older man was dismissive. 'You know your own Eóghanacht family, lady. Wasn't it the Gleann Iubhar branch of your family who, as Kings of Muman, sought to incorporate the Uí Liatháin territory into their own, as they have gradually incorporated the Uí Fidgente and are trying to incorporate the Déisi? Even the Osraige are now on the verge of absorption by your brother's marriage to Princess Gelgéis. All the peoples of the south-west are now being centralised to Cashel's rule. The Uí Liatháin want no more than their independence.'

'So you do mean to raise your people to attack Cashel again?' Fidelma asked.

'We would hope to do so first by negotiation.'

'Really? That is not how you sought to achieve it in the past.'

'But how we would want to achieve it in the future. Each time your warriors have scored victories over our warriors, each time we are defeated, the Eóghanacht unfortunately ensure we rise again by inflicting great suffering on our people, in placing tributes and reparation on us. We can hardly afford to pay what is imposed now. Once we were a rich country, a proud people. Now you ride through our lands as lords. There are deserted farmsteads, decaying villages, empty taverns and houses. The poverty of our nobles is clear and, because they are poor, our workers are also poor and they cry out to be fed. It is a cycle that has to be stopped.'

Fidelma was surprised by the old man's eloquent vehemence.

'Noble words, Scannail,' Caol intervened. 'Words worthy of Scannail the Contentious.'

'Words true of anyone who observes the land and culture they live in,' replied the *seanchaidh*.

'Is this why you live in the world of the ancient past?' Fidelma asked. 'With tales of what once was, your Grey One and ghosts of ancient times. Is it not better to live in the present so that you can make plans for the future?'

Scannail was shaking his head. 'What was once may be so again and be so in the future.'

'You believe it as you wish,' Dego said. 'I hold allegiance to the King and his heirs, who are duly elected by the *derbhfine* of their people. I defend them against they who are in rebellion against them.'

'Such morality,' Scannail sneered. Then he gazed around at his unwelcome guests. 'You have all surprised me here. I don't know how you traced me to my private retreat, as you have done, but it is pointless for me to ask you to explain. But do not think I will attempt to answer any more of your questions. I will not recognise your laws as the nobles who promulgate them are the enemies of the Uí Liatháin.'

'If you knew the history of the law of these kingdoms, you would know that is not so,' Fidelma sighed, an inflection of sorrow in her voice. 'The law is sacrosanct and above kingship. Even the High King of the Five Kingdoms must obey the law. What is greater – a King or his people?'

'The old excuse,' Scannail jeered. 'The people? Because the false answer is that the people ordain the king, the king does not ordain the people. Not so. Not so. The king always ordains himself. Always with a sword in one hand.'

Fidelma hesitated. 'I will not pursue the matter,' she said, uneasily.

Her companions quickly exchanged puzzled glances. It was unlike Fidelma to back away from defence of the law. Even Scannail was surprised.

'Then you will not debate with me?'

'Oh, I did not say that, but I may be the wrong opponent. After all, you have shown your enmity to me in spite of my rank as *dálaigh*, as well as sister to Colgú, the legitimate King of Muman.'

'Then what do you want from me?' The old man was defiant.

'Just to rest and talk with you for a while,' Fidelma smiled thinly.

Scannail moved uneasily. 'Talk? I told you that I will not answer your questions.'

'I hear you. Actually, I told you once before that I was aware of your reputation for great learning and erudition. A *seanchaidh* of renown. So I was wondering what stories you could tell me about a foreign noble of the Britons who claimed to be a descendant of the Eóghanacht?'

The old man looked up at her with surprise. 'You mean the Briton called Rhun?' he asked.

'What can you tell me of him?' Fidelma pressed.

'He lived more than a century ago,' Scannail answered easily. 'So he is nothing to do with anything today. Yet I will answer your questions. Rhun was actually the grandson of a prince of the Britons, in a kingdom called Dyfed. He claimed to be a descendant of Princess Eithne of the Valley of the Yew.'

'Eadulf and I have been in Dyfed among the Britons,' she remarked thoughtfully. 'We knew people thought they had a link with this area.'

'Rhun's grandfather decided to escape the ferocity of the Angles and their Saxon allies, who were attacking the Dyfed kingdom. He fled to Muman with his family and a few other retainers. Among them was his grandson Rhun. They came with riches they had managed to save. Pointing out that they had descended from Eithne, they sought asylum from the Eóghanacht.'

'Were they allowed to settle in the Valley of the Yew?'

'The family received lands here among the Uí Liatháin but only in return for swearing allegiance to the Eóghanacht. The land they were given had been confiscated from the Uí Liatháin. Rhun and his retainers were killed in conflicts with nobles of the Uí Liatháin, who took back the fortress that he had been given, and took also the treasures Rhun and his family had brought from Dyfed.'

'Who seized Rhun's fortress and the treasure?' Fidelma asked, fascinated.

'It was an ancestor of Tigerna Cosraigib. He took back the fortress that Rhun had been given, which was, of course, Dún Guairne.'

This did not surprise Fidelma.

'So, what treasure was it that was brought from Dyfed? Was it a substantial one?' she asked Scannail.

'However substantial it was, it entirely vanished,' the old man said. 'I have heard tales of chests of red gold from the mines of Dyfed, and some made into coins and jewels – the equal to what your artisans make.'

'An interesting story but hardly an unusual one,' Fidelma sighed. 'I imagine the treasure was divided between the Uí Liatháin princes who seized back Dún Guairne. Is that how it vanished?'

'There was little left of it after the Eóghanacht had taken the money in exchange for giving Rhun and his family our land. After Rhun's death there was an attack on Cashel to seize it, but any treasure there was had vanished, leaving only tales of its worth.'

Eadulf was about to remark about wasting time with ancient tales but Fidelma cut him off.

'So the treasure was never found?'

'That is the story,' confirmed the old man. 'I know you wanted to visit Dún Guairne, but I tell the truth when I say it is deserted now apart from those few who remain in the village beneath its shadow. They form a little community, which was once thriving. It still tries to exist mainly from the river that bears the name of the fortress.'

'Why would Princess Lalóg be interested in such matters?' Fidelma asked suddenly.

'She grew up there with her siblings. Does one need an excuse for being interested in what treasures one's forefathers seized?' cried Scannail.

'So you knew of her interest?' Fidelma asked.

'I do not live in total isolation,' he replied scornfully.

Fidelma thought for a moment. 'So Abbot Brocc did not get access to this treasure?' she asked.

'Brocc had been converted to the New Faith. He had converted a long time before his father, Tigerna Cosraigib, was killed.'

'Doubtless Abbot Brocc claimed that he did not know the whereabouts of the treasure.'

'Why would he even be challenged about it?' Scannail seemed puzzled by the questions. 'But there is a rumour that Tigerna Cosraigib met his death at the hands of one of his own *derbhfine* over that very treasure.'

'You mean one of his sons?' Eadulf queried.

'The *derbhfine* means more than just his sons,' Scannail reminded him. 'I have heard such a story. It can probably be discounted.'

'But it might be the reason that Abbot Brocc was murdered.' Eadulf turned excitedly to Fidelma. 'The killer might have thought Brocc had found the treasure and was hiding it.'

'It could be so, but it is unlikely,' replied Fidelma.

'Maybe the Grey One is a suspect,' Caol observed. 'Her followers would want such a treasure to help their cause.'

There was immediate anger from Scannail. 'I tell you, when the Grey One comes into her own, the Uí Liatháin will have a noble of the true blood to rule them.'

Fidelma smiled cynically. 'So the Grey One is a noble?'

'That is for you, as a *dálaigh*, to discover. All I can say is the Grey One does not have such a treasure and will not murder for it. Perhaps, if they had access to the treasure, our people would have more success in recruiting followers to fight against the corruption of the *derbhfine* of Tigerna Cosraigib. I was not lying to you, Fidelma, when I told you that by incarcerating you, the followers of the Grey One only sought your protection.'

'That is for you to prove,' Fidelma grimaced sceptically. 'But right or wrong, we will continue to follow this murder inquiry. We will continue on to Dún Guairne. I think that Conmhaol may have experienced a change of heart and removed himself to that fortress.'

She had said it to judge Scannail's reaction.

'Wasn't he at his *crannóg*?' The old man was surprised.

Fidelma did not reply but looked to Caol.

'Secure our friend. Persuade him to give us the directions we need. Then I suggest we avail ourselves of his refreshments before we continue on.'

That Scannail did not know about what had happened at the homestead of Conmhaol seemed another important piece of the picture she was trying to build.

Scannail was secured and they had a midday meal and drank of their unwilling host's cider before deciding to take a short rest prior to continuing their journey.

A raised voice awoke Fidelma. For a moment she had forgotten where she was. She blinked and came to her senses quickly when she realised it was Caol exclaiming in anger. She swung from the makeshift cot she had used in a side room. She heard Eadulf groan as he started waking up. She hurried into the main room of the cabin. The outside door was open and she saw Dego sitting on the step with Caol bending over him and dabbing at his head with a wet cloth.

'What's happened?' she demanded, although she thought she already knew the answer. 'How badly are you hurt?' she asked Dego, seeing the blood on the cloth.

'He's got a deep abrasion behind the ear,' Caol replied for him. 'We best get Eadulf to examine him.'

Dego looked up at her and groaned.

'My fault. I wasn't expecting it from an old man. It is a shame on my honour.'

'You were not expecting what?'

'That wily *merdrech mac muine . . .* !'

Eadulf had now emerged at Fidelma's side and took a moment to translate the phrase. 'What son of a bush-harlot?' he queried as he bent down. Caol moved out of the way to allow Eadulf to examine his comrade's wound.

'The old *tuiledach*!' Dego muttered. Eadulf realised this was also an uncomplimentary term.

'No use cursing him now,' Fidelma admonished. 'Just say what happened. Scannail freed himself and hit you?'

'It was my turn to watch, as you know. I was sitting by the fire. I fell asleep, just sitting there, and he must have come up behind me and hit me with something really heavy. I don't know how long I was lost to this world before Caol came and found me.'

'But how did he release his bounds?' Caol protested. 'I secured his hands carefully.'

'The point is, he released them,' Fidelma said dryly.

'What woke me was the sound of a horse moving off, and then I found Dego senseless,' Caol added. 'I'd better go to the stables and hope he did not have time to turn out our horses or incapacitate them.'

Fidelma nodded, then turned to Eadulf. 'How bad is it?'

'The broken skin will soon stop bleeding, a possible bruise and bump; the worse thing will be a headache.'

Dego groaned. 'Just wait until I catch up with that *tuiledach*!'

Eadulf rose and was looking round. 'I am sure the old bastard, as Dego has just called him, has some healing herbs about the place. I'll put a moss poultice on the abrasion, which will stop the bleeding quickly. Then I'll mix something to alleviate that headache.'

Caol returned, looking relieved. 'He has taken his own horse but thankfully left ours. Probably he didn't have time to disperse them before we were aroused and chased him. I went to check on his tracks: he was going along by the stream, south-west. It is likely he is heading back to the Grey One's fortress to get help.'

'Most likely,' Fidelma agreed morosely. 'He would doubtless want to warn them, especially as you are now identified as an agent of Prince Finguine. They would need to reflect over what information you could have given him about their plans.'

'But I don't know anything of their plans, apart from going round in grey robes and making prophecies. We know they dislike the family of Tigerna Cosraigib, but whom do they support? The Grey One? Who is she? A noble, but who? Who does she represent?'

'The prophecies are aimed at attacking Cashel,' Fidelma protested. 'Now things seem to be getting violent. Isn't that enough?'

Eadulf had finished securing the poultice to Dego's wound and was busy mixing something in a beaker.

'Old Scannail had a few helpful things, but not everything I wanted. He had valerian and peppermint. I would have used catnip and—'

'Does it work?' Dego interrupted dubiously.

'Well, it won't poison you,' Eadulf grinned, helping the warrior to a chair. 'Sip it and sit there awhile. You will feel better soon.'

Fidelma drew Eadulf and Caol outside. 'Let's see where Caol saw the tracks of Scannail.'

They walked a little way to the stream.

'Will Dego be incapacitated for long?' she asked dropping her voice to a lower tone. She was anxious to move on quickly.

Eadulf shook his head. 'Give him a short time and the head-ache will soon be gone. There are no other injuries. The bleeding will stop shortly. He will still have a sore head and an injured ego at letting an old man best him.'

'Then he can ride with us?'

'All being well.'

'You mean to chase after Scannail?' Caol asked.

'Not if he is going back to the fortress of the Grey One. I think we should continue on with where we were going.'

'Dún Guairne?' Caol asked. 'But there is nothing there now. We have Scannail's word that it is a small, deserted settlement outside the walls of the old fortress.'

'You trust Scannail's word? I must see the place myself. Did you manage to get some directions to Dún Guairne?'

'Scannail let slip it is on the banks of the river, which takes its name from the fortress.' He paused. 'All we have to do is find that river, south of here and to the west, and follow it. Let's hope some local person will identify it.'

'Presumably Scannail is not heading towards Dún Guairne?'

'As far as the tracks lead, his direction is towards the Hill of the Phantoms.'

'We will set off as soon as we can,' Fidelma said. 'Just in case Scannail comes back with his friends. He could even now be hur-rying to warn the Grey One and then return here in force.'

Caol was shaking his head, in slight exasperation.

'I will say this one more time, I never saw more than a half a dozen adherents of that group. I don't think they are a serious military threat against Cashel . . .'

'Not yet,' she replied. 'The Uí Liatháin have had curious alliances and we know the Grey One used mystic messages to focus their minds against Cashel. I am sure Cummasach of the Déisí was not happy when the coup against Cashel fell apart six months ago. They would probably be content to join, or even instigate, a further plot. So we must beware of that.'

'I agree,' Eadulf said. 'With only the Great River dividing the Uí Liatháin and the Déisí as a border, the two could easily join forces and strike at Cashel again.'

'This is why I am anxious about the disappearance of Conmhaol. If he wanted nothing to do with advancing his people then his disappearance is a matter of concern. We must find out whether he left that *crannóg* willingly or unwilling.'

'I was worried at the appearance of that Déisí ship back at Dair Inis,' Dego said, having rejoined them and seemingly feeling better.

'That was just a trader's ship,' Fidelma reminded him.

'A trader with the emblem of a goddess of war?' Dego reminded her sceptically. 'What was the name of the captain – Tóla? He was at Lalóg's village that night and he was talking with the arrogant steward, Cathbarr.'

'But the Déisí have many such ships,' Eadulf said thoughtfully. 'Don't forget that they were often sailing across the seas between here and Dyfed. They are adventurers and so it would not surprise me to see their involvement. I thought you were going to make some point when it turned out that person, whom you mentioned to Scannail, was from the kingdom of Dyfed. I was going to point out that it was the Déisí settlers that actually seized the kingship from the Britons.'

'And that is why I had to shut you up, Eadulf,' Fidelma remarked heavily. 'There are times when your adversary should not be told what you know.'

Eadulf sighed.

'You have often used a quote from your teacher, Brehon Morann. "Do not volunteer information and never let your enemy see how they affect you"?'

'Close enough,' she agreed. 'Now we should prepare to move on in case Scannail returns, bringing his grey companions with him.'

CHAPTER SEVENTEEN

They had ridden for some time and Caol was beginning to get nervous about his incomplete knowledge of the geography of the country when they came across a solitary figure walking along the track with a fishing rod and a plaited-rush bag over his shoulder. The figure halted at the sound of their approach, turned and stood regarding them curiously.

'Can you direct us to the river that passes Dún Guairne or the fortress that bears that name?' Caol greeted.

The man, obviously a middle-aged countryman, examined him thoughtfully. He seemed to take in the fact that two of the party were warriors, before turning his gaze to Fidelma and Eadulf.

'You are not far from it, but the way can be confusing. It is across those western hills and between here and there are marshes and by-ways.'

'That I have already observed,' Eadulf observed dryly.

'Could you guide us?' Fidelma asked.

The man shook his head. He pointed to the opposite side of the track where a dense wood blocked a distant view.

'Beyond those trees, there is my home. I have spent most of the day fishing for our evening meal, which my wife is going to prepare. The day is already darkening. I cannot offer hospitality nor can I accompany you as a guide.'

'Then finding shelter for the night is our urgent need.'

'Keep to this track and, not far from here, you will come to a farmstead called Cúasám Echnach. That is where you might find shelter for the night or a guide to the abandoned fortress you seek.'

Fidelma was puzzled. 'So you know it is abandoned?'

'Everyone knows it has been abandoned these last six months. No prince dwells there now.'

'What did you call this settlement ahead of us. Cúasám Echnach . . .?'

The fisherman grimaced. 'You might have heard the story of what they called Echnach's gold. Echnach means both a sprite and enchanter, if you believe in the ancient spirits. It also indicates moorland and it is on that moorland that the owners of the settlement run their sheep.'

'So Cúasám Echnach is what type of settlement?' Eadulf frowned. 'Moorland and caves – an interesting mix of concepts, but it is in keeping with the strange names that seem to be numerous in this territory.'

'It is a large farmstead. The owner is the lady Báine,' replied the man. Then, before they could question him further, he turned with a wave to them and set off in the direction of the woods.

Caol took the lead again along the trackway. It was not such a distance before he reined in his horse and peered about. He pointed along the valley to a flat treeless area surrounded by low-lying hills.

'That looks like moorland. Quite a few sheep about . . .' Then: 'See, under the shadow on that rise? That's unusual.'

'Unusual?' Eadulf questioned. 'It's just a copse.'

'Unusual because this is moorland and not many trees thrive in this marshy ground,' Fidelma explained.

'There's rowan and willow, from what I can see,' Caol smiled. 'There is a rise in the land and there are some buildings behind the trees. I think this is what that man meant when he told us we would find a place called Cúasám Echnach. That seems to be a homestead. There is a light there. Shall we make our way towards the buildings? We will, at least, get proper directions.'

'It's good that we have these moorland ponies,' Fidelma observed. 'At least they are used to this terrain. But what of your stallion? If Dego leads the way, he can ensure we remain on a track that is dry enough to follow.'

Although it was not really far before the rising hill with its clumps of trees, they needed to traverse a long stretch of grassland and low-growing, uncultivated vegetation, bracken and heather. Here and there were patches of mosses, which they knew were to be avoided. Such areas rested on wet and boggy mud and were likely to swallow the unsuspecting wayfarer.

As they drew near, a couple of figures were visible at the tree line ahead of them. Fidelma saw, from their clothes and demeanour, that the men were workers on the land. They stood arms loose at their sides as they watched the travellers' approach. They were still some way off when one of the men called to them, sending a group of birds flying up in low circles across the heather, calling in alarm.

'What do you seek here, strangers?'

They continued towards the men, although Dego glanced back to Fidelma, wondering whether she should stop.

'We seek hospitality and a pause in our travels,' she called back.

'This is no tavern or traveller's rest,' the man called back. 'This is a homestead.'

'Then we will seek hospitality under the law in the name of a *dálaigh* of the courts,' she replied. 'Is this part of a settlement called Cúasám Echnach?'

At the name the men exchanged glances.

'Who are you?' The question was less demanding in tone now.

Fidelma and her companions drew up to them and halted.

'Just travellers trying to find our way to Dún Guairne. We

were told by a man we met a little way back that we might get directions and even hospitality here.'

'There is nothing at Dún Guairne,' the reply came immediately. 'It has been deserted for some time.'

They had come to the top of the rise on the edge of a section of flat hill crowned with rowan and willow trees. Through the trees they could see various buildings. One, unusually large and rectangular, was clearly a homestead and placed about it were a few more traditional round houses and some farm buildings.

The man who had challenged them was sturdy and looked every inch a farmer in a sleeveless leather jacket and woven plaid trews and leather boots. They now realised that he held a wicked-looking billhook in his right hand and a sharp knife in a leather belt at his waist. His companion was dressed similarly. They were both tanned, with pale blue eyes and a mass of thick curly brown-gold hair. They had similar growths of beard, which must have been shaped by the same hand. They were so alike that they were clearly brothers.

'Who are you?' repeated the one with the billhook.

'As we have said, we are travellers on our way to Dún Guairne.'

Fidelma noticed that both Dego and Caol had their hands resting on their swords.

'We told you it was deserted,' snapped the man. 'Why do you seek it?'

'We are not obliged to answer. Have you never encountered a *dálaigh* before?'

The man looked bewildered and cast a glance at his companion. He had by now caught sight of the fact that both Dego and Caol were clad as professional warriors and that Dego was still wearing the golden torque symbol of the bodyguards of the King of Cashel.

'Is this the place called Cúasám Echnach?' Fidelma repeated with a patient smile.

The man's frown deepened as he considered his reply but then he shrugged.

'That is the territory known as Cúasám Echnach.' He made a sweeping motion of his arm across the flat ground to the surrounding hills. 'It is the homestead of the lady Báine. This is her territory . . .'

'I am sure your lady will follow the spirit of the law of hospitality and not refuse us a place to rest awhile on our journey. I am a *dálaigh,* an advocate of the law courts, travelling to Dún Guairne with my companions.'

The man with the billhook looked distractedly at his companion, hesitated and then, reaching a decision, shrugged.

'If you will follow me, lady,' he said quietly, turning and making his way towards the cluster of buildings that surrounded the rectangular building. It was unusual in such rural areas to find houses built of wooden logs but of rectangular fashion. Usually houses, like the surrounding few, were built of the traditional wooden frames and wattle and daub, with conical thatched roofs. If this was a singular homestead then whoever this woman, Báine, was, she was surely someone of wealth and substance. There were other storage buildings, some open to the elements. One was a kiln and another a smithy. Beyond was a pigsty and some chicken runs, and an enclosure in which some calves were resting.

Fidelma looked around but, other than the two surly farming hands, there was no one about.

They halted their horses at a short distance from the main house, waiting for an instruction from their guides.

The first man, who had done all the speaking, finally said: 'If you and your companions dismount, lady, my brother will take your horses to the shelter over there.' He indicated an area under some willow trees where there was a drinking trough.

Fidelma was aware that both Dego and Caol were making a minute examination of the buildings in case some danger lurked there. But she led the way by dismounting. The horses were taken to the drinking trough by the silent farm worker, while their guide went to the door of the house, picked up a hand bell and shook it three times, sending its peal into the stillness.

There was a movement, surprising them by coming from one of the round houses. They turned towards the shadowy figure that had appeared in the doorway.

Their guide called to her: 'A *dálaigh* seeks hospitality on her way to Dún Guairne, lady. One of her companions bears the tonsure of the New Faith. The other two are clearly warriors, though one is without his right arm but bears the golden collar of the bodyguards of the Eóghanacht King.'

The figure who came forward was scarcely more than a score of years of age. Even Fidelma could appreciate her beauty. A heart-shaped face with delicate features surmounted by long, ash-blond hair, deep blue eyes; even the red lips needed no berry juice to enhance their colouring. While the lift of her chin gave her a determined expression, there were lines at the corner of her mouth that indicated that laughter would sit more naturally on her features than anger. Although she was clad in a simple country dress, Fidelma noticed she had a necklace of semi-precious stones around her neck and her hair was caught back with a band that was probably silk.

The girl halted and examined each one of the group in turn. Protocol dictated that she should not greet them first.

Fidelma stepped forward.

'I am Fidelma of Cashel and this is my husband, Eadulf, of Seaxmund's Ham, in the land of the South Folk . . .'

'Aah . . .' the girl gave a long, sighing interruption, 'you are sister to Colgú of Cashel. I have heard of you, lady, and also of your husband, the Saxon who travels with you.'

Eadulf opened his mouth to protest but the girl had turned back to Fidelma.

'You are legal adviser to Colgú of Cashel. What, then, are you doing in the territory of the Uí Liatháin?'

'I was invited. I am here to inquire into the death of Abbot Brocc.'

The girl's expression did not change. It was as if she already knew the answer. However, she replied: 'Do not the Uí Liatháin have their own judges and advocates?'

'Even if this territory was not considered under tribute to Cashel, I would point out that the law, with one or two minor variations, applies to all the Five Kingdoms and representatives of it have authority in all the territories.'

The girl seemed to consider this for a moment and then shrugged indifferently.

'You are right, of course. Forgive my discourtesy, lady. I have, of course, heard your name spoken as excelling in wisdom and knowledge of the laws.' She turned to Eadulf, 'And, of course, the name of Eadulf is inseparably linked to your own. You are both welcome to my homestead. I suppose it is natural that you would be escorted by a bodyguard of your brother's household. Therefore, I offer you the hospitality of my house.'

'My thanks on behalf of my companions and myself, lady. Before meeting a traveller who directed us here, I had never heard of this place, Cúasám Echnach, nor, as one of your workers informed us, of the lady Báine who, judging by your erudition, must be a *bean-tiarna*. That being so, you must equally forgive my lack of knowledge.'

'It is so that I hold the rank of *bean-tiarna* of this territory.'

'Are you Báine, daughter of—'

'I am Báine,' was the curt response. 'My father was a noble serving the late Prince Tigerna Cosraigib of Dún Guairne. I am informed you are on the way there.'

'We are going to Dún Guairne.'

'It is an abandoned fortress now. My father has been dead these last six months, having answered the call to arms,' returned the girl almost with clenched teeth. 'He died in the conflict.'

'He was a noble serving his prince?' Fidelma asked.

'Like all nobles, he was bound to do so,' the girl replied, then turned and motioned them towards the door of the house. 'Come and you will explain to me what you expect to find at the abandoned fortress and why you came to this place? It is a spot isolated from the main tracks and roads, and one needs to know how one gets here over the moor as it can be dangerous.'

She swung open the door and gestured for them to follow her inside.

They saw the building was quite pleasant, with a central room lined in panels of red yew and with doors leading off to sleeping apartments, and a stone-flagged hearth. Fidelma's eye was immediately caught by several symbols hanging around this central room. Most of them were connected with the goddess Brigit, daughter of Dagda, father of the gods. There were two crescents carved back to back, the ancient symbol of immortality, an image of the sacred oak tree and other little symbols she knew as the *lámh-dia* or household deities.

The keen eyes of the girl saw Fidelma's quick appraisal.

'Before you ask, Fidelma of Cashel, the answer is – yes, I do retain the Old Faith of our people and find no comfort in the strange foreign thoughts that have come from the east.'

'I am aware that most in this territory still do so,' Fidelma replied in a courteous tone. 'I am not travelling through this territory with any other purpose than to resolve the murder of an abbot.'

Báine's expression did not change. She motioned them to be seated, then turned and clapped her hands.

One of the doors opened and an elderly woman entered. She was clearly a retainer. 'Cider and water for our guests,' Báine instructed. 'Also bring some bannock cakes and a dish of honey.'

The woman departed to fulfil the girl's order.

There was an uncomfortable silence before Báine finally reopened the conversation. 'You did not say why you wanted to visit the old fortress.'

The elderly woman returned with jugs of cider and a basket of bannocks with a dish of honey. She set things down before exiting without a word, but Fidelma felt that she and her companions had been very carefully scrutinised.

Báine simply waved a hand to the table as if to indicate that they should help themselves.

'And so?' she asked suddenly. 'Why did you come here?'

'We were merely asking the way to the fortress of Guairne.'

'The fortress is a short ride from here, over the next hill and down by the river.' She waved her hand as if to indicate the hill. 'Why were you going there when everyone knew the place was deserted? You say that you are investigating the murder of Abbot Brocc. What has that to do with anything?'

'He was the son of Prince Tigerna Cosraigib, who dwelt there.'

'He is six months dead,' the girl replied. 'It doesn't explain things.'

Fidelma actually found herself trying to keep a scowl from forming on her features.

'A dálaigh is not answerable to anyone during an investigation.'

'Of course not. Just my curiosity,' Báine replied. If it was meant as an apology it did not sound like one. But there was something irritating in the back of Fildema's mind and she suddenly decided to speak out.

'It was something that Lalóg mentioned.' Fidelma made the comment based on little or no information.

The reaction was immediate.

'Lalóg? You have spoken to her?'

'So you know her?' Fidelma asked quickly.

'Why would I not? She is my mother.'

Fidelma did not find herself surprised by this admission. She had begun to suspect the relationship. In fact, she seemed curiously satisfied as Lalóg had mentioned her daughter who had been at the village with her at the time when Brocc was murdered.

'I heard that you and your mother attended the obsequies of your uncle even though he was of the New Faith. Did your father support Tigerna Cosraigib?'

'Tigerna Cosraigib was ruler of all the Uí Liatháin. Does not the law call on all nobles to support their prince as well as all free clansmen to support their lords? Or are you saying that the Uí Liatháin should ignore the law?'

'It has been known,' Eadulf muttered.

'The graves and confiscated estates of our nobles who did so are also known,' the girl replied softly.

'So none of the nobles here challenged Tigerna Cosraigib? Your uncles, Conmhaol and Brocc, seem to have disagreed.'

'Not in an outright manner.'

'Conmhaol? What of him?'

'You must have already heard that he refused to be appointed by the family council to take the title when my grandfather was killed.'

'When did you say you last saw Conmhaol?'

'I did not say, but I saw him two months ago. It was at that little *crannóg* he retreated into alongside the Tuairigh river with its midges and pests. There were far better places for him to go rather than that lump of land in the middle of a bug-infested swamp. You would not realise how bad it was unless you have been there.'

'The fact is, Báine, we have been there,' Fidelma replied flatly. 'Conmhaol has disappeared. That is why we are heading to Dún Guairne.'

For a moment or two an odd expression appeared on her face. It was almost one of relief.

'I don't understand,' she said. 'If he is not at his *crannóg* you certainly won't find him at Dún Guairne.'

'What makes you so sure?' Fidelma asked. 'We wanted to speak with Conmhaol. We wanted to know more about him and the conflict in his family.'

'I always thought my uncle Conmhaol wanted isolation.'

Fidelma seized on the word. 'Isolation from whom?'

'From the former family and friends of my grandfather, Tigerna Cosraigib. Tigerna Cosraigib may be dead but he did not become Prince of the Uí Liatháin without support. To most of the Uí Liatháin he was a prince to be proud of. He stood for the rights of his people. For many he was the reincarnation of Cú Roí mac Dáiri, the Hound of the Fields, returned from the Otherworld, who was the supernatural warrior equal to Cú Chulainn of Ulaidh.'

'So why didn't one of these supporters become Prince of this territory?' repeated Fidelma. 'It was Abbot Brocc who represented the Uí Liatháin at the peace council after the attempted conspiracy was put down.'

'Are you suggesting that Brocc was a victim of Tigerna Cosraigib's supporters?' Eadulf asked.

'What other purpose would it serve to put the blame on anyone?' replied the girl.

'Brocc – Abbot or not, Prince or not – is deserving of justice, whoever was responsible.'

The girl shrugged. 'Brocc was a strange man. He fought alongside my grandfather at the battle of Cnoc Áine. After which he decided to adopt the New Faith. Even so, he seemed to be my grandfather's favourite. I don't think religion bothered my grandfather, only power and respect. Anyway, I still can't see why you are going to the old fortress of Tigerna Cosraigib. I can't imagine that you would add to your knowledge about how Brocc was killed there because I heard he was killed while taking a bath at the abbey. Most of my family never accepted this New Faith.'

'Yet Conmhaol, when he was ill, always sent for the physician of the abbey, Brother Fisecda. Why was that?'

The girl sniffed. 'Cousin Fisecda had a reputation throughout this territory.'

'Fisecda was your cousin?' Fidelma queried.

'Distant, but a cousin nevertheless.'

'Yet I have heard that Íccaid, who is a member of the *derbhfine*, the family council, was thought to be equally adept in the ways of the healing arts.'

Báine shrugged again. 'Perhaps it is a matter of personal choice? You will have to discuss the matter with Conmhaol.'

'If we can find him. His *crannóg* was totally deserted. There was only one person there.'

'One person?' Báine was tense as if her body had turned to stone.

'One body, I should say. It was that of our erstwhile guide,' Fidelma went on. 'He was the one who had taken us as far as the river and then deserted us at the physician Íccaid's dwelling. The guide was Brother Scatánach.'

The girl let out a gasp.

The sound must have been heard outside as a door swung open and an elderly woman emerged, but Báine immediately dismissed the attendant with a wave of her hand.

'I am all right,' she said shortly. 'That was bad news.'

'Certainly bad news for some people,' Eadulf said with his usual irony.

'You seem acquainted with the young man,' Fidelma observed quietly. 'I apologise, Báine. I had no idea you knew the young religieux well. We understood he was a fisherman's son from a village near the Abbey of Dair Inis, where Brocc was murdered.'

Báine lowered her head. 'He was an arrogant youth,' she remarked. 'He was always trying to suggest he was close to Conmhaol and Fisecda.'

'Íccaid mentioned Fisecda was related to Conmhaol,' muttered Eadulf.

A thought came to Fidelma's mind. 'And was Sister Damnat the daughter of Fisecda? She mentioned she had learnt her healing arts from her father, who was a renowned physician.'

'They are both part of the *derbhfine*,' Báine replied. 'So Scatánach's body was there at Conmhaol's *crannóg*? He was a strange one. He was often allowed to join me and my cousins at lessons as children. That is probably why he felt he was one of us. That was before he went to join Brocc at the abbey to improve his learning.'

'Where did he join you?'

'At Dún Guairne. He used to accompany merchants who trade at the fortress.'

Another idea suddenly entered Fidelma's mind. 'Who was your mentor who taught at those classes which Scatánach joined?'

'An old *seanchaidh*,' the girl replied.

'Scannail?' Fidelma shot the question abruptly.

The look on the girl's face confirmed her guess.

'So Scannail the Contentious taught you?' Fidelma echoed thoughtfully. 'But Scatánach did not retain the Old Faith. He told us that he wanted education, and to receive it and improve his position in life he became a member of the abbey's community. I do not think he really converted to the New Faith. When did you last see Scannail?'

'Not so long ago.'

'Was that when you visited your mother's village at the mouth of the Deep Glen?' Fidelma asked quickly.

'He is always passing there. That is his lifestyle. He is always on a circuit, teaching and reciting his poems and stories. He often came to see me, even here.'

'He came here? On his way to Dún Guairne?'

'Why would he go there?'

'That is not an answer,' Fidelma snapped. 'I demand an answer.'

'I fully know your rights,' the girl replied stiffly. 'We are Uí Liatháin and not yet forbidden to move where we will.'

'But you know the obligation to respond truthfully. What do you know of the Grey Ones?'

Even Caol was surprised by Fidelma's unexpected question.

'Do you mean in myth or reality? I know little about them,' Báine replied defensively. If the question had been meant to throw her off balance, it did not. 'They are part of the folklore of our people because this is how we take our name. They were a powerful influence among the Druids. I have heard that there is currently a group who are trying to revive the concept.'

'So I would be wrong in thinking that you are their leader?' Fidelma was abrupt.

'Why would you ask that?' the girl parried. Her eyes seemed to flash with some angry fire, but she spoke easily.

'Abbot Brocc described a prophetess, who he identified as the Grey One. She was described as a young girl in appearance. She was dressed in grey robes. Her prophecy was correct.'

'Was my uncle Brocc able to positively identify her?' There was a note of cynicism in her voice. 'Are you saying that it was I who threatened my uncle?'

'He was not standing close to the girl. She was speaking down to him from a rock,' admitted Fidelma. 'However, I and my companions were prisoners of the group you call the Grey Ones a day or so ago. I stood before her. Your tutor, Scannail, stood beside her and acted as her mouthpiece. Thus I could not identify her by her speech.'

The expression on the girl's face matched her tone. 'Scannail was with her, you say? And you recognised her?'

'I did not say I recognised her. She was, of course, covered in grey robes and veiled.'

'If she was covered, how do you even know she was a female?'

'By her posture and shape.'

Báine was shaking her head, her anger giving way to amusement.

'Well, I can tell you, Fidelma of Cashel, that you are mistaken. I have heard of these Grey Ones and while they make intriguing claims of being in touch with the mystical world, I prefer to spend my time in more pragmatic matters, such as running my farm here.'

Fidelma frowned. She then gestured towards Caol.

'Have you seen this warrior before? He has ridden with the Grey Ones at the behest of Prince Finguine, my brother's heir apparent, to find out if they form a threat either to the *derbhfine* endorsement or the next prince of the Uí Liatháin or to Cashel.'

'I have never seen this warrior before. Were the Grey Ones recruiting warriors? I thought they were only into magic charms and prophecies? But it must not have been a pleasant assignment for a warrior to betray his honour to become a spy?' She said the words in a sneering manner.

The annoyance was clear on Caol's face. 'You have insulted my honour, for which I could demand an *enechlann,* the compensation for the insult and the contempt in which you made it.'

'There is only one thing that prevents me demanding your immediate removal from my house and denying you hospitality. That you come in the presence of a *dálaig*h.'

Fidelma's companions looked nervously at her, wondering what she would do. However, Fidelma appeared relaxed.

'I do not believe you meant to either insult a renowned Warrior of the Golden Collar in contempt or to provoke a just response. Did I not stress that I am an advocate and you agreed that you understood that?'

'And so?' The girl's reply was still belligerent.

'Then I must instruct you on the rights of an advocate to ask questions directly or through delegation. I have pursued that right and in doing so such questions are made to extract information and not to insult. Therefore, no contempt was shown for this house nor your hospitality, which hospitality is a duty under law, and refusal is answerable to the law.'

The girl flushed. It was clear that the minutiae of law was new to her. She seemed to have trouble digesting the information. It was, surprisingly, Dego who prompted her.

'Do you have an advocate in this territory that you could consult so that they would confirm that the lady Fidelma speaks with accurate authority?'

Báine did not respond. Fidelma spoke pleasantly as she prompted her. 'Do you want to delay for that confirmation or can we proceed?'

The girl considered for a moment and seemed to realise that Fidelma was confident enough and had enough reputation to speak with authority.

'I accept what you say as I hope you will now accept that I told the truth. I am not involved with this esoteric group. On that basis, we can proceed and I will accept there is no breach to the laws of hospitality.'

'Then we will proceed. And you have a question to put.'

'My question is an obvious one and that is how Scatánach led you to Conmhaol's *crannóg* where you then saw his body. I do not follow.'

It took a few moments for Fidelma to tell the story of how they discovered matters in Conmhaol's *crannóg* by Cnoc an Fiagh.

The girl's reactions were now carefully controlled. 'The only body was that of Scatánach and there was no one else? Where was my uncle taken? Where was his household, his attendants?'

'As I said, Báine, the entire *crannóg* was deserted except for the body of the youth. That was one of the reasons why we are going on to Dún Guairne – in order to see if they went there.'

'Why would my uncle go there? He hated that place. He swore he could never go there, even when his father, Tigerna Cosraigib, was reported dead. And many of his *derbhfine* wanted to elect him as senior prince and leader of the Uí Liatháin because of his stand. That is why he hid away in Cnoc an Fiagh.'

'Did you approve of your uncle's action in that respect?' Fidelma queried.

Báine did not hesitate. 'I will be honest. At least he would have been a better leader than his brother.'

'Better than Abbot Brocc?' Eadulf was trying to keep a track of the conversation.

'Uncle Conmhaol is weak and self-centred in many ways, but he is better than my uncle Brocc,' the girl replied.

Fidelma regarded her with interest. 'You have decided views on your uncles. Brocc was a prince of the Uí Liatháin as well as Abbot of Dair Inis. In many families the two roles are not mutually exclusive. Where else would the family council turn after Conmhaol had rejected their support?'

The girl laughed sardonically. 'Look around at these abbeys of your New Faith. Can you name any that were not founded by members of the *flaith,* the noble class? To set up an abbey community you need land, finances and position to stand up to princes and nobles. Of course Brocc sought to accept if the *derbhfine* had agreed to name him as ruler of the Uí Liatháin. What Brocc wanted was power; the power, as a prince, to enforce the New Faith on our people, whether it was wanted or not. The family, those who opposed him, knew there was much arrogance and hatred in him. He was a true son of Tigerna Cosraigib – Lord of the Slaughter.'

CHAPTER EIGHTEEN

'If we understand you correctly, Báine, you are saying that your uncle Abbot Brocc was probably assassinated by someone who feared that if he became Prince of the Uí Liatháin, he would turn out like his father; the father who had earned his nickname Lord of the Slaughter. That he, too, would be implacable? Is that right?'

Báine made a dismissive gesture. 'It seems that those involved in law like logic. You have your logical conclusion.'

'And that logic means that the suspect would be one of those in his family who is opposed to him.'

'Is it not also logical that he was killed because he joined the New Faith and, moreover, that he was abbot of one of the few strong Christian communities in this territory? Most people, those outside the family, would be against him for that.'

'It is a valid point,' Fidelma admitted. 'Yet it does not always follow. When one is given a series of facts there should be only one logical process to reach a conclusion.'

'There is something else to be considered.' It was Eadulf who interrupted with an apologetic glance to Fidelma. 'It has been pointed out that religion was not a factor when the Uí Liatháin joined with their neighbours, the Déisi, in the abortive march on Cashel six months ago. Abbot Brocc did not object to his father's alliance and, although he denied culpability, he allowed seven warships to anchor by the abbey in the great river. So it seems that he supported his father in trying to make war on Cashel.'

Fidelma was thoughtful. 'This may be true, but Abbot Brocc and his librarian, Brother Cróebíne, came to the peace talks, which we both attended. They claimed the Abbey was innocent and not involved in the conflict.'

'That was not necessarily accurate,' Báine said.

Fidelma turned back to her. 'You have confirmed your other uncle, Conmhaol, declined the invitation to be leader of his people. When Brocc came to Cashel and spoke as if he were elected as Prince of the Uí Liatháin, did your family council approve of that?'

'He elected himself but I suppose someone had to speak for us. Conmhaol was weak. We just needed someone stronger to shelter us from the reparations that have brought so much misery. Now we have no representative to speak for us.'

'From what I saw of your farmstead, you have not suffered unduly,' Eadulf could not restrain himself from saying.

The girl started to flush and Fidelma quickly intervened.

'I gather that you did not care much for either of your uncles. You are young, but a member of the *derbhfine* nonetheless. You had a voice but I presume that you did not support either of them?'

The girl surprised them with a burst of bitter laughter. 'We needed someone to stand up for our people and their culture.'

'And you were against the New Faith . . .'

'The faith of the Uí Liatháin is being Uí Liatháin.'

'So you think the murder of your uncle Brocc was something to do with his ambition as much as religion? Eadulf pressed. 'If there is a conflict of ambition then we have to absolve Conmhaol, because he refused to be leader of your people.'

Báine sniffed. 'I would not even trust that. My uncle Conmhaol is also self-absorbed. He wanted to present himself as pious, yet piety was everything that he was not. I would say his assuming the mantle of a caring person was done out of conceit. It was conceit that made him isolate in his cursed island in the swamp. As to his piety, when it came to the treatment of his own wife he used her badly, ordering her to obey him as if she were some *daer-fuidhir*, a slave without rights.'

Fidelma's eyes widened a little. 'He is married?'

'He was. His wife left him and sought a Brehon's judgement. It was found that she could be given an immediate divorce with full compensation, and the return of her *coibche*, her dowry, under any one of the seven laws by which a woman has those rights.'

'Yet you display contradictory emotions of concern for your uncle now that he has disappeared. This does not equate.'

'Have you ever known human emotions to equate logically?' replied the girl defiantly.

'And where love and hate are concerned, we are often dealing with the same emotion,' Fidelma acknowledged with a sad smile. 'Is that what you are saying?'

Báine shrugged. 'I am not into philosophical conundrums. I simply dislike the values that my uncles represented. I am interested in how that affects me. That is what my concern is. I preferred to claim this farmland, which had been my mother's inheritance before her marriage. She was a *banchombarbe*, a female heir with right to the property, so these lands were my inheritance, as I know you will recognise in law. That is why I am also a member of the *derbhfine*.'

'It also means that now Brocc is dead and Conmhaol has disappeared, there might be nothing to stop you declaring yourself to the family council for their support,' Fidelma pointed out.

'I would not dispute that. However, you are so concerned about Conmhaol you have overlooked the heritance of my mother, the daughter of Tigerna Cosraigib. The same laws that apply to me, the laws of female inheritance, would also apply to her. Conmhaol has rejected leadership of the Uí Liatháin and now disappeared.'

'Does Conmhaol's refusal of the endorsement of the *derbhfine* make him ineligible for office in the future?' Eadulf asked, frustrated by the complications of the law. 'That would rule out the theory that he has been abducted to prevent the *derbhfine* endorsing the choice if he stood again.'

It was a possibility that had not occurred to Fidelma because she had not come across such a situation before.

'You must know your family council,' she said to Báine. 'Let us talk about them. Which other relatives are eligible?'

'I have attended only one council since my maturity. I was not impressed. And certainly not all those entitled to attend even bothered to show up, or perhaps their numbers are not many. I do not know.'

'Surely the survivors of Tigerna Cosraigib's family are not so limited?' Fidelma pressed.

The girl gave a short humourless bark of laughter.

'First, my grandfather was not called Lord of the Slaughter for nothing. He made sure that the survivors of his *derbhfine* were limited to those loyal to him. Contingents always went to fight in the Uí Fidgente wars against the Eóghanacht until Prince Donnenach agreed the peace. More relatives were killed in the Déisi campaigns. Others followed their fortunes in Osraige and some even joined the army of Laigin. And if there were some who survived those wars, Tigerna Cosraigib ensured they were no longer threats to his power.'

'So you are saying that your grandfather brooked no rivals?' Eadulf asked.

'Isn't it the same among all nobles and in all lands?' the girl asked.

'So your *derbhfine*, the few survivors of the family of Tigerna

Cosraigib, are the family council because others have become extinct in wars and conflicts?'

'Perhaps this is why I heard no rumours of any contending princes after Conmhaol,' Caol commented.

'There are some more distant, like Íccaid or Cathbarr. They are still valid under the law of the four generations,' the girl acknowledged.

'I suppose it is too much to hope that there is a *seanchaidh* to recite the *forsundud*, the poem in praise of the lineage of your family?' Caol asked. 'We should know the names of everyone who has a right to claim to be Prince of the Uí Liatháin.'

'The only person who could do that would be Scannail, the old *seanchaidh*. He knows all the lines of descent of the four generations.' Báine's tone was almost gloating.

'Scannail?' Fidelma was reflective. 'Now we might have a reason why that page in the abbey records went missing.'

'Scannail could recite from memory the *forsundud*, as they did in ancient times. To recite the *forsundud* from memory is a tradition . . .' Báine halted as she realised that Fidelma probably knew more about such things than she did.

'I recall the page missing from the archives at Dair Inis about Brocc,' Eadulf remarked. 'According to Brother Cróebíne, the librarian, Lalóg, your mother, visited the archives.'

Fidelma gave him a quick glance of disapproval but Báine had heard and she appeared scandalised.

'My mother would have nothing to do with that. Anyway, the sacred *forsundud* would not be committed to writing. That was a prohibition in the Old Faith. Such words are sacred.'

'But not to the New Faith. The page referred to when Brocc was appointed abbot, and his background,' Eadulf felt obliged to explain.

'So you are still going to Dún Guairne? In spite of it being deserted?' Báine changed the conversation abruptly.

Fidelma was silent for a moment, then shook her head, surprising her companions.

'Tomorrow we will start back to Dair Inis. I think we have spent enough time here and, as you say, the place is deserted so there is no point.'

'You think the answers remain at Dair Inis?' Eadulf asked in surprise.

'I believe we can trust Báine and the others who have pointed out that Dún Guairne is deserted. There is no point in going.'

The girl suddenly seemed more relaxed.

Caol shifted his weight in his seat uneasily.

'Something troubles you?' Báine asked.

'We have not resolved the question about Conmhaol. The fact is that the *crannóg* at Cnoc an Fiagh was deserted. Did Conmhaol vacate it or was he abducted?'

'We have already asked the question,' Fidelma sharply pointed out.

'But not decided on an answer.'

'If Conmhaol and his household were abducted and carried off with all the animal livestock and any retainers, what was the purpose?' Fidelma replied. 'It is more likely that he simply decided to remove elsewhere into the adjacent hills. He took his household with him. That makes sense. Conmhaol would feel it necessary to maintain a household.'

Eadulf was surprised, for he thought Fidelma had questioned the idea.

'That would be why his homestead was deserted,' Caol admitted.

Báine was entirely in agreement. 'My uncle claimed that he wanted no involvement with the family. If he did abandon the *crannóg* for a new dwelling, he would obviously take his household and livestock with him. So perhaps he moved further up into the hills to avoid problems? Maybe to the Hill of the Phantoms, to the old ruined fortress.'

'And leave the body of Brother Scatánach? Why kill him?' Dego asked softly.

'It's another conundrum that will not be sorted until Conmhaol is confronted. But we have run out of time,' said Fidelma in a resigned tone, to her companions' surprise. 'As Báine has suggested, Conmhaol was doing things for personal gain.'

'You already have two reasons to consider and you are the *dálaigh*,' the girl replied tersely. 'So the decision is yours.'

Fidelma hesitated only a fraction of time before agreeing. 'We will intrude no further on your hospitality and continue our journey at first light towards Dair Inis. We have to return our ponies to the smithy there anyway and find a boat to take us back upriver.'

Eadulf caught her tone and felt it sounded false.

The elderly, sour-faced housekeeper chose that moment to appear at the door.

'These guests have the hospitality of my house,' Báine smiled. 'They are leaving for Dair Inis in the morning. My suggestion is that you leave journeying until past sun-up. The tracks across the hills will be drier then and the journey made easier.'

Fidelma was surprised at the change in the girl's attitude towards them.

'We are most appreciative and happy to accept your hospitality.'

Báine seemed to realise perhaps she was suddenly too friendly and needed to be more circumspect.

'Do not interpret me wrongly. I am most anxious for you to continue your search for my uncle Conmhaol and to resolve the murder of my other uncle, Brocc. But there is no point in setting off in the darkness of the night. Best to rest here tonight and then have a comfortable journey tomorrow.'

Fidelma answered with thanks for all of her party.

Báine turned to the elderly woman who was waiting quietly with disapproval on her features.

'Have accommodation for this night arranged for the lady Fidelma and her husband as well as for the warriors that accompany her.'

The woman looked scandalised. 'They will stay this night?' she questioned.

'I think that you heard me. They will certainly not sleep out on the marshes,' the girl snapped with irony, suddenly turning into an autocratic princess. 'I have offered them the traditional hospitality of my house. See to it.'

Caol rose. 'I'll attend to our horses for tonight. Where should I take our bags?'

Báine turned to the elderly woman. 'Show the warrior the guest quarters.'

'We would not wish to impose on you any extra problems,' Fidelma said.

'It is no extra problem,' the housekeeper replied.

'Oh, ensure something special is prepared for the *praind*. We will eat at the usual time. When you speak with the stable master, see if his daughter is available to help prepare accommodations and heat the baths for the lady Fidelma and her husband.'

It was clear that Báine had a natural and easy way of issuing instructions, which showed that she was well used to the role of a noble. It was also clear from the suspicious and disapproving look on the elderly woman's face that these instructions did not meet with her approval. Fidelma guessed that the disapproval came from an almost dominating protection for the young noblewoman and not for any other reason.

The woman muttered an acknowledgement and left to fulfil her orders. Báine turned to Fidelma, still maintaining her friendliness and adopting an apologetic gesture.

'I regret we are not a tavern, so we can only supply heated water for one bath, for you and your husband. The weather is still warm enough for the men to use the stream behind the barn. It is where the men on this farmstead bathe. I hope this will meet with your approval.'

'I am sure that will be fine,' Fidelma acknowledged, again thinking the enthusiasm in the other's tone a strange change.

'Good. I hope you do not mind my advice about not leaving early. I suggest that you leave at midday when the sun has ensured the ground is less boggy. That will also allow your horses to be rested.'

When Caol returned, the conversation changed to less contro-versial subjects such as Báine's farmstead – the animals she kept and the crops she grew. They were surprised to learn that, in spite of the marshy land, in two areas the girl grew corn, wheat and barley.

'Running this place must take a lot of work,' Eadulf observed. 'I suppose you grind the cereal grains to make bread and biscuits yourself?'

'Surely,' she agreed. 'My farmstead makes a good living for our workers. We are very self-sufficient.'

The conversation continued until the housekeeper returned to announce the bath had been heated for Fidelma and Eadulf, and one of the outsider workers came to escort Caol and Dego to the stream where they could bathe.

Once inside the bathing house, Fidelma dispensed with the services of the attendant who had appeared to help their prepar-ations. She motioned Eadulf to climb with her into the *debach*, the wooden, tar-sealed vat with its heated waters.

Eadulf could see that Fidelma wanted to say something so that she would not be overheard outside.

'What is it?' he asked, handing her the sweet-smelling soap that had been provided.

'Báine has some plan afoot,' Fidelma confirmed. 'We should warn Dego and Caol when we can.'

'I thought her change of attitude was a bit too sudden,' Eadulf agreed. 'Suspicious and defensive before then, all of a sudden, cordial and hospitable. I could see it was false. Are we in danger? What is the plan?'

'We have to be on our guard. Certainly, the girl knows far more than she admits. She doesn't seem concerned with either the death of her uncle Brocc or the disappearance of her uncle Conmhaol. I think we are near the centre of the spider's web.'

'You still want to return to Dair Inis? I don't think the girl believed that sudden change of plan.'

'My intention is to go to Dún Guairne. The fact that no one wants us to go there – Scannail, Lalóg and now Báine – tells me that we must. Something important is happening, or has happened. Anyway, we will play along with Báine's plans, but we must make sure we get to our saddles before sunrise. Another thing, we must warn Caol and Dego that Báine will want us to indulge in the beverages she will provide at the meal tonight. I believe that she aims for us to be fast asleep when the sun rises in the morning.'

'You think she is that devious?'

'I trust she is not more devious than most, but has some other strategy. But we must not alert her suspicions.'

'I have an excuse that might help' Eadulf smiled. 'I'll point out that this is a special holy day in which believers in the New Faith are not allowed to drink strong alcohol. As she is of the Old Faith she won't realise it.'

'She is intelligent, though,' Fidelma warned him.

They finished their bath and used some of the perfumes that were provided before dressing in the chamber they had previously been shown. The female attendant appeared to ensure all their wants had been catered for and just then a hand bell sounded.

'That will be the call for the *praind*, the evening meal,' the girl advised. 'When you are ready, you may call or just follow the sounds.'

It was not long before Fidelma and Eadulf were back in the main room, where they found a table already set out for the evening meal. Caol and Dego were nervously awaiting their arrival. Báine had already seated herself at the head of the table.

'Were the baths and rest sufficient to your needs, lady?' she asked Fidelma.

'Most pleasant, Báine,' Fidelma replied solemnly. 'And you keep an excellent table.'

'I pride myself on keeping to the traditions of my heritage. However, there is a choice of wines newly arrived from Gaul.'

'A pity, as this is the day we celebrate the life of the Briton Dewi of Dyfed, who founded a community where no alcohol was allowed. So this day we touch no alcoholic drink,' declared Eadulf, turning his gaze to Dego and Caol and letting his eyelid fall for a moment.

The girl had not noticed and motioned them to their places.

They were just finishing the meal, when a sudden harshness of sound interrupted them. The noise was of someone arriving unexpectedly: the protesting whinny of a horse, and voices giving orders. There was no doubt from her expression of surprise that Báine was not expecting an arrival. They heard the dismounted rider striding across the wooden planks of the entrance. It seemed the door was about to open when there was a sharp exchange. When the door did open, the man who entered was one of the two who had originally greeted Fidelma and her companions at the farmhouse.

He glanced around anxiously before addressing Báine.

'Lady, your attention is needed. Tóchell has arrived with a message.'

Báine rose with some alacrity and muttered an excuse before

following the man outside. There were voices raised outside in some animation.

Eadulf glanced at Fidelma, brow raised in question. However, the elderly housekeeper had remained in the room, pretending to be busy, so the look on Fidelma's features warned against anything but any general conversation. It was a short time before the door was opened again and Báine called to her housekeeper to attend her.

As soon as she departed, Fidelma rose, went to the door and stood close beside it in a listening attitude. Then she shrugged and returned.

'I can't hear anything. They must have moved away.'

'What is it?' Eadulf demanded.

'Tóchell was the name of the female attendant of Lalóg,' she reminded him.

A moment later Báine returned. She was looking uncomfortable.

'It was just a neighbour who wanted advice.'

'A late time to call,' Fidelma observed. 'But maybe it is a good time for us to turn in to prepare for our journey back to Dair Inis tomorrow.'

Báine looked relieved.

'We will take your advice and sleep in late,' Fidelma assured her as they began to follow Caol. 'We have had too many long days travelling. I hope the journey back to Dair Inis will be an easy one.'

It was lucky that the guests were housed in adjacent round houses, almost in the same configuration as Íccaid's hospital. Once in the darkness of the guesthouse, Fidelma turned to Dego.

'Go to the stables. Keep out of sight, but see if you can learn anything. The woman Tóchell arrived on horseback. I think she is still here.'

It was only a short time before he returned.

'I didn't see the woman but the two stablemen were chatting away. They said that Cathbarr and his men should be arriving soon,' he said.

'Anything else?'

'Bits and pieces. Tóchell came with a message from Báine's mother. Something about the family council meeting in two days' time. They did not say where. One said, "the problem will now be resolved". I couldn't catch any more.'

'I think I am beginning to see the mystery clearing,' Fidelma said. 'But even if we try to leave before light, the stablemen will be alerted when we get the horses.'

'Earlier, when I went to get the bags, I saw that they had put them in a paddock field behind the stables,' Caol said. 'They just dumped them there and didn't even take off the saddle blankets. The lazy—'

'Wait,' whispered Fidelma. 'Their laziness might be a stroke of luck.' She paused, thinking for a moment. 'I believe we are in danger if we remain. The only thing keeping us safe is that Báine thinks she has distracted us and we are heading back to Dair Inis. So they will allow us to go. But we shall depart long before first light.'

'There is a full moon tonight,' Dego said. 'It's bright, and if we are careful we could have little trouble.'

'If we need to leave, we need to leave at once,' Fidelma agreed. 'Do you think there is a chance of retrieving the horses from that field without disturbance?'

'A chance, if the animals are still down by the far end, where there is a stream. There's also a gate down there so we would not have to come back to the main buildings.'

'Caol and Dego, you go to see if the horses can be made ready quietly. Let's hope they are still at the far end of the field. Come back and tell us if so, and if the way is clear. Then we will bring the bags and leave.'

Caol and Dego left immediately.

Even Eadulf was surprised at this rapid change of plan. 'We will be exhausted before midday without sleep,' he protested.

'Better exhausted than dead,' Fidelma replied.

He said no more but followed her out into the night. Dego was returning with a whispered 'all's well'. He led the way into the shadows with Fidelma and Eadulf at his heels. There was a barred fence to the paddock, so they were able to climb over it without difficulty.

'Keep to the side of the field and work round,' Dego instructed quietly. 'If we try crossing the field in the darkness we might end up in trouble.'

They did not respond, but followed closely.

It was moments later they turned at right angles and saw Caol waiting with the animals.

'I've opened the gate here. The moon is about to leave that cloud bank, which should give us a good start over the hill that is facing you. At least it is not the flat marshland that lies in the other direction.'

'You are sure it is a safe way to wherever we are now going?' Eadulf muttered nervously.

'Let's hope the moon is strong enough for us to see the track and put some distance between ourselves and here,' Fidelma replied. 'We want to go to Dún Guairne, but make some tracks to deceive any followers that we are heading in the opposite direction.'

They exited the field, with Caol, showing his ability as ever, stopping to bend to the gate and close it so that any followers might be confused for a while.

'But where are we heading?' he asked.

'First, we do not head directly to Dún Guairne because that is where they will think we shall be heading.'

'There was another thing I heard the stableman say,' Caol

suddenly said. 'He was worrying about any delay when they should all be at the Hill of the Phantoms for the *derbhfine* to confirm the chosen one.'

'He used the expression "the chosen one"?'

'And this family council is north, at the Hill of the Phantoms, and not at Dún Guairne?' Caol asked.

'I can't help wondering who "the chosen one" is,' Eadulf said.

'Lalóg? I am getting confused again.'

The conversation ceased for a while as Caol and Dego opted to lead the way across some moonlit hills. It was well after midnight but the moonlight was so strong they had no difficulty riding through the strange shadowland. They saw some dark grain barns ahead and it was Fidelma who suggested they might make good shelter for the horses and a place to rest for a while.

Having attended to the horses, they sat down to relax, and exhaustion overcame them without warning. Before she fell asleep Fidelma's last thoughts were on Báine's summons to the *derbhfine*, the family council and its whereabouts. She was now aware that soon the last pieces of the puzzle would be put in place and the entire mystery resolved.

CbAPTeR NINETEEN

The night passed uncomfortably. They had sheltered, with their horses, in the isolated barn. It had once been a grain store but was now empty, rotting and damp. Sleep, after the initial period of exhaustion, was fleeting, and they shared surprise that their departure had been accomplished so easily. No one seemed to have been alerted by their leaving. Now, as the sun began to show itself over the eastern mountains, Caol and Dego were up and foraging the surrounding area to see if there was anything to eat. It was soon evident, however, that the travellers would have to contain their hunger for a while.

As they moved westward, the country become very hilly away from the marsh stretches, which made the going slow. The sun showed it was nearly mid-morning when they came to the brow of a hill and, surprisingly, found a solitary goatherd resting by a small spring. He was elderly, grizzle faced and weather tanned.

'Are we far from Dún Guairne?' Fidelma greeted him.

'Other side of that hill,' the man said, jerking his head in the direction. 'That is the Hill of the Sprites, Cnoc Púca. From there you will see the fortress in the valley below, standing just by a wide river.'

'If it is not an abundance of waters and marshes, then it is a place of goblins and demons surrounding us,' grumbled Eadulf. 'I am sure we have already seen enough places named after them.'

'Remember the Old Faith has not vanished from these hills and gorges yet,' Caol smiled sympathetically.

'Is there a place where we might find fodder for our horses or, indeed, something to keep our own pangs of hunger at bay?' Fidelma asked.

The man looked at their mounts and grimaced. 'Plenty of grasses lower down the hill. You might find straw and even chaff – some of those areas were used for growing cereals in the summer. But food for yourselves . . .? You might find someone who will provide you with something when you get into the settlement by the old fortress.'

'There are people living there? I thought it was deserted.'

'In the settlement. Always there will be people there. But the fortress is deserted by the nobility now.'

Although Caol had to be careful with his stallion, their moorland ponies were as sure footed as always. They managed to climb without problems to the hill that the goatherd had indicated. When they reached the shoulder of the hill, they paused to look down into a broad valley into which three substantial rivers seemed to be flowing. In the centre of the low flatland, the waters met and divided again into two wide rivers flowing south-west and south-east. A large circular stone fortress was set on the south-east river bank. The sun seemed to sparkle on its red limestone battlements.

'We can presume that we have found Dún Guairne,' Eadulf sighed with relief.

No one bothered to reply. Instead, Caol began to lead the way down the hill to the level where one of the substantial rivers provided a barrier.

Eventually, they managed to find a natural ford to cross towards the fortress.

'I never knew a country so filled with rivers and streams,' Eadulf complained again. 'Where can all that water come from?'

Caol waved his hand in a circular motion. 'You are never far from high hills and mountains. Where else does water rise and burst forth into rivers?'

'I have observed that,' Eadulf replied with some irony. 'It would be difficult not to.'

'Look,' Fidelma called. 'If the fortress is deserted by people, at least there seem to be a lot of livestock about the place. I see a little movement around Dún Guairne, and the smoke of fires.'

'Most of the buildings look deserted,' Dego frowned. 'The gates of the fortress stand wide and the animals are wandering in and out.'

The fortress certainly had an abandoned look about it. As they drew closer, they could see it was a traditional circular triple-rampart construction, the great limestone walls of which rose defensively against the surroundings. From the construction Fidelma guessed it was quite ancient, although there was little damage to its walls. It stood not far from the river bank where they saw a collection of buildings of various shapes. There was some human movement here and it was obvious that this was the remains of what had been a fairly large riverside village. Several of the houses were still occupied, judging by the smoke that issued from them.

As Fidelma and her companions drew closer they could see, outside some of these buildings, women were occupied with several tasks. Some were sitting at their doors, hand-spinning wool in an ancient technique. Another woman was cutting vegetables into a cauldron, which was steaming on a fire. One or two men were sitting around, fletching arrows or sharpening wood into points.

The sound of iron striking iron drew the visitors' attention to a building from which acrid smoke came. It was soon evident that it was the village's blacksmith. A middle-aged man, whose appearance and muscular build was typical of men of his art, looked up as they halted before the forge.

The smith surveyed them for a moment. He put down his hammer, taking tongs and placing the metal that he had been working back into the fire. Without hesitation he proceeded to pump the bellows on his fire to restore his charcoal to a glow. The smith turned his head aside and spat on to the burning charcoal. It meant no disrespect, but was the old smiths' way of testing the heat of the coals. Then he stepped back and regarded them.

'Greetings, strangers.' It was a traditional salutation but implied a question.

'Strangers seeking assistance,' replied Fidelma.

'It depends on what assistance you seek?'

'Our horses are in need of fodder,' Fidelma replied.

'Take them round the back. There's a good field there and a dry shed where you'll find hay and even some oats, but that will cost a *screpal*.'

Fidelma swung down from her horse and motioned the others to do so.

'Can we find something to assuage our morning hunger?'

'When you have taken the horses to the field, you could doubtless purchase some bannocks or fruit from yonder cottage where my woman is spinning yarn.'

Fidelma sent Caol and Dego to attend to the horses and suggested Eadulf talk to the smith's wife to negotiate for something they could eat.

'There is something else I would ask of you,' she said to the smith when the others had gone. 'What is your name, by the way?'

'I am called Gobán,' the man replied.

'I should have guessed.' Fidelma smiled broadly. The name meant 'smith' after the smith-god. 'I would like information.'

'If I know the information that you seek, it is yours,' replied the man.

'Just some local information,' Fidelma replied.

'I recognise that voice,' Gobán suddenly said, but almost with a tone of resignation.

Fidelma was puzzled. 'We have never encountered one another before.'

'I meant that I know the sound of a Brehon's voice,' the smith corrected in a tone of acquiescence.

'Well, true that I am a *dálaigh*,' Fidelma said, relaxing. 'But I am sure my questions will not be hard to answer.'

'Ah, questions rather than a question? Questions are always easy to answer once you know the answers.'

'Has there been much activity in the fortress these last few days?'

'There is little activity at the fortress since the old prince was killed. That was back last spring, about six months ago.' He paused and, frowning, brushed the tip of his nose with the edge of his right forefinger. 'But the truth is, recently there have been a few warriors here and others moving about. I do not take much interest in these things. I keep myself to myself.'

'That is unusual for a smith,' she commented. 'It is usually the first place to come to get news. I see animals wandering in and out of the fortress.'

'True, in good times I hear the gossip. In bad times it is best to keep oneself to oneself. I am not responsible for the animals. Doubtless those who left them will come to reclaim them.'

'These warriors gave you the impression that it would be the best course to try to ignore them?'

The smith shrugged, trying to express disinterest. 'There is little more to know.'

'I am sure you can tell me more?' she countered persuasively. 'Who were these warriors and how did they come here?'

The smith exhaled in a deep sigh. For a moment or two Fidelma felt he was not going to answer her and then he shrugged, pausing to stir the greying coals on the fire to try to bring them back to a red glow.

'A few days ago a few boats came upriver and moored over by

the old gates of the fortress. About half a dozen warriors disembarked and, leaving one of their number to look after the boat, they moved in a body north-west. The next day they returned. I am told they had some prisoners with them.'

'Prisoners?'

'I did not see for myself. They brought those animals. I was told that they marched directly back to their boat where the prisoners were placed. They left the animals behind in the fortress grounds. The boats returned back down the river.'

'Did you not enquire who they were, or protest, demanding to know why they had taken prisoners? They must have been local people.'

'One of them, not their commander but someone with authority, warned us to forget everything we had seen.'

'You didn't feel that you should send for the local Brehon? You must have one nearby.'

'Not one lives within three or four days' ride so what use would that be? Anyway, the warning not to say anything was quite specific, to which was added an ancient curse. If we went to alarm anyone about them we would die by the strangling of the sea cat.'

Fidelma knew this was a powerful ancient curse, used by those who lived near the sea. The 'Cat Mara' was a powerful mythical animal that inflicted illness, misfortune and death on those so cursed.

'Well, you have kept your word for you did not go looking for someone to report to, but we came to you.'

The smith grinned. 'I had already worked that out, lady.'

'Is there anyone who could tell us anything further about these people? For example, the type of boat they used.'

The smith shrugged. 'I can tell you one thing, for I know people from that land. There was a man of the Déisi with them. He was in charge of the boats. It's not the first time he has been here. I think they called him Tóla. I'll speak honestly. I think it was wrong for our prince, Tigerna Cosraigib, to form an alliance with Cummasach of the Déisi last spring. The Déisi have never been our friends.'

Fidelma was thoughtful. 'And you say they were warriors, and not merchants?'

'They were warriors.'

Abruptly the smith seemed to catch sight of someone passing behind Fidelma.

'Hey! Temnén! Come here!'

She turned to see a dark, tousled lad of about eleven years of age halting at the sound of the smith's voice and then reluctantly coming forward. It was then they were rejoined by Caol and Dego, who had put the animals into the field indicated by the smith.

'I have done nothing,' were the young boy's first words.

'We have all done something,' replied Gobán in good humour. 'The other day I saw you down at the river speaking to one of those who brought the boats upriver; the craft that were moored by the old fort gates. He was waiting for the return of his companions. That boatman was of the Déisi, wasn't he?'

The boy shrugged. 'It is true I spoke to one of the boatmen. One of them was a Déisi seaman. I did not mean to get into trouble.'

'There is no problem,' Fidelma assured him. 'Just speak the truth.'

Temnén was still hesitant. 'Except for the Déisi boatman, the others were Uí Liatháin. Why do you want to know?'

Fidelma handed the smith a few coins and thanked him for his help before turning to the boy with an encouraging smile.

'Let us walk to the point of the river where they moored their boat. You can show me.'

'There were actually two boats,' the boy corrected, seemingly relieved that he was not to be chastised.

Eadulf had now rejoined them with a plaited-reed bag filled with bannocks and apples and a few slices of cold meat and

cheese, which he handed round. He and the others followed
Fidelma and the boy along the river bank a short distance until
they came to a spot that had clearly been used as a mooring place
for many years by an old open gate in the fortress wall.

'So there were two boats?' prompted Fidelma. 'And they
moored here? Why were you interested in them? Weren't you
warned to forget what you saw?'

'Since the old fort was abandoned, we no longer have as many
boats coming upriver. I wanted to look at them. Anyway, my dad is
a river fisherman and I have always been interested in rivercrafts.'

'So these were rivercraft?'

'I have not seen any such large vessels in this part of the river
since the fortress was abandoned.'

'Large vessels?' Caol queried. 'How can you get large vessels
all the way up here?'

'When you have a broad and lively river, you can get to know
the sort of vessels that pass up and down, or which are so big they
must stay at anchor here because they can go no further. North of
this fortress, the river narrows and eventually goes up into the
spot where it rises. When the fortress was in use there was a
vessel called an *escup*, which would come up from the coast to
deliver wine from overseas.'

'It wasn't a warship?' asked Caol.

'A warship is far too big to navigate as far as this,' replied the
boy, unabashed. 'I speak of merchant vessels.'

'So these rivercrafts were . . . what type?' Caol pressed.

'Two boats of the type that are called *serrcinn*,' the boy
answered immediately.

'You are being very specific, boy.' Caol's voice was toned with
disbelief.

'It seems that you are a clever lad,' Fidelma interrupted, not
wishing to lose the boy's confidence. 'How do you know this?'

'I know this river and was taught much by my dad. We used to go down to the coast where my uncle lives. He works on the ships that sail the ocean. He taught me much.'

'So tell me,' Fidelma went on, 'were the people you saw foreign warriors?'

'Uí Liatháin warriors.'

'Did you see the prisoners they eventually took on board the boat?'

'Oh, yes. The warriors were shouting for us to go to our homes and forget what we had seen. But I saw what happened,' the young boy assured them.

'Then perhaps you will share that knowledge with us?' Fidelma smiled.

The boy pointed to the river. 'First, the two boats were moored here. The warriors went north and it was over a day before they returned with people who they then marched down into the fortress. They had their hands tied behind their backs and the women were made to carry bundles of belongings. They had quite a few animals with them.'

'Marched with hands tied behind them?' Dego pressed.

'Well, they were forced along. They were surrounded by warriors. Dressed like you.' He pointed to Dego.

'Exactly like me?'

'Not exactly,' the boy admitted. 'Not with that gold ring around your neck. But they were warriors, with leather jackets, and they carried swords and daggers. Some of them even carried bows and quivers of arrows. Oh, and most wore grey cloaks with some insignia.'

'So the prisoners were forced on to the boat that was moored here, is that what you are saying?' Fidelma demanded. 'What happened to the animals that came with them?'

'They were let loose in the fortress and the man who shouted at us told us we could look after them until they returned, which would be soon.'

'What happened to the prisoners?' Caol demanded harshly.

The boy took a step backwards at his sharp tone and only then did Caol realise he had spoken in anger. It was mainly in anger at himself as he was supposed to have been keeping watch for strange events to report to Prince Finguine, especially those associated with the Grey Ones. He had thought they were harmless. Now the boy had said these men had worn grey cloaks.

'Sorry, boy.' He tried to sound contrite. 'What I meant to ask was where were the prisoners taken?'

The boy was still nervous of Caol's temper.

'Who were these prisoners?' Eadulf asked in an encouraging tone. 'I don't suppose you recognised any of them?'

'Oh, yes,' the boy returned immediately.

After a few moments' silence waiting for the lad to continue Caol closed his eyes to keep his patience.

'Can you tell us who you recognised?' Fidelma urged.

'I recognised Prince Conmhaol. He lived at Dún Guairne before he went to live at Cnoc an Fiagh. When I was young and the princes lived in the fortress, he was pointed out to me by my father.'

'So your father knew him?'

'My father had to work at the fortress when it needed workers. That was in the days of the old prince. My father always said that Conmhaol was a most important man. Perhaps the most important prince in our territory after his father. There was also his cousin, Fisecda, who was a great healer.'

'You say that they were marched to the boats, which sailed downriver? They were clearly prisoners?'

'Along with some others who I did not know. But I knew Conmhaol and—'

'Temnén!' At the sound of a strong masculine voice the boy turned, and hesitated for a moment before abruptly running off, disappearing into the open gates of the fortress.

A tall man emerged from the nearby smithy carrying some fishing gear. He walked with a confident stride towards the visitors, then examined them each inquisitively without any apprehension in his features.

'Temnén, get along home,' he shouted towards the gates. 'Your mother has need of you.'

'But, Father—' The boy wailed from his cover.

'Home!' snapped the newcomer.

They saw Temnén make off towards the village.

The man turned to them. 'Give you all a good day.' The greeting sounded false in their ears. 'I trust my son has not been telling you imaginary stories?'

Although this was said in attempted good nature, Fidelma could not ignore a note of hostility in the man's tone.

'I hope he has not.' She moved forward and added coldly, 'I am a *dálaigh* and it would be more than disrespectful for anyone to create stories to tell a *dálaigh* when asked questions. So, you are the boy's father?'

The man's attitude seemed to change a little, realising there was authority in her manner. Then he recognised the gold torc on the neck of Dego.

'What questions would you think my son could answer?' the man asked in a more moderate tone.

'He said he saw warriors escorting prisoners to two boats moored just here. The warriors and the prisoners came from north of Dún Guairne.'

'The fortress has been abandoned since Prince Tigerna Cosraigib was killed. That was back in the days of the geese flying north,' the man said after some reflection. 'Aye, that was the period of Giblean.'

'According to your son, he saw among the prisoners Conmhaol and another relative, Fisecda. The same Brother Fisecda who was physician of Dair Inis. They were being led as prisoners with a few others to the boats that were here.'

The fisherman stared at Fidelma. The conflicting expressions on his face confirmed the truth but that, at the same time, it was obviously something he would rather not comment on.

'I suppose others saw this?'

When the man still hesitated, Dego stepped forward and said: 'Come, man, the truth now. You know the penalties for not answering in truth the questions of a *dálaigh*.'

'I know the penalties for interfering in matters connected with the family of Tigerna Cosraigib,' the man muttered.

'Tigerna Cosraigib is dead,' Fidelma pointed out sharply.

'But his family are still alive.'

'So you have two choices. You tell me what you saw or, by refusing, you incur the penalties of the law.'

The fisherman paused a second longer, then shrugged.

'Some of us saw the prisoners taken on board a river boat,' he said, as if the words were being forced out of him. 'Conmhaol and Fisecda were certainly among them. Their hands were bound.'

'So Conmhaol and Fisecda were definitely prisoners?'

'Conmhaol had abandoned Dún Guairne when his father was killed. That was when he went to his *crannóg* at Cnoc an Fiagh. That is further north from here.'

'So your son spoke the truth.' Fidelma smiled thinly.

The man sighed. 'My boy was speaking the truth. We were warned that whoever said anything about it would be cursed. The curse of the Grey One would fall on our village and on each of us, even to the seventh generation.'

'So people here knew the prisoners had been taken? Who did they think these raiders were who took Prince Conmhaol? Was he not in line to become Prince of the Uí Liatháin? Was it not his people's duty to protect him?'

'We heard that he had refused the endorsement of his *derbh-fine*. Therefore he was not the successor to Tigerna Cosraigib.'

'The people who took the prisoners, then – who were they?'

'I suppose they came here as far as the river was navigable and then went overland to Conmhaol's *crannóg*. It is the easiest route.'

'That was not what I meant,' Fidelma replied in an icy tone.

The man seemed reluctant to speak.

'Better the truth than loss of your honour price,' Caol added heavily. 'What is your name, so we know to whom we speak? Don't hide it for we can easily discover it.'

'My name is Tomán,' the man answered uneasily.

'Then let me ask again, Tomán, who did you think these people were?'

'As I say, we heard the old prince's *derbhfine* could not agree on who was to be head of the family and Prince of all the Uí Liatháin. An argument raged, so we heard, and it still has not been agreed who will take residence in Dún Guairne and lead our people. I tell in honesty, *dálaigh*, there are still some who resent the fact that we now have to pay tribute to Cashel and suffer for our past alliances. Some want to reassert the independence of the Uí Liatháin. No one is agreed.'

'Your son said those who came here wore grey cloaks.'

'They could have been anyone . . . even raiders from the coast,' the man replied.

Fidelma was amused. 'I think we know better. I believe some were nobles of the Uí Liatháin. Your son said that you worked in the fortress under the old prince. Do you claim you know nothing about the identity of these raiders?'

'I saw nothing,' the man confirmed stubbornly. 'My son doubtless told you one of the warriors shouted a warning. I have mentioned it also.'

'That you would be cursed? You believe that if you reveal anything, something bad will happen? I suppose you believe in incredible phantoms . . . the Sea Cat or the Grey One. It is embedded in your culture. I suppose that you would tell me, if you could. Who cursed you? Was Scannail in this party?'

It was clear the name had an impact on Tomán. There was nervous hesitation before he spoke.

'I am not that backward,' he muttered. 'Scannail is a *seanchaidh* and would be disregarded for his stories.'

'Then you must have recognised someone who put fear into you?'

Tomán seemed to be mentally struggling with himself. 'We believed that one of those who we recognised was an evil man,' he finally admitted.

'You recognised one of the warriors?'

'Not a warrior, but one of the people acting as though he was in command of them,' Tomán said.

'Why did you recognise him?' Eadulf asked when he hesitated again.

'I did so because his father was once a steward at Dún Guairne. That was when Tigerna Cosraigib was still alive.'

'This man – does he have a name?'

'The father? He was Cetliatha and was a cousin of Tigerna Cosraigib,' Tomán replied.

Fidelma glanced at Eadulf in surprise before turning back to the fisherman.

'Is Cetliatha's son named Cathbarr, who is now steward to Princess Lalóg? She who dwells on the coast near the abbey of Dair Inis.'

Tomán seemed surprised at her knowledge.

'I do not know what he is now, but he served in the bodyguard to Tigerna Cosraigib at Dún Guairne.'

'So Cathbarr was here? He knew Conmhaol had retreated to Cnoc an Fiagh and wanted little or nothing to do with his family. Well, some of his family,' she corrected after a pause.

Dego spoke quietly: 'This means it was Cathbarr who took these raiders to this spot and moored here before going to Conmhaol's *crannóg* to take him, Brother Fisecda and their attendants prisoner. They killed Brother Scatánach. Then they herded the prisoners with the animals to this place.'

'Why leave the animals here?' Eadulf was bewildered.

'They could not take them on the boats. But there is another explanation. They were going to the family council, as we learned at Báine's farmstead. Cathbarr, who led them, knew there would be a decision made there and whomever was chosen would be – remember the words heard last night – "the chosen one". Whoever the chosen one was, he or she meant to reclaim Dún Guairne as the principal fortress. That's why they left the animals here.'

'Is Cathbarr trying to make Conmhaol accept the succession?' queried Caol. 'Otherwise, what would be his motivations? Or does he want the prize to go to Lalóg, whom he serves.'

Tomán shook his head. 'You would discount that notion if you knew Cathbarr. He is staunchly of the Uí Liatháin and one of the leaders that fought at Cnoc Áine with Prince Tigerna Cosraigib. He also negotiated with the Déisi to form the alliance during the last conflict.'

'From the way that Cathbarr behaved when we were at Lalóg's settlement, I would have to agree,' Fidelma said. 'But why make a prisoner of Conmhaol? For what purpose? Forcing someone to change their minds to accept the leadership is inexplicable. What purpose would that serve? I believe the answer lies in the family and involves Conmhaol, but Lalóg as well.'

'Ah, all part of the *derbhfine*. So what is being revealed is a struggle for power among the Uí Liatháin,' Dego summed up.

'It seems that we need to seek out a boat from someone, if we are going to chase Cathbarr and his warriors,' Eadulf suggested.

'And then what?' Fidelma frowned disapprovingly. 'We are talking about facing a large war party apparently commanded by a warrior who has fought us before. This Cathbarr must be as well trained as you, Caol and Dego. And you would not be facing one man but many warriors. We are no match for them.'

'Besides,' Dego added, agreeing with her, 'by this time they will be out at sea and beyond our reach. By the time we reach them, the *derbhfine* will have decided and the entire Uí Liatháin may be roused to join an army to drive any Eóghanacht support out of this territory, or worse.'

'We should try,' Eadulf insisted. 'Is there a boatyard near here? Somewhere we could obtain a boat to follow them?'

'The village is not like it used to be in the old days. There is old Muirgius. He repairs local vessels but mainly boats for river fishing.'

'Well, let's enquire there if he has anything suitable—' Eadulf began.

'It would be a waste of time,' Fidelma interrupted with quiet emphasis. 'We would never catch up with them and, even if we could, and could overcome them, they would never meekly surrender to a *dálaigh*. I have an alternative plan, however, as I am beginning to see what is going on.'

Eadulf's eyes widened. 'You mean you already know the meaning to all this? You know who this "chosen one" is? You know who the Grey One is? You know who killed Abbot Brocc, and why Conmhaol has been taken prisoner? I am simply lost in the possibilities, let alone being able to follow a comprehensible path.'

'Trust me, Eadulf,' she replied, quietly whimsical.

She turned to the fisherman and thanked him for his information. The man accepted her implied dismissal, turned and set off along the river, obviously resuming the purpose of his task with the fishing gear. They watched him walk away before looking expectantly at Fidelma.

'We will go and recover the horses. Then I suggest we depart from here. I will tell you my intentions afterwards. Words can magically be transmitted on the wind . . . can't they, Temnén?' she suddenly said loudly.

The young boy emerged from a clump of nearby bushes.

'I wasn't really listening,' he said defensively.

'Of course not,' Fidelma agreed solemnly.

'Is there going to be a war again?' the boy asked. 'I am old enough to fight now. And is Tigerna Cosraigib going to lead us . . .?'

'The man is dead,' Caol said sharply.

'But they say he was born of the gods, just like the famous Cú Roí or Cú Chullainn. The Grey Old One teaches that he was invincible and he was protected by the magic cloak of the Grey One, goddess of our people.'

'Life is not always as the storytellers would have it,' Fidelma admonished in a kindly fashion. 'Off you go home now, young Temnén. I am sure your mother will have some treat prepared for you.'

The boy turned sulkily away, dragging his heels.

'Let us get our horses and discuss plans where we are assured they will not be transmitted anywhere.'

They made their way back to the smith, who was still at work.

'Did you get all the information you wanted, lady?' he greeted, pausing in adjusting an axe head to a piece of wood.

'We have the information, but not as we wanted,' Fidelma replied. She felt it better not to admit much. 'Can my men collect our horses, for we must be off across country?'

'You are heading to the Great River?'

'To the Abbey of Dair Inis,' she confirmed, 'where we might get a boat to Lios Mór.'

It seemed little time passed before the four of them were mounted and climbing into the eastern hills. It was not much longer when Fidelma called a halt. It was a good spot for

indulging in secrets, on a windswept mound whose grasses had
been pared clean by sheep over the years. There were neither
shrubs, trees nor any growth where prying ears might find cover.
'What now?' Eadulf asked. 'I don't think we have evidence to
bring any suspects to a judgement by a Brehon.'

'Do you know where you are, Caol?' Fidelma demanded,
ignoring Eadulf.

Caol looked around uncertainly. 'You mean the name of this—'

'I mean the direction to where Finnat's homestead is.'

'Oh, yes. It is due north from here. I can find that easily.'

'That is where we shall head first. Will it take us long?'

'If we all had decent mounts we could make it within a day,'
Caol replied. 'However, with these moorland ponies I would estimate at least two days at walking speed for I think we have four
rivers, including that threatening marshland, to cross. It means
taking to high hills and areas like quagmires.'

Fidelma looked at him solemnly. 'Thanks for your optimism,
Caol. The sooner we start, the sooner we arrive.'

'We are almost back where we started.' Eadulf was increas-
ingly bewildered now.

'I will explain later more clearly when we arrive,' she told him.
'We won't be there long for we will all proceed across to the
Abbey of Lios Mór. If Cadan has returned, we will send him back
to alert Prince Finguine, the Chief Brehon and my brother to meet
us at the abbey.'

Eadulf was the first to voice his shock. 'Send for the King as
well as Fithel, the Chief Brehon? You have sorted this mystery
out so far?'

'Some things here are intractable and never will be sorted.
But I will explain when we are more rested. I am looking forward to leaving the territory of the Uí Liatháin. In no area that I
recall do I find the dead dwelling so violently in the minds of the
living.'

CHAPTER TWENTY

The great refectory hall of the Abbey of Lios Mór was not crowded. Only a few senior members were interested in the report that Fidelma was presenting. It was not even a trial, although the Chief Brehon of Muman was presiding and the King and his heir apparent and other dignitaries were present. For a few moments, Fidelma and Eadulf stood on the threshold of the hall, looking around at the small gathering, arranged as if this were a court.

At the far end of the hall there was a raised platform where the Abbot of Lios Mór and his senior staff would usually sit. This time the centre chair was occupied by Fíthel, the Chief Brehon. Next to him was his steward and recorder of the proceedings. On a lower level but immediately below the Chief Brehon was Fidelma's brother, Colgú, King of Muman. On his right was Finguine, Prince of Gleannúir, his heir apparent. On the King's left was Iarnia, the Abbot of Lios Mór, with the stewards and scribes also gathered. With them sat Abbot Cuán of Imleach, Chief Bishop of the kingdom. They had all come at Fidelma's request.

Before them was a table for Fidelma, with Eadulf as her assistant. Standing behind their chairs was Dego, commander of the bodyguard, and two other members of the guard who had joined him at the abbey.

'It's strange being here again,' Eadulf said quietly as they hesitated before entering the hall. 'It was two years ago . . .'

'Fidelma of Cashel,' came the sharp voice of the Chief Brehon, 'we are awaiting you.'

As Fidelma led the way to her allotted position, she caught sight of an elderly man seated next to Caol, among the onlookers. She turned to him.

'It is good to see you, Sárán. I am pleased that you have come safely here.'

'As you requested when you saw me at Íccaid's place, I went to Eochaill and found a boat that brought me up the Great River, all the way here to Lios Mór. I am at your service.'

'I thank you. I need only your presence to ensure I do not misunderstand my knowledge of history.'

'When you are ready, Fidelma,' came the penetrating voice of Fíthel. There was an antagonism between Fíthel and Fidelma, which went back to the time she had applied for the position of Chief Brehon but had been turned down by the Council of Brehons and Fíthel succeeded to the office. She tried to ignore the response that she always felt at the irritating tone he used whenever he sat as judge.

Fidelma turned and made her way to the table where Eadulf now sat with notes to help the case.

'I stand ready,' she intoned solemnly.

'Then proceed.' The Chief Brehon was in a snappish mood.

Fidelma's first action was to take a piece of paper from her *cior bolg* – her comb bag – and hold it aloft in her right hand. It was small and folded.

'I have written here the name of the person behind the killing of Abbot Brocc of Dair Inis. I will hand it to Abbot Iarna to hold until I have finished my presentation. This is the name of the person who arranged and, I believe, took part in the killing of the abbot. I shall argue that Brocc's death was one of *fingal* – the heinous crime of kin-slaying.'

Brehon Fíthel was immediately disapproving. 'That is an unusual procedure. You are known for your dramatics, Fidelma. I have cautioned you several times when you have appeared before me about the use of such affectations. So I caution you again.'

Fidelma tried to keep her expression immobile. 'This is not done for drama but for the purpose of proving what I shall reveal to this hearing. I start by acknowledging that this is not a legal trial. At the end of it, it will be up to the Chief Brehon whether these matters should proceed to a court where all the relevant witnesses should be called to participate. Moreover, in addition, it will be up to the King's Council to discuss the complications of the context in which the act of *fingal* took place. Why? That matter will become clear in my presentation.'

She paused as if to gather her thoughts.

'Primarily this is a hearing of my report on the matters I found at Dair Inis and among the Uí Liatháin. In this, there are several things to consider. We know that the *derbhfine,* the family council of the late Tigerna Cosraigib, the last recognised Prince of the Uí Liatháin, have been unable to appoint a successor. I believe that this is shortly to be resolved and the name on this paper will not only be the new Prince of the Uí Liatháin, but the person who instigated the killing of Abbot Brocc.'

Brehon Fíthel's eyes narrowed. 'I warn you, you tread a precarious path, Fidelma.'

'The path to truth is often precarious,' she replied easily. 'That is why I have asked you, as Chief Brehon, along with King Colgú, his heir apparent and the senior clerics of our kingdom to attend to consider the matter I lay before you. I intend to take you through my thoughts on this investigation, and I believe that before we reach the end of this proceeding, we might have a messenger from the Uí Liatháin to inform the King that a new leader has been approved and installed. If the name is the same as the one I have written here, then, as the Latin judges would say – *quod erat demonstrandum*.'

'We all know you like your Latin sayings,' Brehon Fíthel replied almost grating his teeth. 'Let us keep to our own language, the languages of our laws.'

'I would be more than happy to do so although as we have mostly accepted the New Faith, and to understand it, the work of authority is called *The Book* – or, in Greek, *Byblos* – whose Latin translation is considered the infallible authority of the Faith, we have been impelled to use Latin to make points.'

'Are you come here to teach history?' Fíthel interrupted in a derogatory tone.

'Regretfully, the one fact of history is that no one learns from it,' Fidelma replied evenly. 'I shall be using some points from this *Byblos* because it will be relevant. The Uí Liatháin have not entirely converted to the New Faith but have retained our ancient culture and mythology. This is a source of suspicion and conflict. It bears a relevance to the murder of the abbot. Now, let me hand this paper to Abbot Iarna to hold until I have finished.'

Holding the paper aloft, she strode across to the seated abbot and handed it to him.

'You said Brocc's death was *fingal* – the killing of one by a family member,' Fíthel chided. 'Are you going to explain that?'

'If I may continue, I will.' Fidelma was equally ironic. 'There is another reference work that I shall be using, which I give you notice of so that your steward has time to check out the text. I refer to *Trecheng Breth Féne*.'

'Those are the law texts on treaties between territories.' Fíthel seemed puzzled for a moment. 'I presume that you are acquainted with the regulations about using such treaties? A judge is required to be knowledgeable about them.'

'I am acquainted, otherwise I would not have raised them.'
Fíthel's mouth tightened and he motioned with his hand for the
steward to fetch the texts.

'Let us get on for the sooner we start the sooner we finish,' he
demanded.

Fidelma bowed her head almost mockingly. 'So long as no
aspects of the matter are ignored through haste to end the case,'
she said. Before Fíthel could respond, she continued, 'The simple
facts. Brocc, Abbot of Dair Inis, was murdered. He was a son of
Tigerna Cosraigib, who led the Uí Liatháin rising against Cashel
six months ago and was killed. When Brocc's brother, Conmhaol,
refused the decision of his family council to be successor, you
will recall Abbot Brocc came here to plead the innocence of his
Abbey in the uprising and, beyond his authority, accepted the
reparation imposed on all the Uí Liatháin.'

'Was he not appointed by the *derbhfine* to do so?' Fíthel
queried.

'The family council was divided. That Abbot Brocc had
taken this role upon himself caused disputes and opposition,
especially as Brocc was of the New Faith, while the vast majority of the Uí Liatháin keep to the Old Faith. Brocc returned to
his people with treaty conditions and demands for reparation
from the Uí Liatháin that were not only disliked but turned the
nobles into paupers and the free clansmen into beggars. Many
held Brocc responsible and, if he became leader of his people,
they saw it as a total acceptance of the New Faith. Dair Inis, of
course, was the centre of the New Faith, a place in isolation in
their territory. This meant unrest among the nobles and the
populace. They resorted to bringing forward their old myths
and heroes and, for some, trying to persuade others they had
been resurrected.'

'Like the Grey Ones?' Prince Finguine interrupted. 'That is
why I sent Caol to investigate.'

'Indeed,' Fidelma acknowledged. 'Under these conditions, some members of the family council decided to change the situation.'

'You mean to kill Brocc and put a new leader in his place?' Fíthel asked.

'The family council was in a situation where it seemed no further progress was possible as to their choice of leader. A demonstration had to be made. In accordance with their ancient superstitions, the Grey One had to appear to make a prophecy as to a time when Brocc would die. When it happened and was accurate to the day and time, it was supposed to encourage the Uí Liatháin to rally around the new leader. The people were encouraged to believe that the old deities were supporting them.

'I started with the belief that a prophet who was so accurate on a date and time of death would also be involved in the killing. I was right. But who was this prophet and killer? I began to find out who the members of the family council were. The only *seanchaidh* I encountered was a supporter of the Grey One.

'Conmhaol was a main suspect until I found he really did not want anything to do with his family's internal disputes and certainly not with the leadership of his people. He had truly become a recluse. Brother Fisecda, a cousin, was not only a physician at the abbey but he was a cousin and close friend of Conmhaol and, furthermore, his daughter, Sister Damnat, was a nurse at the abbey. I nearly missed her relationship when she told me. But Conmhaol and Fisecda were abducted by those who killed Brocc, and in the raid to kidnap them, Brother Scatánach of Dair Inis was killed. He had been a go-between for Brocc, Fisecda and Damnat and Conmhaol. This young man overestimated his importance and, sadly, his vulnerability. He even tried to scare us off from consulting a witness by firing an arrow at us.'

'So who was involved in the killing?' Fíthel was frustrated.

'I should remind the learned Brehon that I am not presenting a case in a law court, which would probably make my exposition longer. I am making a report for future legal action.'

Fíthel waved his hand irritably. Fidelma took it as a sign to continue.

'Brocc and Conmhaol had a sister – Lalóg. She was of the Old Faith but presented herself as having friendly relations with her brother, and she was head of a village not far from the abbey. That was who Scatánach tried to stop us seeing with his stupid arrow shot. Lalóg used to visit her brother at the abbey. We heard from the abbey librarian that there were often arguments between the siblings.

'Lalóg has a steward called Cathbarr and we found out that he had been a bodyguard to Tigerna Cosraigib and was a vociferous defender of the Old Faith. He, we learnt from witnesses at Dún Guairne, had led the kidnappers who took Conmhaol and Fisecda prisoners and, I am afraid, was either directly or indirectly responsible for the death of young Brother Scatánach. We also learnt that he was a cousin of Tigerna Cosraigib and therefore a member of the *derbhfine*.'

'So what next?' Fíthel sighed. 'You have named one person who possibly killed this Brother Scatánach during a kidnapping. Was Scatánach a member of the family?'

'He was not. Stupidly, he thought he was indispensable to certain family members. There is another member. She is the daughter of Brocc's sister, Lalóg. Her name is Báine. Again, another fierce defender of the Old Faith just as her mother is. It was her own mother who let slip that Báine was staying with her in the village next to the abbey when Brocc was given the prophecy and then killed to coincide with it. She was the Grey One, the prophetess. She took the role to foretell Brocc's death . . .'

'If it were her, Brocc would have recognised his own niece,' the Chief Brehon pointed out.

'From his position and the fact she was in grey robes, he could not tell. I saw her when I was a prisoner of the Grey Ones and I would not have recognised her. No, there was another principal witness. I met him at Lalóg's village. He was an Uí Liatháin *seanchaidh* called Scannail the Contentious. He made a slip by saying that the Grey One was of the true noble line. Who else but Báine fitted the image?'

'Are you saying that Lalóg, Brocc's own sister, and her daughter were the murderers of Brocc? That the intent was to stop him becoming ruler and then get support from the people to challenge Cashel again?' Finguine's voice had a note of self-satisfaction in it. 'So I was right in sending Caol to find out about the Grey One.'

'Regretfully, I could not find out any specific threat from them,' Caol called out. 'I found out nothing until Fidelma and Eadulf came with Dego and were made prisoner by Scannail and the Grey One.'

'I should record that we owe our liberty to Caol. He organised our escape from the fortress of the Grey One.'

'Who else was involved?'

'Before we speak of the instigator of Brocc's death, I was told that a boat was on its way up the Great River, bearing an envoy to confirm to my brother, King Colgú, who has been approved of as the new Prince of the Uí Liatháin. I will wait until that emissary has arrived and then ask Abbot Iarna to announce what name I have placed upon the paper I gave him.'

The Chief Brehon's brows were darkening, but Fidelma hurried on.

'I also pointed out that any legal process about this matter may only take place within the territory of the Uí Liatháin. If necessary, I am willing to argue the detailed evidence in a legal case at that time. It might necessitate the involvement of the High King and Chief Brehon of the Five Kingdoms. I would also say, it might need an entire *sluagh*, a hosting of the armies of Muman, to support such a hearing. It might not be wise to provoke another war.'

'The law has to be obeyed,' snapped Brehon Fíthel.

Colgú spoke for the first time. 'Do you believe there is a way of dealing with this without another conflict with the Uí Liatháin?'

Fidelma bowed her head to her brother.

'If the name I have written is correct, then we will be attempting to put on trial the Prince of the Uí Liatháin, his family council and the people of Uí Liatháin. While we wait for this envoy, I would like to return to the subject of treaties.'

'Is it necessary?' Fíthel asked in a tired voice.

'I deem it to be so, because we should not just deal with effect, but cause,' Fidelma replied. 'I am pleased to welcome Sárán, a scholar of the Déisi, who survived an illness while researching the history of his people in the Uí Liatháin territory. His recovery is thanks to the physician Íccaid who, coincidentally, is one of the family council of the princes of the Uí Liatháin. I make the point of emphasising the wide divisions of morality within that family. Sárán is preparing a history of his people. *Cogadh Anfóill Oirne* – "The Terrible War Against Us". He will correct me if I have any details wrong.

'Most of you know the history of the Déisi. They were expelled from their homeland in Midhe hundreds of years ago when their prince, Óengus, blinded the High King in one eye. A king with a blemish is disbarred from ruling and so his successor exiled the Déisi. They were doomed to wander without lands of their own, becoming vassals to anyone who exerted power over them.

'When they came seeking land to settle on it was during the time of Óengus mac Nad Froich who, it is recorded, was the first King of Muman to accept the New Faith. Among the Déisi was a beautiful princess named Eithne. The Eóghanacht King fell in love with her but she would marry him only if he granted them territory to settle on in the south-east of the kingdom. They would follow his new religion and he would be accepted as their overlord, to whom they would pay tribute, so long as their own princes and nobles remained rulers of their territory.'

'This story is mostly known. It happened two hundred years ago,' said Fíthel as if the matter was boring. 'It is ancient history.'

'A history whose consequences we live with,' Fidelma said. 'A history that enables us to understand the Uí Liatháin and Déisi unrest.'

'Why so?' Fíthel demanded.

'Is this why, from that time, the Déisi rise up against the Eóghanacht – to get out of paying tribute to Cashel?' Colgú interrupted thoughtfully.

'Yet more complicated,' Fidelma assured her brother. 'The Déisi always felt their expulsion two hundred or more years ago by the High King was unjust. Sárán will maintain, in his history, that the conditions under which they were given lands in this kingdom were also unjust. They should be an independent kingdom.'

'But Muman is a kingdom that, like the entire Five Kingdoms of Éireann, is also divided into five territories, each with its own prince and freedoms under the law,' Colgú reflected. 'I know the Déisi have long since tried to overturn payment of tribute and allegiance to Cashel. But if they became independent, the King of Laigin would quickly use them to attack our kingdom.'

'But what has that to do with the Uí Liatháin?' Brehon Fíthel interposed. 'The Uí Liatháin and Déisi have always hated each other. I recall that, among the Uí Liatháin, the Déisi princess who married the Eóghanacht king who granted them territory is known as Eithne Úathach – the Hateful. What relevance does it have today?'

'Pause and consider,' replied Fidelma. 'When the Déisi arrived here and demanded land to settle, whose land do you think they were given under the terms of Eithne's marriage?'

There was a silence before Colgú spoke.

'I have never thought of there being people there. But this was a long time ago.'

'Once you read Sárán's text it becomes clear,' Fidelma assured him. 'Where the Déisi are now was once part of the Uí Liatháin territory. Those that lived on that land were expelled westward across the Great River. That is where they now live.'

'I do not see any relevance.' Fíthel was again dismissive. 'If you say that this is a source of Uí Liatháin unrest, perhaps I may remind you again that the recent unrest finds the Uí Liatháin as allies with the Déisi against Cashel.'

'History shows that a desperate people will ally itself with anyone,' Fidelma responded. 'Cashel and the Eóghanacht kings are more hateful in Uí Liatháin eyes because they made that bargain with the Déisi. You have probably heard of the short-sighted policy that whoever is the enemy of your enemy is your friend. That is a disastrous concept.'

'So are you saying all the problems among the Uí Liatháin are due to this settlement made two hundred years ago?' Fíthel said in disbelief.

'It is the foundation. Also consider, why is it that the New Faith has made so little headway among the Uí Liatháin? Because the change of faith was a condition of the Déisi colonising their land and trying to impose the New Faith on them. Accepting it was also seen as a badge of subservience. That is why the Uí Liatháin keep to the Old Faith.'

'But some, such as Abbot Brocc, converted,' interrupted Abbot Iarna for the first time.

'And were seen as traitors to their people. Hence leaders like Tigerna Cosraigib rose up to lead their people in bloody conflicts. He was different in trying to link Déisi dislike of the Eóghanacht in a movement to overturn Cashel.'

'Are you blaming the New Faith?' Abbot Iarna asked angrily.

'Not entirely,' Fidelma replied, unabashed. 'When the New Faith was accepted in our laws, it was not expected that the rules of it would so drastically change and that it would challenge the native laws. Rome has continued to change the rules and rituals separating the New Faith from the original concepts that we accepted two hundred years ago.'

'I hope you get to the point as to how you think this impacts on what we are now discussing,' Brehon Fíthel said.

'Oh, it does,' Fidelma replied firmly. 'Those among the Uí Liatháin accepting the New Faith are taught from the Latin translations of Eusebius' *Byblos*, which was fully approved by the Bishop of Rome.'

'What is wrong with that?' Bishop Cuán asked.

'There are two parts to what we call The Book. Unfortunately they often concentrated on pre-Christian ideas: the Laws of Moses, as they are called, found in the texts of Exodus, Leviticus, Deuteronomy and so on, have become focused on retribution, death and blood payment.'

'Wherever they come from, they are in our Book of Faith,' Abbot Iarna declared.

'Not in The Book of the New Faith. And, from reading the Laws of Moses I find it is truly a barbaric and inhumane system. There is no need for me to remind you of the countless times death is imposed on people – eye for eye, tooth for tooth, hand for hand, foot for foot, burning for burning, wound for wound, stripe for stripe. That is what is considered justice.'

'So are you saying we should ignore the *Byblos*?'

'That part of The Book, at least. If we believe in the New Faith, these laws were all rejected by the one who founded it. Did it not say in the Gospel of Matthew that Jesus rejected laws that preached revenge? Teaching us to cut off the hand that steals, blind those that are covetous, kill the person who is responsible for the death of another directly or indirectly, and death not just for killing but even for insulting . . . Look at all the offences that merit death there. It is a system contrary to our laws, yet we are being led slowly into it.'

'This has all been discussed before among the religious.' Fíthel once again was dismissive.

'I have argued it before, and in this very room only a few years ago, when an injustice was being done to the Uí Liatháin,' Fidelma reminded them.

Abbot Iarna, who had sat at that time in judgment, looked uncomfortable.

Fidelma went on, 'The basis of our law was accepted when the New Faith was first recognised by us. Anyone who transgressed the law was allowed to atone for their crimes, even if they caused the death of another. As well as being given the opportunity for rehabilitation in our society, the perpetrator must give compensation to the victims or the relatives of the victims. Vengeance or retribution has only a momentary satisfaction. Only when a killer is shown to be incorrigible, unrepentant and unwilling to provide compensation and pay the fines required by law do we place them in the arms of fate. They are cast adrift in a boat without sail or oar and with food and water for one day. Their fate is left to the winds and the waves.'

'It is clear in our laws,' Brehon Fíthel agreed.

'Then let us look to the *Trecheng Breth Féne*, the laws relating to the treaties between territories particularly, as I referred to before. I have no power, but I can only suggest that we have sown the seeds of resentment being watered each time the Uí Liatháin rise up to, in their opinion, reverse the injustices originally done to them. Instead of dealing with the cause, we have been inclined to seek out laws of revenge.'

'They are in The Book, so what must be done?' Abbot Iarna snapped.

'Go to the words of the founder of the New Faith,' Fidelma

replied. 'It is quite clear that he rejected the teaching of an eye for an eye, a tooth for a tooth. See what the Founder of the New Faith says in Matthew – love your enemy. I have found among the Uí Liatháin there is suffering because the retribution they are forced to pay not only hurts their nobles, but the harm and poverty descends to those under them who barely make an existence from their small plots of land. The King's Council will have to decide what alleviation can be given so that the future will not provide a fuel for continuing generations of unrest and death.'

'Are you saying that even if Abbot Brocc was murdered by his family, and the *derbhfine* make the killer their new leader, we must not call for the retribution of the law, but forgive them?' Brehon Fíthel asked.

'I can only express opinion. This is a matter for the King.' Fidelma glanced briefly at her brother. 'The King will be guided by his full council and advisers. We cannot tear up history and the original wrong, but we cannot keep using it as an excuse for continuing the injustice. The Uí Liatháin must be invited, with the Déisi, to come to an agreement with the Eóghanacht for a future relationship.'

There was a disruption as one of the brethren entered the hall, paused, looked round and, spotting Colgú, came hurrying forward and whispered in his ear before standing back.

Colgú sat upright. 'I am told that a messenger has arrived from Dún Guairne. His name is Scannail, presenting himself as a *seanchaidh* and adviser of the newly appointed Prince of the Uí Liatháin. The new prince has been endorsed by his *derbhfine* and sends his respects to me.'

Everyone was silent as they turned to him in expectation.

'And the name of the new prince?' prompted Fidelma.

There was a moment of non-reaction and then Fidelma turned to Abbot Iarna.

'Will you read the name on the paper I gave you?'

The abbot moved slowly, finding the paper and carefully unfolding it. The motion seemed to take an eternity.

'The name is Cathbarr.'

The expression on Colgú's face made it unnecessary for him to confirm that that was the name of the new prince.